I Wanna Be
Loved by You

I Wanna Be Loved by You

The Grand Russe Hotel

Heather Hiestand

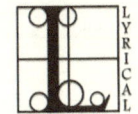

LYRICAL PRESS
Kensington Publishing Corp.
www.kensintonbooks.com

LYRICAL PRESS BOOKS are published by

Kensington Publishing Corp.
119 West 40th Street
New York, NY 10018

All Kensington titles, imprints, and distributed lines are available at special quantity discounts for bulk purchases for sales promotion, premiums, fund-raising, educational, or institutional use.

Special book excerpts or customized printings can also be created to fit specific needs. For details, write or phone the office of the Kensington Sales Manager: Kensington Publishing Corp., 119 West 40th Street, New York, NY 10018. Attn. Sales Department. Phone: 1-800-221-2647.

Lyrical Press and Lyrical Press logo Reg. U.S. Pat. & TM Off.

First Electronic Edition: February 2017
eISBN-13: 978-1-60183-581-9
eISBN-10: 1-60183-581-7

First Print Edition: February 2017
ISBN-13: 978-1-60183-582-6
ISBN-10: 1-60183-582-5

Printed in the United States of America

For Katie and Grim

Acknowledgments

It turns out that writing about spies is complicated! Thank you to Gina Robinson for your sensible thoughts regarding spy heroes. Thank you to Judy Di Canio, Eilis Flynn, Mary Jo Hiestand, David Hiestand, Delle Jacobs, Melissa McClone, Peggy Bird, Marilyn Hull, and Madeline Pruett for your assistance and support. Also, I'd like to thank my editor, Peter Senftleben, and the rest of the Kensington team, with a special shout out to the Social Media team who has worked so hard to launch the Grand Russe; and my agent, Laurie McLean, and the Fuse Literary team, for their support of the Grand Russe series.

Chapter One

Outside London, afternoon, January 9, 1925

Sadie Loudon pressed her hands down the sides of her slightly too-short uniform skirt when she saw Mrs. Curtis. She'd shortened the hem to make it saucier, but the above-calf length created problems when she bent over. January was no time to have a breeze snaking up her bare thighs. However, the increased tips in this seedy inn where she was a new chambermaid more than made up for the discomfort.

"Clean up that mess in the lobby, ducks," the housekeeper said, brushing frizzy locks of graying hair behind her ears. "We'll run off our customers."

Sadie clucked her tongue when she saw the pile of paper in the middle of the small hotel lobby. "Who dumped that rubbish there?"

"No idea," Mrs. Curtis sighed. "We're too close to the Richmond train station for comfort."

Sadie set her mop and bucket in the corner and went to pick up the papers. Her shoes crunched on a broken tile in the checkerboard pattern as she walked across the floor. She looked back to see Mrs. Curtis wincing at the noise.

As she picked up the first piece of cheap paper, the headline, in large, heavy type, stood out: UNITE THE WORKERS! She scanned the text, which said, "Not a penny off the workers' wages, not a penny tax on food!"

The words meant little to her. She had only started her first proper, paying job on Monday. No paycheck had been issued to her yet. As far as she was concerned, these labor unions trying to create unrest were merely creating more work for her.

"I'll be sorting out the Reading Room," Mrs. Curtis called. "Have a tidy in room 301 when you're done in here. They just went to tea."

Sadie made a face at the floor. Dreadful 301 and their nasty poodles. Cleaning the foul-smelling room took four times longer than any of the others. She clenched her fist, ruffling the leaflets, then stooped to gather the rest.

A slam sounded behind her, as if a guest had opened the upstairs door in a rush. Someone hurtled down the steps. She glanced up to see a bearded man in gray trousers, a baggy black coat, and a Russian *budenovka* hat barreling toward her. Dropping the leaflets, she attempted to stand.

The running man crashed into her. She fell backward, her arms going wide. Her back hit the tile, legs going up in the air. Pain radiated through her skull and shoulders. She panted, too startled to do anything else.

More noise on the stairs. More crunching on the tiles. The front door banged open. Steps slowed. Another man, this one in a slim, hand-tailored, pinstriped suit, looked down at her. His bowed lips curled when he saw her silver knickers, exposed by the skirt hovering somewhere around her waist. He was clean-shaven and rather young, with gray-blue eyes that regarded her dispassionately, despite the smile.

Sadie pulled her knees together and dropped her feet to the ground. "Help me up!" she begged, cautiously pulling her arms to her sides.

The man narrowed his eyes at her, then glanced toward the door. "My apologies, darling," he said in a lazy but polished accent that somehow hid a hint of a wink. Without looking back, he ran after the first man, his highly polished oxfords gleaming from her floor-level vantage point. He pushed through the door, coat-less, running into the cold after his quarry.

Slowly, she put her hands to the tiles and pushed herself up. Her back ached and her head spun. "Well, I like that," she muttered. "Such cheek." She pushed her skirt down and stared uneasily at the leaflets.

Bolsheviks were labor agitators, weren't they? That first man was a Bolshevik, judging from the hat. As much as he had frightened her, the complete calm in the second man's eyes bothered her the most. She had a sense that nothing could break through his defenses. Goodness, though, he'd been a handsome one.

Shivering, she rose shakily to her feet and staggered to the battered reception desk. Old Ben, the hall porter, appeared as if from nowhere.

"Sadie, love, what's happened to you?" Old Ben stepped up to the other side of the desk.

"I was knocked down."

"By a guest?" Old Ben stared uneasily at the small lobby.

"They came from upstairs." She described both men, lavishing most of the details on the second man, with his broad shoulders, long legs, and memorable face.

"I don't recall either of them," he said. "I'll have to investigate. Why don't you ask Mrs. Curtis for a headache powder and have a lie-down in your room?"

Sadie wanted to say yes, but she wasn't a well-trained vicar's granddaughter for nothing. "I still have work to do. After I clean room 301, perhaps."

"No, love, have a lie-down first. Half an hour."

"I will then. I do ache dreadfully." She smiled and hobbled toward the stairs. When she saw one of the leaflets, curled up in the corner of the lobby, she picked it up and tucked it into her pocket. She had a vague sense that she needed to be better informed about labor issues.

The thin winter sunlight faded over the rooftops as night came on. Les Valentin Drake handed a copy of *Motion Picture Magazine* to Yuri Gadisov, the owner of the newsstand a block away from the Richmond Inn. "This isn't my bestseller, that's *Photoplay*, but it's an excellent publication."

Gadisov, a corpulent ex-lorry driver who'd immigrated to England five years before, made a congested noise and took the magazine. "I think they would sell better around the Green. Girls on this street don't have the money for American imports."

"Girls are obsessed with American stars," Les said, not bothering to push. He didn't have orders to sell to Gadisov. His objective was to receive an invitation to Gadisov's father-in-law's birthday party the next night.

Gadisov lifted his shoulders. "Maybe I should take one copy of each to see what sells. You never know, eh?"

"You never know," Les agreed, thickening his faint Russian accent. He'd developed it based on his grandmother's accent, remembered from childhood.

Gadisov glanced at the beautiful redhead on the cover. "I still don't like short hair on women, Valentin."

"Of course not," Les agreed. "A woman's crowning glory."

"Yes," Gadisov sniffed. "A man like you must be looking for a wife, eh?"

"Do you have someone in mind?" Les asked, pulling out an order pad and filling out Gadisov's purchases.

"Would you like a nice Russian girl?" Gadisov asked. "Or do you want an English girl?"

"Russian, naturally," Les said. "A girl who knows how to brew a proper cup of tea."

"Nothing but the samovar," Gadisov agreed. "You should come to a party with me tomorrow night. My wife is from a large family. Lots of pretty girls will be there."

"I'd like that," Les said with a cheerful wink. *Got him.* Gadisov's father-in-law was reputed to be involved in a local Bolshevik cell and Secret Intelligence had been looking for an in for months. He handed Gadisov his order form and the man counted out a few coins in payment.

"Here is the address." Gadisov wrote it across the form.

"Very good. I'll see you and your lovely family tomorrow. *Spasibo.*" Les shook hands with the man and walked a block south.

Five minutes later, he stared out through the window panes of the telephone booth across the street from the Richmond Inn. His eyes felt gritty from a day mostly spent outside in the winter wind, most of it without his coat. He'd had to retrieve his coat from the café where he'd left it when the labor provocateur he was following moved more quickly than he expected. He'd chased him through the inn right after that but he had vanished hours ago. He'd stayed behind the man as far as the Thames but his quarry had disappeared into the brush along the river banks, which was inhabited by tramps of the dangerously unstable Great War–veteran type.

The Bolshie hadn't been worth pursuing. His section head had agreed with him when they met early that afternoon at a safe house in Chiswick, but Les had been sent back to Richmond to collect a copy of the flyer for the file. Also, he had the never-ending task of developing his cover persona as a commercial traveler dealing in American magazines.

He'd meant to go newsstand to newsstand in Richmond, selling copies of *Photoplay* today. Some of them were owned by Russians and he was always looking to build relations there. The Secret Intelligence Service had set him up in business, partly with the intent of using his magazines to pass messages coded in invisible ink to undercover agents. At the end of the day, he had to leave a copy of the December 1924 *Photoplay* on a bench in Waterloo Station. Cover model Lois Wilson's beautiful chin was marred with a small inkblot, the clue to the other agent that this magazine contained orders inside.

Les wished he knew what the orders were for. Presumably something more glamorous than magazine sales. He set down the telephone receiver and checked his case, making sure a clean copy of the January issue was on top, then opened the door. Dodging cars, he strode across the street and entered the Richmond Inn for the second time that day.

"It's you!" gasped a young woman at the reception desk. A middle-aged couple turned away as she spoke, the wife staring hard at Les, her tongue in the corner of her mouth, before her husband tugged her toward the staircase.

Les recognized the hotel employee from earlier, though his main recollection was of a pair of silver knickers and a set of deliciously rounded thighs above gartered stockings. But his photographic memory had catalogued all of her. Not Yuri Gadisov's feminine ideal. A real looker, her thick dark blond hair was cropped into a fashionable bob, tucked under at the ends. She wore a black chambermaid uniform, although the skirt was a bit skimpy. He grinned when he remembered the undergarments again. If he'd run past at just a slightly different angle, he might have been able to see right up the loose fabric to the feminine treasures hidden beneath.

When he refocused on her, he saw her cheeks were flushed scarlet. "I'm so sorry I couldn't aid you earlier today," he said, taking her plump, unresisting hand in his. He noted that her skin seemed much too soft for a chambermaid, and catalogued a mole at the base of her middle finger on the back on her right hand.

Her voice came out breathless. "Who was that man you were chasing?"

"A very bad man," Les said, careful not to let his assumed Russian accent creep in. "Obviously, since he hurt you, darling. Is your head aching?"

She wrinkled her nose. "It hurt dreadfully at first, but I rested. They are very nice here, kinder than some of the guests."

"I'm sure." He rubbed his thumb across her throbbing pulse. "Do you happen to have any of those flyers? I wanted to take one to the police."

"Are you going to have them make a sketch of his face?" she asked eagerly. "Do you need me to go to the police with you?"

He smiled tenderly. He doubted she would remember anything but the man's Russian hat and his beard. He, on the other hand, had caught the precise details of the man's eyes, nose shape, and distinctive ripped earlobe, since the earflaps of his hat had been buttoned up. "I wouldn't want to waste any more of your valuable time."

"I did keep a copy of the flyer," she said, surprising him.

He'd been afraid he'd have to go through the bins. "Very intelligent of you."

Her cheeks pinked again. She had a pointed chin that spoke of mischief in the making, but her eyes were a transparent green blue that, along with her dimples, encouraged trust.

"How old are you, darling?" he asked.

"Twenty." She paused. Her fingers spasmed in his hand. "Well, I'm twenty tomorrow, it's my birthday."

So honest, this adorable little flapper. "What are you doing to celebrate?"

"Nothing. I only moved here on Monday." Her tongue darted out and touched her lower lip for an instant. "From Bagshot. I don't know anyone."

His decision was made in an instant. Despite his claim to be looking for a wife, a date would protect him from having to flirt unwisely in the Russian community. Also, he couldn't resist this intelligent, dramatic, extremely attractive girl. "Then you must come with me. I was invited to a birthday party here tomorrow."

"At the hotel?" She made a face, demonstrating her opinion of any party that might be held here.

"No, darling, in Richmond. In a private home."

Her fingers curled in his palm. "Oh, I don't know."

"Very respectable," he assured her. "A matron's party. The mother-in-law of a local businessman."

She tilted her head. He could see she was considering, hovering toward going. "Oh. What do you do?"

"I sell American movie magazines."

Her eyes lit. "I love movie magazines. What do you have?"

He squeezed her hand gently, then released it. Then, he opened his case and pulled out the January *Photoplay*. "Have a sample copy."

"Oh, I never. Thank you." She stroked the cover.

He went into his patter. "Do you think the hotel might want to subscribe? I have other magazines too, but this is the most popular."

"I couldn't say." She took the magazine from him and set it on the counter, then opened the cover. "My stars, look at that silver fox coat."

He leaned in to look. Really, he should read the blasted things. "You'd look lovely in it."

She laughed. "Listen to us. A traveling salesman and a chambermaid wasting time over a photograph of a fur coat. As if either of us will ever see such a thing."

"You never know. You're much prettier than the model."

"I am?" She dimpled.

"Of course. I've always preferred blondes to brunettes anyway."

"Many men do," she agreed, bending over the desk a couple of inches. She turned the page of the magazine.

"The model has no chin," Les added, wondering if she was trying to show him her breasts. Her uniform didn't really allow for it, though. "I bet you have a marvelous profile."

She tilted her head so he could see her profile. *Eating out of his hand now.* He had no idea what use to make of the little chambermaid, though. It didn't seem likely anyone important would ever stay at this inn. On the other hand, there was a thriving Russian community around here and wherever there were Russians, there were Bolsheviks in the crowd. So, he'd develop her as a source in case he found a use for her later.

"See, a perfect profile," he said jovially. "Lovely straight nose, chin and jawline perfect for your face, and the most kissable lips."

Her lips parted in surprise. "Mr. err—"

He had to think quickly. The Russians knew him as Valentin Dragunov. Valentin was indeed his real name. Dragunov was up the family tree somewhere, although his true full name was Leslie

Valentin Drake. He'd best use his working name with this girl. "Rake, darling. Haven't I mentioned that? Lester V. Rake."

"What does the V stand for?"

"Never you mind," he said with a comical wince. "What is your name?"

"Sadie Loudon."

In his mind, he linked the picture of this pretty girl to South London, which included Richmond, where she lived. That way he'd remember her name, since "South London" was close to "Sadie Loudon." "A very pretty name."

She wrinkled her nose. "Commonplace. I sound like a chamber-maid, don't I?"

"Not with that accent," he assured her. "No, you'll move on to better things, find a husband if you like."

Flipping past a page of upcoming American movie releases, she pretended to ignore his suggestion. "I only took this job after a fight with my grandfather. I was doing secretarial work for him before."

Now a secretary was a valuable asset indeed. They had access to everything their guv touched, while being such a low-level employee that they were rarely suspected. And, often women, they were easily swayed with romance. If he could lead this girl into the right sort of job, he could make his career. "Are you hoping to return to secretarial work?"

"No. I like working with my hands, I think. But not cleaning." She made a disgusted face. "You wouldn't believe what some of our guests do to their rooms."

The memory of a blood-spattered guest room in Lambeth, where a couple of Russian gangsters had fought to the death, flashed into his thoughts. But this young girl had seen nothing of the potential ugliness of life, the world he was immersed in. And he needed to keep her ignorant of it.

"I can well imagine," he agreed. "Listen, darling, I need to toddle off and sell magazines now, but I'll pick you up around seven tomorrow night. Good?"

"Yes," she agreed. She was quiet for a moment, then smiled brilliantly. "Thank you for the invitation, Mr. Rake."

"Les," he said, all but bowled over by the force of that smile. Sadie Loudon had charisma in spades. "I hope you shall call me Les."

"That's awfully forward," she said seriously. "I was raised by a vicar, you see. I'm not as modern of a girl as you might think."

"Your grandfather is a vicar?"

She nodded.

She'd be a patriot, then. He'd have to investigate her family. It wouldn't be difficult, as her surname wasn't a terribly common one. "I bet he is loads more conservative than you."

She tucked her chin into her hand and stared at a magazine photo of actress Bessie Love in a very low-cut dress. "I could have married his curate and just settled for life there."

"Any man would be lucky to marry a girl as pretty as you," Les said, knowing it was the expected phrase.

Her very white teeth flashed. He noted her lips were full and not at all chapped by the January weather. She took care of herself. Vain.

"I flirted with the idea, but I wanted to see more of the world. My older sister left home last month. I didn't realize how unbearable life would be without her."

"Where did she go?"

"Up to London proper. She planned the thing better than me."

"You can go there too. Stick with me. I'm in and out of all kinds of establishments. I'll keep an ear to the ground for a position for you."

"That's just the berries," she exclaimed. "Thank you so much."

He smiled. "I'll see you tomorrow then, Miss Sadie Loudon." He slid one finger along the smooth curve of her cheek and felt her shudder under his touch. Oh, she was delicious.

Sadie smiled happily at herself in the mirror in an empty bedroom in the inn. Luckily, she was a much better seamstress than her sister, Alecia. She didn't have a mirror in her own postage stamp of a room. Unlike Alecia, she refused to sew baggy, practical dresses. Her dance frock was her best approximation of a Lanvin dress she'd seen in a magazine, with black-and-white triangles on top of sleekly shaped silver fabric. The result was attractive, well-fitted, and modern, though demure. It wasn't low-cut like Bessie Love's dress in the American magazine, but she was no old-fashioned and sweet little Mary Pickford either.

In fact, her sister believed that she'd stolen their grandfather's curate's affection away from her, but Sadie didn't see it that way. In a post-war world where men were still scarce, a girl had to accentuate her best assets, and if Albert Warren had preferred a fun-loving girl who liked to spend time doting on him, to quiet, busy-with-parish-business Alecia, that wasn't her fault. She'd simply played the game of love better. There had been no declarations between Albert and her sister. Even now, when she realized the curate had been better suited to her sister, she had no regrets.

She took one last look at her teeth, to make sure none of her red lipstick had rubbed off on them, then ran downstairs as fast as she could in her two-inch heeled shoes.

"Happy Birthday, Sadie!" Old Ben called from his post next to the reception desk as she trotted across the checkerboard floor.

"Thank you!" She waved at him then went through the door, still tying the sash around her coat.

Les Rake stood next to a beautiful two-seater sports car. He wore evening dress underneath a long gray wool driving coat and a matching cap and looked like he belonged on the cover of a movie magazine himself. She knew right then and there that she'd landed a date with money. The car, sparkling new, was made for speed.

"What is that?" she asked, making her voice breathless and admiring, which was not difficult.

"A Bentley 3-Litre. Just a Blue Label, I'm afraid, but she goes up to eighty miles per hour like a dream, and I've had her to eighty-five."

She put her hand to her cheek. "Goodness. Hard to keep your hat on."

He grinned, exposing a good ten upper teeth. An automobile aficionado to be certain.

"Silly of me to think someone who traveled a great deal for his work didn't have a car," she said, running a gloved finger lightly over a gleaming headlight.

"I keep her in London for the most part."

London. What a dream. Of course he lived there. "She's a girl?"

"A lady, to be sure." He chuckled and bent to kiss her cheek. "Happy Birthday, Sadie."

She took a breath of his cologne. Something expensive and peppery. "Thank you."

He opened the door so she could slide onto the smooth khaki leather seat, then went to the other side. She smiled and leaned her head back. Albert hadn't had a car. A week away from Bagshot and she was celebrating her birthday in style with a handsome date. Leaving home had been the right decision.

Les started the car as he explained they didn't have far to go. The house where the party was taking place was on the west side off of Richmond Green. He parked about a block away from the party, saying he didn't want to be fenced in by all the other partygoers, and before she knew it, they were walking down Old Palace Lane to a row of modest, two-story white terraced houses.

"Here we are," he said. "Mind those tiny front steps."

As soon as he said this, the steps came into view. She heard the sound of a gramophone, playing dance music. Exactly what a girl should hear on her birthday. Clutching Les's arm tightly, hoping she looked as film star-fashionable as he did, she walked next to a damp hedge. It brushed her arm, leaving a wet stain and the scent of evergreen as they passed.

Les stopped walking and pulled out a handkerchief, brushing the damp off her sleeve. "There you go, darling."

She smiled at him, pleased by how closely he paid attention to her. Then, he helped her up the steps into an overly warm room full of Russians.

"Vodka?" he asked. "Tea?" No one had looked at them yet.

She never drank alcohol. It made her already round face swell. "What kind of tea?"

"Russian tea. It's smoky. Have you tried it?"

She brushed her short hair off her face and unpinned her hat. "Do you think they have lemonade?" It was too warm for tea. Not to mention smoky tea sounded disgusting.

"Probably." He flashed that devastating grin at her. "For the children. Maybe we can find a bottle of bubbly?"

"Lemonade," she said, firmly.

"There's a place for coats," he said. "I don't see anyone wearing theirs."

She unbuttoned her coat and began to slide it off her shoulders. Expertly, he stepped behind her to receive it, his hand on one of her arms. Such a gentleman.

A song ended and the dancers realigned. People moved in and out of the center of the room. A voice shouted over the already loud room, booming loud enough to be heard over the gramophone. "Valentin!"

Les's hand tightened on her arm. He surprised her by pulling her coat off one arm and sliding it across the other, to hide their hands. "Here, take this."

"What?" she asked, confused.

"It's my ring. Put it on your wedding finger."

"What?" she repeated.

"Do it." He said it in such a firm voice that she complied, entirely flustered and not a little upset.

He pulled her coat the rest of the way off, but to her surprise, he took it from her with a calm smile, no sign of agitation or stress.

"Pretend to be my wife. If the subject comes up."

Had he even moved his lips? She had heard the words well enough.

"Valentin!" came the call again.

"Yuri!" Les walked over to the great, balding bear of a man who had shouted and clasped his arms. "*Dobryj vyechyer.*"

Sadie blinked hard and stared down at the little gold ring on her finger. Had her date just said something in Russian? While his looks were film star handsome, she hadn't thought him an actor. What was he playing at? The two continued to speak, complete physical opposites, one, tall, middle-aged, red-faced, enormous, exuberant, the other slim, young, pale, and comparatively reserved.

Another man joined them. He was yet another type. About thirty, older than she thought Les to be. He wore a variation of the *budenovka* hat the man Les had chased through the inn had worn on his head. In a minute, Les and the younger man detached from the older and they walked over to her.

"This is Semyon," Les said. "Semyon, this is my wife, Sadie."

She could have sworn he spoke good English but now he had a faint Russian accent. What were they doing, some kind of theatrical production? Had he brought her to a Russian home to mock the family?

Semyon didn't seem like a fun bloke, however. He didn't smile as he inclined his head. Nor did he speak to her, just spoke a few more phrases in Russian to Les.

"Semyon tells me there is a better party in Chelsea, tonight, Sadie darling. Younger crowd, you know." He winked. "Adult lemonade."

Sadie glanced around. It was true, nearly everyone here was over forty, and it was her birthday. Also, she knew her way back to the inn from here. "We could stay here and dance. The records are good."

"Mazurka," Semyon said heavily. "Polka. Always these Polish dances here."

"I like them. At least so far."

"It will destroy your nerves," he said, unsmiling.

"Glory," Sadie said, putting on her brightest smile despite her nervousness. She glanced at Les and he nodded slightly. While she didn't understand what was going on, she knew he needed her to go with him. And she wasn't ready to let go of him yet, a man who lived in London and might be her ticket to a different kind of life, with dancing and Chelsea parties. "To the other party we must go, then."

"Good girl," Les said approvingly. "We'll have a much better time there. Let's put your coat back on, darling."

As he helped her slide the coat back over her arms, she caught sight of that ring she now wore on her fourth finger. Gold, with a black stone in the center. A 'V' was cut into it. V for what. Valentin? Who was Valentin?

Chapter Two

Sadie touched her handbag as they left the Russian party, feeling for the coins at the bottom through the thin fabric, her escape if something went wrong. She was desperate to figure out why her date suddenly had an accent. Questions tipped her tongue. But the Russian man, Semyon, followed them out the door and said several sentences to Les in Russian, who clearly understood him. He walked the block to the car with them and Les opened the passenger door.

Semyon squeezed into the seat next to her, pushing her close to Les on the plush bench. He smelled of spilled spirits and cucumbers. A little of fish, as well.

"Where do you work?" she asked, as Les started the car.

"Mac Fisheries," he said, proving he understood English. It explained the slight smell.

Les patted her knee in a familiar fashion, reminding her she was pretending to be his wife. She wanted to fire questions at him, Semyon's presence or not, when Les had to brake alongside a cemetery to let people cross the road, but then he turned to her.

To her surprise, he reached under her right leg and came up with a rectangular box. "Happy Birthday, darling. I thought you might need these. I'm sorry I forgot to give them to you before."

Forgetting the sight of the grave monuments alongside them, she took the box and squinted at it. "Hermès? Glory." She opened the box and found a butter-soft pair of beige leather driving gloves. Her breath caught in her chest. French gloves. She had been given French gloves for her birthday. The only other gift she'd received was an extra roll at breakfast. When she and her sister moved in with their grandparents after their parents died in the sinking of the *Lusitania*, presents had been outlawed. All the money spent on gifts previously had to go toward the poor boxes, the curse of having a vicar grand-father.

She forgot about the Russian accent, the fake wedding ring. She wanted to belong to a man who thought to buy her fancy gloves. Her old knitted mittens were off in a flash, and she slid on the new gloves. Flexing her fingers, she sighed with happiness. "Thank you, Les."

He squeezed her knee again then winked and drove on. She placed her old mittens in the Hermès box and tucked it under the seat, then rested her head on his shoulder. Semyon made some comment to Les that made him chuckle and respond. She listened to the cadence of the foreign language, trying to pick out words, but it made absolutely no sense to her.

Not twenty minutes later they were parking in front of a row of white-stone and brown-brick-faced terraced houses in Chelsea. "Where is the party?" she asked.

"In a basement flat. This is where the artistic types live," Les said.

"Whose party is it?"

"That never matters. It's who is there. Probably a mix of artists, Bright Young Things, and socialists."

"Where do we fit in?" she asked, extending her lushly gloved hand to Les so he could help her out.

Raindrops slid off her tight-fitting hat as she stepped onto the pavement. When had it begun to rain? Semyon slammed the street-side door and crossed over to them.

"Are you an artist, a Bright Young Thing, or a socialist?" Les asked.

"I'm a young matron of means," she said uncertainly. She'd like to be a Bright Young Thing. Her sister had gone to London in search of the flapper lifestyle, a strange dream for quiet Alecia, who'd taken a position as secretary to a couple of famous actors. But then, her sister was smart.

Les nodded his approval, then glanced at Semyon. She crossed her arms, knowing she'd never have the truth out of him while the Russian was present, and followed the two men past a couple of the houses. Semyon glanced at a door number then grasped the gate hiding a flight of steps leading to the basement level and went down. They followed him into an exceedingly small flat. In the back, past the bedroom, was a tiny reception room, which was open, despite the rain, to a postage stamp-size courtyard that nonetheless nearly doubled the party space. A fox-trotting couple danced back into the flat, cawing with laughter and shaking the rain off. The woman's bare back was covered with gooseflesh.

Les swiped an open bottle of champagne off a table and reached for glasses, then poured for two. He handed a glass to Semyon then took a sip of his. "I had better find you some lemonade, darling."

She tossed her head. "I'll find it myself." The kitchen was in full display to the right of the courtyard. No baize door hiding it in a flat of this size. She found a jug of water on the counter with some teacups and decided that was good enough. When she'd drunk her fill she leaned against the wall and watched Les talk with two men who approached him, both of the scruffy variety, rather than the foppish evening dress–wearing fashionable young men who were dancing with scantily clad girls.

"*Spasibo*," she said, trying out the one word of Russian she knew. She blushed when a slightly older girl stared at her quizzically.

"It's thank you in Russian," she explained.

"I know. I'm married to a Russian," the girl said, tucking a stray lock of black hair behind her ear. "Oh, I must have lost a pin somewhere."

"Impossible to find in this crush."

"Yes, and the flat belongs to a man," the girl agreed. "No spare pins in the lavatory."

"I'm Sadie Loudon," she said impulsively. "I mean, Sadie Rake."

"Newlywed?" the girl inquired.

Sadie pulled off her gloves and flashed the signet ring. "Very newly wed, I'm afraid. I keep forgetting."

The girl smiled. "Doris Ikanov. We married last spring. Which one is your husband?"

Sadie lifted her chin in Les's direction. He'd taken off his hat, and his sandy brown hair flopped charmingly over his brow. She noticed the hint of a beard was starting to show.

"Very handsome," Mrs. Ikanov said, her eyes widening.

Sadie nodded. "And your husband?"

"He is speaking to yours, in fact."

"The one with black hair?" He had a heavily lined forehead, but nicely full lips and beautifully shaped eyes.

The other woman nodded and Sadie said, "I approve."

They smiled at each other. "Do you live in Chelsea? Oh, is that water?"

"Yes, in the jug."

"I'm parched." Mrs. Ikanov walked into the kitchen and poured herself a teacup full.

"I was, too. Something about the rain makes me thirsty. But no, I live in Richmond. I have a live-in position."

"You're in service?"

"No, not that old-fashioned. A hotel."

"Oh, I see. Your husband doesn't mind?"

"He travels for work a great deal. Selling magazines." Sadie felt herself slipping deeper into her role. "He always has such stories to tell when he comes back."

"I would imagine so. Does he live in the hotel, too?"

"No," Les said, coming up to her. He slid his arm around Sadie's waist.

She realized she still wore her coat. Quickly, she unknotted her sash as he said, "We have a flat in the Primrose Hill area."

"I love the view there," Mrs. Ikanov enthused. "We live in Acton because my husband works for a soap company there."

Sadie could see the moment her pretend-husband lost interest in the woman. His eyes half-shuttered, then his gaze wandered toward the open terrace doors.

He walked away with their coats. When he returned, he said, "Shall we dance, darling? I know you wanted to and they just put on a new record."

"Yes, of course," she said, setting down her teacup on the edge of the counter. She smiled at Mrs. Ikanov then took his arm.

When Les pulled her close to him, she tilted her head into proper dance position. Her cheek brushed his bristly jaw. She sighed with happiness. Albert the curate had been all but hairless. This was a proper man. She shouldn't get in over her head, especially since Les was, at the very least, a liar, but there was nothing wrong with a nice time, a few kisses on her birthday. The full story could come out another day.

The record skipped. Several voices complained and a man ran to the gramophone to change the record. "Bees Knees" came on. It had been a massive hit a year or two ago and she remembered twirling around with Alecia at a friend's house, all the girls dancing together. She grinned up at Les and he smiled back, looking a bit surprised.

"Good memories," she whispered in his ear. "We used to play this song in the afternoons."

"In the vicarage?" he asked.

"No." She shook her head. "No music in the vicarage."

"What's wrong? You lost your smile."

She rubbed her cheek on his jaw again and closed her eyes. "I just realized how much I've missed my sister. It was so lonely in the house without her. It was either marry Albert or run away."

"And you ran?"

"Yes."

"Who is this Albert?" he inquired.

"The curate."

He chuckled, the sound sending rumbles down her body. Her nipples peaked, a delicious sensation. He pulled her even closer, just what she wanted, as the hoof-like percussion part of the song began. She could stay like this forever.

"Never marry a curate, darling. He'll never keep you warm at night."

She smiled, her face hidden against his cheek, feeling quite relaxed, even without champagne. They danced through five songs. Les ignored Semyon's attempt to catch his attention, and kept going until she said, "I'm gasping, Les, and not for a gasper."

"Need some more lemonade?" he teased.

She pulled a face. "No lemonade here, only water."

"I Dream of a Castle in Spain" came on. She stepped back.

"Don't you like this song?"

"No, the tango bores me. I like fast dances."

He glanced at her, then squeezed her hand. "Let's go."

"What about your friend?" She injected a slight amount of sarcasm.

"He can stay. This is hardly a blow. I'm happy to leave."

She noticed his accent was gone again. What was going on? "Were you hoping this would be a wild party? Do I seem like that kind of girl?"

He tugged her hand, and she followed him out of the room and down the hallway toward the single bedroom where Les had left their coats. The door was cracked and others were inside.

A thickset Russian man wiped sweat off his brow. This was Mr. Ikanov. Mrs. Ikanov stood next to him. She smiled widely at Sadie.

"Oh, Mrs. Rake! I'm so happy to see you again."

"We couldn't dance anymore," Sadie confided, fanning herself.

"Oh, I know. The heat. Too many people for one small room. I've never understood girls who dance holding cigarettes. I know it is all the rage but it makes the air unbearable."

"I quite agree," Sadie said, as Mr. Ikanov coughed.

Mrs. Ikanov smiled shyly and held out a scrap of paper. "I wondered if you'd like to have tea with me one day during the week?"

"Oh, thank you," Sadie said. "But I work, you see."

"Yes, of course." Mrs. Ikanov blushed. "When you have a free day. I'll come in, even to Richmond. It would be so lovely to have a friend with a husband like mine."

Sadie glanced at Les. He was oddly expressionless, his pale gray-blue eyes assessing the Ikanovs. When he caught her gaze, he came to life.

"So busy, my bride," he said. "She is happy to make new friends, Mrs. Ikanov. I'll be sure to have her contact you when she is given a day off."

"Saturday must be the day," Mr. Ikanov said. "Dinner next week, perhaps?"

"This is Mrs. Rake's birthday," Les said. "Special circumstances."

"Oh!" Mrs. Ikanov smiled. "Many happy returns!"

"Thank you." Sadie beamed as Les helped her with her coat, then handed her the beautiful new gloves. She tucked the scrap of paper carefully into her handbag, then nodded goodbye to the couple as Les escorted her from the small bedroom.

When they were back in his car, alone at last, Les said, "Your birthday is waning, Sadie. Where do you want to go next?"

"How about the place where you buy your accents?" she asked. She had to needle him, though she was aware of being in a strange place, and in his car, at that. No one she knew was aware of her whereabouts.

"My accents? What do you mean?" he asked as he started the car.

"Sometimes you sound English and other times you sound Russian."

"Oh that." He glanced at her and chuckled, then pulled away from the curb. "My grandmother was Russian. She raised me. I imagine I start speaking with her accent when I'm around Russians. Is that what happened?"

"Yes," she admitted. "When you spoke to me you sounded English. Quite plummy, really, but then you'd have a faint accent."

"I did attend Oxford," he said modestly. "There is no mystery about the accent."

"Did you lose your parents young like I did?"

"When were you orphaned?"

"Ten years ago, nearly."

"You were very young. Admittedly, I was younger. My mother died when I was seven, and my father when I was at school."

"And then your grandmother took you in? Like my grandparents. Now it's just Grandfather. My grandmother has passed away."

"Yes, I'm all alone now. No brothers or sisters."

"I'm sorry. That's hard."

"We're both rather alone in the world."

They had driven about five miles from the party. She had no idea where they were, but they went down several leafy roads before parking in front of a row of terraced houses similar to the ones they had left.

"I thought we could take a walk if you like," he suggested.

Just as he said it, rain splattered on the windshield again. He pulled off his gray cashmere muffler and tucked it around her neck. "There, you'll be fine."

She smiled and allowed him to help her from the car. Between the gloves and the muffler, she was as warm as butter on toast. And when he put his arm around her, she felt even cozier. He was careful to walk under the trees as much as possible, to keep her dry. It didn't work very well because most of the leaves were gone, but she felt cozy, nonetheless, like these London streets were laid out just for her and her adventure with this unusual, elegant man.

"How old are you?" she asked.

"Twenty-five. Why do you ask?"

"Just curious."

"Too young for the war, just barely," he said.

"Oh, I never wondered that."

"No?"

"Men who were in the war, the ones who are just a little older than you? They are either very quiet, stern almost, or rather frantic with gaiety."

"What am I?" He squeezed her shoulder.

"Something in between, I suppose." A mystery, still, though he had explained the accent. Eventually, they emerged from the tree-lined streets into a large green space. She felt a bit out of breath from climbing up the slope, or maybe it was the view of the city, spread out before them. Lights lining the streets twinkled. "Is this Primrose Hill?"

"Yes, of course. Nothing else like it in London. I live near where we parked."

She giggled. "I suppose I do, too. Do you want your ring back? Were those married-only parties? Is that why you made me wear it?"

He stroked her shoulder. "I suppose I wanted to feel connected to you."

She remembered the look in his eyes when he'd seen Semyon, and knew there was a bit more to the story, but she understood loneliness. "It's fun to playact, to be someone else. But sometimes, I just want to be me."

He pulled her against the warmth of his body. She rested her cheek against his shoulder. They were even closer than when they had danced. But she was too shy to wrap her arms around him. He was a stranger. She took off her new glove and pulled off the signet ring, then pressed it into his palm.

"Time for a divorce?"

"Yes," she agreed, smoothing her glove back on. "Do you need these back as well?"

"No, the gloves really are your birthday gift." His lips curved into a lopsided grin. "One last kiss before we part forever?"

She giggled and tilted her face up to his. "We shouldn't separate without one."

"Have you been kissed before, Sadie?" His warm breath, laced with champagne, tickled her upper lip.

She pressed her lips together to cure the tickle. "A few pecks from the curate. He didn't know what he was doing, though."

"And you do?"

"I could tell," she said pertly. "I've kissed my own hand better than he kissed me."

"Hmmm." His lips moved closer to hers, just an inch apart.

A solemn moment. This could be her first real, proper kiss. The bottom dropped out of her stomach and she felt lightheaded with nerves. How could he want her to make the final move? "I don't know—"

He silenced her protest by pressing his mouth to hers. One arm pulled her waist snugly against his pelvis, while the other arm cradling her shoulders loosened, so that she dipped back. The pressure of his mouth increased against hers and her lips parted willingly. A gust of wind blew around them, bringing raindrops. But she wrapped her arms around his neck, clinging to the sensation of his mouth against hers, feeling as warm as if it were August and not January.

Until the rain began in earnest, that was. He pulled away from her, leaving her face still tilted up. A fat drop of rain caught her in the eye. She had to remove her arms from his neck to wipe the moisture away.

"The problem with these tight fitting cloche hats is they don't protect your face," he said. "We'd better return to the car."

She couldn't think of anything to say, still dazzled by their kiss. He seemed to understand, and put his arm around her, directing her to the path that would take them back to their car. As they descended the slope, she wondered if he would ask her to take the next step with him and try to bring her to his flat. She'd all but told him she was a girl alone in the world.

Instead, he talked lightly about the music they had danced to, *The Thief of Bagdad*, a movie he'd seen recently, and an elaborate birthday party he'd been to as a child in the Insect Room at the London Zoo.

"I want to go to the new Aquarium," she said, in an attempt to add to the conversation.

"That just opened last spring, didn't it? I haven't been either. I'm not always in London, of course."

They reached the street and he directed her toward his car, not even glancing at the sleepy buildings around them. A little disappointed, but also relieved that he'd treated her like a lady, Sadie allowed him to help her into the car.

The seat was chilly, but she warmed up as soon as he slid in next to her and started the engine. Halfway through the drive she unwound his muffler.

"You can keep it," he said. "It looks adorable on you, that elfin chin popping out over the wool. The color makes your eyes even more blue, too."

She felt her cheeks warm. "You're too generous, Les. I can't allow you to keep giving me gifts."

"I like giving you gifts. There isn't anyone else to, right?"

She didn't want to remember that. Her sister couldn't afford idle purchases and her grandfather expected all spare money to go into the church roof fund. He liked to say his granddaughters weren't peacocks. "What about you? Who gives you birthday gifts?"

"No one anymore," Les said, his hands easy on the steering wheel.

"I'm sorry. At least we found each other." She smiled at him. "Speaking of elfin, did you know your ears are a little bit pointed?"

He chuckled as she took off a glove and brushed a finger over the tip of his ear.

"Ticklish?" she asked.

"It's not a place I'm normally touched."

She jiggled her finger against his soft skin again, then, suddenly shy, put her glove back on. "You must think I'm terribly silly."

"I appreciate your sense of fun. I spend a lot of time projecting bonhomie at the world, since I'm a salesman. It's nice to be with someone I'm at ease with. I'm not making all the effort in order for us to enjoy each other's company."

"That's quite a speech about the life of a salesman." She thought about her own first week as a chambermaid. Most of the time, she had her head down working. If guests passed her in the halls, she moved against the wall and looked away, as instructed.

"It's work, and these days, you can't be too choosy."

She knew he had money. His luxury car and the location of his flat told her that. But maybe it was all inherited. It would be rude to ask for details.

All too soon, they were pulling up to the Richmond Inn. Her birthday adventure was coming to a close. As he pulled the car under the awning over the inn's entrance, she said, "Thank you so much for taking me to the parties. I had a lovely time." She fluttered her lashes at him. "Especially on Primrose Hill."

He flashed his teeth at her. "That was my favorite too, Sadie."

She waited for him to ask her out again, but he didn't. Maybe he had to go back on the road soon, but she had no way to contact him. Not that a girl could, of course. He would decide if he wanted to see her again. It seemed much easier to be courted by someone your family knew, someone local. But she'd never met anyone like Lester Rake. Leaning into his arm, she said, "Thank you for making my birthday special. I will treasure these lovely gloves and your scarf. Are you sure I should keep it?"

"Absolutely." He slid one finger up the back of her gloved hand, then curled the muffler higher on her neck. "Thank you for such a magical evening. I'll get your door."

He helped her out of the car, squeezing her hand, then Old Ben was at the door, gesturing her in. She glanced back, hoping Les was staring at her, but he'd already returned to the car. Where she stood with him was anyone's guess. For herself, she didn't think she'd ever be able to forget that magnificent kiss at the apex of London.

On Sunday afternoon, Les sat across from his section head, Douglas Childers, Lord Walling, a titled aristocrat known around the Secret Intelligence Service only as Glass, in a one-bedroom flat in Cosway Street, Marylebone, used for operative meetings. Glass always liked to start with a convivial cup of tea in the small conservatory, saying there was precious enough civility in espionage as it was.

"Well then, on to business, shall we?" he said, setting his china cup down with a tiny clink against the saucer. His large hands made the regular-sized cup look like it belonged to a girl's play tea set.

Les shifted on his hard decorative iron chair. "Yes, sir. Were you able to read my report about this Richmond business?"

"Indeed." Glass steepled his long fingers against his chin. "Tell me more about Semyon Kozyrev."

Les followed suit and set down his half-filled cup. He didn't like the malty Assam anyway. "I haven't asked anything of him yet. I'm merely developing the friendship. Honestly, it might be more trouble than it's worth."

Glass winced slightly. He didn't believe in wasting time on anything. Les thought it might be because he'd lost three older brothers in the war. Glass kept his private life very quiet, but Les knew that much. "Why?"

"Semyon invited me out to dinner with his wife and sister about two weeks ago, so I told him I was married to avoid complications."

"That's where this Sadie Loudon came in?"

Les glanced out the window. While there was plenty of light coming from the slanting windows, they were only a couple of feet away from another block of flats. "Yes. Typical flapper, up for anything if it comes with a well-dressed man in an expensive car who is willing to pay for dinner."

Glass smiled. "What do we know about her?"

Les tilted his head back and forth. "She's a good actress. Threw herself into playacting as my wife."

Glass made a note on his clipboard. "She didn't ask questions?"

"I gave her a couple of gifts." Les shrugged. "A game girl. Poor, not much family, first job. Just grateful to go dancing, really."

"She's twenty?"

"Just had her birthday yesterday," Les confirmed. "The important thing is that Semyon's appearance at the Timur Pesin party meant I didn't get anywhere near my target."

"If you can run Semyon, you don't need to be close to the Bolshevik cell," Glass said, unperturbed. "Keep working on that relationship. He's important."

Les shook his head. "I can't do that without Sadie Loudon. What I am going to do, tell Semyon she died?"

"If she's game, I don't see the problem."

Les pushed his irritatingly floppy hair out of his eyes. If it wasn't for the fact that his late father had had exactly the same kind of hair, he'd have cut it short. As it was, it had become rather a trademark, which meant that if he had to change identities, cutting his hair short would be an easy disguise. "She's not one of us."

"She's a simple, silly, English girl, right? Devoted to her country and all that. It's not a problem. Just use her in Richmond when you're dealing with Semyon. You don't need to reveal anything."

Les remembered that kiss on top of Primrose Hill. He'd woken up with his toes still curled, not to mention an aching erection. "Very well."

Glass opened a folder, lips pursed. "Scratch that. I have a new assignment for you. You'll have to involve Sadie Loudon, I'm afraid."

"Semyon?"

"He could be there. We need you to go up to Hull. Sell a few magazines, but primarily, you are to look for the flyer printer. The report came in just before I left and I didn't see it until now. That Bolshie flyer you picked up was printed on paper only available in the Hull area."

"Bolshevik hotbed, Hull."

"Exactly. You'll need to bring Miss Loudon along in case you run across Semyon."

"Why? My cover is as a commercial traveler. I wouldn't take my wife along."

Glass flipped a page. His heavy black eyebrows moved together for a moment, then relaxed again. "Semyon's wife is Irina Kozyrev, correct?"

He didn't know where Glass was leading this conversation. "Yes, but I've never met her."

"Assuming you can't take Mrs. Kozyrev to bed, the next best thing is to have your wife befriend her. If this Miss Loudon is the silly, friendly type, she's a perfect way to reach Irina Kozyrev."

"She did get us asked to dinner with a mixed Russian-English couple," Les admitted, concerned by the path this conversation was taking. Sadie was a green girl. Running her as a source was one thing, but actively having her take part in deception was quite another. She had no spycraft, no experience. "She is personable."

"I saw that in your report. Too bad it didn't appear, at first glance, that the Ikanovs were of value."

Les realized his thoughts were much too focused on Sadie. "You never know who they might be related to, but there was nothing there at first glance. Back to the main point, why is Semyon's wife important?"

Glass's already deep-set eyes shadowed. "She is the daughter of Mikhail Lashevich."

Les schooled his features carefully, but a vein had begun to rat-a-tat at his temple. "You must be joking, sir."

Chapter Three

Glass drummed his fingers on the iron table, clearly not surprised by Les's reaction to the stunning news. "Yes, our old enemy, Mikhail Lashevich, the devious pet assassin of Lenin. His daughter Irina is Semyon Kozyrev's wife."

"Well I'll be a monkey's uncle," Les said. His throat felt dry but he didn't want any more of the loathsome tea his section head favored. Lashevich had killed several British spies working in Russia in the past half-decade. He was a nightmare shared by nervous operatives everywhere.

"Must be five o'clock somewhere," Glass said, noticing his discomfort. "I think we've a bottle of brandy around here."

Les chuckled, forcing away old, bad memories. "Think I need a restorative for shock, do you?"

Glass grinned and pushed his chair back. The mischievous look lightened his eyes by a decade. He was probably about thirty, but his war experience had matured him beyond his years. Still, Les had seen how Glass's tall frame and distinguished manner attracted a lady's eye. "You went pale, my lad. Pale as a virgin bride."

Sadie picked up a thin envelope from her sister. Even now, away from home, Sunday was family day. She called her grandfather every Sunday night, and she saved the most recent missive from Alecia so she'd have something to open.

After propping her pillow up against the iron headboard of her bed, Sadie opened the letter and began to read. She couldn't hold back her whoop of joy. Her gaze unfocused as she took the one-second glance around the tiny room she shared with another chambermaid.

The manager of the Grand Russe Hotel in London, on Park Lane no less, was offering her a chambermaid position.

Alecia wrote that it wasn't bed and board, but they could share her bed in her hotel room for now while Sadie uncovered where the other chambermaids resided. She leaned her head back against the wall. *London.* It would be lovely to amass a little nest egg before she went, because there were sure to be expenses, but no doubt it would be at least a week before she'd begin. She'd have a couple of weeks pay and she'd be certain not to spend a penny of it between now and then.

Sitting up, she rubbed her tongue between her teeth as she considered how to get up to London. It wasn't far, but she wouldn't be able to go until she had time off. Unfortunately, her half day wasn't until Wednesday. She consoled herself with the thought that Wednesday was only three days away, and the job was hers. She only needed to make arrangements with Mr. Peter Eyre, the Grand Russe Hotel's manager, for a start date.

Jumping off the bed, she went to the trunk at the base of her bed and began pulling out clothes. Did she have anything smart enough for London?

The approach to Wednesday seemed to last three weeks instead of three days. The cap on her joy was the hideous, disgusting mess the evil poodles had deposited in room 301 the day before. She'd spent two extra hours cleaning. Mrs. Curtis had promised she'd be paid for the hours, but she'd lost sleep because she'd had to hand wash her filthy uniform, and then she'd had to work in a damp skirt.

When she went upstairs to change after the morning round of tidying the public areas, she was still shaking with cold. Physical labor hadn't kept her warm. *You never should have shortened your skirt, Sadie my girl.*

In her room, she pulled on fresh everything in the hopes it would feel warmer. Over her underthings she draped her newest dress. The cream fabric made her hair and eyes brighten a bit. She didn't neglect the new gloves and muffler. They were so much nicer than her old coat and hat.

She half-wished she could pack up her meager belongings and just start at the Grand Russe tomorrow, but that might not be what Mr. Eyre had in mind, and she ought to give Mrs. Curtis a couple of days to find a replacement. It wouldn't be hard, with the state of employment as it was.

"You must have sensed me coming," said a voice from the bottom of the stairs as she reached the lobby.

Her heartrate sped up. "Why it's Les Rake," she said, playing coy. How exciting that he'd reappeared.

He wore another of his fancy suits, topped by a coat with a cozy fur collar. She couldn't begin to calculate the expense of his wardrobe. It put hers to shame, and compared to her sister, she was positively frivolous.

"What are you up to? I remember you said you had a half day on Wednesday and I thought I'd stop by."

Her gaze went to his lips. She remembered the warmth of them against hers on that cold night. Her knees melted a little, but her voice was composed. "Selling magazines in town again?"

"No, I came just for you." He looked at her calmly, then smiled. His sharp cheekbones bracketed his mouth.

He was such a sheik. She put a hand to her chest as her heart went pitty-pat. "That's very kind, Mr. Rake. I was on my way to London."

"I'll run you up," he offered. "But it's Les, surely." He tilted his head.

"Les," she said, unable to suppress her own smile. She tucked her hand around his arm. "How kind of you."

The lobby was deserted as they walked out. His car was parked right in front. She sighed over the sleek automobile. What would they think of the new chambermaid arriving in such style? Her sister wouldn't even notice, of course. She never recognized money.

Her grandfather had repeatedly asked both of them to pay more attention to certain members of the parish. Assist certain elderly ladies in and out of their benches and that kind of thing. Sadie had understood it was a matter of the elderly persons' money, but Alecia had been naïve to the end, even asking why they helped a couple of the women when they were such antidotes, when there were other much more pleasant persons in the parish.

Les helped her into the car. When he entered on the other side, she snuggled up to him.

Les smiled to himself as the eager girl pressed her shoulder to his arm, her thigh to his.

"How is your family?" he asked politely as he started the car. They were heading to Kings Cross Station. He half-listened to her prattle along about her weekly phone call to her grandfather the night before.

"You didn't tell him about your date with me?" he asked, amused.

She shrugged. "I didn't know if I'd ever see you again, what with you traveling."

He patted her knee. "You must have known how well we got along. Of course I'd come calling for you again."

She touched her head to his shoulder for a moment. "I hoped, of course."

He wrapped his arm around the back of the seat. They passed the cemetery and headed toward Chiswick, passing an overburdened lorry. He found life ran more smoothly when he focused on nothing but business, but Sadie Loudon was easy to like.

His attention drifted as she continued to talk, considering his best approach in Hull. A day out with the missus? Why would anyone go to Yorkshire for a day holiday from London? It took hours. No, they had to be going to a rally at the docks there. Glass's contacts had indicated there might be one. From whom might he have heard of it? He was only beginning to build his contacts. He mentally shuffled through his list, but was distracted by Sadie mentioning the Grand Russe Hotel.

The Secret Intelligence Service had been working to put eyes and ears into the place since it opened late the previous year. Les didn't know if they'd managed it yet.

"Sorry. What were you saying?" he asked. "I was distracted by that farmer blocking the road with his horse-drawn wagon."

"So old-fashioned," Sadie agreed. "What I was saying was, the manager of the Grand Russe has personally offered me a post."

"You don't say," Les said, as they pulled into a free spot on the street near Kings Cross Station. "We'll catch the train from here."

"Where did you want to go? To the Aquarium like we mentioned?" she asked.

"No, Yorkshire," he said absently as he walked around the car. Wind fought him for control of the passenger door. He had to wrestle it open. "I have a meeting in Hull."

"I can't go to Yorkshire," she protested. "I have to go to the Grand Russe!"

He took her arm and helped her onto the pavement. She wobbled as a gust of wind snatched at her. "You said the job is waiting for you. Why do you have to go now?"

"It's my half day."

"Write to the manager," Les said. "Plan your start date by letter. He won't want you popping in. A letter is more polite."

A line appeared between her perfectly arched brows. "Do you think so?"

"Absolutely. Much more professional. Take it from me, darling. I have much more experience with the world of business than you do."

She bit her lip as they entered the busy railway station. "I suppose you are right."

He pressed his case home, helping her to make the decision he wanted. "If you like, I'll take you over to the hotel, but the manager might think you impertinent."

She bit her lip. "I don't want that."

"I'll tell you what. You can write a letter to him on the train and I'll post it for you. On your next half day, I'll take you to the hotel if you haven't had a response."

"That makes sense. But still. Hull? In January?"

"I have a meeting," he said. "But we'll dine on the train. We'll have a wonderful time. I'll buy us first-class tickets."

She brightened immediately as he thought she would. "I've never been in first class. Yes, I suppose I would like to have an adventure, rather than chase a position that is, after all, mine for the taking."

"There you go, then," he said, leading her to a store so they could buy newspapers and writing paper. When the train arrived, he found an empty compartment and settled them in. She spent the first couple of minutes trying out each of the plush seats, then curled up next to him as the train jerked and pulled out from the station. The excited smile hadn't left her face since she'd decided.

He stood when they reached the edge of London proper and took off his coat, then helped her with hers. When he sat down again he draped their coats over their legs to keep them warm. He could feel her warmth radiate from her shoulder to his arm. She was staying very close to him, quivering despite her happiness. He reached into a coat pocket and took out his piece de resistance and gave it to the obviously nervous girl.

"This is for you. A late birthday present."

She took the box, her smile brightening. "Oh, Les, you've given me so much already."

He was pleased to hear her calling him "Les" again. "Just a little something to apologize for my behavior that night."

She tugged off the ribbon and opened the box, then stared down at the contents.

"It's a Russian nesting doll. Separate the top from the bottom."

She pulled out the squat wooden figure. About five inches, it was painted with the face of a wrinkled old woman wearing traditional peasant black.

"Pull the top part off," he said again.

She tugged them apart, then squealed when she saw another doll inside. "This one looks younger."

"The matron inside the widow," he confirmed.

Quickly, she repeated her action, and found a smaller doll. "A girl this time."

"I think there is one more."

She separated the girl, wearing a necklace of flowers and a colorful dress, and found a solid baby doll inside. "How adorable. What a lovely gift, Les. Is it Russian?"

"Yes. I wanted you to know a little more about my heritage," he said, staring out the window as the train moved into open country-side. Smoke blew past the window from the engine.

"Are you Russian?"

"One quarter Russian. My father's mother," he confirmed.

"Did your father have a Russian name?"

"Valentin. Yes."

"That's where your ring came from."

In response, he pulled off the signet ring and placed it back on her finger.

She smiled and examined it, the doll still in pieces on her lap. "What is your real accent? The Oxford man or the Russian?"

"Both, I suppose."

"Who is the real Les?"

That was a question he'd never be able to answer. When a spy looked in the mirror, what face did he really see? He'd been recruited by the Secret Intelligence Service at nineteen, still at Oxford, just as the war ended. After two years of being a courier locally, he was sent to Russia. It was 1921 and he'd spent a couple of months getting there, a couple of months setting up his cover and getting his accent right, then nine months in the army under fake identification. The worst part had not been gathering intelligence on the state of the Russian army, but trying to get the information he gathered out of the country. By the end of that time, more than a year total, his health had been broken due to the poor food, limited sleep, and harsh conditions, not to mention a tragic love affair. He'd headed back out, a dangerous journey, with most of his intel still trapped in his head. Returning to London in early 1923 had been a disquieting experience after the deprivation of his time out of England. It had been nearly two years since he returned. He'd regained his health but then his grandmother had become ill and died. Les had lost most of a year between his health and his grandmother's. Glass had put him back to work as a courier a year ago. Then he'd received his new sales cover three months before. There had been a lot of discussion around whether or not he should have ever been to Russia in his cover. He was operating under three identities. His own, Lester Rake, and Valentin. They'd decided Valentin had been a child in Russia and had left after his Russian army service. Lester Rake had no interest in Russia.

Now, he was doing something very dangerous, letting a very young woman in on the secret of his two identities. But Glass had thought it was worth it. Les wasn't sure he agreed, but Sadie's potential value had jumped at this notion that she might go to work at the Grand Russe soon. She could be the eyes and ears they needed at a hotel that was attracting all manner of wealthy, scandalous, celebrity, and most important of all, *foreign* guests.

"Les?" she asked, rather more gently that he might have expected.

"Sorry. Woolgathering."

She tugged his arm and pulled him down until she could nuzzle her cheek against his. "Did you lose your grandmother recently?"

He nodded. His throat seemed to have closed on him. "A year ago. Her heart. She had a bad attack and was bedridden after that for quite a while before she died."

"And you were her only family, and now you are quite alone in the world."

"Yes, I suppose I am."

"Except for a pretend wife." She grinned at him.

He smiled back. "You are a winning character, Sadie Loudon. How could I resist trying on the role of your husband?"

Her flush didn't just cover her cheeks with a dusty pink. Her neck reddened, too. "You aren't the first man who wanted to marry me, but you are most handsome, I must admit."

He glanced through the windows of the compartment. No one was nearby, so he tilted his head, replacing cheek to cheek with lips against lips. Her mouth parted in surprise. He kept the kiss light, almost teasing, but lengthened it voluptuously, until he could feel her breathe against his mouth. She was so healthy, so wholesome, nothing like his tragic Russian mistress, who lived in a town of hovels near the base. He'd been stricken down with cholera, but she had died. His lost Natalia.

Natalia had not expected a wedding from him. He wondered if Glass realized Sadie would expect this false matrimony to become a marriage proposal. A fake wife in England was a lot different than a fake one elsewhere. He'd end up not being able to work here and would need a new foreign posting.

He shuddered at the idea of returning to Russia. An operative posted there wouldn't live to be old. Not with the likes of Mikhail Lashevich around.

Sadie pulled back from their kiss and stroked his shoulder. "You're shaking. Poor Les."

"Emotion, darling. Haven't you ever met a man who made you quiver?"

She stared at him. Such an innocent, this girl. She'd be convinced he loved her, and was love-desperate enough herself to love him back for that reason alone.

Sadie was still dazed as they exited the train. The five-arch roof over the vast platforms told her Hull was no provincial outpost, but a bustling transit center. Unfortunately, despite the imposing Italian Renaissance-style building of the station and nearby hotel, the area smelled strongly of fish.

She couldn't keep her thoughts on the locale though. They kept returning to the man leading her who knew where in this bustling city. She'd had very little exposure to men. A butcher in Bagshot had professed his love, but he wasn't her social equal. She'd run into one young man repeatedly for about eight months at social events locally and they had flirted a lot, but then his father had inherited some property in the South of England and the entire family had moved away. She'd never heard from the youth again. And then there had been Albert. She was so much more outgoing than her sister that she'd never realized how narrow her experience truly was.

"You remember Semyon?" Les asked as they walked across the street, heading east.

"Of course."

"His wife lives full-time in Hull and we might encounter them," Les said. "Let's pretend to be married again, shall we?"

She played with the ring he'd placed on her finger. "Are you going to pretend to be Russian too?"

He grinned at her. "Why not?"

"Silly man," she muttered. "I hope this entire exercise isn't a part of some elaborate scavenger hunt. Kidnap a vicar's granddaughter or something?"

"Stop playing with the ring," he said.

She did as he asked, not seeing the value in doing otherwise. Her wages hadn't been paid yet and she didn't have the money for a train ticket home. She was trapped. Her concern made her bold. "Are you afraid of Semyon? He seemed a dark character."

Les gave what sounded like a forced laugh. "More afraid of the women in his life. He wanted me to date his sister. With a face like his, I can only imagine what his sister looks like."

"Oh, I see. This seems such an elaborate ruse though. What about honesty?"

"Such a vicar's granddaughter," he teased. "You want me to tell the man he's ugly?"

"No, of course not, but pretending things like marriage is only going to tie us into knots."

"Trust me for today, will you? We've sent off your letter to the Grand Russe, and now you have nothing to worry about." He wrapped his hand around her upper arm. "We'll find a café and have something to eat without the floor moving under our feet."

She nodded, not convinced any of this was a good idea, but she'd already committed herself by rashly climbing the steps onto the train in the first place. "That sounds good. I could hardly manage a cup of tea on the train."

"I noticed. Windy day."

Her stomach rumbled at the discussion of food. She'd always had a healthy appetite. "A plate of eggs and toast sounds delightful. Then what do you have in mind?"

His nostrils flared as he breathed in. She'd already decided she wouldn't be breathing too deeply in this port town. Salt air and seaweed were one thing, but she could already smell the decaying fish and fuel, heavy in her lungs.

"Let's not go toward the river," she said. "Does it smell better somewhere else?"

"No, they have sewer trouble in the city center," he told her. "We're better off down here."

Two men walked by them, speaking Russian. She realized a cluster of old women with apple-doll faces were probably Russian too.

"Did your grandmother live in Hull?" she asked, realizing he might have wanted to show her his heritage, since he already seemed to be in love with her.

"For a time," he said. "This is an important connection point to Russia."

She smiled at him. "I appreciate you sharing your family history with me."

His gaze was already drifting off. "Why don't we go to the Ship's Hound? They have good coffee and borsht."

"What's that?"

"A Russian soup."

Les played with Sadie's hand as they sat at a table in front of the window at the Ship's Hound, drawing circles around her knuckles. She seemed to expect his attention, her hand steady in his. Her demeanor had changed to self-assurance, a woman who was cherished. It wasn't wearing his ring that had caused the change. She hadn't acted like this on Saturday night. Was she consciously playing a role?

Sadie pushed her bowl away, her soup only half eaten, and pulled the box with her nesting doll from her handbag. She separated the dolls then put them together, lining the quartet up on the table.

"I hadn't expected to see you here."

Les looked up. Semyon stood next to the table, holding a tray. Next to him was a beauty, a slender woman of about thirty, taller than Semyon. This must be Irina. He unpacked his most suave smile and rose. "I was sent up here by my company to sell some magazines."

"They read in Yorkshire? I hadn't noticed." Semyon spoke in Russian.

Les answered in kind. "But there are printers here. Do you know any of them?"

Semyon's eyes narrowed. "What do you know about printers?"

Heart beating fast, Les pulled the flyer he'd retrieved from Sadie from his pocket and handed it to Semyon.

Semyon set down his tray, took the piece of paper, and perused it. "The date is wrong. The rally was changed to today, down on the small wharf by the Albert dock."

Coal stink instead of fish. There were such better places to live in England. "Did you come up to go to it?"

"Why do you care? You sell to merchants, don't you? You aren't a newsboy."

Les thought fast as Sadie stared at them. "I'm interested in worker's rights. Do you know how much money my company's owner has? While I'm all but living on a train, begging for my shillings."

"Is that why your wife is along?"

His brain continued to churn out answers. While whole fiction was dangerous, the fact that they weren't married meant everything was a tissue of lies. "We had to set mouse traps last night. She can't stand to see the poor dead things, so I brought her with me." Thankfully Sadie didn't speak a word of Russian.

"A sensitive soul."

Les nodded. "Yes. You should hear her speak about the atrocious way some dog owners treat their pets. Is this your lovely wife?"

"Yes, this is Mrs. Kozyrev."

Les nodded politely. Semyon's wife could scarcely bother to glance at him. She seemed to be fixated on Sadie's dolls. "Sadie," he hissed.

His pretend wife glanced up. He pointed at the dolls. "I think Mrs. Kozyrev would like to see your present."

Sadie gestured politely to the chair across from her at the four seat table. All three of them sat as she turned the painted side of her dolls to face Mrs. Kozyrev.

The older woman picked up each of the four dolls in turn. "I had many of these when I was a child in Russia." She spoke in English. "I had to leave them all behind."

"I'm sorry," Sadie said. "The war?"

The woman shook her head. "No, I only left after Lenin died."

Sadie radiated empathy. "I'm afraid I don't know anything about Russian politics."

"That is best for wives." Mrs. Kozyrev's lips twisted as she took a soup bowl off the tray. "Politics are not a woman's game. We are too soft-hearted."

Les glanced between the two women. His gut told him that they were not compatible. Sadie was too fresh and uneducated to appeal to this cosmopolitan refugee. Not like the young wife from Acton who was desperate for a friend. When Glass had given him orders he hadn't accounted for Sadie's youth. She was only a chambermaid, after all.

"What time is the rally?" he asked Semyon in Russian.

He responded in kind. "In an hour. Will I see you there?"

Les nodded. "I need to pay a couple of sales calls on bookshops here and then we will go to the docks. Will your wife come along?"

Semyon nodded and took his own bowl of soup off the tray. "She is very political."

"Mrs. Rake is not educated in these matters." Les spooned up the last couple bites of his borsht. There likely wouldn't be time for food later.

"She'll learn," Semyon said. "What is her background?"

"Orphan," Les said, not wanting to reveal more.

"English through and through, right?"

Les nodded and put his and Sadie's bowls on Semyon's tray, then poured overbrewed tea from the pot into his empty cup.

"Why did you marry her? Money?"

Les was glad they were still speaking in Russian. He let his gaze peruse the length of the skinny brown bow detail on Sadie's cream dress. The ribbon slid down her chest between her breasts, revealing their buoyant shape underneath the thin fabric. He glanced back at Semyon, who smirked.

"A young man must have his pleasures," Semyon said.

"Your wife is very beautiful," Les told him. Sadie's eyes went to him. The color matched the stormy sea now. He realized he had missed an exchange between her and Irina Kozyrev. When he glanced next to him he saw Irina was putting the nesting doll together, then, when at last the matryoshka was back together, she put the doll into the gift box and placed the lid on top, then slid it into her handbag.

Shocked, he let his hurt show as he moved his gaze back to Sadie. She shook her head slightly, as if warning him of danger. Next to her, Semyon was devouring his soup. Sadie pushed a plate of brown bread to him and he took a piece without looking up.

Les stared at his erstwhile wife. Had she given Irina the dolls because she was afraid of her, or was there some deeper game? What had the girl sensed about her role here? Irina set her handbag on her lap, her lips curving with genuine satisfaction. With a last look at Les, Sadie deliberately moved her attention to the other woman, smiling. Irina laughed.

Sadie had done the unexpected and turned the assassin's daughter into an ally, it seemed.

Chapter Four

Sadie watched Irina Kozyrev devour her borscht while she listened to their two companions speak in Russian, a language she had no familiarity with. Les was using his hands a lot when he spoke, something he didn't do when talking in English. Mrs. Kozyrev had gone from seeming to have no appetite for food at all, to an intense hunger. The woman ate the rest of the bread on the plates too, enough for three people, then drank two cups of tea.

She had a level of acquisitive lust that Sadie had only seen in children, children who were as likely to steal a friend's doll as to build a friendship just to have access to a favored toy. Unscrupulous, possessive desire.

Sadie had thought it best to make a gift of the doll, rather than find it had been "lost" by the end of the day. She had no idea if Mrs. Kozyrev would appreciate the gesture, or if merely wanting the possession would make it hers in her mind, but these people seemed important to Les. He'd left that Richmond party to follow Semyon on her birthday, and now they'd come some five hours on a train, apparently to follow him again.

She didn't understand at all, as it seemed to have nothing to do with Les's job. But her best hope of returning home in one piece was to make whatever Les needed possible, so they could return to the train. Then, when she was safe in Richmond, she could explain that his behavior had been outrageous and he owed her an apology, an explanation, or she'd never see him again.

"*Matryoshka*," Mrs. Kozyrev said. "That is what they are called in Russian."

"The dolls?" Sadie asked.

The woman nodded and poured a third cup of tea. Sadie was thirsty herself, but the pot was empty now.

"I had fine examples of course, not tourist garbage like yours, but still, it was made in my homeland."

Sadie nodded, years of life as a vicar's daughter, forced to bow and scrape to wealthy elderly parishioners, accustoming her to casual insults. She glanced over to Les and saw he'd had the same practice. Despite having nothing to eat or do, he looked entirely serene. "Do you think we could have more hot water?" she asked him.

He jumped to his feet, lifting the tray from the center of the table. She appreciated his athleticism. The fabric of his trousers stretched across powerful thighs whenever he moved. He had large feet, which made him seem more firmly planted into the earth than most men, but despite that, he moved with grace. She had loved dancing with him, kissing him, but his character had an air of danger that kept her on edge.

After he returned with the water, they passed another twenty minutes with the Kozyrevs, chatting lightly about Russian art, about which Sadie knew nothing. Then Semyon tapped his watch and Les pushed back his chair.

"We are going to take a walk," Les said. "There is a meeting we'd like to attend."

"What about your work?" Sadie asked.

"I can stop in at one bookshop on the way," he said, glancing at Semyon. The other man nodded. "That will appease my employer."

"Then what?"

"Back on the train. You have to work in the morning."

She nodded. "Thank you for remembering."

"Absolutely."

"I must have something to do when you travel," she said, aware that two sets of Kozyrev eyes were on them, and that they were pretending to be married for reasons she did not understand. Her best idea now would be to pat his hand or offer some other kind of familiarity, but she had no easy way to reach him since he was across the table with Semyon.

"Very well," Semyon turned to Les and said in accented English. "If you must do your work, you need to leave now. We do not want to miss the speeches."

Mrs. Kozyrev rolled her eyes, and Sadie realized she was not going to enjoy this outing at all.

"Stay with us," Semyon ordered. "Let your husband do his work. We will meet him at the dock."

Sadie's eyes went wide. She looked at Les, assuming he'd protest, but he was already standing, pulling his coat on. He couldn't leave her in an unfamiliar town in Yorkshire with strangers!

But he could, and he did. He walked around the table, bussed her cheek, and said, "See you soon." His eyes did not meet hers as he spoke to Semyon rapidly in Russian. She only recognized the name of a railway company, then he strode out of the door, swinging his magazine case.

Semyon leaned forward and said something to his wife. She lifted the teapot and poured fresh tea for all three of them. He took out a flask and doctored his tea and his wife's. Sadie waved away the alcohol and stared glumly at the table. She wondered if she should send a cable to her grandfather now, asking for help.

Something told her, though, that she could trust Lester Rake. Why, she couldn't say. Something about his eyes, the way his gaze was so steady on her. Inside him was an unflappable place and she had to trust that no matter how crazy things seemed. She'd only known him a few days but she felt safe with him. Les, yes, but not Semyon, and definitely not his wife. She wasn't going anywhere with them but to this wharf where the railway company had its warehouse.

"There must be a toy store here for Russians," Mrs. Kozyrev said. "That would have more dolls."

Sadie stared into her cup as Semyon responded to his wife in Russian, twirling the last half inch of dark tea inside, wishing she could read her tea leaves and see what her future held. She tilted her head this way and that, trying to see shapes in the matted leaves.

"Do you know Hull?" the other woman asked, her voice coming back to the forefront.

Sadie showed her the contents of her teacup. "Does that look like a glove to you?"

Mrs. Kozyrev regarded her like she was a spider building a web on a lace curtain. She leaned forward. "Do you know Hull?" she repeated.

Sadie felt slapped. Who did this woman think she was? "No." Her voice was clipped, a rebuke.

"There must be a telephone subscriber list, or some kind of directory," she said, as if hoping Sadie would find one for her.

"My husband won't need much of a head start," Sadie said, pushing back her chair. "Shouldn't we be going?"

Semyon stared at her blankly for a moment, then nodded. "Why did you come to Hull?"

She took a moment to translate his heavy accent. "I hadn't planned on it. But my Les, he brought me along."

"You work at a hotel?"

"Yes." She felt the desire to be as unimportant as possible to this man, so she didn't mention her exciting opportunity. "I'm one of the masses toiling. At the Richmond Inn."

"Your husband, his accent." Semyon grunted. "England is so class conscious. You do not seem his equal."

She froze in her chair. "My grandfather, my father, for that matter, was a gentleman."

"Not a coal miner then, or a simple greengrocer?"

She shook her head. "I was orphaned young. I thought it best to make my own way."

He frowned, and she realized she'd made a mistake. She forced a smile. "But then I met my Les. A whirlwind courtship."

He smiled back, exposing a missing tooth on the top right side. His eyes drifted south. "Yes, he does appreciate what you have to offer."

She felt a desperate urge to bathe. He made her feel unclean. But she couldn't react. She was dependent on him to find Les so she could go home. Never again. Les was one thing, but his creepy friends were another.

"You are much too pretty to have remained unwed for long," Mrs. Kozyrev opined. She then said something to her husband in Russian and rose to her feet, gesturing to Sadie. "Come."

Reluctantly, Sadie followed her into the back of the restaurant. The small washroom was damp and icy. She watched the other woman pull a small mirror from her handbag and repaint her lips a vibrant shade of red. Her own lipstick was back at the hotel, forgotten in the basket on the top of her trunk. Since her grandfather didn't like makeup, she hadn't developed the habit of carrying any in her handbag. Now, with a man like Les taking her anywhere at any time, she needed to be better prepared. If she stayed with him, she'd be one of those women who carried a knitting bag with her everywhere she went, just to have something to do.

"You are smiling," Mrs. Kozyrev observed. "Why?"

"I was thinking I should take up knitting like a proper married lady."

The other woman frowned. "I do not knit."

No, you're too busy being avaricious. Sadie shivered as the woman put away her lipstick and powder. They returned to Semyon and left the restaurant, heading toward the docks. Even before they reached the bookshop where they were meeting Les, Sadie could smell seaweed and clay, with a faint tang of vinegar.

Les, standing outside the shop door, greeted them with a ready smile.

"Sell anything?" Semyon asked in English.

"I unloaded ten magazines that I had on hand, but I couldn't persuade the man to take on any subscriptions."

Sadie took his arm. "At least your case is lighter now."

Les nodded absently. They turned a corner and Sadie's nose was assaulted by the heavy stench of fuel. She could hear roaring sounds, which turned out to be a gathered crowd.

"Did we have the time wrong?" Les asked Semyon.

The man shrugged. Sadie began to be able to make out the words on the signs men were waving. "Solidarity" was a common theme. "Strike" was another. "Worker's Rights" held great popularity.

She understood there was a lot of unrest around the coal miners. "Why are they protesting here?"

"It's a regional transport hub," Les said.

She clutched his arm tighter. "Why did we come here? I don't like this." The men looked so dirty, like they never washed their clothing or hair. The scent of coal in the warehouses, the trains, the sea smells, it all turned her stomach. She was a long way from Bagshot.

"Stay close to the Kozyrevs," he said. He stared at his hand holding his case in disfavor. "I'd like to hear the speeches."

"There are speeches?" she asked faintly. "I thought we'd take a look and then go back to the train station."

"No, this will go on for a couple of hours," Les said. "Come, let's move closer."

Semyon cleared a path through the crowd, leading them steadily through the protesters to a distant spot on the actual dock thrust into the Humber where a platform had been raised and a banner was held by two poles stuck into barrels. A man was imprecating the crowd from the platform. Sadie couldn't hear a word but was struck by the man's thick mustache and pointed beard. He looked like Lenin, the assassinated Russian revolutionary, although he spoke like an Englishman.

Or, as she listened to him shout from the platform, she realized he sounded like a Russian, but with an English accent. All his talk of worker inequality excited the crowd, but it meant nothing to her. At twenty, she had most of what she wanted, and knew the rest would come if she chose a husband wisely. She would fight for the right man, instead of hoping for one to choose her, like her sister had. Sadie Loudon wasn't going to be a surplus woman, like so many a decade or so older than she were, thanks to the war.

"Stirring stuff," Les muttered next to her. He sounded sarcastic. "Here, take this. I'm going to go right up front."

She took the case on autopilot, distracted by a woman, obviously pregnant, begging her husband not to raise a sign into the air. They were better dressed than most, and she imagined the man might work for the train company rather than as a miner.

Les had moved away from her by then. She pushed deeper into the crowd in front of the dock. She couldn't risk losing sight of him. When she saw him again, he was speaking to an unusually tall fellow. Another speaker came onto the platform and orated about wage slavery. The crowd around her rallied to his cry. She pressed forward again, trying to keep the tall fellow in sight. Off to the right, where the warehouses began, a row of cars pushed through the crowd. Uniformed police constables poured out of them as they stopped.

Woman were more prevalent close to the platform. Some had the light of holy fire in their eyes, true believers in the cause. A couple even had children in tow, picnic baskets, like a cold January day on the river was a good excuse for an outing. Had Les imagined something like this for their date? A picnic?

Someone groaned.

Sadie stopped her forward movement when she saw another pregnant woman, breathing hard, clutching a basket. She dropped Les's sample case and grabbed the woman before she doubled over.

"You need to leave here," she told the woman, trying to speak under the roar of the crowd. "The police have arrived."

The pregnant woman frowned, shaking out her skirt. Spots of tar had smeared on it. "The fabric is going to be ruined." The distant expression on her face intensified and she put her hand to her belly.

"Are you in labor?" Sadie asked, disbelieving. She set the basket down on top of Les's case and grabbed the woman around the waist, just as the crowd surged forward. They were carried several feet closer to the platform.

Sadie craned her neck, trying to see what was going on. The police were still on the edge of the crowd but she couldn't see much. On the platform, the man had spittle in the corners of his mouth as he screamed something about lies and freedom and revolution.

She turned around, trying to protect the woman's belly. Her eyes scanned for Les, for the tall man who'd been next to him. "Oh, thank God." She spotted the tall man. Despite his height, he looked like a boxer, with the characteristic reset nose and damaged ears.

"Let's go that way," Sadie said, pointing. She tried to walk at a diagonal, very hard to do moving backward. The crowd pushed again, shouting. Signs waved in the air all around her. The wind whipped one out of a slight man's hand. It hit another man a couple of feet away from Sadie, knocking the cap from his head. The man went to his knees. Sadie stumbled against someone else. She grabbed for the pregnant woman, whose eyes were vague as she focused on whatever was happening inside her body.

Someone ripped her handbag from her arm just as she saw the tall men. "Les!" she screamed.

A hole appeared in the crowd. She saw Les, still dapper from tie to the tip of his head, though his coat was inexplicably filthy. He pointed at her and called something out, but she couldn't hear him. She turned sideways, trying to pull the woman along in her wake. Les pushed forward, his arm out, blocking men from moving forward.

She heard whistles, police whistles. The crowd moved in a new direction, almost a spiral. Some were trying to leave, some were trying to get closer to the platform. Les reached them.

"I think she's having a baby," Sadie cried, gesturing to the woman's belly.

"Go toward the police," Les said, his expression determined as he came to help.

The wind brought sprinkles of rain, or maybe sea water. It sounded like thousands of pieces of paper rustling. She couldn't be sure, but the sky had gone charcoal. With Les at the woman's front and her at the woman's back, they began to propel her toward the constables. Thanks to the crowd, they made little headway. They went in the direction of the police cars, but also even closer to the platform. The banner whipped in the wind. She heard the planks creaking. Waves dashed against the pilings, sending sludge over the dock. The speaker gripped the book in his hand and waved it over his head. The wind grabbed it, sending it flying into the crowd. The man stumbled and another man grabbed for his arm.

The pregnant woman groaned, recapturing Sadie's attention. She caught Les's gaze. He glanced over the woman. She knew he was trying to decide if he could carry her, but the woman was already bulky without her pregnant condition.

"Where's Semyon?" she called. Even better, she wondered where the boxer was. He could carry the woman.

Les shook his head then leaned over the pregnant woman's ear, trying to speak to her. Sadie saw the boxer and waved her hand at him. Did Les know him? Would he help? She hadn't seen the Kozyrevs for at least ten minutes.

The strong wind slapped at the banner. One side separated from the pole. The pole holding the banner tipped. The barrel and whatever was inside keeping the pole upright didn't hold. It fell into the crowd.

Sadie screamed as she was spun around and covered her head with her hands to protect it. People pressed away in all directions. She pulled her hands from her eyes, unsure of how they'd arrived there. The pregnant woman hummed, holding her belly, uninjured, but Les had fallen face first onto the wooden plank of the dock, the pole over his back.

Sadie's vision dimmed. Her diaphragm froze, cutting off her scream. Fighting black spots in front of her eyes, she ran forward, terrified, and tried to lift the pole off of Les's back. It was so heavy.

She could roll it. Would that hurt him more? Two men jumped off the podium and helped her. They heaved the pole to the side. It clicked on the wood as it rolled.

"What do I do?" Sadie sobbed, staring down at Les's unmoving form.

"I dinna see a head wound, miss," one of the men said.

"He's lost his hat," she said nonsensically. "Does he look cold?" She stripped off her coat and began to lay it over him.

"Make a pad and put it by his head. We'll turn him over," the other man said.

She did as he suggested and they rolled him over. He had livid scratches on his face from falling onto the dock. His eyes were half-closed. An older woman appeared and knelt by Les's unmoving form. She put her cheek to his mouth.

"He's breathing," the woman reported. When she looked up, her attention was captured by the pregnant woman. "You have your hands full here. I'll take the woman in labor."

The man with the Scottish accent pointed. "They've ambulances behind the police cars."

"Can we carry him to an ambulance?" Sadie asked. The nurse had already taken the pregnant woman by the hand and was leading her off.

The man with the Lenin facial hair walked up to them. "A comrade fallen for the cause. May I have his name, please?"

Sadie stared at the man. "We need to get him to the ambulance. Will you help?"

The Scotsman rolled his eyes. "Orville Percy makes speeches. He doesn't lift."

"His name?" asked the man impatiently. "Don't let your husband die in vain, Mrs—"

The crowd roared off to the right. The policemen were moving.

"We need to get yer husband to the ambulance now, before some other fellow takes it," said the Scotsman. "Help me with his shoulders. I'll take his legs."

Sadie thought frantically. What would Les want? She decided he'd come here for a reason and she should respect that. "Lester Rake," she told Orville Percy as she pushed her arms under Les's right shoulder, scraping her knuckles on the splintery wooden planks. "He's a salesman and his name is Lester Rake. But he's not going to die."

* * *

Les could hear the crying. It seemed like every time he woke up, Aunt Tatty was crumpled into the arm chair next to his bed. He turned his head on the pillow, choking up himself, missing his mother, too. Something was wrong though. The pillowcase didn't smell like lavender and it scratched his cheek.

"Les?" Rustling. "Nurse? My husband's eyelids are fluttering."

He heard a young woman's voice, a Surrey accent, not Aunt Tatty's middle-aged Hampshire tones, interspersed with sobs. Someone was talking about her husband.

He moved his head again, slowly coming to full consciousness, though he wasn't ready to open his eyes. *Hospital.* He must be in hospital. Trying to remember why seemed like too much work.

"He's moved his head," the young woman said, as shuffling footsteps came to a stop nearby. "And blinked."

"It's been a long five days for you, dear," said another voice, strained and tired, older and slower than Aunt Tatty's. "It's suprisin' to have good news after all this time."

As Les thought about losing five days, his thoughts moving at turtle-speed, the young woman said, "The doctor said he would wake up when the swelling went down."

"It's the Lord's will," the woman said.

Les identified her as a Yorkshire woman. West, he thought, working class, probably a nurse at the hospital. So he was in Yorkshire. That did ring a bell. *Hull.* He'd have sat up with the sudden remembering, but he felt much too weak. He settled for opening his eyes.

The woman at his bedside had her hand on his pillow. Her hand had his father's V signet ring where a wedding ring ought to be. He recognized the ring, but who was the girl? She smiled tenderly at him.

"Les? It's Sadie." Her voice trembled a little. "Your wife? Mrs. Lester Rake?"

He wasn't married. But, he considered, he was a spy. She must be his cover. Was she a spy too? She looked so young. "How old are you?" he asked, his voice sounding aged and raspy.

"Silly man. I'm twenty. Do you remember? We went to that party with Semyon on my birthday?" Her voice was light as she patted his arm, but her greenish blue eyes were troubled.

She was trying to tell him his history. *Semyon.* The full name, with autobiographical details, snapped into his head. Semyon Kozyrev, husband of Irina, labor organizer, funded by the Russians. He'd been attempting to develop the man into a source. No chance of turning him. No, Les remembered he'd been trying to infiltrate the labor organization. He'd been sent to Hull to deepen his connection to the Kozyrevs, introduce Sadie to Irina.

"Sadie?" Should he use a Russian accent? His usual accent. How his head hurt, like it had been squeezed like a sponge and left to shrivel.

"Yes, darling." She smiled at him.

Awfully pretty, this blonde. Why had Glass wanted to inflict an assassin's daughter on this appealing young English lass? For their great work, he supposed. Patriotism over the individual. "Five days? What happened to your job?"

"I couldn't leave you. It was my fault. You had no money, no identification."

He worked his throat, trying to sort it out. "Water?"

"Just a sip now," the nurse cautioned as Sadie eagerly brought a smudged glass to his lips.

He was only allowed to drink an inch. "Have the Kozyrevs been helping you?" he asked slowly.

Sadie shook her head. Her head movement made the room spin around his eyes. "Yes, a little." She leaned closer. "I'm afraid of them, Les. I couldn't leave you. A wife wouldn't. Plus, someone stole my handbag and I lost your sample case. Everything is gone. Your wallet, any money either of us had. Except your keys. No one stole those."

Slowly, he lifted his hand to his head. The Kozyrevs. She was right to fear them. She had no idea who he really was; he remembered now. He'd somehow charmed this girl into pretending to be the wife of a commercial traveler. He'd promised to have her home and back to work by morning.

"You need to gather your strength," the nurse said, pulling up his blanket. "Don't worry about home quite yet."

"Sadie? What about you?" he asked. "Five days?"

She smiled wearily. "I slept here, but Mrs. Kozyrev brought me clothes and food once a day. I've become quite a nurse these five days, tending to you."

Which is why he wasn't dead. She'd been force-feeding him. "You've kept me alive."

"Of course."

He ran his tongue along his foul teeth, trying to find moisture. "I am so sorry, Sadie."

She patted his arm. "I couldn't leave my husband, you silly man."

What would she have done if he'd died? He hoped Semyon would have paid her way back to London. He could smell the scents of illness, the vomit, urine, and blood, hear the groans and wheezes and snores, as he came into full consciousness. No privacy here.

"Ah, here's Doctor," the nurse said.

"He's awake, then, eh? Your faith was justified, Mrs. Rake," drawled a young man with a tongue depressor tucked into a suit pocket. He stopped at the bed and stared down at Les.

Overwhelmed, he allowed himself to lapse into semi-sleep after the doctor poked and prodded him. Saving Sadie would have to wait for a little while. At least she looked a lot better than he felt.

"Well, well, well."

Les heard the Russian accent sometime later, and fought his way out of brain fog. He heard the click of a woman's heeled shoes on the floor. A heavy object was dropped by his bed.

"Mrs. Kozyrev!" Sadie exclaimed. "Isn't it wonderful?"

"I am most happy for you," the woman said.

"It's been dreadful. Les has only just regained consciousness. What would we have done without you?"

He opened his eyes a crack to see Irina Kozyrev gazing down at him, a little smile playing across carmine lips. "So sick-making to see a strong man in his prime struck down."

Les felt a frisson of fear. He clenched his stomach muscles, hoping he was strong enough to sit up. He wasn't. What did the Kozyrevs want with him now? Had they somehow learned he was a spy?

Chapter Five

"There you are. Stay strong, dearest." Sadie hovered next to Les, though Semyon Kozyrev was doing most of the helping as her fake-husband climbed the first step onto the train at the station in Hull. He coughed as heavy smoke wafted through the chilly air.

They were finally going back to London, more than a week after having gone north for one day. He'd steadily improved since he'd woken up, although he'd said little in the past few days. She understood this. What were they to say to one another? She wasn't really his wife and everything they said was heard by others.

Les coughed again as he took in another lungful of coal-laden smoke. She pressed herself against his back so he wouldn't fall out of the train. Agonizingly slowly, he climbed another step. When he reached the top, Semyon jumped back down and his wife handed up Les's sample case. Her handbag and his wallet had never reappeared, but at least the Kozyrevs had found the expensive leather case. She didn't want Les to lose his position.

"Thank you." She waved down to the Kozyrevs, who lived in Hull.

"Here is some reading material for you." Semyon handed up some newspapers.

"Thank you again." She glanced down and saw the top newspaper was folded to an article detailing the mass protests in Russia in the honor of Vladimir Lenin's first death anniversary.

Semyon nodded at her and stepped back from the train. She and Les moved into the passage and made it into the third-class compartment just as the train began to chug out of the station. He was pale and out of breath and as much collapsed onto the bench as sat.

She stared at her beautiful leather gloves, the birthday gift from

Les a little less than two weeks before. They clashed with the orange and blue knitted handbag she'd found discarded in the charity clothing box. The nurses had been kindness personified during their stay at the hospital. On her second day there, she'd agreed to clean the ward every morning in return for sleeping in a trundle bed next to Les at night, but it was easy work.

Finally, when the doctor said Les was well enough to attempt the journey home, the nurses had taken up a collection for their train fare. The Kozyrevs had paid the part of Les's hospital bill not covered by her cleaning.

She'd had a weak moment where she'd whispered in Les's ear, asking if he had any relatives they could apply to for help, but he'd shaken his head no. So he had no living relatives, and she had only one she could contact and was too embarrassed to do so. The truth was, cleaning here was no more disgusting than cleaning up after those poodles at the Richmond Inn, and she hoped a letter from the Grand Russe Hotel was waiting for her, since she'd no doubt lost the Richmond Inn position.

When she opened the newspaper, two small rectangles of paper dropped out. She lifted one and saw it appeared to be a membership card for the League of British Workers. Mr. Lester Valentin Rake was typed onto the member line on one card. Mrs. Sadie Rake was typed onto the other. A box was checked on each for January dues.

She handed them to Les. "What's this?"

He perused the card, then took the other one from her unresisting hand. "Congratulations, you've been accepted."

"What do you mean?"

"These are basically an invitation. As you can see, they've paid for, or given us credit for, the first month's dues."

"It's already the twenty-second."

He nodded, then closed his eyes as if his head movement nauseated him. "Yes, we really join if we pay the next month's dues."

"What is the League of British Workers? Is that the group that held the rally?"

"No." He licked his lower lip.

She remembered that mouth so hungry against hers, but it seemed like forever ago. Ironically, she had been so intimate with his body. She knew every nook and cranny, had washed its unresisting angles and curves. He was a beautiful man, despite the hidden scars, evidence of a harder past than she could have imagined. Yes, she knew his body, but not his mind.

"What is this League, then? Some pet project of the Kozyrevs?"

He smiled. "I assume it is exactly that. I'll ask around."

"It doesn't make any sense, you know. A League of British Workers should have English members, not Russian."

"Words can be very deceptive, Mrs. Rake," he said. "Sometimes organizations are named the opposite of what they really are."

"Are you a Bolshevik?" she asked in a low voice. "I found that flyer from the day we met in your sample case. I remember you were chasing that Russian man."

Les's mouth twisted. "I owed him money."

She didn't believe him, but he wasn't well enough to confront. "You looked like you were having fun, but he didn't."

"Russians aren't very good at having fun," he said. "And I'd had a look at you."

She blushed, remembering the way he'd charmed her, the way she'd followed him anywhere. "Why do you want to be friends with the Kozyrevs? I gave Irina my nesting doll because it seemed like you really wanted me to befriend her."

"Where did you get that idea?"

"The way you looked from her to me and back again. You had a plan. Maybe it's joining this League. But I don't understand why it's so important for you to be Russian. You have only one Russian grandparent. Shouldn't you simply try to be British?"

"It's not that simple," Les said softly. "Think of this. Semyon knew me as Valentin, but now he has the rest of my name. He must have found my wallet, and kept it."

"You are as afraid of him as I was of his wife," Sadie said.

"Agreed," he said. "I have to protect you, now."

You're telling me. Sadie shook her head. She and her sister had spent hours dissecting every little detail of their small lives in Bagshot. This man lived life on a larger scale, but he rarely spoke at all. She'd spent more than a week at his bedside, even seen his man parts numerous times, and yet she knew no more about him than she'd known on her birthday. Could she trust him? What kind of mess had he pulled her in to?

Les fell asleep against her shoulder before she could pull herself out of her thoughts. He slept all the hours the train moved through the center of England. She read the papers Semyon had provided, forcing herself to pay attention to everything Russian-related. There was a trade mission in London, for instance.

When she tired of reading, she schemed. After twelve days at Les's bedside, the least she should receive out of the experience was a marriage proposal. She deserved to be his wife after all of this, and it would be good for him too, since he'd fallen in love with her by the time they arrived in Hull, based on what he'd said to her then. She'd lost her position because of him and the Lord only knew how disappointed her grandfather would be by her behavior. She needed to vanish off the face of the earth until she had a proper ring on her finger, her marriage listed in the books of some parish. Finally, she fell asleep too, thinking about spending her life with Lester Rake, and woke up with a mouth of cotton wool and fuzzy vision as the train pulled into the station. She recognized the tall stone and glass edifice of Kings Cross.

Touching Les's shoulder, she said, "We're home. You need to gather your strength now."

He sighed. "I'll get it back, darling. I've been in worse shape than this. We should have taken the time to find my car."

She waited until they were in the taxicab moving toward Primrose Hill before she followed up on his remark. "Worse shape than this? How is that possible? You nearly died. And your car can wait for another day. I wouldn't want you driving and I don't know how."

He patted her hand on the seat between them. His movements were disjointed, not the actions of a man with energy. "I was in the army. We weren't fed well. I've traveled to Russia and back."

With Les's wallet missing, she'd made up most of his biographical details at the hospital. He'd told her he was twenty-five. "You were in the Great War?"

He shook his head. "No, I'm twenty-five. I just missed the fight, went to University instead."

She frowned. "And then you joined the army?"

He grinned tiredly. "The Russian Army, darling."

She glanced away, trying to control her emotions. He'd gone to University, then moved to Russia and joined the army there? What kind of man was he? If the story were even true.

Light had fled the sky by the time they reached Primrose Hill. She paid the driver she could scarcely see with the last of the nurse collection money when they reached the converted Edwardian house where Les had his flat. Les accepted her help to exit the taxicab, then walked arm-in-arm with her to the front door of his building.

"I really hope the keys in your pocket went to this flat," she said.

He nodded. "Yes. We were lucky there."

She opened the case for him and pulled out the keys. The door swung part way open then stuck. Mail had piled up in a white snow-like drift around the door. She knelt down and gathered everything, then set it on a marble-topped half table to the side of the door. It had a mail sorter but there was too much mail to fit in the slots.

The entryway was a separate room of its own, very modern, with a narrow flight of steps to one side and passages leading off in two directions. A grand mirror opposite the door made the room appear larger than it was, but still, she could have fit most of her bedroom at the Richmond Inn into it.

"The garden is to the left and the bedrooms are to the right," Les said with a yawn.

"Let's go right to your bed," she said, wrapping her arm around him.

"My bedroom is the last one, the fourth door," he said sleepily. "Sheets will be stale, I'm afraid."

She patted his back. "I don't think you'll mind. We'll find you some pajamas and you'll be asleep as soon as your head touches the pillow." They took their first steps. She remembered finding it hard to keep up with him when they'd gone up Primrose Hill. Now, she had to slow to match him.

He found a reservoir of that rakish charm. "What about you? Are you going to lay your head down next to mine?"

She blushed. "I'll stay here for now. You need me to care for you and I'm out of a job after what happened. I assume there is more than one bedroom?"

"There are three total, but I use one as a study."

"I'll take the other so you don't have to share your pillow. But while you sleep, I'm going to take your keys and go over to the Grand Russe Hotel. Maybe they will take pity on me even though I don't have the response to my letter. Plus, my sister lives there. I can borrow clothes."

He pointed. "This is my bedroom door. We just passed the bathroom and before that were the other two bedrooms. What about the Richmond Inn, or even your grandfather?"

"I don't want to leave you for that long. I need to get food for us somehow. Maybe I should stop in at your office for you and explain?" There was no way she was going to speak to her grandfather until she had a resolved story about her relationship with Les.

She helped him move into his bedroom. His steps had slowed measurably by the time he reached the bed.

"I can sleep in my clothing." He sat on the bed.

"No. You rode the train in those clothes. They're filthy. Can you take your coat off?" She went to a highboy dresser that was part of a matched bedroom set constructed from a dark, masculine wood. Expecting him to tell her which drawer to focus on, she opened one drawer, then another, not really looking, but he didn't say anything. The third drawer from the bottom held striped pajama sets in Indian cotton. She pulled out a set and then went back up the drawers and found socks. The flat was decidedly chilly.

"I need to turn on the heat." She turned back to him. His eyes were half-mast, but they snapped open when she took off his tie then unbuttoned his coat.

"Turn on the radiator. It's just outside the loo door." He yawned. "I should take off my own clothing."

"Think of me as your nurse. I've done this sort of thing often enough for you in the last couple of weeks."

He looked more alert. "You did?"

"Yes. I had nowhere to go, so I took care of you like a wife would."

He clasped her hand, his fingers cold. "I'm so sorry, Sadie. This is not the kind of time I wanted to give a pretty girl."

"You didn't plan to be hit over the head while trying to help me rescue a pregnant woman," she said tartly, getting his waistcoat unbuttoned.

"What happened to her, I wonder? You know, I really don't remember much of what happened. Just scattered images."

"I don't know. She wasn't injured, just frightened, I think. Or maybe she was having labor pains. I don't have any medical training."

"But you are an expert in me now." He regarded her, a little dreamy-eyed.

She smiled tenderly. "Yes."

He yawned. "You have the keys. You see that little monkeywood box on the top of the dresser?"

She looked over and saw a mid-sized reddish box. "Yes." She wrapped the pajama shirt around his shoulders then helped him put his arms in.

"Take all the money in it. Taxicabs, grocery. I don't know if it will extend to fresh clothing for you, but a pair of stockings, at least. Spend it all."

"What if you've lost your position, Les? Is that all the money you have?"

"No." He yawned. "Bank account. Don't worry, darling. I can sell anything. I won't be sacked."

She helped him with his trousers and pajama bottoms, reflecting that he could indeed sell anything. How had she come to this, helping a man with his clothes?

By the time she had the covers tucked under his arms, he was asleep, snoring softly. She returned to the highboy and took all the money she found, about five pounds, and the keys. Tossing them into her orange and blue knitted handbag, she returned to the entryway and tucked everything into her coat pockets.

"Oh, I feel grubby," she muttered to herself. She'd made a parcel of her original clothing, but in the end, she'd taken nothing from Mrs. Kozyrev but the dress she wore. She needed to wash her original clothes and indeed, what she wore. In the bathroom, she did the best she could to tidy herself and make sure she didn't smell. An iron would have helped. Les's flat was a maisonette with the parlor and kitchen upstairs. She didn't want to be gone too long though, knowing he would wake up hungry since he hadn't eaten since Hull.

No lipstick, no powder. She glanced at herself one last time in the mirror over the mail table. At least she had a nice muffler and gloves. Maybe she could find her sister and borrow her makeup before she went to the hotel manager's office.

Once outside, she had no trouble finding a taxicab, and received directions to the closest greengrocer's shop for when she returned.

The Grand Russe Hotel was on Park Lane, a very prestigious part of London with many fine hotels. The taxicab pulled up under an awning and the door was opened by a dark-skinned man in a resplendent Russian red coat and matching hat.

"Welcome to the Grande Russe Hotel," he said in an American accent, large white teeth flashing in his face.

"Hello." She paid the driver as the doorman shut the door.

"No luggage?"

"No. I'm here to see my sister, Alecia Loudon. Do you have any idea how I can reach her?"

"Ask at the reception desk. If she's on the main floor, the hall porter will be able to locate her for you."

"Do you know her? My sister?" Sadie's attention was distracted by the sight of two constables disappearing through the front door.

"I know who she is, miss. Works for those Marvins, the theatrical couple."

She nodded eagerly. "Yes, that's her."

The doorman touched his cap. "Pretty girl. Doesn't leave the hotel much."

"I think the Marvins keep her very busy."

He opened the hotel door for two ladies in fur coats and turbans. They ignored him, walking right past him then toward the street. "I expect so, with the command performance taking place a couple of hours from now."

"Oh. I've come at exactly the wrong time, haven't I? She'll be run off her feet." Sadie bit her lip. "I was hoping to borrow some clothes."

"Expect so, miss. Tomorrow might be better." He straightened his collar.

"What about Mr. Peter Eyre? Do you think I could speak to him?"

The man bent slightly, to bring his mouth closer to Sadie's ear. "I'm not sure what's been going on around here, miss, but this is not a normal day. We've got government folks comin' in, lots of Russians movin' around."

"Russians?"

"Trade delegation staying here. I tell you, film stars are less work."

"Good to know." She nodded solemnly. "Well, thank you, mister."

He inclined his head. "It's John, Miss. Johnnie Miles."

"You must be a long way from home."

"We all are, if we ain't with our mommas." He grinned at her.

"Wish me luck," she said breezily. "I might be working here myself soon."

"Good luck then, Miss Loudon."

"Sadie Loudon," she said and offered Johnnie her hand. He looked at her, confusion pleating his brow, but took it. She smiled and walked toward the double doors. A constable opened it for her and she stepped into the famed hotel.

While she didn't consider herself a superstitious person, the hotel's energy felt off from the moment she entered. She knew it had only reopened at the end of the previous year, due to a complete refurbishment after the mysterious multiple murders of young film actresses some two and a half years ago. The Grand Hall was magnificent, reminding her of a train station in its breadth and grandeur. Busy, too, with bellboys rushing around, well-dressed folks walking in and out of the famously opulent Coffee Room. The walls seemed to echo with conversations, some of which might have taken place minutes ago, or even days. She was pretty sure she recognized the sharply coiffed woman who walked out of the hair Salon holding a tiny black dog. Honor Page, the film actress. If the chambermaid position was still available, she might be cleaning the room of someone as famous as that very soon.

She pulled off her muffler. Some kind of central heating kept even a space this large too warm for outdoor clothes. The hotel employees were dressed in what appeared to be heavy wool, Russian-style coats, but they didn't appear to be overheated. Maybe it was simply her nerves.

Glancing around, she found the reception desk and went to it. A middle-aged man with thinning blond hair stood behind the desk. His badge said "Lionel Dew, Night Manager."

"Mr. Dew," she said. "Can you tell me where Alecia Loudon is this evening? She works for the Marvins."

He regarded her with a stiff, militaristic air. "Do you have an invitation, miss? No one is being allowed on the floor without an official invitation or a room key."

She shook her head. "No. I had a letter from her, suggesting I see Mr. Eyre about a position as chambermaid. I wrote him more than a week ago."

"Mr. Eyre does not hire chambermaids," he said. "You'll need to leave an application." He reached under the desk and pulled out a piece of paper. "Here you go. Fill that out and we'll keep it on file for three months."

She didn't like the sound of that. "Do you think I'll be able to see Miss Loudon tomorrow?"

"It will be easier to navigate the hotel tomorrow, I should think so, yes," he said. "It's not every night we have a theatrical performance in the hotel."

She nodded. "I understand. Thank you for your time." She took the applicant form, considering whether she should go into the Reading Room and fill it out straightaway. Something about the atmosphere seemed so wrong, however, that she was torn between filling it out to ensure it was clean and unbent, and getting out of there as quickly as possible.

Forcing herself to remain calm, she went into the Reading Room and borrowed a pen from an elderly gentleman who was dozing over a newspaper crossword puzzle. She filled it out, using Les's address, knowing this could make her unreachable very soon. She put Alecia down as a reference.

"Here you go, Mr. Dew," she said, going back to the front desk.

He took the paper without so much as raising his unibrow of sparse blond hair, and put it under the desk. She thanked him and left, never so happy to leave a building in her life. She'd been in mausoleums with better atmosphere. How could Alecia stand it?

Johnnie helped her into another taxicab. "You didn't stay long."

"I couldn't see my sister or Mr. Eyre," she said ruefully. "It sounds like this is anything but a normal evening at the Grande Russe."

"When those Russians moved in everything changed," he confided. "And they ain't leaving anytime soon. We just have to get by. It's a lot of money for the hotel."

"Did I really see Honor Page?" she asked.

Johnnie nodded solemnly. "Staying with her husband, Mr. Teddy Fortress."

"I love his movies, even more than Charlie Chaplin's."

"Yes, miss. I haven't seen them myself, only been in England four months, but I hear they are very funny. Maybe you'll go to the pictures with me sometime, if you come to work here?"

"Maybe," she said with a smile. When she was in the taxicab driving away, she debated with herself over whether or not she should have said she was married. It was confusing to have more than one identity.

Another hour and a half later, she was back at Les's flat with groceries. She left them in the entryway and went into the master bedroom to check on Les, but he was fast asleep. So she took the groceries upstairs and made herself a plate of eggs, tomatoes, and sausages, setting the remains on the back of the stove for Les.

After she ate, she found the spare bedroom, noting that he wasn't well prepared for guests. She found a sheet in the linen closet and made up the small bed in the room. He was still asleep and she decided to let him be. After all, he knew where his own kitchen was if he woke hungry. She was ready for a proper night's rest herself.

"I don't think you should go out." Sadie looked him up and down critically the next morning, her hands on her hips.

He'd already turned the poor girl into a proper wife. Even an experienced wife couldn't find fault with his suit, however. Was she a virgin? He thought so, but she wouldn't stay so for long, with her willingness to take risks with strange men. He felt a moment of concern for her, but at the moment, caring for him kept her out of trouble. When he thought of the sorts of things he was willing to do when he was twenty, his heart sank into his stomach, though. He had the scars to show for the results of his choices.

"I need to. I want to keep my position, remember?"

"I can go with you. Carry your case."

He cupped her cheek with the hand that wasn't holding his case. "A good night's sleep did wonders. I'm not even dizzy right now. The bruising on my chest looks much better, too."

"You're a grown man and I can't stop you, but I'll be here to help you pick up the pieces when you return."

"What are you going to do?" he asked.

"I'm going to borrow your dressing gown and wash and iron my clothes. I left your address with my Grand Russe application."

If he had more energy, the thought of a naked Sadie in his paisley dressing gown would have sent the blood rushing south. Even in his condition, his cock twitched a bit at that idea. "Anything else?" His voice went husky.

"I had your milk and eggs delivery restarted when the man came to the door this morning. I thought I'd make scones."

"Perfect. I'll be home for tea. Assuming my car is where I left it the day we went north. Otherwise I'll be hunting it down."

He whistled jauntily as he clapped his hat onto his head, trying to prove to them both that he was well, and went out the door. Thankfully, there was a taxicab stopped on the street and he was heading toward Marylebone almost immediately.

Once he entered the street with the flat Glass used, he found a telephone box and called his contact number. He was told his section head would be along within half an hour. After he entered the flat, he made tea on the small stove, but then was too tired to drink it.

Some time later, the sound of the door opening woke him. He opened his eyes just as Glass entered the room and stood, tightening his tie.

Glass clasped his hand warmly. "I thought we'd lost you, Les."

"Not this time."

"How are you feeling?" Glass lifted the tea cozy and touched the pot. He grunted and poured overbrewed tea for them both.

"Tired. I must have fallen asleep for ten minutes or so."

"Your coloring is off. Concussion?"

"I think I'm past all that now. I was mostly unconscious until Monday, but it's Friday now."

"You need to eat. Build up your strength."

"Sadie is still with me, courtesy of me costing her her job, so she says, but I think she's afraid to leave me alone."

"A good woman is hard to find," Glass said, sitting down. He pushed the other chair out with his foot. "Tell me everything. I'll write it down to spare you making a written report of your own."

"Thank you, sir." Les told his story.

Glass chuckled at the end as Les reported how Sadie had gone to the Grand Russe Hotel to hunt for her promised job the day before. "Poor Sadie Loudon. She just runs headfirst into trouble."

"What do you mean?"

Glass's expression became serious. "There was a bomb at the Grand Russe yesterday. If Special Branch hadn't been notified in time, the entire hotel might have exploded. Your Sadie could have died."

Chapter Six

"Sadie isn't mine. We've been playacting sure, thanks to the Kozyrev situation, but that's it." Les spun his teacup. His training kept him from reacting outwardly to the shocking news about the hotel bomb that could have taken Sadie's life. He didn't remember drinking the contents of his cup, but it was empty now, with just one tea leaf decorating the inside.

"Haven't slept with her?" His section head asked from his position on the other side of the iron table.

"No. No opportunity." Obviously. His hands were shaking. He was a wreck.

Glass raised his thick eyebrows. He seemed to find the answer amusing. "You need to finish that business. Get engaged to her, if you have to. We need eyes and ears inside the Grand Russe. Between the bomb attempt and all the Russians both as guests and employees, that place is a hotbed of trouble."

"You want me to keep Sadie close?"

Glass pulled a brown paper bag from his pocket and shook out a few roasted nuts. "Keep her living with you. Why not? Don't tell her you're feeling better. Make her feel needed. But also make sure she gets that job. Of course she was turned away yesterday. They were much too busy to see her. She must have walked in just as they were pulling explosives out of the place."

Les's stomach, empty but for the black tea, rumbled uncomfortably at the notion that Sadie could have been hurt. "I don't think she'll leave me," he said. "I'm not sure what she's thinking. She did try to see her sister, but she won't contact her grandfather. He's a vicar."

"She's put herself in a position that would be anathema to a man of God with a parish looking on," Glass said, handing him the bag. "Get engaged. That will cheer her up."

Les poured nuts into his hand. "Yes, sir."

As Les popped the first one into his mouth, Glass said, "Now, on to the heart of the business. As you can imagine, we have a bomber to find."

"You didn't get him?"

"No, we rounded up most of the Russian cell. A strange business. Still trying to sort out the reports."

"Anything I can do to help?"

Glass's answer was another question. "How are you getting along with the Bolshies?"

Les opened his case and took out the two membership cards for the League of British Workers.

Glass grinned. "Well, well, well. Good work."

"Not sure this is relevant to the Grand Russe though. That is Russian trade. I'm trying to infiltrate the labor side of things. The ones who want strikes and disruption."

"Yes, but there are only so many bombers to go around. The higher-ups in any Russian-funded organization are going to have a conduit to the experts."

"Yes, sir."

"As you know, we've been woefully short-staffed since the war ended. With an issue this serious, we need every man available on the hunt. Continue to work your networks, but you'll also receive assignments directly related to finding this bomb builder Konstantin."

"Very well."

"You'll be working with Robert McCall of Special Branch. Wouldn't want you to find the bomber and not be able to arrest him."

"Very good. What about Sadie? The Kozyrevs think she's my wife."

"I noticed the membership card. Since she's so attached to you, I think an engagement is enough for now. After all, if she can't get that position at the Grand Russe, her use to you isn't what it could be."

"She's a good actress."

"I'll have a thorough investigation done." Glass shrugged. "Maybe we'll make an operative of her."

He didn't like the idea of silly, sexy Sadie being thrust into danger. Yes, she was resourceful, but she didn't seem very athletic. He'd danced with her enough to know she was enthusiastic but lacking style.

Glass snapped his fingers. "Come back to me, Les. Your eyes were closing."

Les blinked. "Sorry. Is there anything else?"

Glass opened a folder. Les noted several photographs in a pile. "These are the Russian diplomats in town. Memorize their faces."

Les spun the folder around and looked through the photographs. One of the best tools an operative had was a perfect memory. Luckily, he possessed one. Once memorized, he never forgot a face. "Got them," he said, passing the folder back. "What should we do about the Kozyrevs for now?"

"Get in touch with Semyon and find out when the next League meeting is. You'll want to make sure to pay those February dues. Have Miss Loudon send a thank you note to Irina for her kindness. Other than that, the League and the Kozyrevs may have to go back into the files since they are out of sight in Hull. Too few resources."

"I'll see if Sadie has their address. I don't have it, but they must have assumed I'd have a way to get in touch with the League."

Glass examined the membership cards. "Probably done by the same printer that was used for those flyers. I recognize the damaged E."

Les said, "You're right. I must be more tired than I expected."

"Go home, take some rest. McCall will contact you. Treat him like a friend. No need for Sadie to understand the full picture."

"Very well. I'll need a ring for Sadie. She likes gifts."

"I'll have something sent over. But it will have to be cheap. Budgets, you know."

Les nodded.

"Does Semyon have your address?"

"Since I make a point of interacting with every Russian bookseller, he can always find me. His network is as good as mine. Also, he probably acquired my wallet in Hull but I can't be sure since it wasn't returned to me."

Glass twisted the corner of his mouth at the information. "Keep an eye on that." He grinned. "And congratulations on your engagement."

"Funny," Les muttered.

*　*　*

Sadie, aware that Les was asleep downstairs on Saturday morning, stayed in stocking feet as she moved around the parlor, dusting and straightening. She hadn't been raised to be either idle or untidy, but Les had the usual bachelor habits. Newspapers strewn about, two weeks old now, books piled higgledy-piggledy on tables or floors, some with bookmarkers torn from newsprint. One extremely disgusting piece of newsprint that had been used to wrap fish and chips some weeks ago. Thankfully it was too early for ants, because she found a couple of fish coating bits next to the chair. When she finished straightening she began to sweep the rug, making a tidy pile of crumbs and other debris on the floorboards at the edge of the room.

"Sadie, darling, what are you up to?"

She glanced up, pleased to hear Les's voice back to its usual heartiness. He hadn't yet dressed, and she should be shocked by the sight of his bare feet and pajamas.

"Good heavens, what is that on your head?"

She patted it. "Just your largest handkerchief. I didn't want dust in my hair."

"We all share a maid in this building. I get her on Thursdays."

"She hasn't been in the past two Thursdays, I can guarantee you that," Sadie said, hands on hips as she surveyed the room. "No respectable woman would have left a fish and chips wrapper on the floor. No wonder it smells greasy in here."

"Right you are. I let her in, you see. She doesn't have the keys."

"And we came here on a Thursday. I can't live like this for five days, Les."

"Why don't you toss those crumbs in a bin and have a nice bath?" He stepped into the room, careful to skirt her pile, and ran his hands up and down her upper arms. "You've had a busy day."

"I did?"

"Yes, but you need to return to the Grand Russe."

"I do?" Sadie felt stupid.

"You still haven't seen your sister, and there's the position to check on."

"Didn't you see the papers? There was mysterious police activity at the hotel on Thursday, when I was there. I know it was true, I saw them myself."

"Yes, but that was two days ago. It's bound to be fine now."

She shivered. "What if someone was killed there?"

"No one was killed. And remember those delicious movie stars. You want to see them, don't you?"

His blue-gray eyes had a mesmerizing effect on her, especially so close. As she watched his face, his eyes half-closed into a sleepy sexuality, he pulled her against his dressing gown, dusty apron and all. When his head tilted, placing his clever lips just at the level of her mouth, she didn't resist, but wrapped her arms around his neck, remembering how it had felt the first time.

She gasped when her breasts pressed against his chest, nipples already budding, and he took her open-mouthed, their first kiss since she'd almost lost him. His tongue slid along hers and she caressed him right back, feeling liquid all over. This was how girls fell, fell happily and completely.

She felt like a wife but wasn't. Her head was such a mess. He pulled back, sucking her lower lip between his teeth. When he nipped, he had her full attention again, then he dipped his head down to caress her neck.

"That's nice," she whispered, letting her head fall back. He cradled it in one large palm while he nibbled and licked around her neck, kissed the base of her throat. She took it all in stride, feeling glorious, until his other hand went to her bottom and squeezed. Her eyes snapped open and she stepped back.

"Les!"

"Sorry, sorry," he said, his eyes wide and unfocused. "Carried away, human nature."

She put both hands to her chest. Her heart was pounding. "There's such a thing as too far."

"I know. You're a good girl, Sadie." He rubbed his head as he stepped back. Was it hurting?

"I'm not that good," she admitted. "But I was never around boys enough to find myself in trouble."

One side of his mouth curved up in a boyishly mischievous smile. "You've fallen into it, good and proper."

"And how," she agreed. "But there's cleaning to be done, and I've scattered dust all over your dressing gown."

"There's a woman who will collect my washing and bring it back Monday. I call her landlady. I'll gather up a load, sheets and everything."

"I'll do all that. Do I just set the bundle outside of your door?"

He nodded. "I'll do it though. I need to move a bit."

Her body still quivered, but the ordinary conversation calmed her. "You must have a spare of everything then."

"Yes. I'll call right away."

"I'll fix you some breakfast." She hurried after him as he moved into the kitchen.

"That would be wonderful. I'd murder for a cuppa."

"What?"

He held up a finger. She noticed his hair was standing up directly on his scalp on the back of his head. She didn't remember doing that. "The blower is downstairs. I have to go downstairs to make the call about the laundry. I'll be back in a tick."

"I'll have a tray ready for you." She shook her head, amused, as he walked out, and went to open the icebox. Was it exhaustion from his injury, or the effect of her kisses making him so confused? In his dressing gown, she couldn't escape the scent of him: his soap, his hair, his body. She could still taste him on her lips. She'd never been overwhelmed by a man's sheer physical presence before, and the sensation dizzied her.

Blinking, she realized she had a hunk of cheese in one hand and a sticky bottle of chutney in the other. She didn't remember picking up either of them.

Forty minutes later, she had him fed and herself tidied and ready to leave for the Grand Russe. "Are you certain you can handle the laundry yourself?"

"I've still twenty minutes to gather the pile," he said. "I'm moving more slowly than usual, but I'm better."

"I know you are." She pulled on her glove, then caressed his arm.

"We'll stick together, you and I, right?" Les asked.

"Of course. I'm not going to leave you until you are one hundred percent well. What kind of a nurse would I be otherwise?"

"You have a plan to leave me?" He looked troubled, adorably so. Though he'd changed into day clothes, he had yet to tidy his hair. If it wasn't for the fact that he also needed to shave, he'd look like a lad.

"I always thought I'd live with my sister if we both went up to London. But, you know, she has a beau, I think. She's mentioned someone a couple of times in letters."

"Maybe she'll be married before you."

Sadie cleared her throat. *Not likely.* "It would only be fair. She's older, you know."

She held her head high as she left the flat, Les's spare set of flat keys jangling in her pocket.

Sadie was still out, hopefully acquiring that chambermaid position at the hotel, when Les heard his door knocker banging. He'd made his bed, but had been lounging on it, staring at the wall. Not a very effective way to spend a day. He'd meant to be reading a Russian-language newspaper to keep his skills up.

When he opened the door, he found a stocky man a couple of years older than himself, dressed in a nice but unmemorable dark suit but a rather exuberant striped tie. Les approved, because it kept attention off of the man's face. All he had to do was change the tie and he'd be unnoticed.

"Mr. Drake," the man said, and held out his hand. "Robert Mc-Call, Special Branch."

Les took his hand. "Come in." He shut the door after the man entered. "Keep in mind that I have a lady staying here who thinks my name is Rake."

Detective McCall's thin lips widened into a smile. "Is this Miss Loudon?"

"Yes. I'm in quite a pickle there. Not sure how it's going to resolve."

McCall looked him over with seasoned police eyes. "You're not one hundred percent."

"What's giving me away?" Les inquired.

"Your skin is the wrong color. Are you sure you're ready for this?"

"I served in the Russian army," Les said. "I can work three quarters dead. What are we going to do?"

"Stake out the Russian Tea Rooms in Kensington. It's a known hangout for this bomber Konstantin and we've been told he lives upstairs."

"You are asking me to drink tea and sit? And for this you think I'm not ready?" Les gave the police detective a cold stare.

"I don't like dead weight," the detective said. "If we have to chase someone, you'd best be ready to do it."

"You needn't fuss. I'm ready for anything." He considered. "I'll be Valentin Dragunov. That's my Russian name. You?"

"I don't have undercover identities," McCall said laconically. "I'll simply be your mate. What is Dragunov's story?"

"Mostly unemployed wheelwright. No usual haunts."

"Was Dragunov the name you used in the Russian army?"

Les nodded. "Dragunov immigrated after his army service. He's older than me too, and enlisted at sixteen at the end of Russia's time in the war."

McCall rolled his eyes. "Very well. Change your clothes. I don't think a Russian would be caught dead in that sweater."

Les looked down at his cozy white Irish wool. The Aran sweater had been hand knit for him by the widow of a fellow operative. It had taken two months to make. She'd made six of them for her late husband's colleagues, a year's worth of mourning and keeping her hands busy. "A Russian is desperate enough to wear anything he might find, these days, but I'll put on a cheap suit. Have a seat if you like, won't take but a minute."

The door opened and Sadie came in. She squealed when she saw Les and ran into his arms. "Mr. Eyre gave me the position! I start tomorrow."

He hugged her back. Sadie continued to surprise him in all the best ways. "Excellent, darling. Let's go out to a café and celebrate."

She bounced a little and looked at McCall, standing there silently. Les gestured at him. "This is my friend."

McCall stood. "Robbie O'Donnell," he said with a hint of Irish brogue.

"There must be more cafes in Primrose Hill than we could count," Sadie said. "Which one is your favorite?"

"I thought we'd go to South Kensington," Les said. "I've been wanting to visit the Russian Tea Rooms."

"Right near the Natural History Museum, if that suits you," McCall said enthusiastically.

"More Russian heritage?" Sadie asked, having lost a little of her sparkle.

"I want you to try tea from a samovar," Les said. "There's nothing like it."

McCall shuddered, then winked at Sadie.

"I'll dress quickly," Les said. He narrowed his eyes. "Be good, Robbie."

Ten minutes later, they were in a cab heading south past Regent's and Hyde Parks. "Let's loop past the Grand Russe Hotel," Les told the taxicab driver, curious to see how close it was to the restaurant. In terms of driving distance, the hotel turned out to be at the halfway point between his home and the tea rooms.

"I still don't see why the mustache was necessary," Sadie complained.

She hadn't mentioned the working class attire, but his fake bride didn't like his fake mustache?

"It is," he said.

"I don't like handlebar mustaches," she said. "And it isn't effective, because your eyes and nose make your face, not your lips."

McCall glanced at her in surprise and lifted his eyebrows in Les's direction. "It hides the shape of his mouth. His upper lip is distinctive, Mrs. Dragunov."

"Dragunov has a mustache," Les growled, wondering what the driver thought of the conversation. Given that costume parties were all the rage, hopefully he thought they were speaking about one.

Sadie harrumphed as the taxicab pulled up in front of a mottled gray building on a corner. Six stories were visible. The building was a mismatched jangle of form and none of the attached buildings on the block made sense together. Les counted three storefronts in his target building as they exited. The entrance to the apartments seemed to be through a door on the right side.

"Do we know which apartment Konstantin is meant to be in?" Les asked. "There are quite a few."

"Who is Konstantin?" Sadie asked.

"An old friend," Les muttered. "He's about thirty-five, with a graying beard. A great beast of a man."

"What are we up to, Les?" Sadie asked.

Les wrapped his hand around her arm. "Valentin Dragunov, darling."

"Valentin again," Sadie said, glancing down at the "V" ring she still wore. "Right. But the rest of it is new."

"We're just having tea at the tea room. Relax, darling," Les told Sadie.

McCall squinted at the pair of them, then shrugged and opened the door. They were greeted by a curly dark-haired woman with small eyes and thin lips. Les already knew who she was: Anna Wolkova, the daughter of a Russian Imperial Navy man whose family had stayed in London when the Revolution occurred. She had opened the tea room in 1923 and it was a center for White Russians, but if McCall was correct, the Bolshies were moving in, too.

Wolkova took them to a table in the rear and gave them menus. They weren't dressed for display in her front window.

"Now what?" Sadie whispered.

"We have tea and celebrate your new position," Les said. "When do you start work?"

"On Monday."

"Did you see your sister?"

"No. She lost her position. Her life is very complicated at the moment, it seems. I did see the manager, Peter Eyre, though. He's a fright."

"Why do you say that?" McCall asked, losing his accent.

Les raised his eyebrows and McCall shook his head in self-loathing.

Sadie didn't seem to notice. "He's a hard man. Exotic but English, very aristocratic manner but I felt like he was undressing me with his eyes."

"You do have quite the figure, my lass," McCall said, exaggerating his Irish accent this time.

"Ignore Robbie," Les said, patting Sadie's hand. "He's the worst sort of ladies' man."

"What do you mean?" McCall asked.

"You're the sort of ladies' man the ladies don't like," Les growled.

McCall chuckled heartily as a waiter came to take their order. Les ordered blinis with caviar and a smoked fish and cheese plate, along with tea for all three of them.

"No cake? No buns?" Sadie asked.

"Sugar is bad for the teeth," Les said.

She grimaced at him. "I'm going to make a trifle when we return home."

McCall chuckled. They listened to Sadie make elaborate plans for her trifle, difficult to manage as she wouldn't be able to purchase the berries she wanted in January. However, even Les's mouth was watering by the time their smoky black tea arrived.

Sadie helped herself to a generous dollop of cream. McCall followed suit, but Les liked his tea black, the way he was used to drinking it. The flavor did not go with sweets.

He was biting into a blini and starting to enjoy himself, despite a slight buzzing in his ears, when a man walked into the tea room alone. The hostess took him to a table near them as Les catalogued the man's features and matched them to the photographs he had stored in his brain. He'd seen this man's distinctively hooked nose recently.

Leaning toward McCall, he said, "That's one of Ovolensky's trade delegation."

McCall leaned back, holding his tea, looking more relaxed than before. "A Bolshie in a White establishment?"

"Who is Ovolensky?" Sadie asked.

"Georgy Ovolensky." Les spoke so low that his lips barely moved. "Head of a Russian trade delegation staying at the Grand Russe Hotel."

Sadie frowned as Les stared at the Russian again. Fedor was the man's first name, but Glass hadn't known his surname. "Looking for a taste of home, perhaps?"

Sadie glanced around. Les put his hand on her knee under the table, stilling her instantly.

"What is it?" she asked.

"Did you see that man at the hotel?" Les asked. "Three o'clock."

She picked up on what he meant right away. "No, I didn't see him, but I was only at the reception desk and in Mr. Eyre's office."

"He's staying there," Les said. "Someone to keep an eye on."

Sadie laughed. "I'm going to spy on the hotel guests?"

McCall's eyes widened.

Les forced a laugh. He must be more exhausted than he realized. "No, darling, of course not. But we know him, you see."

"He doesn't seem to recognize you," she observed.

"We're much too lowly," McCall explained. "He's an important man. A Russian like your friend Dragunov needs to know who is who in his native community."

"Are you teasing me?" she asked plaintively. "I thought we were celebrating my new position, and you're both talking nonsense."

Les patted her knee again. "Do you want to return home and make your trifle? I'll put you in a taxicab and give you the money for any berries you can find."

"I'll use jam," she sniffed. "And eat every bit myself."

McCall thrust out his chest in mock despair. "But I want some, too."

"Not until you learn to behave," she said. "The pair of you are nothing but big teases. Caviar and smoked fish. Really? Even the cheese tastes moldy."

"We Russians are deprived," Les said. "Do you have any idea how miserable the Bolsheviks have made my homeland?"

"Shhh, laddie," McCall said.

Les glanced casually at Fedor's table, but the man's attention was on a table with three women eating scones. One of them had jam on her cheek. Les took some coins from his pocket and placed them in Sadie's hand. "For the taxi fare and your jam," he said. "I'll be home in a couple of hours."

Sadie blinked, clearly confused, but now that they had actually spotted someone important, this was no place for her. He had his hands full with McCall's buffoonery. "I should do a bit of shopping before it is too late. We do not have much in the icebox for tomorrow."

He pulled some more coins out of his pocket and handed them to her. She mock curtsied at him and walked out, head held high.

"Very pretty, your wife," McCall said in a smarmy tone.

Les ignored him because another man had just approached Fedor. He memorized the face. "Recognize him?"

McCall bit into a blini and shook his head in the negative, then pulled out a notebook and began to sketch the face. They waited for another half an hour, but no one else joined the two men. When their waiter glared at them, they paid their bill and left.

"Perfect timing, anyway," Les said. "My section head should be at our meeting place this time of day."

"Very good," McCall said. "But we were hoping to spot Konstantin."

"We aren't going to catch him sitting in the Russian Tea Rooms. We need to set up across the street, so we can see the door to the flats above."

"Fair enough. The only problem is that St. Augustine's Church is across the street. How are we going to see that door from the church?"

Les stared at the church's Victorian Gothic façade, set considerably back from the street. "I have fantastic French naval binoculars."

"Stained glass windows," McCall countered.

Les swore when he saw McCall was correct. He was truly off his game. "We need to survey the building and discover out where Konstantin's hideout is."

Chapter Seven

"You sell magazines," Glass pointed out, leaning away from the tea table in the Marylebone flat some forty minutes later. "Go into the building and sell door-to-door. You have the stock."

"As Lester Rake or Dragunov?" Les asked, scratching at his fake mustache.

Glass considered Les's face. His brow furrowed. "Dragunov has the mustache."

Les ignored the furry discomfort on his face. "Yes, but Sadie thinks my eyes and nose are my most prominent features and the mustache isn't much of a disguise."

"I can't wait to meet her," Glass said with a roll of his eyes. "Does Rake wear glasses? A hat?"

"Hat."

"Make sure it shadows your eyes." Glass shrugged and poured more tea for both of them. His own dark brown eyes had shadows underneath. He hadn't had much sleep recently. "Lose the mustache, go as Rake."

"But Rake doesn't sell door-to-door."

Glass sighed. "Rake has been in hospital, out of work, for two weeks. He needs some fast money, so he's selling door-to-door. Good enough. We need to find Konstantin."

"Any word on his next target, or if there is one?" Les had finished McCall's sketch of the man with Fedor. It lay on the table between them.

"We received some intel from our in-Russia operatives that indicate the Bolsheviks are considering English cultural targets."

"The Natural History Museum?" Les suggested. "It's near the Russian Tea Rooms."

"That would be a lot of bomb. Large building." Glass rubbed his right eyebrow. It had a slight scar running through it, left over from his war service.

"So you have no idea of possible targets."

"No. Could be hotels. They tried the Grand Russe."

"Not the Bolsheviks. The Whites hired Konstantin."

"Yes, yes. He's a cipher. That group of Whites is all we have. Fedor may have nothing to do with Konstantin, but him being seen nearby is a bad sign."

"Any Russian might reasonably go to a restaurant owned by and targeted toward Russians," Les argued.

"I hear what you are saying. I hope this other man with Fedor, when we identify him, can lead us to a greater understanding of the situation. For now, I want you in that building, selling magazines. I'm pleased that Sadie has the position at the Grand Russe. We'll see that bear fruit, I'm certain."

"Are you going to bring her in, attempt to recruit her?"

"For now, keep her close. I don't have the budget to pay her. She isn't going anywhere, right? I haven't located a ring for you yet. Hopefully by Tuesday."

"I'll continue to court her. I haven't had to propose, just look wan."

"That can't be much of a stretch. You don't look well, Leslie. Go home and make an early night of it."

"Very funny." Les hated his full first name.

Glass grinned and picked up the sketch. "I'll send this around. Good work."

Sadie's first day as a chambermaid at the Grand Russe went well. She was assigned by her supervisor, Olga Novikov, to the second floor, which was the first floor with guest rooms. The second floor held the least important guests, out of the six guest room floors.

While she hadn't seen her sister, Olga had told her that Alecia had moved into the same boarding house where she lived, to care for an elderly woman. Olga suggested she write Alecia a note during her lunch and she'd deliver it that evening. Sadie had eagerly complied and hoped Olga would bring her a return missive in the morning.

She arrived home at six-thirty, feeling exhausted after a ten-hour workday. A couple, arm-in-arm, were entering Les's building. She hung back, tired as she was, not wanting the neighbors to see her entering his flat. It wasn't respectable. She hoped the buses would make more sense to her tomorrow and she'd be through the front door sooner, but she'd taken one going the wrong way around St. James's Park and that had cost her a half hour.

In Les's entryway, she saw his coat on the steps going upstairs, damp with rain. He'd been outside again, in his condition. Was the man deliberately attempting not to recover completely? After she kicked off her shoes, not the most practical for chambermaid duties, and took off her coat, she went upstairs, to find Les, not wan and re-laxing on a sofa, but standing over a golf putter, considering his ap-proach to the chipped teacup he was using for a hole.

Sadie had been contemplating, not especially happily, a busy evening of preparing dinner, planning breakfast, and fluffing Les's pillows, while being much more inclined to put up her feet and enjoy one of Les's magazines while nibbling from a Rowntree's Dairy Box of chocolates. Having put in a full day of work, she was irritated by not having the money for said chocolate. "If you're well enough to be playing at golf, I guess it is time for me to move out."

"Sadie!" he exclaimed, cocking his putter over his shoulder like a rifle and coming toward her.

"As soon as I get my things from Richmond," she said piously. "I expect to hear from my sister tomorrow morning. After that I can make arrangements."

"Darling, you mustn't." He leaned the putter against the wall and rubbed his hands down her arms. "Look at me. My color is all wrong. If you weren't taking such good care of me I'd still be in bed."

"You still don't have much pink in your cheeks," she admitted. "But if you know that, you should be in bed!"

"I needed to move around a bit." He snaked one arm around her waist and clasped her other hand, then danced her side-to-side. "It's unhealthy to lie around all day."

"You went out," she accused. "I saw your wet coat. And what a place to leave it, by the way. Take it into the bathroom and hang it over the tub at least."

He grinned sheepishly. "See, I need you. I'm not minding prop-erly, yet."

She loved the feeling of being in his arms. He wore that Irish sweater again, and it turned him into a furnace, exactly what she wanted to cozy up to after the cold return to the flat. "I doubt you ever did."

"All kidding aside, darling, you can't afford a place like this. Are you hoping to live with your sister?"

Of course not. She wanted his kisses. She wanted his caresses. She wanted to marry him. "She's not at the hotel anymore. She's caring for an old lady at a boarding house. Olga lives there too."

"Olga?"

"She's in charge of the chambermaids. Very Russian and formal."

"Fascinating," Les murmured, dropping his chin onto her hair and dancing her around again. "See, I can't even hold my head up."

"I can't keep living with a man who doesn't need me to nurse him," she said, moving her head out from underneath him.

He stopped dancing and let go of her. She watched as a number of thoughts danced behind his eyes, fluttering away before some kind of expression showed on his face. Before she could step away, he ran his index finger down the plump line of her cheek. "Sadie, darling, we had fun together before my head injury, right?"

"I suppose."

"We had fun together at the tea room yesterday."

"Not especially," she muttered, biting her lip.

"I admit old Robbie is a bit much to take."

"I never know what is real where you are concerned," she admitted.

"You and me, that's real. That existed before all this Russian silliness. I admit I let things go too far, but you and me, that's real and serious, I promise you."

"I can't live in sin, Les. My grandfather—"

"Is a vicar," he finished. "I know, darling, I know. Give me a little more time to sort it out, will you?" He let go of her and put his hand to his forehead. He swayed a little.

She wrapped her arm around his waist and tugged him toward the sofa. "You'd better sit down."

"I should return to bed."

She knew he could playact all too well, but he did look pale. Her nursing instincts won. "I don't want you going down those stairs while you're dizzy. Rest quietly. I'll fix you a cup of cocoa and we won't talk about this again until after I'm home from work tomorrow. You stay home, promise me?"

Les met Glass in the Marylebone flat at four the next afternoon. He'd spent close to six hours around Harrington Road, selling magazines. Ironically, he'd sold out. Camden was a hotbed of bored women who liked movie magazines and didn't want to walk to the shops.

He'd made sure not to leave his bedroom until Sadie left for the Grand Russe that morning, not wanting to discuss her moving out again. And frankly, pretending to be ill made him feel ill.

He set his case on the bench just inside the flat door and took off his coat. That had been a near miss with Sadie the night before. Blimey, he didn't have the ring yet. He didn't want to propose to the girl, but it was obvious the moment would have to come. Yes, she was game, good fun, wonderful to kiss, but marriage? They barely knew each other, and she didn't know his secrets. What kind of marriage did Glass expect him to have with her?

"Woolgathering?" Sarcasm warred with the natural gravel in his section head's voice.

Les glanced up. Glass had folded his large frame into the front doorway. He lifted his eyebrows at Les.

"Sadie threatened to move out last night."

"Did you propose?"

Les pulled off his shoes, damp with rain. "No ring yet, guv."

"Guv." Glass snorted. "I'm sure you'll have it today sometime. Don't lose it. It's a real diamond."

"Is it being delivered to my flat?"

Glass nodded and flicked his wrist. "Come in, have a cuppa, tell me about your morning."

Five minutes later they had steaming cups of black Irish Breakfast tea on the table in front of them and Les was summing up. "Three flats where no one answered. Two flats where a woman answered and I had no sense of who else might live there."

Glass leaned over his tea. His cheek tightened as he worked through some internal problem. "I spoke to Quex. We're afraid that Ovolensky's man is helping Konstantin somehow, despite the fact that Konstantin tried to kill Ovolensky."

"I've read the reports. It seems as if Konstantin attempted to turn this cell of Whites into Bolshies."

"Charismatic bloke," Glass agreed.

"Is there a chance that was his goal, rather than the bombing? That perhaps he never intended the bomb to go off?"

"It seems unlikely." Glass lifted his teacup. "But Ovolensky is an advance team. It's not until April that the main delegation arrives. He might be expendable. He's the only main player in his group, after all."

"Should I keep working the building? I expect he's in one of the five flats we haven't thoroughly investigated."

Glass finished off his tea and set his cup down. "Les, we've discovered that Alecia Loudon, Sadie's sister, is engaged to Vera Saltykova's brother, Ivan Salter. Vera was a member of the White cell and is still missing. Additionally, we need eyes and ears in the Grand Russe. Sadie, as a chambermaid, is perfectly placed to keep an eye on Ovolensky."

Les poured more tea into Glass's cup. "Actually, that isn't true. Ovolensky is on the seventh floor and she's cleaning on the second. They've started her at the bottom."

"We have to start somewhere. I want you to gather Sadie completely to your side."

"She wants to move out. She knows I'm shamming."

Glass's cheeks made half-moons at the corners of his mouth as he chuckled. "She does, eh? I don't. I don't think you are on your game at all."

"I'll keep playing sick," Les said in measured tones. "I'll give her the ring when it arrives."

"I want you to marry Sadie."

Les wrapped his fingers around the edge of the table. "You what? Seriously?"

"You'll receive a wedding ring too. We'll have a fake special license made up. You'll marry her under your false name."

"She's a nice girl, Glass. Why don't you simply recruit her?"

"We can't risk nerves and there's no time for training."

"There never is time for training," Les muttered.

"She's barely twenty, just out of the vicarage. A bit of a thrill seeker, I'd say, and a nurturer. I hope we can bring her to agent status, but for now, I want you to run her."

"And ruin her," Les said. "Who will marry her for real after this?"

"In the end, she'll mature into one of us, I hope. You're a good foot soldier in the war against Russia, my friend. Sadie is important, but we can't have her sharing confidences with her sister or this Ivan Salter, the Russian fiancé. Her loyalty and confidences need to come entirely to you."

Les ran his hand through his hair, fighting for the detachment that allowed him to live a double life. Why had this one woman broken his façade? It must be the head injury affecting him. It couldn't be her.

Sadie arrived home with a filet of haddock and half a pound of potatoes. She'd taken the right bus this time and had jumped off in front of a greengrocer's. Her travel couldn't have been smoother and her dinner plans were simple but she was still exhausted. On a day like today what she wouldn't give to have a housekeeper and a kitchen maid like her grandfather had. Les had an efficient and very modern kitchen, but there still wasn't anyone to put food on a plate for her.

As she sneaked into the flat, avoiding the neighbors, she fantasized that Les had spent the day relaxing, then nipped down to the greengrocer and had prepared them a nice hot soup for dinner. But, it wasn't to be. Against her orders, she found the flat dark and cold. Les wasn't around.

She stamped her foot as she took off her coat in the entry hall. Why, she should bundle up her meager possessions now and leave. He claimed he was too ill for her to go, yet ignored her order to rest!

Hunger won out over good sense. She went into his bedroom and found a pair of thick woolen socks to put over her freezing toes and stomped upstairs to make dinner, wracking her brain for ideas on how she could afford to live in London and work at the Grand Russe without relying on Les's flat.

By the time the potatoes were fork-tender, she had tea made and the haddock fried. She'd opened a tin of peas she'd found on a shelf, rather pleased with herself. Her grandfather's kitchen help couldn't have done better. And for after? She'd bought a Cadbury's flake bar for a treat.

"Something smells good." Les walked into the room, damp and weary.

"You look like you worked a full day," she said disapprovingly.

"My guv was on the blower first thing, ordering me out the door. I have to sell my quota."

She regretted her anger. *Poor Les.* "Did you do it?"

He nodded. "Not on my usual patch, though. I sold door-to-door, but it's good to refresh the old skills."

"You shouldn't have worked so hard," she scolded. "Come and sit down." Glory, what was she to do with the man? She couldn't afford this flat, or any flat, for that matter. Alecia couldn't live with her either. She had to share a bedroom with her elderly charge and then, of all the funny things, she was going to be married! Her sister had found a husband. With a first name like Ivan, he had to be Russian. Funny that they'd both found Russian men.

She regarded Les as he picked up his fork.

"Could you open a bottle of wine?" he asked.

"I wouldn't know how," she admitted.

"Never mind then. There must be a bottle of beer somewhere."

She found a bottle of Guinness stout and pried off the top for him.

"Thanks, darling."

She sat across from him with her plate and tea, feeling both virtuous and domestic.

"I want to speak to you about something important," he said, after inhaling half of his plate. "Any more peas?"

"That's important?"

"No. I wanted more though."

She shook her head. "Sorry, there was only the one can."

"Do you need more money for groceries?"

She warred with her urge to demand he do half the shopping and cooking, and reminded herself that he wasn't well enough to work and do the chores. Ugh! She wasn't his maid, or his wife, or even his girlfriend. But she was starting to feel like a fool. Why was she so drawn to him? "You can have the rest of my peas." She shoved her plate at him and ran blindly out of the room, her feet sliding on the polished wood floor.

Sometime later, with no idea how long she'd sat in a corner of the sofa closest to the gramophone, she was shocked when Les wrapped a blanket around her, then knelt at her feet. When she sniffed, he placed a handkerchief into her hand.

"Darling," he said.

When she put down the handkerchief, she saw he looked adorably rumpled. She wanted to hide her face against his neck and let him make it all better. Being a chambermaid at the Grand Russe was exhausting. Olga was a far more demanding taskmistress than Mrs. Curtis had been. The rooms had to fairly sparkle by the time she left them. At least there weren't any poodles.

"What?" she sniffed. She forced herself to sit up. "I should do the washing up."

"I can do it."

"You should rest."

He took one of her hands away from where it clutched the top of her apron and held it in his. "Darling, I know it seems hard right now, so unsettled, but I told you that you were important to me, right?"

She sniffed and wiped her eyes. "I'm just so confused. I can't go and live with Alecia like I'd hoped, not ever. She's engaged."

"Then you should be engaged too," he said.

"What?" she asked. Her voice came out little girlish, but her heart leapt into her throat. Had she heard him properly?

"Why don't we announce our engagement?" he asked. "It makes sense. I'd be a fool to lose you."

"You would?" She hiccupped. Embarrassed, she covered her mouth with her hand.

He smiled tenderly. "Of course, darling. Beautiful, ready for anything, the perfect nurse, good cook. I could walk a thousand miles and not find another like you. Why not get engaged?"

"Why not?" she echoed. After all, he did love her and she was falling in love with him, too. She must be, to risk her reputation and do everything for him without recompense. Where was a girl like her going to find a posh man like him? Her sister was marrying an immigrant night watchman. She would be doing better than Alecia. More importantly, Les needed her. He barely took time to rest as it was. He was obviously a slave to his company.

"Is that a yes?"

"Yes, I'll marry you." She smiled and let the handkerchief drop into her lap.

He went pale for a moment, but then rallied with a happy smile. "Oh, I'm so delighted." He put his hands on her knees, rose, and angled in for a kiss.

The telephone buzzed. His face was still just far enough away that she saw him blink. Dazed, she watched him stand up and walk to the staircase. He'd just proposed, she'd accepted, and he stopped to answer the telephone. She let her head fall against the sofa cushion. That poor man wasn't thinking straight.

He returned a couple minutes later. "I'm sorry, darling, but I have to go out."

She struggled up. "What? Now?"

"My company, you know. Guv is being an absolute beast. Wants me out hand selling."

"Tonight? In the rain?"

He shrugged. "Testing my loyalty."

"But your health," she protested.

He patted his belly. "After that lovely meal, I'm quite restored."

She stood. "Oh, Les. I'm so sorry."

He put his hands on her upper arms and rubbed briskly. "Have a quiet night, darling, will you? We'll celebrate tomorrow evening. I've put some more cash into that box in my room. Take what you need." He kissed her cheek and went out of the parlor, whistling.

Bemused, she entered the kitchen and began to clean up dinner, noting that he had eaten not just his own food, but everything left on her plate as well, not just the peas. She had to make him man-size portions. Her fiancé. She smiled and hugged herself. If only she could telephone Alecia and share the news. Her gamble had paid off. The fact that her decisions in Hull had more to do with her fear of the creepy Kozyrevs than anything else was pushed to the back of her mind.

Les met Robert McCall outside the door leading to the flats at Harrington Road. "What's the story?"

"We increased foot patrols in the neighborhood to keep a general eye on the building," McCall said, all business for once. His breath puffed white clouds into the air. "And we had circulated photographs, drawings, everything we had of the Russian problem."

"Who was spotted?"

"Fedor. We've learned his last name. It's Verenich."

"First the tea rooms, and now he's in the building?"

McCall cocked his head and waggled his eyebrows. "A constable followed him and watched him break into a flat. It was one of the ones where no one answered the door earlier."

"Moron," Les said. "To let himself be watched. Poor spycraft."

"More a heavy than a spy, I think. Did you notice his shoulders?"

"And his paunch," Les said. "Strong man gone to seed."

"He had a gun on him," McCall said.

"Where is he now?"

"In the flat. There was no way to take him out quietly, not under the circumstances. The constable was on his own. No telephone in the flat."

"Can I search it?"

"Yes, after we get Fedor out of there. Come down to the station when you're done and have a chat with him. We'll have to release him quickly, due to his diplomatic status."

Les nodded as the door to the building opened. He turned his back to the door as three men came out, one of them cursing in Russian. When the three had entered a taxicab together and departed, he and McCall went upstairs.

They found a sparely furnished bedsit built in an L shape. The only amenity was that the flat came with its own bathroom. Les took in the sparse furnishings in a glance: a wood table with two chairs, a cot that looked like army issue. "And a chest."

"A chest," McCall agreed, beginning a tapping pattern on the wooden floorboards, searching for a cache.

Les went to the windows, which were just a couple of feet away from the next building, and closed the curtains. Then, he checked the chest for booby traps. He didn't find any, and when he opened the chest, there was nothing but clothing, serviceable, cheap, and hand-made. Oversized.

"He sleeps here and works somewhere else," Les said, defeated after twenty minutes. The floor was solid, as was every other aspect of the flat. Konstantin didn't appear to eat here, either.

"This may be more of a safe house than a home," McCall said.

"It's neither now." Les shook his head. "The toiletries and the clothing belong to the same man. But he's careful. I haven't found so much as a stray hair, even on the blankets."

"I can't believe we've cost ourselves our only lead," McCall said, kicking one of the table legs. The cheap wood creaked its protest.

"Not quite yet. Off to New Scotland Yard to see what we can get out of Fedor," Les said with a yawn. The long day was having its toll on his weakened body.

They went downstairs, nodding to the constable outside keeping watch, and climbed into the waiting car. When they arrived at the Norman Shaw buildings, they were ushered into a passageway outside of an interrogation room.

"He claims to barely speak English," said a uniformed constable outside. "Other than insisting he must be released, he's staring at the wall."

"Turn him around," Les instructed. "He must not see me."

"Yes, sir." At a nod from McCall, the constable returned inside the room to make the arrangements.

Chapter Eight

Sadie stretched her toes to the far end of the bathtub and sighed with pleasure. This was what she needed after two days of intensive chambermaid duty, to start her day with a luxurious bath. She stretched her neck from side to side and fanned her fingers through the warm water. Les's bedroom door was still closed. She hadn't heard a peep from him, but it was early yet. After she was done, she'd nip upstairs and make them a nice breakfast and treat him to breakfast in bed. No more bachelor ways for her man. Maybe they'd discuss wedding plans. As far as she was concerned, she'd best be Mrs. Lester Rake by the end of February.

She heard a door opening somewhere on the floor. Les must be up. He'd want the bathroom. She stood in the tub and found a towel, then dressed quickly. Later on today, she'd have to return to the Richmond Inn and get her things. She couldn't stand to wear the two dresses in her possession any more.

Five minutes later, she was opening the bathroom door. Les was in the entry hall, his hair standing on end. He must have just taken off his hat. His eyes were bloodshot and he had a day's growth of beard.

"Were you out all night?" she asked in shock.

"Afraid so."

"Les, your health," she exclaimed, coming toward him. She rested her hand on his arm. "Let's get you to bed. Did your boss make you stay out drinking or something?"

She tried not to let him see she had breathed him in as well. At least he didn't smell of perfume, just old cigarettes, dust, and spirits.

"Why aren't you at work? It's gone nine A.M. now." He unbuttoned his coat, making a face as the smell of it wafted into the air.

"We are engaged. Surely you can't expect me to work outside the home?"

His look at her was incredulous. "Yes, I can. Go to work."

"Les!" She protested, outraged. "It's unseemly."

"I've lost two weeks' wages and you need a new wardrobe." He swayed a little. "What about our honeymoon? Don't you want smart things? You need to bring clothes to our marriage, at least."

She wrapped her arm around his waist, concerned with his appearance. "I see," she said, chastened. "But I want to take care of you. You aren't doing a very good job on your own."

He smiled wearily at her. "I owe you my life, darling. I know that. But for now, we need to stop speaking. I need to find my bed and you need to go to the Grand Russe."

She bit her lip. There was no point arguing now. "I didn't have breakfast yet," she said in a little girl voice.

"I'll go down and get a taxicab for you while you butter some bread. It will have to do. Two minutes, Sadie," he warned.

"Very well," she sniffed. "But I cannot work for the hotel and take care of your flat, and you, properly. When I come home tonight I am packing my things."

He said nothing, just held his coat together with one hand while he opened the front door.

Twenty minutes later, resentful, she walked down the stairs to the Grand Russe's basement and into the staff lounge. She went to her peg and took her uniform into a private bathroom to dress. When she returned to hang her things, she found her supervisor and Mr. Eyre waiting for her.

"Sadie!" Mr. Eyre's half-closed eyelids and air of utter perfection intimidated her, but his words were kind. "Are you well? We were worried about you."

Sadie frowned. He seemed to care more than Les did. She sniffed. "I'm sorry, sir. My fiancé is recovering from a head injury and he didn't come home last night. I was too concerned to leave until he appeared."

Olga's full lips compressed. Her supervisor was beautiful and distinguished enough to play a queen in the pictures, someone like Mary, Queen of Scots. "You are unmarried and live with a man?"

"I didn't have anywhere else to go," Sadie explained. "I thought

I'd live with Alecia, but you know I can't now. My fiancé has a large flat. Three bedrooms."

Mr. Eyre patted Olga's shoulder. "Do not trouble yourself, Miss Novikov. Sadie is a respectable girl. Does your fiancé have a telephone?"

"Yes, sir."

"Then please use it to notify us if you have another crisis," he said. "Would you like me to call our hotel doctor to look in on your fiancé?"

"No, sir. But thank you."

Olga muttered something in Russian, then turned away and gestured imperiously over her shoulder for Sadie to follow. Definitely Mary, Queen of Scots. Sadie lowered her eyes and trotted behind her supervisor, feeling Mr. Eyre's gaze follow. He gave her the shivers, despite being young, refined, and handsome.

Les checked his watch. Sadie should be home any moment. He lit two tapers in the center of the kitchen table, which was carefully laid out with covered dishes from a restaurant across the street. A waiter had arrived with a fine French beef and onion dish, along with a side of creamed turnips and potatoes. They had a lemon tart for dessert, and the waiter had decanted a half bottle of red wine.

He knew Sadie wasn't a drinker, but he'd need the wine, even if she didn't. Tonight he needed to finish his proposal and put a ring on this girl's finger. He'd been left with no choice in the matter.

Glass had personally delivered a very convincing-looking special license to him. His section head had been wearing false hair and a delivery uniform. Les hadn't recognized him at first. He'd doubted such a tall man with a distinctive way of animating his face could disguise himself completely, but Glass had done it.

Or maybe Les was still not quite on his game. Regardless, Glass had reminded him of the possible importance of Sadie's position. He'd been horrified to learn Sadie hadn't gone into work this morning and told Les he had to keep Sadie there for now. For sure, he couldn't allow her to become pregnant. She was unwilling to work as it was. A baby coming would make her leave work for certain. Some marriage he had to look forward to. What he did for his country.

He stood over the table and breathed in the scent of warm beeswax.

If he concentrated, he could isolate it from the flavors of the French cuisine, taking him back to his mother's dressing table when he was a child. She'd liked to sit with a candle before she'd go to bed in the evenings, saying the light was soothing to her eyes. It hadn't been until after she died that his father had told him the truth: the entire marriage had been a setup. His father had married her to keep an eye on the inner workings of her family. His grandmother on his mother's side had been Irish and her brothers were all part of the Irish Home Rule movement.

Now he was marrying Sadie to keep an eye on Russians. Well, not really marrying. She wasn't important enough to marry for real, like his mother had been.

The front door opened and closed. *Show time*. Sadie had arrived home. He locked his thoughts away in the mental box he'd created five years before when he started espionage work, and took on the persona of Lester Rake, about to plan a wedding.

He heard clattering, as if Sadie was throwing her shoes around the entry hall. Probably kicking them off in a fit of childish temper since he'd dared to force her to work. Then, he heard footsteps coming up the stairs. When she entered the kitchen, he saw she had a wrapped package of something. He moved into place behind the table.

She blinked as she saw the candles and covered dishes. Her eyes narrowed as she held up her package. "I bought sausages."

He leaned across the table and took the package from her. "Breakfast."

"Yes." She stared at the candles again.

"I thought you might like a nice meal. It's from the restaurant across the street." He could tell from her unsmiling face that their rather brutal discussion of the morning had not been forgotten.

"Why? It's expensive."

"We should celebrate. I was trying to propose to you last night, you know."

"You did." She glanced up at him.

He smiled. "But, darling, I never finished." He came around the table and pulled out a chair. "Here, sit."

She seated herself and allowed him to pour wine for them both. "Just a sip. It doesn't agree with me."

"I understand." He sat as soon as he had the covers off of the dishes.

"It looks delicious," she admitted.

"Let's eat. You must be hungry. I hope you had a decent lunch."

"I had to work through because of coming in late," she said, each word forced out reluctantly. "But I didn't get the sack."

"I'm glad to hear it."

"I really can't believe you don't think I have enough to do in this flat though. And it's economical. You won't have to pay for a cleaner, or for expensive restaurant meals. I can do all that."

He and Glass had not factored in the idea that Sadie might not want to work. But she had to. "I'm sorry, but you're a modern girl with a new job and why shouldn't you work? I travel a lot and you'll be bored."

"I'll go with you," she insisted. "Look at what happened in Hull. If you're going to have these foolish impulses, I need to protect you from yourself."

He grinned. "In that case, we'll get married tomorrow!"

She smiled for the first time since she had come in. "It takes weeks."

"Not with a special license."

"Which is not inexpensive," she pointed out.

"Can I tell you a secret?" he said, making it up as he went along.

"What's that?"

"I can't manage these late nights with my supervisor. Either I stay his drinking companion when he's on a bender, or I marry. Married men have more opportunity in my company, and aren't expected to make a circuit of public houses at night. For all his waywardness, my company owner is a family man at heart. He likes to have his men marry. And he very much disapproves of the sort of arrangement we have."

"Which is?"

He shrugged. "Living in sin." He leaned forward. "If he found out you were living here, I would be fired."

Her mouth dropped open. "I can't support you on a chambermaid wage, Les."

He pulled the special license from his pocket. "We really can be married tomorrow. No more worries for you, and I won't risk being sacked. What do you say?"

She took the paper, frowning, her lips moving as she read. "Such applesauce. Was this really necessary?"

He grinned. "Don't you want to marry me?"

"Of course." She sounded uncertain.

"It's all set up for tomorrow night."

"I thought my grandfather would officiate," she said, her hand shaking. "I know that is what my sister is planning."

"Don't you want to beat your sister to the altar?" he asked, poking at Sadie's vanity.

She bit her lip. "We can't risk your career. It would break my heart to lose this lovely flat."

"Very well," he said solemnly, ignoring that his fake fiancée had just put his flat over his person. "Meet me at the Peace Chapel in Marylebone as soon as you are done for the day, tomorrow. We'll marry then."

"Can't we wait until Saturday night? That way we'd at least have a quiet twenty-four hours or so when we don't have to work."

He pulled the ring box from his pocket and took her unresisting hand. Her eyes widened as he opened the ring box to show her the diamond solitaire on a gold band. She sighed with happiness as he slid it on her finger. "No. I can't wait another day."

"I knew you were in love with me," she sighed, staring at her ring. "Oh, it's beautiful, Les. Is it a family heirloom?"

"Of course," he lied. "My mother's."

"You haven't told me about her," she said absently.

"She was lovely. Died much too young."

"My mother too," she said, holding her hand this way and that, admiring how the candlelight sparkled off the stone.

Les wondered how much Glass had invested in this ring, and how many fingers it would eventually adorn during its life as a Secret Intelligence Service marital weapon. For that matter, had his mother's engagement ring been the same? It was probably in a bank vault along with the rest of his family's valuables. He'd never cared much about jewelry.

"We'll have our own family soon enough. Perhaps Alecia and I will have babies right about the same time and they can grow up together. That would be nice." Her gaze had gone soft and dreamy.

Not if he could help it.

The next evening, Sadie's taxicab pulled up in front of the tiny Peace Chapel in Marylebone. It was nothing more than a storefront.

She'd given Olga a note for Alecia, to tell her about the wedding tonight, but her sister would never be able to come here in time, even if she could leave the elderly woman she was caring for.

She opened the front door, which was unlocked, and found a small anteroom. Through a cheap door, she found a small, Spartan chapel, with an altar toward the back and folding chairs in the rest of the room. Four men were present. Les, Robbie O'Donnell, a slightly older tall fellow in an expensive suit, and a stoop-backed man with a clerical collar. Les had supplied himself and his witnesses. She had no one. For a moment, she even wished for her friends from the Richmond Inn, Mrs. Curtis and Old Ben, to be present, but she had burned those bridges by taking off for Hull so precipitously. She'd made her bed with Lester Rake and now she needed to lie in it.

At least he was a handsome fellow who dressed well. If she occasionally felt like he was looking through her rather than at her, well, that was just her insecurities talking. He obviously had fallen in love with her. Just like she had with him. That fluttering sensation in her belly was happy nerves, excitement. Tonight she'd be a wife, his wife, Mrs. Lester Rake.

The ceremony only took five minutes. He put a slim gold ring on her finger, and Robbie solemnly gave her a thicker band for Les's finger. He must have chosen it himself when he'd bought her ring. The other man, Lord Walling, a proper aristocrat, shook her hand solemnly when the ceremony was through. They all signed the paperwork and then went for dinner at an Italian restaurant near Soho Square. The men shared two bottles of wine and became very merry, teasing Les mercilessly. She was confused and scarcely touched her pasta. Robbie was a friend, but who was Lord Walling? His supervisor? The owner of his company? He was well-dressed enough to be wealthy, but didn't have the looks of a heavy drinker. They were too busy trading quips to ever make the relationships clear. Meanwhile, Sadie was fawned over by the waiters, who brought her so many different desserts to celebrate her bridal status that she felt sleepy from so much heavy, alcohol-soaked cake.

They shared a taxicab back to Primrose Hill, and let the new Rake couple off alone in front of his building. Robbie and Lord Walling shook both of their hands very enthusiastically, then the taxicab drove off, wheels grinding against old leaves and water on the street, leaving them alone in the rain.

Sadie held onto Les's arm lightly as they entered his flat. Hers too, now. She actually had a London home, a proper husband. If only her sister had been at her wedding. She pulled off her gloves so she could check on her rings.

When he closed the front door behind him, she said uncertainly, "I should move my things from the guest bedroom into your room."

He yawned hugely. "Don't worry about it tonight, Sadie, It's very late and you have to work tomorrow."

"I didn't hear Lord Walling say that you have the day off either. Is he your supervisor or the company owner?"

"Supervisor," Les said, yawning again. "And you are right. I'm off to bed."

She watched, dumbfounded, as he pulled off his coat and gloves, then set his hat on the newel post leading upstairs. "I must admit I didn't have time to prepare properly for our wedding night. Could I have a quick bath? I—" she blushed.

He looked at her with those pale gray-blue eyes. Once again, she had the uncomfortable sensation that he was looking through her instead of at her. But then, his expression changed. He came to her and grasped her upper arms.

He smiled boyishly, exposing his perfect teeth, his hair flopping down over his brow. "Darling, I'm still injured. We're going to have to take this wedding in multiple parts. Tonight the ceremony. We'll plan a little party with your family soon. And the wedding night will have to wait a bit."

"It will?" Her heart began to pound uncomfortably.

"You are comfortable in the guest room?"

Tears pricked her eyes. "Of course, but my place is with you now."

"We have a lot to become used to. You don't want to listen to my snores quite yet, and I can sleep later in the morning than you can. So let's be easy on each other."

"But, Les," she protested.

"Just for a little while." He nodded and stepped back, releasing her arms. "You know I'm right. Listen to your husband."

"You're supposed to treat me like your wife," she whispered, feeling so lost.

"I am. This is kindness, darling, truly."

She blushed furiously. "You weren't injured down there."

His lips curved. "You'll find that a great deal of sexuality comes from here." He tapped his forehead. "Rather than, err, down there. And where was I injured?"

"Your poor head," she said dutifully.

He nodded. "Be a good darling and go to bed. I'm sure you are as tired as I am. Write your sister tomorrow and your grandfather, and let's make plans. You should meet her fiancé, too."

"Very well," she said dolefully. Yes, she was tired, but she'd had certain expectations.

"Wonderful. Dinner with a trio of Loudons. I cannot wait."

"Salter," she added. "The fiancé's name is Ivan Salter."

"Salter isn't Russian, but Ivan is. Is he part-Russian, part-English like me?"

Sadie shrugged. "I haven't met him. He works the night shift."

"Oh? Is he employed at the Grand Russe?"

She nodded, feeling sleepy now that she'd lost the battle for a wedding night. "In Security. Alecia said he's being promoted but for now he's working his old hours because his former position hasn't been filled."

Les's gaze wandered away. He'd lost interest in the conversation.

"Well." She forced a smile. "Time for bed, Mr. Rake." She lifted herself to her tiptoes and kissed him on the cheek.

"You can do better than that." He grinned and wrapped his arms around her, pulling her body flush against his. "Mrs. Rake."

Their lips touched, lingered against each other. Sadie felt the tips of her breasts tighten. She longed to be his wife in truth. But just as she steeled herself to make a pitch on her behalf, he thrust her away and turned.

"Good night, darling. Go straight to bed."

A couple of seconds later, she heard his bedroom door open and shut. Her wedding night was effectively over. Her eyes filled with tears. She wiped them away, angry at herself. Her cheeks and jaw hurt and her feet were sore and cold.

She sniffed. In the morning, she'd take every shilling from that box on his chest and use the money to buy herself a smart new pair of shoes. A wedding present. She deserved that much. Mrs. Lester Rake, indeed.

"It has been a week since the bombing attempt. What progress have you made?" Peter Eyre sat behind his desk at the Grand Russe.

He pulled his Dunhill lighter from his pocket and offered a Pall Mall cigarette to Detective Inspector Dent of Special Branch.

Dent was about fifteen years older than he was, still handsome, although the lines of cynicism were thickly etched on his forehead. He looked to be in excellent physical condition, and as he waved the cigarette away, Peter remembered he'd promised himself to cut back and take better care of himself. Youth didn't last long, but there was no reason to shorten it even more by pure foolishness.

"Not smoking, eh?" Peter tossed his lighter in one hand and caught it in the other.

"Mouth feels like an ashtray already."

"Long day?"

Dent nodded. "Won't say no to a drink."

"Very well." Peter pushed his chair back and went to his drinks cabinet. "Champagne?"

"I'm not one of your Society pals. How about a vodka on the rocks?"

"Vodka, eh? The spirit of the Grand Russe Hotel?"

"Why did your family rename the hotel?" Dent asked. He smirked when Peter turned to him. "Come now, Eyre, not that Eyre is your real name. I've been on the case a week now. I've learned quite a bit about you."

"Then you ought to know the hotel was renamed after the famed ballet company."

"Why?"

"The ballet, *The Sleeping Princess*, as performed by the Ballets Russes, inspired the redesigned décor."

"Why?"

Peter dropped ice into the small tumbler and poured the clear liquor, then added a slice of preserved orange peel. "My brother loved ballet."

"Where is Noel?"

Peter gritted his teeth. "At the East Suffolk and Ipswich Hospital."

"He was a sniper in the war?"

Peter nodded. "He lost his sight, right at the end of the war. Made it all the way through, almost."

"A pity. Everything going his way, then this. How old is he now?"

"Let's see. He was born in 1888. A Christmas infant."

"Late thirties, then. Waste of a life. Effectively over when he enlisted."

Peter shrugged. "I expect you want me to say how happy I am to be so much younger, but I'd have fought."

Dent sneered. "Too soft by half, I'd say."

"Never," Peter said. "But I've risen to the occasion. After all, my brother has not."

"He's blind."

"Hysterical blindness, not medical." Peter winced. He shouldn't have admitted that. His parents would be terribly disappointed. But this was a police detective. Dent would know the truth already.

"They say far more officers broke than enlisted men," Dent said. "A very strange war. And now, an even stranger war, this issue with Russia."

"You must think my family courted disaster, naming the hotel as we did."

"I think it was a mistake," Dent said candidly. "But now we have to deal with it."

"What is the latest?"

"We have learned that Ovolensky's men are hunting for Konstantin. He managed the technical aspects of the attempt to bomb this hotel last week."

Peter frowned as he made himself a screwdriver. "But Ovolensky is here to lay groundwork for an Anglo-Russian trade conference this spring."

"Never trust a Russian to be what he claims." He pulled a folded piece of paper from his pocket. "This is our best approximation of Konstantin's appearance, but we have yet to spot him."

Peter glanced over the photo. It could have been any stocky man thirty-five or older with a beard and even he knew that was the easiest part of a disguise to remove. "This is worthless, but Ivan Salter thinks he saw Konstantin again yesterday. They met once."

"Where did he see him?"

"In the hotel. The Coffee Room. Just before eight in the morning when his shift ends."

Dent swore. "And you didn't think to tell us?"

"He wasn't sure."

"Bloody hell, man, do you want Konstantin to finish the job and level this place?"

Peter frowned. "Does Special Branch or the Secret Intelligence Service have eyes and ears in the hotel?"

"I can't answer that."

"Surely I have a right to know. If I knew who your man was, I could quietly tell him when there is a suspicion and have it handled immediately. We could have nabbed the maybe-Konstantin right away." He paused. "I'm sure you've done your best to recruit Ivan Salter. He didn't report in?"

Dent didn't answer.

Peter reached for a fresh cigarette. "Salter himself is suspicious that one of our night watchmen, Tim Swankle, is more than he seems."

Dent took a sip of his drink and shifted in his chair.

"The problem is," Peter continued, "that they are all new. The hotel only reopened in December. I don't have a lot to go on."

"It's not your business to know who we might have in place," Dent said, setting down his glass after one sip. "I'm sorry. I'll be in touch."

He walked out. Peter tossed the contents of his own drink down his throat, feeling the burn and the outrage. How was he supposed to keep his hotel, employees, and customers safe with no information? He had the distinct feeling that the Metropolitan Police didn't trust *him*.

Chapter Nine

Les's eyes burned as he sat up in bed early the morning after his wedding night. His first day as a "married" man and he'd been awake all night, for the wrong reasons. Thoughts of his virgin bride tormented him, but he couldn't take advantage of what she so freely offered to her new husband. The betrayal would be more than even he could stand. He couldn't repeat his father's mistakes. Honoring his mother's memory meant choosing to treat Sadie differently.

When he heard doors open and close, he ducked into the bathroom and shaved, then dressed. Sadie was still in the kitchen when he went in.

"You're up early." She sat at the table, eating buttered toast. "Didn't you sleep well?"

He heard the chill beneath her words. "I thought I might take you to work."

"Why?"

"Newsstands around the park. I'd be back in my supervisor's good graces if I sold our magazines into those."

She nodded. "Have you thought about making an actual sales plan?"

He sat across from her, drinking in the sight of her creamy skin and full lips. Hardening instantaneously, he knew himself for a sentimental fool. He could have spent the night with her, and she'd have been grateful. Sleeping with her would have been better for his cover besides. "What do you mean?"

"You seem to go where the wind blows. I know you're a gifted salesman. If you were systematic about it, you might be truly successful, even be promoted into management of your company."

He grinned. "Less than fifteen hours of marriage and you're already ambitious for me?"

"You know I can't be a chambermaid forever. The babies will come, when you're feeling better." She glanced down at her toast, blushing.

"No child bride you," he muttered. "There's a clever mind behind that pretty face."

She kept her eyes on her toast, making her impossible to read, but he saw the little clench of her shoulders. She hadn't liked what he said. Why? Because he'd seen the real her, or because she'd taken it as an insult?

He pushed back from the table. "We should go."

"Are you going to come in?" she asked.

"Why not? All your unmarried colleagues ought to know you aren't a spinster anymore."

She nodded. "As you wish. I left my shoes downstairs. I look forward to meeting the neighbors too, now that I can flash my wedding ring."

He hadn't realized she'd been feeling self-conscious. Another crime. He put on his coat while she buckled her shoes, noting the leather was worn on the tips and she winced when she backed her right heel into the shoe. "You need different shoes."

"I know."

While she put on her coat, he went into his bedroom and found a stash of pound notes taped to the underside of his sock drawer. He pulled back the tape and peeled off two notes, then put everything back the way it was and returned to the hallway.

"Here," he said, thrusting the notes at her. "Buy yourself new shoes after work."

She stared at the notes. "I can buy shoes for half that."

"Two pair, then, but buy something very comfortable. You have to be on your feet all day."

"When I'm not on my knees." She sighed as she pulled on her gloves.

Sadie had no idea how crazy she was making him. On her knees, indeed.

He kept his gaze fixed out of the window during the taxicab ride to the hotel, and was pleased when she took him through the basement staff entrance without comment. Knowing the layout of the hotel might come in handy one day. The basement level was what he expected of any large business, dank and poorly lit.

"The original bathrooms are that way. Can you imagine? Only four, in the basement no less, for the entire hotel?"

"At least you don't have to worry about chamber pots these days."

"Yes, we do, on the lower floors." She shuddered as they walked down the dim passage. "The staff lounge is in here."

They walked into a bustling space full of women in dark dresses, hanging coats on pegs. The space wasn't decorated with anything much, just old furniture and a cork board with notices.

A tall and slim blonde with a very regal carriage crossed her arms over her chest when she saw them enter. Sadie smiled at her tentatively and pulled Les along with her.

"Olga, this is my new husband, Lester Rake. Les, Miss Novikov is in charge of the chambermaids."

"Novikov?" Les frowned. He knew that name. Aristocratic. "You must have a title, Miss Novikov. I am partly Russian myself."

"In Russia I was called Her Serene Highness," she said with a nod. "But those days are over now."

Her accent was rather slight. She had been well educated, despite the turmoil during her youth. He thought her about his age, definitely older than Sadie. Her face had no lines, but her eyes held stories.

"May I call you Your Serene Highness?" he asked.

Her upper lip curled. "Not even if we were in Russia. It could get me killed."

"Of course, Miss Novikov," he said. "We wouldn't want that." At least she was unlikely to be sympathetic to Bolsheviks.

"Who were your people in Russia?"

"I am a Dragunov."

"I do not believe I ever knew anyone with that name."

"Not a distinguished lineage," he admitted. "Wheelwrights and other skilled laborers."

"Good with their hands, your people?"

"Yes." He forced a smile. "How I ended up in sales I'll never know."

"Your parents?"

"Deceased." He put his hand on Sadie's shoulder. "I'm all alone in the world. I am so very lucky to have found my Sadie."

"Such a precipitous marriage," she commented.

"I'm sure you are aware of our living arrangements. I could not subject my darling girl to censure. She's much too respectable for that."

Olga made a noncommittal noise. "Her shift commences in one minute. Unless you are here to give her notice."

"Not at all," he said with a smile. "I travel for work and she's new to London. I am hoping her position will give her the opportunity to make friends."

Olga's eyelids lowered, giving her a superior air. "I see. We are not especially close here. The hotel has not been open for long."

Les forced enthusiasm he didn't feel into his voice. "Then she is in at the start. Very exciting."

"Yes, well." Olga's gaze wandered somewhere over his right shoulder.

He turned to Sadie and kissed her cheek. "Have a wonderful day, darling, and remember to buy shoes. Don't worry about dinner for me."

"You won't be home?"

"I'll manage if you are not home," he said. "Perhaps Miss Novikov would like to shop with you and you will eat with her."

Olga glanced between the two of them, and Les realized he'd pushed it too far. A newlywed man wouldn't be encouraging his wife of one day to dine with another woman.

"I'll probably be asleep," he backpedaled. "My injuries have kept me rather low, of late."

"I am sorry to hear that," Olga said in a disinterested manner.

The clock chimed. All of the women scurried through the door as their shift began.

"Do you know the way out?" Sadie asked.

He smiled. "Don't you worry about me." He kept his gaze on her just in case she turned around, the portrait of an adoring husband, and watched the last of the women depart. For a moment he was alone, but any minute there might be an influx of people leaving from the previous shift.

Olga was very suspicious of him. Was she protective of all the chambermaids, or did she have a specific issue with their situation? Perhaps she was merely a jealous virgin. Les knew he was an attractive man who was good with women. It was a part of spycraft. But since he'd chosen a partner, for now at least, he had to be careful with his behavior. He wasn't used to this new role. The Kozyrevs had a lot to answer for. He wished for a moment that he was still focused on infiltrating the labor movement, rather than this London mess.

For certain, he wasn't going to be allowed to hang about the Grand Russe like some kind of stage-door Johnnie. Sadie would expect him to be at work and Olga would be generally suspicious. He'd even have to leave town for days on end for his cover. Did Glass know what kind of complication he'd created in Les's life with this arrangement?

Les made a quick circuit of the staff lounge, then prowled around the basement, thoroughly mapping the space for himself. He noted all of the exits and entrances, stairs and elevators, nooks and crannies. Then, he went upstairs, curious to see if he'd be noticed coming out of the staff staircase on to the main floor.

He wasn't. A pity. He'd have thought staff would be more diligent when they'd almost been bombed just over a week before.

Sadie was buttoning her coat at the end of her shift when Olga came up to her in the staff lounge. Olga glanced at the thin gold band and engagement ring on Sadie's ring finger.

"Did you really marry him?" her supervisor asked.

"Yes. He purchased a special license." She twisted the lovely diamond engagement ring so that it lined up perfectly with the front of her finger. It would be better to leave it at home and just wear her wedding ring, but she'd had it for such a short time. "I think I should buy a chain and keep my rings around my neck at work."

"Your tips will be better if gentlemen guests think you are single," Olga said.

"I suppose so. But I'm not really working for the money. Les wants me to make friends. He's afraid I'll be lonely. Alecia is so busy with that Mrs. Plash and I don't know anyone else."

"Doesn't your husband have friends?"

"We've been to tea with his friend Robbie, but he's single. Another man came to our wedding, but he's Les's supervisor. Then there's a married couple we've spent time with, but they live in Hull apparently." Sadie fidgeted. "We met another couple who seem nice. They live in Acton. Maybe I can invite them to dinner soon."

Olga nodded slowly. "I am glad to hear these things, but my heart tells me that your Les is a bad man."

Sadie's fingers tingled, pins and needles, as her shoulders froze into an odd position, tightening her muscles. "Whatever do you mean?"

"Please don't be offended," Olga said. "We were betrayed, my maid and me, when we were escaping my fiancé's murderer in Russia. By a confidence man. My maid, she sacrificed herself to save me. I am afraid Les is like that man."

Sadie's heart thumped in her chest double-time. As much as she hated to admit it, Les did have some odd characteristics, the Russian aspect being only one of them. "Why?"

"He has an insincere look in his eyes. A cold look." Olga stared hard at Sadie.

She resented Olga's words, but the woman did have life experience she lacked. "If you are right, what should I do?"

"If you need help, see Peter Eyre," Olga said. "He'll protect you as if you are family, assuming you do a good job here. No more late mornings."

Sadie nodded. "I didn't think I'd be working again, you see."

"It's time to behave like you are grown," Olga said. "No more childishness. Face your responsibilities and your realities."

"What am I going to do about Les?" Sadie asked.

"I assume you love him," Olga said. "I imagine you do what every wife does, hope for the best, behave impeccably, and hide away a bit of cash so if he leaves you flat, you'll be able to get by."

"Glory, what a cynical attitude." Sadie forced a laugh.

"These are uncertain times. You can have everything and lose it all."

Sadie knew Olga referred to her lost life as a Russian princess, but what came to her, really, was the sight of Les, crumpled on that dock in Hull. Her handbag gone, and them both far away from home. The situation had worked out for them, but what about next time? "I don't think he needs my salary. I'll set that aside for emergencies."

"Smart," Olga said. "Don't quit your job here until it is absolutely necessary. I don't trust that man."

Sadie wanted to confess everything to Olga in that moment, but she kept her own counsel. Surely she would learn to understand Les in time. After all, he must love her. He'd married her.

After her shift, she took a bus to a department store and used the money Les had given her to buy two new pairs of shoes. It would have been even nicer if he'd been there to help her choose them. Both pairs she bought were low-heeled and comfortable. One black and one gray, not very exciting really, except that it was fun to buy something new. At least she'd have something to report in her letter to Alecia that night.

Instead of going to dinner alone, she went home, hoping Les would be there and awake. She did have to work in the morning, but after that, they had an entire day and a half to celebrate their marriage properly.

As she opened the front door, she wondered if she should have bought something wedding-night appropriate instead of the second pair of shoes. Her hand trembled as she closed the door. What was she afraid of? Marriage night jitters were common, but almost every girl had a wedding night and lived to tell the tale.

The flat was silent as only an uninhabited space could be. She could even hear a single car going by outside, and rain on the pavement in the small garden space. While she was quite sure Les wasn't home, she checked his bedroom anyway. Empty.

She ran herself a bath and put on his dressing gown after, surrounding herself with Les's scent. He was probably going to eat out, but with whom? And why wasn't he taking care of himself, so he'd be prepared for their proper wedding night? Shaking her head, she went upstairs to fix herself the last of the eggs.

A few hours later, she was dozing in an armchair next to the popping and hissing but warm radiator when the front door opened. A couple of minutes later, Les came up the stairs.

Caught in a vague dream that drifted from the Hull docks to Primrose Hill to that party in the Chelsea basement flat, Sadie was startled to see the outline of his broad shoulders appear in the doorway.

"Who were you with so late?" she demanded, still confused from her dream. "Another woman?"

"Of course not, darling," he said, coming closer, bringing cold and the scent of coal dust and rain. "Why would you say that? Have you ever seen me look at another woman?"

She rubbed the sleep from her eyes. "I'm sorry. Bad dream. What are you doing out so late?"

"It's only eight. I had a quick bite at a pub with Robbie."

"Why?"

"I happened to be right where he lives at the end of my day."

"Where is that?"

"Camden. Are you working tomorrow?"

"Yes, the chambermaids work five and a half days. I have half-Saturday and all day Sunday off."

He nodded. "We'll have to do something fun tomorrow. Dinner and dancing? A film?"

She yawned. "A film, I should think. You aren't well enough to dance."

"All that twirling wouldn't do me any favors. Anything to eat around here?"

"You just ate with Robbie," she said.

"Right," he said with an air of distraction, making her wonder if he was quite all right.

She sat up, yawning again. "There is a packet of biscuits in the cupboard."

He brightened at that. "Tea and biscuits?"

"Yes. You sit down and I'll fix us up a tray. We'll have a quiet little chat together and then go to bed." She saw his look of alarm. "Separate bedrooms again, I think. You're all done in. I can see that."

He smiled and held out his hand to help her up from the chair. "I'm sure I'll be better soon, love."

She walked away smiling. He'd never called her "love" before.

"You're sure you can get in?" Detective McCall folded his newspaper and put it under his arm.

Les leaned against the tree in Hyde Park that McCall stood under, looking out toward Marble Arch. "I know where the employee entrance is. The shift starts in five minutes and there seemed to be a lull between one ending and one starting. If we get through the door exactly five minutes from now, I think we'll be fine."

"Excellent." McCall rubbed his hands together. He wore a nondescript suit today, his working uniform. No overcoat, but they'd have nowhere to stash coats when they were in.

"What do we know?"

"Ivan Salter, the security man for the Grand Russe, the only bloke we have not had under arrest who has seen Konstantin, thinks he was at the Grand Russe a couple of days ago right about this time of day." McCall ran an index finger down the side of his nose. "Now, Konstantin was in the Coffee Room."

"What's the importance of that?"

"Free food. I don't know how they keep out the transients. I expect anyone well-dressed can get in there. It's meant to have coffee and toast for guests and there are waiters who presumably know the guests."

"Konstantin has a helper among the waiters?"

"Could be. Or he's around a lot and staff is used to him, think he's a guest. Or he is one."

Les sighed dramatically.

"I know. You've memorized the sketch?"

"It's worthless. All the focus on the beard. Salt-and-pepper beard that's too young for the rest of his face."

"He looks like everyone else," McCall said, baring his teeth. "A Bolshie bomber who looks like everyone else."

"Is Salter one of ours?"

McCall shook his head. "He is the hotel's man. Salter is much too Russian to trust the government."

"He's engaged to Sadie's sister."

McCall's eyes widened, then he chuckled deep in his throat. "You espionage types. I have to admire how you manipulate people. You met him socially yet?"

Les shook his head. "It will come. We'll make use of Salter whether he knows it or not."

McCall glanced at his watch. "One minute to go."

"Let's cross the street." They had to dodge a bus and a truck, but made it into the alley behind the hotel without any trouble, then went down the stairs to the employee entrance. As Les suspected, the door was unlocked.

"Now what?" McCall pushed open the door.

Les followed him inside. "I have the entire area mapped in my head. I can see why Konstantin would find it easy to get to the Coffee Room. The staff staircase lets out just before it on the corridor."

"That's why you think Konstantin might have a nest down here?"

"He's not at his flat. And there are bathrooms down here."

"What else?"

"What I'm really curious to see, is if there are any access points to the Metro or the sewers."

"Shouldn't be," McCall said.

"I know," Les agreed. "But can you imagine?"

"Give me the tour," McCall said.

They took twenty minutes to traverse the main corridors. McCall knew the ground floor quite well, and announced what they were underneath at every key point. "No sign of anyone sleeping down here," he said, after they closed the last of the four bathroom doors.

"Time to check those three oddball doors I've found."

McCall nodded and they returned to an area underneath the reception area. "Door is locked."

Les smirked and pulled out a set of lock picks. "Time me."

"Forty seconds," McCall announced when the lock snicked open. "Don't switch to a life of crime anytime soon, mate."

Les pulled a small torch from his pocket and pointed it through the door. "Looks clean."

"And deep," McCall said. "I heard a rumor that Peter Eyre lives in secret chambers behind his office. I'm starting to believe it."

Les switched off his light and put up his hand. "Noise ahead," he whispered in McCall's ear.

"Rat?"

"Shadow," Les said.

McCall unsnapped the holster under his suit coat and pulled out his Webley semi-automatic pistol.

Les put his hand over the bulb of his torch and switched it back on. He allowed a thin thread of light to escape, enough for them to both move forward on either side of the passage. Ahead of them, Les heard the sound again. Water dripping? A pipe, maybe, not a person at all. But then, he heard rustling. A rat?

After five more feet forward, he allowed more light. Another door.

"Must be right underneath Eyre's secret lair," McCall said.

Les put his torch between his teeth and turned the knob, expecting it to be locked. It wasn't. McCall shook his head. Les agreed. He didn't like it either.

He lifted his torch and swept it around the door.

"No cobwebs," McCall said, putting his back against the wall.

Les opened the door in a smooth motion, then swept the space with his light.

"Hands where I can see them!" McCall said, seeing something Les could not.

No one spoke but Les heard breathing, then footsteps moving away.

McCall swore and dashed into the dark. Les followed him, keeping his torch trained on the ground. Twenty feet in, they found a wall. The passage went both ways.

"We have to stay together," Les said. "Which way?"

"Toward the park. Metro that way, right? Sewers the other?"

"Hard to know sometimes," Les muttered. They slowed down and continued forward. A door slammed ahead of them. Les sent his torchlight in an arc around the space and found two doors.

McCall sniffed the air. "What is that? Cordite?"

Les tried a door. "Locked."

"Open it," McCall said. "We might be chasing a bomber."

Les had the lock picked in thirty seconds this time. McCall moved to the wall again, as he opened the door and swept the space with his flashlight.

McCall swore when he saw what Les had revealed. Boxes of supplies. And crates. Some of them marked Dynamite.

Chapter Ten

Les flashed his torch around the dark room, highlighting each box as the light settled on it. Hellfire, what evil had they uncovered in the Grand Russe's basement?

"This looks more like a sodding storage cache than a bomb site." Detective McCall put his pistol in his holster and pulled out a torch of his own. He swore again. "A cot. You were right. I think Konstantin was holed up here with his precious belongings."

"Should we go after him?" Les asked, glancing at the clumped blankets at the foot of the stained mattress. "Or get your men in here to clean this up?"

"See if there's a direct way out of the hotel from this area," McCall suggested. "Then get some help. We can't run the risk of letting him get back in here to remove the goods."

"You want to go?"

"You have a weapon?"

"Not a gun."

"You go. I'm going to protect all this."

Les nodded. "I'll talk to the first constable I see, or just call Special Branch. Who should I ask for?"

"Detective Inspector Dent. He's in charge of the Grand Russe investigation."

Les patted McCall's arm and returned to the passage outside of the room. His torch was just heavy enough to use as a weapon, and he had a couple of knives secreted on his person too. What he really wanted was a glimpse of Konstantin, if indeed that was who he was after.

Sadie hummed an old ragtime tune as she pulled the tray with three pork chops from the oven. She'd learned from her late grandmother to sear them in a pan first and then finish them off in the oven, which had dramatically improved the quality of her pork meals. She set the tray on the stove top then bent down again to retrieve her potatoes. The front door downstairs opened just as she shut the oven door.

She swept off her apron and slid her feet into her new black shoes. Not much other beautification was possible before Sunday. Tomorrow she hoped to retrieve her clothing. She and Alecia had agreed to meet at the train station in the morning and they had a busy day planned. Meanwhile, she had done her best with her new lipstick and powder, hoping that Les would see she'd made an effort.

Would he finally feel well enough to make her his wife in every way?

When he appeared in the doorway, she wasn't sure what to think. "You have leaves in your hair!" she exclaimed.

He put his hand to his head and pulled a curled brown leaf from his hair. "Missed that."

She stepped up to him and ran her fingers through his wavy bangs, dislodging a twig and a couple of leaf bits. "What happened to you?"

"Lost my hat."

"And your coat." He stayed still, allowing her to run her hands through his hair. She needed a comb. Her fingers caught on tangles. "Oh, dear. You need to wash it."

His eyes fluttered closed. "Don't stop. That feels delightful."

She stroked his head, learning the narrow shape of his skull under his thick, wavy sand and mud colored curls. His hair was slightly damp too, and smelled like felt, cold, and something mechanical. "Did you sell a lot of magazines today?"

"No. I took a walk with Robbie. Trying to rebuild my strength."

Odd choice. "You must have been in a park."

"We were in and out of Hyde Park."

"Just across from the Grand Russe? Did you come in to say hello?"

"I don't think Olga would appreciate that. She didn't seem to like me much."

"She's extremely reserved," Sadie said. "But kind, too. She passes letters back and forth between Alecia and me every day."

Les tilted his head away from her, effectively ending her ministrations. She let her hands drop. "Are you going to see your sister?"

"Yes. We're going to take the train to Bagshot tomorrow, go to service at Grandfather's church. Hopefully I'll have time to pack up my things from the Richmond Inn. Will you come with us?"

"No. I played too much today. I need to catch up."

"You can't sell magazines on a Sunday," she protested.

"My accounts, darling. I have paperwork up to here." He put his hand to his neck as if to prevent her from touching him again.

Her enthusiasm dimmed, but she still had a great deal to look forward to. "I see. Well, I'm so happy to be seeing my sister. I'll let you escape this time."

"You should plan a dinner with her and her fiancé," Les suggested. "Does Her Serene Highness have a beau?"

"I don't think so, but I'm not sure my cooking is up to royal standards anyway."

"Let's give it a try. Do I smell pork chops?"

She nodded and went to fetch the food and bring it to the table. She'd never understood why her grandmother wasted dishes by transferring food from the cooking vessels to prettier serving dishes, but she wanted to please Les so she attended to all the small details, even pouring him a glass of wine that she hoped went with her food.

He employed his fork and knife enthusiastically, praising the crispness of the potatoes and the juiciness of her pork chop. She thought her gravy was too salty, but he didn't complain. Her attempts at small talk were ignored as he ate at a rapid pace. He finished every bite of the meat, even what she had left on her plate, then pushed back from the table with a happy sigh.

"That will have me back in fighting condition," he said. "Thank you."

"Where are you going?" Since she'd only worked a half day, she wasn't exhausted. "We should see a film or something."

He yawned. "Oh, I don't think so. Not tonight."

"I looked through your records. We could dance."

"Darling," he protested. "I'm a wounded man."

"Not too wounded to tramp about with Robbie all day." As she stared at him, irritated, his expression changed. Even his body seemed to soften.

He walked toward her and slid his arms around her waist. "Sadie, darling, am I neglecting you? Relax, I'll help you do the dishes and then we'll put a record on. Happy?"

She smiled, glad he did want to spend time with her. "Perfectly."

* * *

Les attempted to discreetly stretch his calves as he dried the dishes. He'd chased Konstantin or whoever it was through the bowels of the Grand Russe and into a hatchway leading into an old construction tunnel. After an hour, he'd lost him. There had been too many choices of hatchways and he'd found the wrong one. He'd come up from underground near the Hyde Park Corner Metro entrance, amazed that he'd been below so long, and had called Detective Inspector Dent at the first telephone box he found. He'd spent the rest of the day walking the area around the hotel, watching for suspicious activity, but now that he knew about the tunnels, he realized Konstantin was moving into the hotel through them, not through the actual hotel entrances.

He knew the next day would be full of meetings of higher-ups between the Service and Special Branch, trying to decide what to do about this new development. Was Sadie, or any other employee, safe in the hotel? He knew the basement would be swept clean of weapons caches. Where would Konstantin hide next?

His fingers slid along the still soapy rim of a serving platter and he dropped it. He bent down just as Sadie did the same and grabbed for the platter. He fumbled it and Sadie caught the other edge. They bumped heads as it slid through her fingers as well, but they were low enough to the ground by then that it didn't crack as it hit the rug protecting the linoleum in front of the sink.

Les's thigh spasmed and he sat abruptly. Sadie collapsed next to him and rubbed her forehead. "Sorry about that," he said.

"I didn't rinse the soap properly," she admitted.

He rubbed her forehead. "I didn't mean to wreak my revenge on your poor head."

She moved her head back and forth against his hand, like a cat. The poor girl was desperate for affection and he was afraid to give her any. For all his attempts to remain aloof, the closeness of her to him, all night, every night, just a wall's length away from him, drove him wild and made it hard to sleep. Just for the asking, he could have this luscious, curvy female in his bed. If only he was a very slightly less honorable man.

The muscles in his thigh twitched again. He grabbed at it, kneading the muscles.

"What's wrong?"

"Too much exercise."

"Let me." Her slightly damp hands moved to his thigh, leaving wet marks on his trousers as she dug surprisingly strong fingers into his muscles.

"Mmmm." He let his head fall back against a cupboard as she soothed his muscle.

"Sit on your bum," she instructed. "You aren't helping anything by crouching."

He complied, stretching out his legs. Her head was bent underneath his, and he could smell the chamomile she must have used to rinse her hair. How innocent was she? The position she was in could easily lead to other things, although he'd indicated he was too beat up to think of any of that.

But, he wasn't. As the fire left his leg, warmth spread to other parts of his body. And with her in the position she was, he couldn't hide the evidence of how he felt. He stared at her neck, the soft down on the back of the smooth skin, and couldn't help himself. He lowered his lips a scant inch and kissed her there, then nuzzled his nose into her hair.

When she didn't protest, he wrapped his arms around her waist. She turned, her face against his chest, and crawled into his lap until they were face-to-face.

"What?" he asked.

"This." She cupped his cheeks with her hands and kissed him, very sweetly.

He was long past sweet. Her lips were closed. He licked along them, tasting the coffee they'd had after their meal. When she parted, he swept in, taking her with harsh possessiveness. He could feel the heat of her body against his chest. Blood pumped into his erection. He took one of her hands from his cheeks and pulled it down his chest. Her mouth pulled away from his as he pressed her hand against him. She'd moved her head far enough away from him that he could see the surprise in her big blue eyes.

"Do you know what this is?" he asked harshly.

"Your man part."

"I'm aching for you, Sadie."

"What does that mean?"

"It means in this moment, I feel like I'm going to die if I don't touch you."

Her tongue darted out, kitten-like. She licked the corner of her mouth. "On the kitchen floor?"

"I don't care where we are." He felt like his cock would break if he didn't adjust himself. To hell with it. She thought she was his wife. He undid his trousers and righted his rock-hard appendage.

Her eyes went wide when she saw him peeking out of the top of his trousers.

"Sorry," he said, tucking his shirt back in.

Her gaze had gone fiery. She pushed his shirt out of the way. "No, I want to see." She stroked the slit in his head, then pushed his trousers and drawers out of the way as she slid her hand down the length.

"Sadie," he protested.

"You have hair there too, just like I do." She grinned at him. "I always visualized my wedding night, with me in a white gown, on the bed, in the dark, not being able to see anything."

"Then what?" he rasped. She was still stroking him, up and down, lightly. The sensation wasn't getting him off but it was making him crazy, these feather-light strokes. Sensual, maddening.

"Then my husband would get into bed next to me. I don't know what he would be wearing. Gently, he'd pull up my gown, and come to kneel between my legs." Her voice caught and she squeezed the head of his cock.

His head fell back, his throat dry with passion. "Go on."

She squeezed him again. "The fabric would be around my waist and he'd lower himself over me, the weight of my husband pressing me into the mattress."

"Oh?"

"My fingers are wet."

"That's normal, darling."

She rubbed her fingers around his head, then slid her fingers down again with more pressure this time. "You'd kiss my neck, I mean, my husband. Like you did the back of my neck."

"You like your neck being kissed?" Each word felt like a boulder being spit from his mouth. The back of his head touched the cupboard. His eyes closed.

"Yes. It's nice." Her fingers slid back up. She squeezed him again.

He could feel it coming, his complete surrender to her touch. His hips jerked. So much, so little, human contact, it didn't matter. "Oh, Sadie."

"What?"

"Don't stop," He groaned, moving against her hand, wantonly intent. When he stiffened and lost himself, she stilled her hand despite his command. He grabbed her hand with his own and forced her to keep moving along his length until he'd stopped coming. Sweaty, panting, he barely noticed her standing, finding the kitchen towel, wiping her hand.

When she knelt next to him, he said, "Had you ever done that before?"

She shook her head. "Of course not. I wasn't that naughty of a girl. I didn't even know to do that."

He smiled, his eyes still closed. "The things you learn."

"You seemed to enjoy that quite a lot."

"Indeed."

She put her hand on his chest. "Does it feel as good as that looked when you make love?"

He opened his eyes. "Better, Sadie, even better."

"Was this the thing that men do to themselves?"

"Men certainly can. Women too. Haven't you ever given yourself pleasure?"

"I'm a vicar's granddaughter," she said piously. "I wouldn't know how."

"I'll teach you, but not here." He put his hand on the rug to start levering himself up, and felt crumbs crunch against his fingers. "Somewhere cleaner."

She looked nervous. "I'm sorry, I haven't had much time."

"No, darling, you aren't the maid here. We need to get help for you." He closed his eyes for a moment, knowing he'd opened the window to the usual. "The Thursday girl, maybe more."

"All we need to do is have me leave my position," she argued. "I can't make more than help would cost us here. It's not like before the war."

"I want you to make friends," he said. "Enough about that, darling. Trust me."

She harrumphed. "Now what? You look sleepy."

He fastened his trousers and stood, then offered his hand to help her up. "It's a side effect of completion. Very relaxing."

"You do seem relaxed," she agreed. "Now what? Would you like a bath?"

"Sadie." He chuckled. "I can't leave you unsatisfied. Come into the bedroom with me. You should learn your own body."

"We're going to have our wedding night?" Her voice had an endearing tremble.

He smiled. "We're going to start. Let's do the things we might have done while we were engaged, if life had been a little different."

Her brows came together. "I know about petting."

He chuckled. "Isn't that what you just did, saying you'd never done it before?"

"I mean, I know what men hope for."

He put his arms around her. "Don't you hope for it, too? Don't you feel the longing to be touched?"

She didn't speak, but her adorable little tongue darted out again to touch the corner of her mouth. He was learning her signals.

"Good girls can speak about these things when they are wives," he said.

"I'm a very new wife," she whispered. "And not very much of one."

"That's not true." He gathered her close and kissed the top of her head.

"I love you, you know," she said in the same small voice, as if trying to reassure herself.

He closed his eyes and breathed in her chamomile scent. Her love was an illusion; she didn't really know him. Unfortunately, his entire life was like that. But even a spy needed comfort sometimes.

"I'll do anything to make you happy." She tilted her head to meet his eyes.

The spy part of him instantly became suspicious. Why was she trying so hard? Did she have secrets of her own? He shook his head a little. He needed to stay in the moment with her, and cement their relationship. Her goal would be the same. She didn't know the wedding had been a farce. Of course, she was merely trying to make their marriage real. She'd committed the rest of her life to him, for better or worse. He didn't think vicars' granddaughters took to divorce very easily.

Silence could be dangerous. He had to respond, but he couldn't tell her he loved her. No matter the circumstance, he had to save some things for his private life, his future, to the extent he had one. He took Sadie's hand and kissed it. "Come along, Mrs. Rake. Let's go downstairs."

They stood and he put his arm around her waist, guiding her downstairs. He didn't really want to take her into his bedroom, though he had intended to do just that. But at the last instant, he opened the door of the guest room and ushered her in, even though the bed was small. It was best not to fall asleep with her. What might make him justify making love to her in the wee hours? It wouldn't take much. A cold night, an erection, and a soft, scented, willing female.

"I wish I had something proper to wear," she said, turning to him. "Something enticing."

He found a match and lit the candles in a pair of brass candlesticks that were on a tall, narrow chest he kept miscellaneous items in, like spare bullets. She stayed by the door. The room seemed very small and he felt nervous and relaxed at the same time.

"Have you ever let a man take your clothes off?"

She shook her head, throwing shadows on the wall.

He stepped forward. "Have you ever let a man touch your breasts?"

Her voice was tremulous. "I'm not going to ask you those questions. Anything that happened was before we met."

He smiled. "Oh, Sadie, I'm not worried. I just want to know where to begin."

"Oh. Well, I'm glad you know what to do."

He gathered she'd let someone touch her breasts, but only clothed. So she'd been a bit adventurous for a vicar's granddaughter. "Sit down on the bed."

She did as he asked, making the mattress squeak. He liked that she was neat. Her bed was made, and what little clothing and possessions she owned were folded away somewhere. In fact, there was nothing really of her in the room at all. For some reason, this made him sad. A woman ought to have things around her. Had being orphaned and having to live with her grandparents made her feel like she never really belonged anywhere?

"What is your favorite color?" he asked.

"Orange."

He winced. "Why?"

"It's cheerful. I had an afghan my mother knit for me when I was a little girl. Orange and brown stripes. It fell completely apart a couple of years ago, but I slept with it for years."

"Do you knit? You could make one."

"It wouldn't be the same."

He knelt at her feet and unbuckled her shoes. "Your feet are like icicles."

"It's still January."

He squeezed her narrow feet in his hands then began to massage them, trying to bring warmth to her extremities. "I think you should definitely knit us some afghans, even if they aren't orange and brown."

"What colors would you like?"

"Green and blue, maybe."

She tilted her head. "That would be nice. I can't knit as fast as my grandmother could, but I could have a couple finished before spring. It would be nice to knit while we listen to the radio. What would you do?"

Sharpen his knives. Clean his guns. "Read, I suppose. I like to read Russian newspapers to keep my language skills up."

"Will you teach me Russian?"

He chuckled and squeezed her feet again. They seemed slightly warmer already. "No. It's not a pretty tongue."

"Say something."

"*Privet*, Sadie."

"What is that?"

"Just hello." He abandoned her feet and stroked her ankles. "*Vy shchekotki?*"

"That was a question," she announced. "What?"

He moved his fingers up her calves, feather-light. "Are you ticklish?"

"Oh," she breathed.

"What is the answer?" He let his fingers drift back down her calves, then moved to her shins.

"I'm not going to tell you," she said, as he reached the backs of her knees. She shuddered and tried to pull away.

"Got you." He chuckled and took off her garters, then rolled down her ivory stockings while she was distracted.

"See, you aren't so very old-fashioned. If you were, your stockings would be black."

"I haven't worn black stockings since I was fifteen," she scoffed. "Even in Bagshot."

He pushed her skirt up to mid-thigh and kissed the tops of her legs. She inhaled sharply but didn't protest. While he refused to allow himself the right to take the ultimate liberty with her sweet young body, he didn't see what would be wrong with giving her pleasure. He inched her skirt up more, until he could feel the heat between her legs and smell the scent of her arousal. His cock went hard again, as if she'd never given him completion, and his hand trembled as it moved straight to the top of her knickers. She lifted her hips to let him pull them down, breathing hard.

"Shhh," he crooned. "You'll like this, I promise."

"Of c-c-course," she stuttered. "It's our wedding night."

He closed his eyes tightly when she said it, but could still feel her under his fingers, and the scent of her sex filled his nostrils. No, he couldn't stop now. She deserved the same pleasure she'd given him. He tugged her forward. The back of her head slid down the wall as she gave herself completely over to him. When she was flat on the bed, he stroked his hands up the insides of her thighs until the flickering candlelight danced over the curls just above her legs. He kissed her there, then slid his fingers over her soft maiden lips. She was so wet, and her thighs were trembling.

"Sweet Sadie," he murmured, then kissed those soft, scented lips before parting them and setting to the work of, if not taking her virginity, at least making her aware of the power of her own body to bring her pleasure.

She didn't last long. Untutored but eager, she was easy to arouse. While a more experienced woman might need a more thorough approach, she only needed soft strokes, kisses, the touch of his tongue against her. When he put his hands on her bottom and pulled her taut against him, she moved against him and cried out, then softly wrapped her arms around the back of his head. He moved his mouth to her thigh and rested.

When her shaking had stopped, he leaned back on his heels and put his hands on his thighs. His erection wanted attention, but he knew he needed to stop. Her sweet taste and compliance made him even more aware of how easy it would be to abuse her trust. Without saying a word, he went into the bathroom to have a cold wash.

Sadie folded the last of her sweaters on the top of her grandmother's old valise and closed it. She felt droopy and it made perfect sense to sit next to her luggage on her old bed at the Richmond Inn. Two feet away, her sister closed the trunk at the end of the bed. Sadie was thrilled to have reunited with her sister, even if Les had stayed away.

"Empty," Alecia said, pushing a fallen pin back into the thick blond coil at the nape of her neck. "I think you are packed. The people here seemed nice."

"Yes, Mrs. Curtis seemed genuinely happy that I'd run away to be married." Her London coworkers were so much more sophisticated.

"Even if it didn't exactly happen that way," Alecia said ruefully.

"It's a better story. Besides, my husband behaved honorably at the first moment he could. A special license." The phrase "my husband" still felt exceedingly odd on Sadie's tongue. She had expected to wake this morning feeling much more married after the intimacies they'd shared the night before, but she hadn't after the way he'd left her.

"Very posh," Alecia said. "I'm glad your Les did the right thing."

"I wasn't ashamed to face Grandfather today," Sadie agreed.

"I thought you were less conventional than me," Alecia said with a smile.

Sadie had thought the same, but London wasn't Bagshot. "Is it usual not to sleep in the same room as one's husband?"

"If you have a great deal of money, I think that is usual," Alecia said. "My former employers, the Marvins, didn't share a bedroom."

"Have they been married long?"

"Close to twenty years."

"I don't share my husband's bedroom. Of course, he's been injured and we don't have exactly the same schedule."

Alecia frowned and sat beside her. "Do you have a bedroom of your own?"

"Yes. The guest room. It has a small bed."

Alecia lowered her voice. "Do you want to share a room?"

"Not if it damages his recovery." Sadie winced. "Sometimes Les still seems unwell, but I don't know."

"He had a head injury," Alecia said. "He might still have periods of dizziness or even nausea."

"He was in bed for many days. I'm sure he doesn't feel back to normal. He was so vital when I met him. Positively bursting with vigor."

Alecia nodded. "What else?"

Sadie took her sister's hand, feeling her eyes fill up with tears. "I think I'm still a virgin. I shouldn't speak of this, and he did, well, do things with me last night, but we've been married for days and this isn't normal."

"You don't know that," Alecia said, putting her other hand on top of her sister's hand and squeezing it. "One never speaks of one's wedding night, or of sleeping arrangements, or anything, really."

"I suppose you are right. It just seemed the natural order of things."

"I expect, if you are having some intimacies, that your marriage is going to be fine."

Sadie knew her sister well enough to see the concern in her eyes, though. "What?"

"I don't want to hurt your feelings, and Mr. Rake was injured," Alecia said.

"But—" Sadie said impatiently. "Out with it."

"It's just that Ivan and I." Alecia paused, her pretty face going red. "We can't keep our hands off each other, not when we are alone. We have succumbed to our, well, our mutual needs."

Sadie gasped. "You've become lovers?"

Alecia nodded. "I'm sorry, Sadie. But everyone is different. I'm sure as we have more married friends we'll learn more about what is normal, but for now we only have the two of us."

"We need friends with experience."

Alecia nodded. "I'll take you to Emmeline Plash. She's no virgin. She's Peter Eyre's mistress. Who better to speak about sexual matters?"

Chapter Eleven

Alecia lived in a boarding house on Montagu Square, in a three-room suite with Edith Plash and her thirty-four-year-old daughter, Emmeline. Sadie's supervisor at the Grand Russe, Olga, lived in the house as well.

"When I first moved into the Grand Russe with my former employers," Alecia said as they climbed the steps to the boarding house's front door, "the Plashes lived there as well. But Mrs. Plash is a very confused elderly person and she'd leave their suite and hide and do strange things. Eventually Mr. Eyre had enough and sent them here."

"Did he dismiss Emmeline as his mistress?"

"I'm not really sure," Alecia said in a low voice. "They have known each other since childhood. Their relationship has a very long story behind it."

"Why didn't he marry her?"

Alecia opened the door. "She's a fair amount older and she was in love with Mr. Eyre's brother."

Sadie followed her into the front hallway. "Did he die in the war?"

"No, but he was badly injured." Alecia waved at an elderly man sitting next to a gramophone in the parlor. He nodded his head cheerfully, then went back to tapping his hand on his armrest to the beat of a foxtrot.

"That's sad. He was too injured to marry?"

Alecia led her up the stairs. "I don't really know. They are secretive people. I take care of Mrs. Plash as best as I can. Emmeline can be very friendly and charming or utterly aloof. I never know what to expect."

She pulled out a key and unlocked the first door on the right. They entered a sitting room both larger and more nicely furnished than Sadie would have expected from a boarding house.

"This is lovely," Sadie said.

"Yes."

A brassy blonde of middling height walked into the sitting room. She was dressed for dinner and dancing in a black fringed frock and black sequined headband. In one hand, she held a long cigarette holder with an unlit cigarette. Her face was heavily made-up, making her look closer to forty than thirty.

She extended a thin arm to Sadie. "Who is this darling child? Not your sister, Alecia?"

"Yes, this is Sadie. We were finally able to see one another. Sadie, Miss Emmeline Plash."

"How lovely," Emmeline cooed. "Alecia, Mother is having one of her spells. You'll need to stay with her every minute tonight or she's likely to wander."

Alecia nodded. "Is she awake?"

"Yes, and asking for tea."

Alecia nodded. "I'm sorry, Sadie, but I'll have to dash."

Sadie gave her sister a hug. "Thank you so much for helping me to pack. I'll see you next Sunday?"

"Yes, I hope so." Her sister smiled.

Sadie noticed that even her sister's walk was more confident as she went down the passageway. Her truly gorgeous pink T-strap shoes didn't hurt either, giving her normally dowdy sister some modern appeal, though her handmade dress was an old one Sadie recognized.

"Do you have anything to wear for dinner?" Emmeline inquired. "I might be dining alone otherwise."

"Nothing that would be acceptable outside of a vicarage," Sadie said, then frowned, surprised by the invitation. "Oh, I do have the dress I wore on my birthday." She opened her valise, with the remnants of her Richmond Inn life, and rummaged through it, then held up the dress.

Emmeline rolled her eyes dramatically. "Child, you cannot wear that at the Grand Russe. No, let's find you something. I think we're the same size."

Sadie followed her, bemused. While they were the same height, only the looseness of today's fashion would allow them to fit in the same dress. For one thing, she had a bosom.

Emmeline had no such concerns, however. She went to her closet and pulled out a fuchsia-colored sleeveless velvet dress with a two-tiered skirt. "I can't wear this one. It makes my skin look ghastly."

Sadie wondered if Emmeline's makeup was heavy in order to hide damage, pocks, or something else. She lifted the upper tier of skirt and held it against her wrist. "I think it will be fine on me. Are you sure you want me to borrow it?"

"Oh yes, then I don't have to go alone. My cousins are often there, but there is no guarantee. When I lived at the Grand Russe, I'd just go back to my room and order in from the Restaurant, but now that I'm in exile, that doesn't work."

"You do realize I'm a chambermaid at the Grand Russe?" Sadie said tentatively.

"Of course, but your sister was a mere secretary, and Peter had no problem with her being in the Coffee Room. As long as you're pretty enough it's fine." Emmeline thrust the dress at her.

Sadie changed her dress quickly and borrowed a minimum of cosmetics, but refused the cigarette holder Emmeline offered. Her grandfather had forbid them cigarettes long ago, saying smoking mothers led to unhealthy babies, and she'd noticed Les didn't smoke either.

Emmeline didn't even let her say goodbye to Alecia. In a wink, they were downstairs getting into a taxicab, leaving Sadie's things, even though the hotel was less than a mile away. Sadie didn't think Emmeline stayed thin by exercising.

Johnnie Miles, the Grand Russe doorman, opened the taxicab door for them when they arrived. Sadie saw him pay the driver. Emmeline didn't appear to notice. Johnnie did a comical double take when she stepped out from the cab as well.

He flashed his brilliant white teeth at her and tapped his fingers against his red cap. "Why, Miss Loudon. I didn't see you there. Your sister inside too?"

"No, Johnnie, but didn't you hear? I'm Mrs. Rake now."

"You done got yourself married? Well, who'd have thought? Congratulations!" His mouth curved into a smile, but Sadie noticed it didn't reach his eyes.

"Sadie," Emmeline said impatiently.

Sadie nodded at Johnnie and followed Emmeline into the Grand

Russe. She hadn't been in the Grand Hall too often and this was the first time she'd entered without being focused on obtaining a position. The sheer opulence of the green-and-red Russian décor struck her. She wondered how Olga felt, coming to work in a place that must look like the Russian palaces of her childhood. A page boy darted past her in a gold coat and ruby red trousers. Three flappers who would have been right at home on a movie set sat on a banquette next to a table holding a magnificent floral display. Fashionable couples queued around the Restaurant, having their names taken for the next seating. The air smelled like cigarette smoke and perfume.

"Come," Emmeline said, gesturing impatiently with her cigarette. Sadie followed her to the double height entryway of the Coffee Room. Some said it was the most decadent room in the hotel. Utterly modern, the walls were papered in a stunning geometric white-and-blue pattern that ought to have clashed with the beautiful parquet floor but didn't. Along the walls were silver-painted sideboards with metal urns of coffee and tea, and appetizers. A bar with an attendant was in one corner. A four-piece band was in the other.

Sadie knew the room was filled with tables in the morning, but at this time of day, half the tables were cleared away so there could be dancing before Maystone's, the nightclub on the alley-side of the hotel, was in full swing.

Sadie's stomach rumbled. She could see stuffed mushrooms on a tray on the sideboard against the wall. Other trays held some kind of olive spread on toast, as well as deviled eggs. She wanted to devour every cucumber sandwich left on a half-picked over tray and thrust her fingers into the bowl of salted nuts. All of it looked delicious, but Emmeline tugged her toward the bar instead of the sideboards.

She ordered champagne in an exaggeratedly high voice, looking at everyone in the room from the corners of her heavily blackened eyelashes. "My cousins are here," she said in Sadie's ear.

"Where?" Sadie glanced around, wondering what the male version of Emmeline would be.

"They are just about your age. Gerald and Harold. Very boring brown hair that they are each doing their best to drown in a slick of oil? It's too sick-making, the family hair, you see."

Sadie saw two young men in evening dress approaching them. They both had heavy-lidded eyes. She realized Emmeline probably had the same eyes, and that was part of why she looked so much older than her real age with all the makeup and the naturally sleepy expression.

"What ho, Emmy?" One of them asked. His eyes were pale blue, but that seemed to be all that distinguished him from his brown-eyed brother.

Emmeline handed Sadie a champagne flute and, thirsty from a long day, she drained the slim glass without thinking. The blue-eyed boy smiled at her. "Drink up, what? I'll get you another."

Sadie blinked at her empty glass. Oh, her face would be puffy in the morning. "I should eat."

Emmeline emptied her own glass and handed it to her cousin, who returned to the bar. "No, you should dance. Gerald, dance with my friend."

The brown-eyed youth smirked lazily and held out his hand. Sadie recognized the distinctive opening notes of "Royal Garden Blues" and grinned at him. This was exactly what she needed to take her mind off her troubles.

After the song ended, she drank the glass of bubbly that Gerald gave her, then popped a stuffed mushroom into her mouth before he moved her back onto the dance floor. They danced three songs in a row, and on the last song, she saw Emmeline enter the floor with Peter Eyre. He put the boys, with their expensive clothing and carefully styled hair, to shame. Eyre was more exotic than they, more polished. Sadie could tell every aspect of his wardrobe was top-of-the-line and he had a certain something, some kind of inner glow that brought attention to him in any room.

Her husband had the opposite quality. While Eyre would always stand apart, Les seemed to coax people to him. It was an entirely different form of charisma. With Eyre, she'd be too nervous to even dance with him, for fear she'd trip and make a fool of herself. Les made her bold.

Was Eyre actually bad for Emmeline? Maybe he was partly responsible for her frantic quality. He was perfection and she had the look of someone falling apart, even in the expensive clothes. Her fingers were stained from her cigarettes and her shoes hadn't been polished expertly.

Distracted by her thoughts, she drank the glass of champagne Gerald brought her without thinking.

"You'd better sit down. Your face is getting red."

Sadie put her hands to her cheeks, and felt the heat. "Oh, I become so blotchy when I drink. I shouldn't."

A girl of eighteen or so dashed out of a group of similarly finely dressed friends, all in the latest French fashions and fur coats. "Gerald," she shrieked. "You cake-eater!"

"You biscuit!" he called back. "Come give us a dance."

He left Sadie standing on the edge of the dance floor. She supposed her wedding ring made her uninteresting, even in an expensive dress. But she'd wanted a husband. It would be nicer if he was actually by her side, though, instead of who knew where.

After that, not wanting to think about her troubled marriage, she threw caution to the wind. When one of the friends of the fashionable "biscuit" asked her to dance, she danced twice with him, then had champagne. Then Gerald was at her side. More champagne. Another hour later, she found herself dashing out of the hotel, a part of the group, and going into Maystone's, where a full band was playing, including a brilliant piano player. Sadie was entranced by the music, the dresses, the Bright Young Things, people she'd read about but never seen before. Film people, like Honor Page and Tallulah Bankhead, were holding court at small tables. She saw someone that Gerald said was a famous theatrical producer with a scantily dressed girl in her mid-teens.

Around midnight, in full courage, she danced with Peter Eyre.

"Do you like music as much as your sister does?" he asked.

Sadie shook her head. The room spun. Or maybe Eyre had spun her. "I like all kinds of fun."

He cocked his eyebrows and tightened his grip on her. "Where is your husband?"

"Husband." The word seemed thick on Sadie's tongue. "Some husband." She put her head against Eyre's shoulder, deciding she liked him.

Her head felt good and floaty, and the fabric of his coat cooled her heated cheeks. She lifted her nose and nuzzled his cheek. "You smell good," she whispered. "What is that?"

"Sandalwood, Sadie." He took one of her hands back into his own. It seemed to have wrapped around his neck.

She giggled and nuzzled him, then set her lips against his jaw.

"Sadie!" Emmeline appeared out of nowhere, and started rubbing Eyre's face. "You're getting lipstick all over Peter."

Sadie blinked. "What's wrong?"

"We need to get her home," Eyre said. "She's half cut."

Sadie pulled her hand from his grasp and wrapped it around his neck again. "You don't mind a little lipstick, do you?"

"Hey, now," Emmeline said sharply. "Stop that." She tugged Sadie's arm off of Eyre's neck.

Sadie let go of Eyre completely and stumbled back, bumping into another dancing couple. A cornet solo began, bleating out what Emmeline said next. But there was no mistaking the kiss Emmeline planted on Eyre's mouth.

She was marking her territory. Sadie realized she'd been terribly forward. She brought her hands to her face and saw her wedding ring. *Glory*. Drinking was always a mistake.

"Dearie me, we have a sitter," someone said in an arch aristocratic voice. Hands inserted themselves under her arms and she was hauled off the dance floor.

"Do you know where she lives?"

"Primrose Hill, her sister said."

Sadie blinked blearily, saw two Peter Eyres. She wagged her finger. "One of you is quite enough, thank you."

"What?" he said. "I can't understand her."

She decided she wanted to sit.

"Dearie me, not again," said that arch voice.

Peter Eyre picked her up. Sadie could see the irritation in Emmeline's eyes, and wanted to warn Eyre of her jealousy, but he smelled so good, and she felt secure. She passed out.

Les had both pillows on his bed bunched under the back of his head as he tried to catch up on his reading. A spy needed to know just about everything, but a spy who was also a magazine seller needed to know his stock. At least, that was his excuse for reading the film magazines. His reason for being up in the wee hours, though, was his missing wife. At least he wasn't presently involved in anything dangerous enough that he had to worry about her being kidnapped or hurt because of his work.

He yawned and set down *Photoplay*. When was his strength

going to return? He was tiring of the old man antics of his body. While he ought to do something about Sadie, he couldn't find the brain cells to decide what. Go to the Richmond Inn where Sadie had gone that morning, to gather her possessions? Track down her sister who lived on Montagu Square somewhere?

He heard a thump against the front door. He frowned. It was early, but too early for newspapers or bottles to be delivered. He tugged his dressing gown from the foot of his bed and pushed the covers back.

The radiator in the hallway gurgled, fighting against the cold night as he passed by. A key rasped in the lock ahead of him. On his right, he took a quick step into Sadie's dark room and felt the bed. It was empty. He moved down the hall as the front door opened, expecting her.

Instead, the shape in the darkness was much too bulky.

"There now," a man's voice said. "Let's get you to bed."

Les saw red. He'd been trying to be a gentleman with Sadie, and she'd brought a man home? Some innocent. He turned on the hall light just as she giggled.

Blinking hard, he saw a man, coat and hatless, setting down his giggling wife. She wore an expensive rose-colored dress he'd never seen before, under her usual coat. Giggling again, she rocked on her heels and the man caught her under her arms.

"Are we dancing?" she asked in a drunken slur, throwing her arms around him.

Les rushed forward and grabbed for her, pulling her away. When the other man made a noise of protest and didn't let go, Les flathanded him in the forehead. The man's head slanted back abruptly and he let go of Sadie.

She was dead weight, still giggling, and smelled like cigarettes and champagne.

"How much champagne did you pour down my wife?" Les protested, getting a better grip around her waist. "You do know she's married?"

The other man held up his hands, palms-out. "I'm Peter Eyre, the manager of the Grand Russe. I'm afraid your wife overindulged this evening."

Les stared hard at the man. A real golden chap, handsome, polished, wealthy. He wanted to take another swing just on principle, but he needed Sadie at the Grand Russe. "I'm sorry I hit you."

Eyre rubbed his forehead, then lifted his eyebrows. "Could have been worse. I'd have hated for you to break my nose."

Les fisted his hands, seeing red. "If you wanted sex with my wife, why didn't you take her to your rooms? You were already at the hotel."

"I wasn't taking advantage. I was merely bringing her home," Eyre said, lifting his chin arrogantly. "I felt responsible. I know Sadie's sister rather well and fully realize how innocent the Loudon girls are. She doesn't belong in Maystone's any more than Alecia."

Sadie sagged in Les's arms. He glanced down and saw she'd gone green. "Go into the bathroom," he ordered. "You're going to be sick."

She didn't move.

"You'd better take her," Eyre said. "Unless you want to clean your floor. Come and see me tomorrow at the hotel. We'll discuss this."

Les swore under his breath, but turned, his bare feet cold on the wood floor, hoisting Sadie into his arms. With as much dignity as possible, he dashed into the bathroom and set Sadie down just in time. He couldn't hear anything over the retching, but by the time he was able to return to the hall, Eyre was long gone.

Les woke late on Monday morning. A good ten seconds passed before he remembered the scene from some six or seven hours before. He heard a faint buzzing noise down the passage. Sadie's alarm clock. His own clock showed it was nine-thirty. Had she forgotten to turn off her clock when she left for work?

He reached for his dressing gown then remembered it had been soiled. Rubbing his hands down his arms, he went out of his bedroom and turned up the radiator, then opened Sadie's door. The alarm clock was indeed buzzing, but Sadie was still in the bed. She'd avoided going to work again.

This was the second time, and surely Eyre would fire her now. How could he make her understand how important her job was without revealing the truth about himself?

Muttering under his breath, he went into the bathroom and turned the tap on. He filled her glass and went and set it on the table beside her small bed, then turned off the alarm clock. If she was still this soundly asleep, there was no point waking her up.

He'd have to see Peter Eyre himself, and try to save Sadie's job, even though it was obvious she wouldn't be in today.

Forty minutes later, he stared down a young man named Hugh Moth at the Grand Russe reception desk. "He said he'd see me this morning." He glanced over the clerk's head at the green-and-red stenciled designs above the key and mail racks.

"He's very busy. You can speak to the Reading Room manager about purchasing magazines, but I think they only bring in newspapers. However, there is the newsstand just outside. Have you tried there?"

Les frowned. "How do you know I sell magazines?"

"You're Sadie's fellow, aren't you? I heard her name was Sadie Rake, now. Didn't see her downstairs this morning when I came in."

"She's ill, and I'm not here to sell magazines."

"Then you should see Olga."

He suppressed a shudder. "I definitely should not. Mr. Eyre is expecting me."

The bones of Hugh's wrist peeked out of his white shirt cuff as he rubbed his chin. "I will see if he is available," he said in a doubtful voice.

Les waited while the young man made his way through a door behind him. Eyre had both office and living quarters back there. And down below was where they had found the weapons cache.

A couple of minutes later Hugh returned, followed by Peter Eyre. He wore a Savile Row suit, the image of a prosperous London businessman, right down to the lit cigarette in his fingers. No sign of a hangover.

"Please come back, Rake," Eyre said, lifting the hinged part of the desk. He brought Les through a large room with a switchboard and a number of women at the controls to an inner office with a couple of men at desks. Then, finally, they were at Eyre's private office.

Eyre gestured to a chair in front of his desk, then seated himself behind it. Les could feel the man attempting to diminish him and wished he could be frank. But here he was, playing the salesman with the wayward wife.

"I hope you don't blame your wife too harshly for the events of early this morning," Peter said. "Emmeline is a corruptor of innocents."

"Who is Emmeline?" Les asked as he sat down.

Eyre's desk was piled high, and not just with cigarette butts and glasses. Paperwork overflowed from two different trays. "The woman who brought Sadie to the Coffee Room, and then to the nightclub last night."

"Sadie was at a nightclub?"

Eyre pushed papers around, found a matchbook, tossed it into a drawer. "Yes, Maystone's, the club here, I'm afraid. Emmeline and her cousins were tossing back the bubbly and Sadie was swept up in it. I don't think she's used to imbibing."

"I've never even seen her drink. She's refused it before."

"Emmeline could drive a saint to spirits," Eyre said, tapping the photo of a blonde in a silver frame that clung to the far left edge of his desk. "I've known her my entire life. I thought she would marry my brother."

"What happened?" Les asked, always ready to learn more about anyone in an important position.

"She wrote him a Dear John letter when he was posted at the front. Noel was a sniper, you see."

"Oh?" he coaxed.

"Yes. Broke his heart. The next day he became suicidally heroic and was gassed." Eyre's words had slowed as he spoke.

Les winced. The effects of being gassed were bad enough that death might have been preferable. "Poor soul. Did he survive?"

Eyre toyed with his expensive lighter. "Yes, without too much lung damage. He was sent back out and it went downhill from there."

"Why did she do it?"

He set the lighter down and his hands disappeared under his desk. "She wanted a good time and felt being tied to him was holding her back, I suppose. She'd been engaged and broken it off a couple of times already. I don't know why he wanted her to marry him, but he said the word in a letter and she broke it off in the next one."

Flighty bitch. "Not very patriotic to do that to a soldier."

"She's seen unhappier days since, to be certain. No one thought the war would last so long or cost so many boys their lives."

Les's cover didn't include his service time in Russia. "Are you glad we are of an age to have missed it all, to live ordinary lives?"

Eyre lit a cigarette off the butt of his last one. "Now I have to live for two of us, Noel and me. And Emmeline's brother died. My best friend when we were young. So I take care of her, as best I can. We've driven each other mad for years. It's been torture, really. She's eight years older than me, and doesn't have nearly as much money as my family, these days, with all the men dead. I pay her bills when she runs out of cash for the quarter. I'm even paying for Sadie's sister to care for Emmeline's mother."

"Her brother would expect it of you."

"Yes, I suppose he would. Not marry her, with the age difference, but the rest."

Les chuckled. He'd learned enough. "Such confidences between strangers. I must speak to you about my wife."

"I told Olga she wouldn't be in today. She had to make do with one less girl. It's fine." Eyre gestured gracefully with his cigarette. "I took Sadie on as a favor to Alecia, not because we really needed someone right away."

Les catalogued that away, both as evidence of the appeal of the Loudon girls, and of Eyre's character. "I'm sorry that she's been so unreliable."

"She only just entered the work world. Women aren't trained to it like we are." Eyre pushed back his chair and stood up. "Do you need her to keep working?"

"She's not a girl who will want to stay home alone in my flat," he lied. "She needs friends, connections, pin money. From what I've seen, she didn't leave her grandfather's house with much."

Eyre nodded. "Olga is a good person to learn from. A reliable friend, a survivor. There are a lot of good people here."

Les couldn't help needling the man. "And danger too, it seems."

"Yes, I admit we've had some unrest around here. Comes with the name, I suppose. We get Russian diplomats and their enemies."

"Did they catch the people who tried to bomb the hotel?"

Eyre's smile was rueful. "I had hoped we kept that quiet."

Not in his world. "Sadie first came here that very day, so we heard about it."

Eyre looked down. "The police caught most everyone."

He played innocent. "Most?"

"There are still persons at large. But we have reason to believe that the British diplomats that were attending a command performance here were the real targets, not the Russians we have as guests. So I'm not too worried."

Naïve? "Maybe you should be," Les said.

"Yet you don't want me to sack your wife," Eyre said.

Les shrugged. "Maybe I need the money."

Eyre's eyelids lowered and the smoke rising from his cigarette hid his eyes from view. "Maybe you don't love her, either."

Chapter Twelve

Les's lungs seemed to still, leaving him frozen. He stared at Peter Eyre. "Surely you don't think that. We were just married."

The hotel manager moved out from behind his desk and perched on the edge in front of Les. "I expect a shouting match from a man like you. I just admitted there could be danger to your wife here in the hotel."

"No you didn't," Les said. *Keep the goal in mind, man.* "You said as long as the British diplomats stay out of the hotel, the Russians are safe enough. I'm not scared. I'm standing here in your office."

"True."

"Of course I love Sadie," he added.

The corner of Eyre's mouth turned up. "Such a short courtship, you two. From what I've heard, a decent man would be obligated to marry the girl under your circumstances. I wouldn't blame you for not loving her. We're men of the world. She's a beauty, of course, but marriage?" Eyre placed his cigarette in a battered brass ashtray.

"She saved my life," Les said. "She's good as gold, my Sadie. What point are you trying to make?"

"I'm trying to sort you out, Rake," Eyre said evenly. "You're married to my chambermaid. Her sister is engaged to my head of security. You might say you're one of the family, but you're a puzzle. I will figure you out eventually, though."

Les forced himself to relax in his chair. He understood that Eyre, standing over him behind the desk, was attempting to intimidate him. Playing his role, he allowed it. "You need a salesman on staff?" he asked. "Hoping to entice me away from my present post?"

"Don't count on it," Eyre said. "I won't hire just anyone. I turned Alecia down initially when she asked me for work."

That was a genuine surprise. "Why?"

Eyre settled into his perch and knocked over the photograph of Emmeline. He didn't seem to notice. "She didn't suit, but Sadie does. Sadie is a charmer, and we need that around here. The guests like personality at a hotel like this. And Sadie is a creature of the modern age, more so than Alecia."

"I haven't met her yet."

"Lovely girl, very lovely," Eyre said. "You should have seen her, when she borrowed gowns from the actress she worked for. But she just disappears in her everyday clothing. Not Sadie. Sadie is too vivacious ever to disappear. She'll keep you on your toes, old thing."

"She has so far, undeniably. I should return home and check in on her."

"I can just imagine her sore head," Eyre said, chuckling. "We'll see her tomorrow."

"Thank you for letting her keep her position," Les said, holding out his hand.

"I have spent years cleaning up behind Emmeline. Just one more day of it."

Les left the office after shaking Eyre's hand, thinking he'd played it a little too dull. Should he have made a scene about his wife's employer letting her dance with strange men in a nightclub? If Sadie had followed him to Hull because he was irresistible, behaving too colorlessly around the Grand Russe could backfire on him. The problem was, he didn't know how to play a husband. Even to a girl as desirable as Sadie. The Secret Intelligence Service didn't give husband lessons. Being a seducer was usually much more valuable.

Sadie woke to the smell of eggs and tea. She turned over in her bed, blinking. Les picked up the empty water glass he'd filled some hours before, and set down a tray on the bedside table. The bed dipped as he sat next to her.

"Do you think you can eat? You've been in bed close to a dozen hours."

"Aren't you at work today?" she asked, dazed.

"I was out. Filled orders for a couple of shops. Saw Peter Eyre."

Her memory was fuzzy. "Was he here?"

"He brought you home after spending some time with you at a nightclub."

She remembered dancing. Emmeline Plash and her cousins. "I never drink, but they kept giving me champagne and I was thirsty."

"Once you say yes to the first couple drinks it becomes very easy to continue."

"I found that out." She sat up. The room spun.

Les wrapped his arm around her shoulders and pushed himself back against the headboard. She cuddled up against him, trying to decipher the signals of her own body. "I want to eat, but I could get sick."

"It's better to try. How about a bite of toast?"

She considered that. "Yes, the thought doesn't nauseate me."

He handed her a buttered round and she took it, gingerly placing it between her teeth. His hand tightened around her shoulder as she bit down but he said nothing. When she dared to tilt her head in his direction, his expression was serene.

"Aren't you angry?" she asked.

"You were foolish," he told her. "But anyone can fall into bad company once and drink too much. Nothing happened except you risked your position again. It's lucky that Peter Eyre came to your rescue."

She remembered hanging on him, Emmeline doing the same. If he'd been a different kind of man, what might have happened? She shuddered. "I am so sorry. I couldn't have behaved less like a wife had I tried to make a mistake."

He kissed the top of her head, then made a face. "I'm not used to you smelling of cigarettes."

"Why don't you smoke? Most men do."

"I did before I went to Russia. I didn't like the tobacco there and lost the habit."

"I see. I'm surprised I don't come home from the Grand Russe reeking of it. Everyone smokes there."

"I hadn't noticed, but then, I haven't been myself. Things do need to change, Sadie, between you and me. If we are going to go on."

"I know you're right," she said. But she felt forgiven, as she sat there, leaning against him, eating her toast, even though he said nothing more. It was enough for now.

Les checked Sadie's room on Tuesday morning before he left to meet Glass in Marylebone. The room sparkled. She'd felt much better by evening and had done some cleaning. Apparently she'd gone to work as well. He'd been afraid that she'd approach the question of what was going on with their physical relationship but thankfully she hadn't had the energy for that. He knew where they were going, and he felt bad for her. What would happen when Glass ordered him to discard her?

He puzzled over his feelings as the taxicab drove him to Marylebone, rain dotting the windshield, the February wind blowing tree branches on the sides of the road. His claim of love for Sadie to Peter Eyre hadn't accounted for anything. His heart was as barren as the trees, where she was concerned. There wasn't a single soul alive on this earth whom he loved. Precisely the best way for a secret agent to live. Not for him the tangles of Lord Walling's family. He only had memories.

But it was the memories that taunted him, as always. And Sadie, when she was gone, would taunt him too. If he'd been a different kind of man, they might have been good together. Instead, she'd had her first night of carousing, and he couldn't claim that frustration with him wouldn't lead her down the same path again, no matter her apology yesterday. Especially with this Emmeline Plash in Alecia Loudon's orbit. He wondered what sort of man Alecia's fiancé was, to think it a good idea for Alecia to work for the Plashes. Not very strong, or perhaps Alecia had an entirely different kind of character than Sadie.

"Just a quick word today," Glass said when Les walked into the flat. He didn't have tea brewed, although he was seated at the usual table.

"What?" Les asked, sitting down across from him.

"I want you to move into the Grand Russe."

"Why? I've got Sadie." Surely the break with her didn't have to happen so soon.

Glass's eyebrows lifted. "What does that matter? Take her with you. We need to watch Ovolensky's group more carefully, especially in light of the weapons cache."

"What are you looking for specifically?"

"I want you listening," Glass said. His fingers touched the table as if hunting for his missing tea cup. "Take Peter Eyre into your confidence. I liked the sound of your conversation as you reported last night. He sounds like a reasonable chap."

"You want me to tell him I'm Secret Intelligence Service?"

"It won't be the first secret the man has kept," Glass said. "His family has served the crown for nearly fifty years in one way or another."

"What about Sadie, is she to know?" Les stared out the window, but nothing caught his attention.

Glass cleared his throat. "No. Say you are going to have your flat redecorated and you can have a honeymoon at the hotel."

"Redecorated? She thinks part of the reason she has to work is because I don't have the money to keep her."

"You got a bonus." Glass grinned and tugged his ear. "Selling magazines."

"A bonus? I've only been out of hospital for a week and a half."

"A bonus for work before that," Glass said. "What does she know about it? Tell her it's too much of a bachelor domicile and you'll move into the hotel while she chooses wallpaper and paint."

"Pushing the bounds of credibility," Les muttered.

"She'll believe anything you tell her," Glass predicted. He splayed his fingers on the table. "You're the husband. What you say, goes. She'll hear more living there, besides."

"She's given me nothing so far. She's cleaning the lowest floor with the most transient guests."

"It takes time to develop a source, but we need to move more quickly. So you're in. Go." Glass closed a folder that had been open in front of him.

Les rolled his eyes. "What about the basement?"

"Now, that's a problem, and we need to know if Ovolensky's men are abetting the local Bolshies. Of course, one thing may have nothing to do with the other, if Konstantin was getting in through tunnels. The hotel was closed for quite a while there after the Starlet Murders a few years back, so people could have been exploring." He shrugged. "Why not the Bolshies?"

"Do we have any idea where Konstantin is holed up? Who is helping him?"

"No. We don't even really know what he looks like, or if that was truly him you saw."

"It was dark and I only saw the back of the man," Les reflected.

"Prowl the hotel," Glass said. "Link up with your future brother-in-law, Ivan Salter, the security head, and develop him as a source.

Get to know every inch of the Grand Russe, and all the players. But mostly, get a microphone into the wall of the Russians' suite and listen."

"Am I still a salesman?"

Glass cocked his head. "I'm promoting you to management, and your first job is to restructure the sales force. So you can stay in the hotel and think."

"Sadie will love that," Les said dryly. And he worried about all the additional contact he would have with his beautiful bride. How was he going to stop himself from making love with her if he couldn't escape at will?

"Sadie did arrive on time to work this morning," Peter Eyre said, setting his cigarette in his ashtray. His desk had been straightened, the picture of Emmeline moved to a less precarious spot. "Did you feel the need to check on her?"

Les shifted in his chair in front of the desk, wondering at the impression he'd given the Grand Russe Hotel manager. At least the man had agreed to see him, frankly confusing his reception desk man, Hugh Moth. "No, in fact, she is probably off shift by now. I didn't come to speak about her."

There was a knock on the door jamb and a tall, dark-haired man of about forty years with deep circles under his eyes entered the room.

Peter Eyre stood. "Detective Inspector Dent."

The man nodded and shook Eyre's hand, then sat down next to Les. Eyre glanced at Les, looking the faintest bit uncertain for the first time.

"Always a pleasure, Mr. Rake," Eyre said, "but I'm afraid we'll have to conduct our business another time."

"Actually, Mr. Rake is the business," Dent said. "We're going to need a suite on your seventh floor for him."

Eyre reseated himself, picked up his cigarette and took a deep drag. He double-blinked as he processed the information, but his mouth didn't twitch. "Mr. Rake is Special Branch?"

Dent shook his head slowly. "You don't need to know what he is."

"Nor does Sadie," Les added, capturing Eyre's gaze.

A pained expression crossed Eyre's face, then vanished, leaving his features blank. "One moment." He left the room, leaving the door open, then returned with a ledger. After returning to his chair, he set the ledger down and flipped through pages. "Do you know how long you'll need a suite, Detective Inspector?"

Dent glanced at Les. "The Russians are here until May, correct?"

Eyre nodded, keeping one finger on a page. "As long as that?"

"We'll need a suite that shares a wall with the Russians," Les said. "I don't know for how long."

Eyre flipped through several more pages. His hands were slow, deliberate. The fingers didn't shake. "The Artists Suite will open today. It is booked again on the fourth, but it's your best option. We'll have to do something different with the American film star who was meant to be moving in."

"Yes," Dent said dryly.

"I need to get ears into the suite Ovolensky is in," Les said. "Is there a vent or anything in between these two suites?"

Eyre pulled a different ledger from a shelf behind him. Les could see it contained carefully drawn schematics. "The Piano Suite, where Ovolensky is, and the Artists Suite, do have a connecting door between the sitting rooms. Can you work with that?"

Les nodded. "It gives us a place to start. We'll need to have our technicians ready to go as soon as Ovolensky leaves next."

Eyre closed the ledger. "Very well. Have your men in place. I'm sure we can make the Artists Suite available in an hour or two."

Dent leaned over Eyre's desk and selected a cigarette from an open case. "As few people as possible need to know about this."

Eyre closed the case. "Ivan Salter works nights. If your men can wait until evening, Ovolensky never dines in his room. We can have Salter keep an eye out and notify your men so they can make the changes."

Les appreciated how easily Salter had fallen into his lap. His future fake brother-in-law, soon to be a source whether he knew it or not. "Make sure Salter understands that he can't tell Alecia Loudon anything. And all of the installation work needs to be done when Sadie isn't around."

"She doesn't know the truth about you?"

"No," Les said, in a do-not-ask-questions tone.

"What are you going to tell her?" Eyre asked. "Bloody hell, I should have known something about you was off."

Les shrugged. "It's the honeymoon we didn't have. Also, you've been told I'm a commercial traveler?"

Eyre nodded.

He frowned. "I've been promoted to management. We'll move in late tonight. About nine P.M.?"

"If your men can install the listening device by then," Eyre agreed.

"It's quite a new technology, but our chaps know what they are doing," Les said. "We'll stay out of your way and you stay out of ours."

"I've no choice," Eyre said. "But I hope you know what you're doing, for Sadie's sake."

"I have no intention of hurting her," Les said, meeting Eyre's gaze squarely.

"I'd like to believe that," Eyre said. "But I don't."

"I just unpacked my things from the Richmond Inn," Sadie protested, gesturing to the small chest of drawers in the Primrose Hill flat guest room. Why on earth was she still a chambermaid if her husband could afford a suite on the Grand Russe's seventh floor?

"You had only one valise," Les said. "And two dresses from our Hull adventure. It won't take you ten minutes to gather your clothing."

That wasn't the point. "Why are we moving?"

"Lord Walling wants us to have a honeymoon," Les said. "He's paying for the suite for a few days."

"That's ridiculous," Sadie said.

Les shrugged. "It never pays to uncover the motivations of rich men. Just spend their money, I always say."

"Ridiculous," Sadie muttered again. "If he'd just give you the money, it would probably buy a motorcar. Or a new wardrobe for me. And your kitchen implements are decidedly lacking, Les."

Les offered her a winning grin. "Just enjoy our bit of luxury, darling. A suite at the Grand Russe. Did you ever imagine you'd be able to stay in one?"

"Of course not. Did you?"

"It's a promotion, darling. And a reward. Rich men don't need money, so they don't understand other people's use of it. A stay on the seventh floor of such a storied hotel is a reward a rich man understands."

"On a Tuesday? With no warning?"

Les sat down on Sadie's bed. "Yes, on a Tuesday with no warning. Pack up, that's what I'm going to do. And think of this. You can sleep in an extra half hour now, because you don't need but to go down the lift to be at work. No cooking either."

"How long do we stay?" Sadie asked, liking the notion of the sleep. She didn't care so much about the cooking, having the idea that too much hotel food might add pounds to her already generous figure.

"I don't know, but I will be around more. I'm going to be staring at charts, figuring out how to restructure the company's sales force."

"Olga is going to find this exceedingly strange," she said.

"Think of it as an opportunity to spend time with your future brother-in-law," Les suggested. "Ivan works nights, correct? So you've never even met him."

"True. I don't know when the wedding is going to be, either. Alecia is committed to caring for Mrs. Plash for the rest of her life."

"It's a real opportunity for us," Les said with enthusiasm, pointedly ignoring her mention of a Plash. "This flat is too large for newlyweds. We need to be in tighter surroundings so we're forced to see each other more."

Sadie felt more troubled than pleased by that. Newlyweds shouldn't need forcing to be together. What was wrong with her marriage? Was it simply that Les still didn't feel well?

Les turned around, suitcase in hand. Sadie had disappeared again to wander the corridor of the Grand Russe's seventh floor. While he had admired the vibrant art decorating both the corridor walls and the suite, she had kept a steady eye on the doors, hoping celebrities would pop out. She'd heard a rumor that the reclusive American film star Lon Chaney and his wife were in residence. Mae Murray had been seen in the halls as well, and the famed comedian Teddy Fortress with his starlet wife Honor Page had been guests for some time.

He set the suitcase on a shelf in the closet in the sitting room and went to check the adjoining door between their suite and Ovolensky's. The technicians had discovered paintings on both sides to the right of the door, and concealed the microphone on the Piano Suite side and the recorder on the Artists Suite side. Les pulled the painting back, which had been reinstalled on a hinge, and checked to make sure that the disk was in place. It would be his job to change and check them.

He thought he heard a noise on the other side of the door. Ovolensky might be returning from dinner. He switched on the apparatus. The disk began to turn. He pushed the painting flat against the wall as Sadie opened the door of their suite.

"We have Russians next door," she announced. "I saw Teddy Fortress in the hall. I wonder who else is staying here. I'm going to get an education in high society."

"I thought we were going to stay in and enjoy our honeymoon," Les said.

"I thought you were going to reorganize your sales force," she said, looking grumpy.

"I'll work when you work." He faked a yawn. "Speaking of work, it is rather late. I think I'll turn in."

"Which bedroom is yours?" she asked.

"There is only one."

Her lips parted, then she pressed them firmly together. "It is rather late," she said in a squeaky voice.

"I'll bathe," he told her. "Just go to sleep when you're ready. I'll try not to disturb you when I come to bed."

"I need to clean my teeth, wash my face."

"Very well. I can wait." He sat down on the bright white sofa in the center of the room and picked up one of the movie magazines. The cover model might have been the young woman in a fox stole and enormous hat he'd seen walking toward them in the corridor when they first arrived. He checked the name but it didn't ring a bell, then held up the magazine to Sadie. "Recognize her?"

Sadie peered at the cover. "Not really, but I think she's only done about three movies. British movies, not American."

"I think she might be staying here."

Sadie brightened. "What room?"

"We'll find out tomorrow. Bed, Sadie. You have to work in the morning."

Her feet dragged on the carpet as she left the room. He only had five years on her, but in some moments they felt like twenty. She wouldn't work at the Grand Russe for long. Too flighty. The thought of what would happen when Glass told him to discard her and move on gnawed at the back of his brain. What a cruel thing to do to a girl. He hoped the disappointment didn't change her.

The next morning, Sadie was dusting on the second floor when Olga checked in with her.

"You look out of sorts," her supervisor observed.

"I didn't sleep well. We moved into the Grand Russe last night, did you hear?"

"And you didn't sleep well? On one of our beds?"

Sadie gestured at her to shut the hotel room door. Olga complied, then leaned against it.

"Can I tell you a secret?" Sadie asked.

"What?" Olga thrust her hands into her apron pockets.

"Last night was the first time we'd shared a bed," Sadie said, tucking her dust cloth into her box. "I'd never shared a bed with any- one before, even my sister. The mattress kept moving, and he'd breathe in my ear. It was unnerving. I don't think my eyes closed all night."

"What was the arrangement before?" Olga asked.

"I slept in the room next to his at the flat," Sadie explained. "He hasn't been well. The head injury, and being confined to bed for more than a week. He needed more sleep than I do."

"Certainly." Olga's expression didn't change.

"Yes, and I was quite irritated, getting out of bed while he stayed fast asleep. My alarm didn't even wake him."

"Poor man."

Sadie frowned. She wanted the sympathy. She'd been doing the hard work of caring for him while he convalesced.

"Why did you move into the hotel?"

"He was promoted and this was a gift from his manager. I don't know for how long. He has a strange relationship with his supervisor. He's a real lord."

Olga nodded. "Aristocrats can be very eccentric. Inbreeding."

"Les has been promoted," Sadie repeated. "Why can't I leave my position? He keeps saying I need to make friends, but isn't that more properly through our church, or others who live in our building? Do I really need to be friendly with chambermaids?"

Olga regarded her unsmilingly, and Sadie realized she might have offered the other woman an insult. "Not that I consider myself any better. I just mean, I ought to be friendly with other young wives, not single girls."

"I think you ought to continue to cultivate your own independence."

Sadie knew she'd insulted the woman again, but surely Olga could be married if she wanted, with her looks. "Why?"

"You never know what might happen. When I was eighteen, I was wealthy, part of an important family, and engaged to be married to a Russian prince equal in rank to myself. That was seven years ago. Everything collapsed under my feet. I lost my family, my country."

"But this is England," Sadie protested.

"At seventeen, I thought my world as secure as you feel yours is. Foolish, I admit, but I knew nothing about politics, even in a time as fraught as that."

"What happened to your fiancé? Did he break it off?"

"He was killed. Many were," Olga said simply. "What happens to you if your young husband dies? Do you have a source of money, a nice nest egg tucked away in case he's been living on credit?"

Sadie shook her head. "I only took my first position a few weeks ago."

"Stop protesting and keep working," Olga advised. "At least until you have some money put away, where no one else can find it. There are things that can go wrong in life, and money can fix many of them."

Sadie nodded. "You are wiser than me. I know that. But I want more hours in the day. I want to be young. Living in a vicarage was no fun."

"You chose your life, your marriage."

"Events took over my better judgment. It was only a second date," Sadie said. "A second date that took me to Hull for the day. Once I put my foot on that train, everything changed. If it hadn't been for that, I'd have been working here a week or more earlier, and perfectly content."

"But you did. See, even in England, things can change so very quickly. I don't think you should regret putting your foot on that train. If you hadn't, your Mr. Rake would have died on that dock. Is that what you would rather have had happen?" Olga opened the door and stepped out, leaving Sadie to imagine the could-have-beens.

No, she would not have wanted Les to die. What she wanted was for them both to live. She took a look around the room and decided she'd finished with it for the day. After she picked up her box she opened the door and went into the corridor, checking her list for the next room to be tidied.

Her hip bumped something. She reached out to steady it and grazed a still burning cigarette with her finger. She put her finger to her mouth to soothe the burn, and pushed the ash can into place. A wad of paper was wedged between the can and the wall. She bent down and reached for it, finding more paper. Banknotes. Pound notes, and quite a few of them. She rifled through the stash. How strange. There were more than fifty of them, and she'd discovered them in a most unusual place. Around her, the hallway was silent. She had no way of knowing how long the banknotes had been there or who had left them. Staring at the money, she knew this could be the nest egg Olga said she needed, and no one would ever know she had it if she kept the money. However, she would lose her job if someone reported the money missing and it was discovered she'd kept it. Since Les considered her job to be so important, she'd better turn it in.

Chapter Thirteen

L es yawned and checked the alarm clock. Seeing it was ten A.M., he set his paperwork aside, a made-up and crossed-out fantasy of an organizational chart, just in case Sadie asked what he'd been doing. He'd particularly enjoyed making up names. While it was common in intelligence work for agents and supervisors alike to have nicknames, they didn't sound like they came out of Dickens. Douglas Childers was called *Glass* in the Secret Intelligence Service, but Les had called him Dentition Chilblain in his chart. Not much of a joke but it amused him. Besides, it could be said that Glass had both perfect teeth and a chilly demeanor. If you crossed him, you could end up with scars from the encounter, as German Intelligence agents had discovered during the war. Glass's exploits as a young officer a decade ago were legendary.

Les wasn't sure if Sadie would come up to the suite during her lunch break, so he decided to listen to the most recent surveillance disks while it was still safely mid-morning. He hoped she didn't return during her work hours, as he wasn't sure how much contact he could handle with his beautiful wife.

Sleeping, or not sleeping as it were, next to her had been torture. He'd been too aware of that curvy body underneath a sateen nightgown. She had warmed the sheets and perfumed the air. He'd faked sleep, hoping it would fool his body into slumbering, but that had only worked for a couple of hours. She'd startled him out of his rest when she'd rolled over about two in the morning and settled the toes of her left foot into the hollow behind his knee. That soft, warm touch had given him a raging erection that no amount of mental dousing could quench. By the time her alarm had gone off, his jaw ached from clenching his teeth. He'd faked sleep to keep from engaging her as she readied herself for work, and only then had finally achieved a couple hours of rest.

He had gone through three disks the previous night, so he loaded them, one by one, onto the portable gramophone in the bedroom and listened, relaxed in an easy chair, part of a pair in a breakfast nook in front of the one window. The first two disks were full of Russian-language chatter. He appreciated the practice of listening to native speakers conversing, though they said nothing of interest.

On the third disk, however, someone new entered the room. The conversation changed. Three men were present, two of them very drunk. The newest arrival let out a string of curses as he mentioned the hotel.

Les's eyebrows raised as the man made fun of the hotel staff, with special venom being directed toward Princess Olga Novikov. The man didn't seem to know who she was, but apparently he'd propositioned Olga for the night and she'd turned him down. Les made a mental note to let Peter Eyre know about it. She might not like him, but he wouldn't want her being raped or injured.

Next, the man insulted the food in the Restaurant, comparing the caviar unfavorably to what was available in Moscow. Eyre would want to know that as well.

The next part of the conversation didn't make a great deal of sense. They'd been talking about what passed for Russian food in London, then the sober man said something about macaroni pasta, hardly a Russian delicacy. Les frowned and moved the needle back. Something about the accents on the radio? What did that have to do with pasta?

He sat up straight when he heard the name "Konstantin." Was someone in Ovolensky's party in cahoots with the bomber? He needed surveillance on the door so he could see who was going in and out of Ovolensky's suite.

He lifted the gramophone needle and scratched notes on his pad. Macaroni pasta, or rather, noodles, which is what the man had actually said. Konstantin the bomber. The radio.

He closed his eyes and rubbed his temples. There was something just outside his thoughts, something trying to make a connection. Macaroni. Pasta. Noodles. Maca. Roni. Marconi.

His eyelids popped open. Marconi House. On . . . the . . . Strand. Noodles. Pasta. Strand?

He knew about Marconi House. The BBC had once made their broadcasts from that location. They still had radio transmitters on site. Was Konstantin going to bomb it? Were Ovolensky's men, Bolsheviks all, in cahoots?

Les pushed back his chair, energized, and removed the disk from the machine. He slotted all three of them into paper holders and tucked them into a Gladstone bag, then put on his shoes. While he had hours before Glass would be in the Marylebone flat, he had other ways and means of contacting Secret Intelligence. A telephone call to a certain number would send a courier to pick up the disks from a dead drop in Hyde Park. He'd call from downstairs. Another set of ears needed to listen to the third disk, and they needed to have a man on the seventh floor by evening.

Before he left, he put a cup to the wall. No sound of anyone. That was another reason they needed surveillance. He didn't know when to record. Unless he stayed in the room every minute. Maybe he should do that. Fake a cold and tell Sadie he needed to stay in bed. He'd still need a messenger in that case though, to move the disks through town. Glass would have to decide what he wanted to have Les do.

"Where did the money come from?" Emmeline Plash asked. She poured tea from a plain white china pot, dribbling liquid onto the table without noticing.

Sadie smiled, glad they were at the boarding house and not damaging a Grand Russe Hotel tea table, and tucked the bank notes back into her handbag. When she'd gone back to her room on the seventh floor after speaking to Mr. Eyre, Les hadn't been there. Too excited by her reward to sit around, she'd taken a taxicab over to Montagu Place to see her sister.

Unfortunately, Alecia was busy with Emmeline's mother, who was having an agitated spell, common at that time of night, but Emmeline had been eager for a chat.

"I found a wad of bank notes," Sadie said.

"And you kept them?" Emmaline frowned at the table and swiped at the tea puddle with her handkerchief, then dropped it next to the teapot.

"No, I took them to my supervisor, who sent me to Mr. Eyre. He thanked me for my honesty and gave me ten pounds as a finder's fee. The rest went into his safe until he can figure out who it belongs to."

"What are you going to do with it?" Emmaline pulled the sugar bowl toward her and picked up the tongs.

"My supervisor would tell me to tuck it away for an emergency, but I want some new clothes. I haven't had the heart to ask my husband for more money."

"He doesn't give you an allowance?" Emmaline lifted a sugar lump toward Sadie but she shook her head.

"No, I'll have my wages. But he did buy me shoes. He was very generous when we first knew each other. Gloves, a muffler, a Russian doll. One present after another. And loads of housekeeping money since."

"It's different with boyfriends," Emmeline said knowingly, stirring her tea with the tongs. "What do you want to purchase?"

"My nightgowns are a disgrace." Sadie wondered why the older woman was so absent-minded today. "I have nothing pretty, and, well, I am a wife."

"Absolutely," Emmeline agreed. "I know just the place. Very discreet, very French. We'll find you something that has your husband panting harder than a dog in August."

Two hours later, Sadie had a beautiful dusky pink lace and satin nightgown in her possession, along with a lace robe and a pair of cream and silk lace pajamas that were the cat's meow. Emmeline had told her that if she wanted to be truly seductive, she could leave off the pajama trousers and just wear the top. The mere idea had made Sadie blush, and think of what Les could do with the easy access to the most private parts of her body. Emmeline had bought nothing but a new pair of ice-blue step-ins to replace a ruined pair that matched a camisole in her possession, and declared herself in desperate need of bubbly to restore herself.

Sadie separated from Emmeline as soon as they ran across Gerald and Harold in the corridor outside the Coffee Room. The last thing she needed was to drink again, only three days after the last disaster. Her face had only just lost the puffiness. She returned dutifully to her suite on the seventh floor, only to find Les wasn't even there. At the dinner hour, no less. They were supposed to be honeymooning. Furious, she pulled on the dress she'd worn on her first date with Les, applied a fresh coat of lipstick, combed her hair, and went back downstairs.

The Coffee Room crowd was sparse, given the early hour. Sadie filled a plate and sat in a corner to watch the three couples who were dancing. Before the first song was complete, the tune broke off. The clarinet player in the band played a trill with rising pitch. It sounded vaguely familiar, and as the dancers clapped, Sadie saw Teddy Fortress and Honor Page entering the room, him in evening dress, her mint-green gown covered by a white feather stole. The film star had a glittering silver and gold headpiece and her comedian husband held a lit cigar. He smiled delightedly at the crowd, then tripped, spinning around in a circle then landing, cat-like, at the table of a young couple. The crowd laughed and applauded. Sadie recognized the bit, and the trill, from one of his hit movies.

Miss Page looked bored as she followed her husband to the table. The music began again, the old hit "Avalon." Gerald came up and held out his hand. Sadie took it, happy to dance, ready to forget her troubles. Still, though, as she followed Gerald through some fast footwork, she wished it was Les holding her in his arms.

After Gerald came Harold. A bass saxophone joined the piano, clarinet and drums as the room began to fill. Even on a Wednesday night the room was popular. Sadie heard the distinctive brays of the Bright Young Things as a scattering of them appeared. By the time Teddy Fortress himself danced with her, the floor was full of a dozen or more couples dancing. A puddle of champagne dampened the corner of the floor and a couple of thin young men giggled hysterically, rolling along the wall.

"I think we missed our dinner reservation," Teddy said, tightening his hold on her waist. "Haven't I seen you somewhere before?"

"I'm in the Artists Suite," Sadie said.

"Ah, yes. You should have lunch with my wife one day. She has a couple weeks respite before her next production begins."

"That would be lovely," Sadie agreed, wide-eyed. "Are you filming?"

"That I am, but we stopped early today. Trouble with the backdrops."

Sadie nodded as if she knew exactly what he was speaking about. Actually, she did know, from reading Les's movie magazines. "They didn't look realistic?"

Teddy chuckled and pulled his cigar from his mouth and held it over Sadie's shoulder. "Made the Eiffel Tower look like a great hulking spider."

"Oh, dear," Sadie said breezily, as he twirled her by the band. "They need some new artistic talent."

"Any good art in your suite?" Teddy asked. "All Russian, I suppose."

"I'm ashamed to admit I haven't looked at it much. We only arrived yesterday evening."

"No artistic eye?"

"Actually, the sitting room has a number of Georges Barbier ballet watercolors," Sadie said. Olga talked about art a great deal. "But that won't help you."

"No, he's in France," Teddy said. "But if there is any good art by Russian immigrants working here, well, starving artists and all that."

"I'll investigate. I recognized the Barbier work because it is in other rooms as well."

"Of course. The Ballets Russes," Teddy said. "Is your husband in the arts?"

"Sales." She took her hand off his shoulder momentarily to prevent a stray thread on her dress from curling around his shirt button. "He sells movie magazines, or at least, he used to."

Teddy chuckled and dragged on his cigar. "Trouble, my wee bird of paradise?"

Les opened the door to the suite at eight-thirty. He had an expensive bouquet of greenhouse roses and a good story about a lorry crash on the Embankment that was actually true, though he hadn't been anywhere near it. Instead, he'd spent all afternoon and into the evening conferring with Secret Intelligence about the possible threat to Marconi House, instead of romancing his fake wife.

"Sadie?" he called into the darkness.

Nothing. He turned on a lamp. It illuminated a framed watercolor of ballet star Vaslav Nijinsky at his most fey, but no Sadie. He set down his valise and the bouquet, then went to the wall, quickly pulling aside the Firebird painting to show the eavesdropping apparatus. The disk had long since stopped spinning. He put his ear to the wall. Nothing. Ovolensky and his men were out to dinner as usual at this time of night.

He heard a knock on the door and went to open it. In the doorway stood a tall, rangy Russian in the hotel's night watchman uniform. Noting hair that was black as night and sensual lips, Les was most arrested by the piercing blue eyes of the man.

"Salter?"

"Rake," the Russian replied.

Les stepped aside so he could enter. As he shut the door, he said, "One moment, please." He walked quickly into the bedroom, to make sure Sadie wasn't there. Was she kidnapped? Drunk again?

He went back into the room. "I apologize. I just arrived home to find my wife missing."

"She's in the Coffee Room," Salter said in a heavy accent.

"Have you met her?"

Salter shook his head. "I have seen her portrait. Alecia has it framed."

"I see. Is she with Emmeline Plash?"

"She was dancing," Salter said. "Miss Plash is in the room."

"Wonderful," Les muttered. "What do you think of Miss Plash?"

Salter's eyelids drooped. "She is my wife's employer."

"I'd have said that was Peter Eyre."

"He pays her wage," Salter agreed. "However, she answers to Miss Plash. A complicated woman, but under the circumstances I cannot say more."

Les forced himself to return to his main interest. His work. "Eyre has told you we need to keep an eye on Ovolensky and his men?"

Salter's upper lip curled. "That goes without saying."

"Your fellow countryman," Les said.

"My cousin," Salter added. "Did you know that? He had my parents murdered."

Les had read the dossier that afternoon, had learned the full story of Salter's revolutionary sisters and hapless parents, how he'd fled with one sister from Russia after the murder of another, and ultimately arrived in London. But he didn't want to reveal more than he had to. After all, that sister was now missing, and she had been part of the plot to bomb the hotel. Les didn't trust the man nearly as much as Peter Eyre did. "What do you know about me?"

Salter shrugged. "You are with the government, are part of the investigation. I am on your side. I want Ovolensky gone."

Les nodded. "We need to know when the suite is occupied, so we can listen. We have a microphone in the wall, but we have to know when to record. Manpower is limited and we can't keep a man here all the time."

"Does your wife know?"

"She does not."

"If she's as bright as Alecia, you won't be able to keep that a secret for long."

"The more people who know a secret, the less of a secret it is."

"I don't believe in secrets," Salter said. "Secrets destroy."

"Are you going to tell Sadie the truth about me?" Les asked.

Salter met his eyes, then shook his head. "What do you want the watchmen to do when they see people going in and out of the suite?"

Les pulled a sheaf of newsprint from his bag and handed it to Salter. "Have the watchman slide a *Daily Mail* under my door when they enter. Then send a note to the reception desk that the newspaper has been delivered. They will know if no one is in the suite here and have a telephone number they can call."

"Why don't you simply stay in?"

"I will as much as I can, but we're stretched paper thin. There will be another man here. McCall. He's Special Branch. You can trust him as you trust me."

Salter nodded.

"Any word from your sister?" Les asked casually.

"She's no longer a part of this," Salter said. "She's far away and I hope making a new life for herself."

"She might have been able to help us," Les said.

Salter's intent gaze fell upon Les. He felt the charisma of the man and understood why he'd been promoted to security head despite his family tie to a revolutionary. "You could have imprisoned her, but it would merely have wasted her life. I don't believe she had anything useful to offer."

"What do you know?" Les asked.

"I've seen Konstantin," Salter said. "I'm one of the few who has."

Les nodded. "Then it's a good thing you are on our side and not his."

"I am British now, despite my accent," Salter said. "And soon, we will be family. When Mrs. Plash dies, Alecia and I will marry immediately."

"Wonderful," Les said. "Happy to hear it. Now, if you don't mind, I need to retrieve my wife."

"One question."

"Yes?"

Salter lost his air of assurance. "One of the watchmen, Tim Swankle, isn't what he seems. Is he one of yours?"

Les considered. "I haven't heard the name."

"I don't think we should trust him."

"Very well. I'll look into it."

Salter raised his eyebrows at the discarded bouquet. "You'd better put these in water. Shall I have a vase sent up?"

"Certainly." Les opened the door and escorted Salter from the room. After he locked the door behind him, he slipped the recorded disk into its paper sleeve and put it in his bag, then readied the system so that it was only a moment's work to start it again when the Russians returned. After all, when he came back, he wouldn't be alone and he didn't want Sadie to see what he was doing.

He went into the bathroom and splashed water on his face. Stubble covered his cheeks and chin. In the mirror, his haunted, pale face reminded himself of the Russian soldier he had been, not the prosperous English gentleman he was now. He needed sleep and a shave, but worry about Sadie drinking with Emmeline Plash again drove him out of the room and downstairs.

On the ground floor, he could hear foxtrot music filling every nook and cranny, originating from the jazz band in the Coffee Room. One of the bellboys snapped his fingers as he rushed by, a damp dog nipping at his trouser hem. He must have taken the beast for a walk. A chill breeze swept in from the front doors as Les moved past a chattering crowd on the way to the lift. He stiffened, not allowing himself to shiver.

Outside the Coffee Room's double doors, he smelled perfume, coffee, and cigarettes. A waiter passed by the door opening with a tray laden with champagne bottles and glasses. Les peered in. Scattered tables were full of the fashionably dressed. Many couples danced on the parquet floor that covered about a third of the room, hiding the band, though not the music.

He scanned the room while moving toward the sideboard that always contained food, realizing part of his problem that night might be hunger. Glass never seemed to have an appetite and therefore one rarely ate at meetings with him. He picked up a deviled egg with a sprinkling of onion on top just as he spotted Sadie.

She wore the dress from that first night, when they'd gone to the Chelsea party. Silver fabric, not very enticing, really, but with black-and-white triangles that gave it style. Sparkle. Just like she sparkled. Her partner, the film star Teddy Fortress, had molded her into his arms and she looked like she belonged there, as full of light and life as him.

Fortress had a cigar in one hand, behind her back, and a champagne flute in the other. If it wasn't for Sadie's natural grace, it would have seemed awkward to dance with a man not using his hands, but she made it work by holding his wrist.

As Les chewed the egg and swallowed, he saw the ash from Fortress's cigar, along her back, was about to drop onto her dress. He dashed forward to rescue her. He grabbed Sadie's shoulder and spun her around. She stumbled. Fortress barked something. The crowd of dancers moved away from them, leaving a circle of floor empty.

Sadie's mouth was open, her gaze radiating hurt. And anger.

"The cigar," Les said. "He was going to burn you."

Fortress's ruddy face went cold. "I'd never have done so, sir. And who are you to suggest such a thing?"

"The lady's husband," Les snapped. "No cigars on the dance floor."

Fortress stepped closer and put his face very close to Les's. Life experience meant that no one could ever bully him. He didn't move except to wrap his hand around his wife's arm and pull her slightly behind him.

"It never pays to tell someone like me what to do," Fortress snarled, his always ruddy face darkening. "I'll have you tossed from the hotel."

"It wasn't me about to burn someone," Les retorted, holding his ground. He wanted to punch the inebriated comedian in the nose. In the background, a lady screamed dramatically. He heard rushing feet, and Peter Eyre appeared, without his habitual cigarette, Emmeline Plash weaving slightly, a couple of steps behind him.

Eyre looked cosmopolitan and unruffled as usual in flawless

evening dress. "Gentlemen? Emmeline, why don't you take Sadie to my office?"

"She's returning to our room," Les stated. "With me."

"I demand satisfaction, sir," Fortress said theatrically.

His wife, Miss Page, appeared, lacquered black hair gleaming under her expensive headpiece. She threw her arms around Fortress dramatically, spilling his champagne. The flute fell out of his hand when she knocked it and it fell to the dance floor, splintering.

The band finally stopped playing. Eyre lifted his hand and signaled to a waiter. The little group stepped aside as the man rushed forward with a broom and dustpan.

"Satisfaction," Les said sarcastically. "I'll demand satisfaction myself for your attempt to damage my wife's person."

"I did no such thing."

"You were about to burn her with your cigar," he snapped. "Plenty of witnesses."

Eyre put his hand on Les's shoulder. "You look all done in, my friend. Why don't you and your wife go upstairs? I'll have a tray sent up."

"I demand you eject these persons from this hotel," Fortress's wife said, still wrapped around her husband. For good measure, she added a quiver.

Eyre smiled politely. "This man was merely attempting to save his wife from a burn. An accident on your husband's part, I'm sure. Nothing deliberate. Why don't we all have dinner tomorrow night and make friends?"

"What a lovely idea, Peter," Emmeline cooed, stumbling a little as she wrapped her hands around his arm.

Eyre reached into his pocket and pulled out his cigarette case.

Sadie nodded. "We should, Les. That sounds delightful. Mr. Fortress would certainly never harm me, and Miss Page, I'm such a fan of your work. What an honor it would be to dine with you."

Les could hear the nervousness in her voice. The poor girl, with her new, all but unknown husband of uncertain temper. At least he'd been trying to defend her.

Les dragged out his most disaffected, posh accent. "I'll accept if the gentleman will. I'd hate to find ourselves with pistols at dawn."

Fortress nodded, though he still sneered.

"Then it's all settled," Eyre said, putting a cigarette to his lips. "Tomorrow evening, eight P.M., in the Restaurant."

Les put his arms around Sadie's shoulders and drew her away. He didn't speak as they walked toward the lift, but could hear his stomach growling. While he could control every aspect of his outward appearance, he'd never been able to stop his stomach from doing what it would.

"Have you eaten?" Sadie asked, when they reached the lift and the small space seemed to make the sounds of his stomach echo.

"I had just swallowed my first deviled egg when I saw that bastard's cigar," Les said.

"We'll order a tray," Sadie said, staring at the wall. "You have to keep your strength up."

"And you, my dear, need to decide if you are going to be a flapper or a wife. I won't have this type of display." Les saw the lift operator's eyebrows fly up before the man turned completely toward the wall.

The lift stopped and he opened the door. Sadie marched out of the tiny space and down the hall, shoulders rigid. When she reached their suite door she pulled her key from a pocket hidden under the sash of her dress and unlocked the door.

"You wore that dress on our first date," Les said, following her in. "And now you're dancing with film stars in it?"

"I'm a flapper!" She flapped her hands over her head.

"No. You are married to me. Let's make this work."

"I never know where you are," she shouted. "Whether we're going to eat together or even see each other. Why not go downstairs with a friend? I learned my lesson about the champagne. I didn't have any."

He gritted his teeth. "You danced with an unsuitable partner."

She put her hands on her hips. "Teddy Fortress is married. I danced with everyone. You overreacted, Les!"

He heard a whisker of sound and whipped around. A newspaper was being slipped under his door. The Russians had returned. He needed to get to his post and turn on the recording device. Experience told him that the most telling conversations often happened right when people entered a room, the thoughts that had been stored up while they were reaching a private place.

"Very well, Sadie," he said. "Why don't you have a bath? I need a minute to gather my thoughts and order food. Do you want anything?"

Her eyes narrowed. "I thought we were fighting. Mr. Eyre is sending food."

"I'm too tired for the dramatics," he said, injecting weariness into his voice. "Go, now. We'll speak in a few minutes."

She blinked hard, as if holding back tears. He needed her out of the room, so he took her arm and pulled her toward the bathroom, then patted her rear. "Go."

Chapter Fourteen

Les's pat on Sadie's bottom kicked her into high gear. Unused to such an intimate touch, she trotted away from him, reaching the bathroom first. Without looking back, she shut the door, creating a barrier between them. Grateful for the respite, Les went to switch on the recording device and see if he could hear anything. He pulled the painting open and turned it on, then lifted his listening device to the wall.

Two men were speaking in Russian. One of them complained about the quality of the wine served in the Soho restaurant they'd eaten in, while the other mentioned the curvaceous woman at the next table and ruminated about what he'd like to do to her breasts. The man was a poet, which made Les's brain flash to his own wife's curves, the breasts he'd never seen.

Glasses clinked, probably the sound of vodka being poured. The door opened again and a third man entered the room. Les recognized the voice. Fedor Verenich. More glasses were poured. The conversation turned to the quality of the hotel towels. Code? Or were they really speaking about towels?

Les set down his device and listened to his own suite. Sadie must still be in the bathroom. He returned to his post, just in time to hear the name Mikhail Lashevich. Lashevich, the famed assassin. Irina Kozyrev's father. Les swore. Was the Bolshevik Hand of Death in London?

He listened intently as Fedor expressed admiration for Lashevich's way with a knife. Clearly he'd seen the man's handiwork up close, but that didn't mean the assassin was here. The conversation changed again, this time to the results of a cricket match. Why would a bunch of Russian thugs care about cricket? It must be code. He needed to have the conversation analyzed further.

Using his own code, he wrote on the newspaper and shoved it outside the door for Salter to retrieve. Someone would appear to retrieve the disks first thing in the morning so he didn't have to leave.

A door opened in his suite. He quickly moved away from the wall, shutting the painting. Leaning against it, he heard the snick of the mechanism locking it into place. He saw nothing at first, as if Sadie hovered in the hall instead of choosing a room to enter. But then, a ghostly figure appeared in the hallway. When she passed next to a lamp, he saw what she was wearing, a tea length negligee of pink satin and ecru lace. The cut was modest, but he could see her thighs, shadowy underneath the fabric as she moved. A panel of lace was cut into the satin down her breastbone, leaving her breasts entirely covered. But it was early February and she was chilled. He could see her nipples pucker underneath the thin fabric. Would her arms be dotted with gooseflesh when he touched her?

She was on tiptoes as she darted into the room.

"Where did that come from?" he asked in a low voice, feeling as if he might frighten her off.

She stopped, and crossed her arms under her generous curves. "There you are. I didn't see you."

He'd turned most of the lights off, worried about light showing through the wall where the microphone had been inserted. The dim light from only a couple of small lamps set the mood now.

"You're wearing perfume?" he asked as he drifted closer, slowly, unthreateningly. His mouth had gone dry. Her hair was damp, waved from the shower, plastered darkly to her fine skull, making her chin look especially determined, her cheekbones defined.

"No, just soap, but it's nice soap. Jasmine, I think."

"You look like a movie siren, like that vamp Nita Naldi." The fabric was ribbed around her ribs, giving it the look of corsetry. Her hips flared below her small waist, molding the satin.

She giggled and let her heels touch the floor. Her fingers skimmed her sides. "I received a bonus today and decided to spend it on you."

"Well done, Mrs. Rake," he murmured, giving her the blatantly appreciative stare she seemed to want. "A bonus, you say?"

"I found some money on the first floor. Mr. Eyre gave me a finder's fee because I turned it in to him."

"Honesty pays," Les said. He snaked his arm around Sadie's waist and pulled her against him. Just as he was lowering his mouth for a kiss, he heard something bang against the wall separating their suite from the Russians.

"What was that?" Sadie asked.

"Maybe the Russians are fighting," Les said.

"I'm surprised you haven't tried to befriend them, with your interest in your heritage." Sadie put her palms on the lapels of Les's coat.

"They are rough men, for diplomats." He glanced down, trying to see what he could of his wife's cleavage. This negligee had been bought by an amateur in the arts of love. It hid too much flesh. His fingers itched to take it off her.

The crashing against the wall came again. "I should bathe," he said. "Why don't you go into the bedroom and I will join you in twenty minutes or so?"

"You could come into the bedroom with me now." Her tone was shy, her gaze hopeful.

He gave into temptation and let his hands drift from her back up to her shoulders, then very slowly, he moved them down the front of her gown, to cover her breasts. "Wait for me," he said. "I'll be in shortly."

"Very well," she breathed, not moving.

He squeezed her breasts gently and she jumped back. Chuckling, he bent forward to kiss her cheek. "Too rough."

Her color was high, her pupils dilated. "It's time, Les. Make a wife of me."

Oh, hell. Les's mind blanked of the things he needed to do. The investigation, the wall, the recordings. His sudden, sharp erection was almost painful. Coherent thought fled. His hands moved to his coat and he tore it off, then loosened his tie. She stepped to him and tugged it over his head while he found the lacy bottom of her skirt with his knee, rucking it up until his hands could gather it and pull the garment off of her. In the lamplight she was a perfect hourglass-shaped goddess, eternal woman personified. Naked, she turned, the lamplight catching the smooth ivory globes of her bottom. She glanced over her shoulder at his half-naked form, a siren calling her lover, and darted into the bedroom.

He had the rest of his clothes off between one heartbeat and the next, then followed her, no other action possible. She stopped by the bed and turned back. Her chest rose and fell. Steam from her bath still warmed the room and he could smell jasmine even more strongly. Moving toward the bed, he grasped the blankets and pulled them all back, exposing the pillows. She sat on the sheet, her gaze on his. He set his knee on the bed next to her bottom and leaned over her so that she was forced to tumble backward, one vertebra at a time touching the bed until her head rested on the flat surface.

Though he wanted to plunder, he forced himself to remember her innocence and be gentle. His lips found the hollow of her throat. He kissed down her breastbone and dipped into her belly. Then he moved up again, circling one breast, then the other, before teasing her neck, finding the tender spots that made her squirm or gasp or pant. Minutes passed before he took her mouth for the first time, setting his weight against her torso. Her legs bent, her knees locking around his flanks. She'd lost any fear of touching him. It had been a week now since she'd become Mrs. Rake. Her feet came up, rubbing along his bottom and locking around his back at the ankles while she kissed him fervently, her hands pulling at his hair. He found her damp, heated opening and teased it with his erection.

She broke their kiss long enough to say his name.

"Sadie," he murmured.

"Glory." Hands still fisted in his hair, she found his mouth again.

This woman was built for love. She needed him. He couldn't deny himself. His hips canted forward, his erection nudging its way inside her. He tried to move tentatively, to slide in and out, a mere inch deeper each time, but she thrust her tongue into his mouth and slid it along his. His few remaining thoughts splintered and his instincts took over. He dove home, sliding deep inside her tight, perfect cavern, the warmth and sleekness all but overwhelming. Squeezing his eyes shut against the sensation, he balanced himself on his forearms and begged himself not to spill too soon.

Sadie's hands had stilled in his hair. Slowly, she moved her fingers down the back on his head, and settled her arms around his neck.

"Are you well?" he whispered.

"I'm perfect. It didn't hurt at all." She tucked her face against his shoulder.

He found it easier to continue without her soft mouth on his. The mechanics of thrusting, of discovering what made her tense or cry out took precedence for a time. Thoroughly in the moment, he was surprised to find his own energies gathering. The urge to spill upon him, he seated himself deeply then followed the dictates of his body to move hard, fast. Sadie's answering cries indicated she was ready for him. He felt her rhythmic undulations as she came apart and he followed her down, his face buried in her fragrant hair. *Heaven.*

No matter what happened now, he'd committed to this marriage, this woman. It was only when, sated and satisfied, he'd moved onto his back, tugging her with him so that she rested across his chest, that he remembered she wasn't really his wife, that he'd given into the fantasy that she believed. But he found it hard to judge himself harshly. Virgin or not, she'd been ready for love. He knew he hadn't even hurt her. There wouldn't be any blood on their sheets. No, the bloody mess here was what leaving her would cost them both when the time came.

Sadie's eyes opened, even though her brain willed them not to do it. Ugh. She could see watery light around the edges of the curtains. But she was so perfectly comfortable. The bed maintained the perfect temperature; she had just the right number of blankets on her. Les breathed steadily at her side. Only a couple of nights and she was already used to the sound so close to her ear. In the hospital she'd listened for him, always afraid his breathing would stop, but that fear was long gone now, despite his continuing lack of perfect robust health.

The alarm clock made that pre-buzzing sound that indicated the full alarm was about to blare. She hit the top to turn it off and sat up. The blanket and sheet fell to her lap. She realized her breasts were uncovered. When she turned to dangle her legs off the bed, she felt unusual stiffness in parts of her body. Stickiness, too. Her eyes widened. She and Les had made love the night before. Leaping to her feet, she spun around. Her husband was only a vague dark lump in the bed. She danced her way to the bathroom. Marriage was wonderful. A month ago, she'd been a chambermaid in a downscale inn in Richmond. Now she was a Londoner, a married lady, waking up in a grand hotel. She'd danced with a film star the night before, then she'd had relations with her handsome husband. Grinning, she shook her head at herself in the mirror and ran a comb through her bed-rumpled curls, then began to heat the water for a quick bath.

She might only be a chambermaid, but she was having dinner with two film stars, Peter Eyre, and Emmeline that night. Surely she wouldn't be a chambermaid for long.

As she bathed, her thoughts went to the mysterious Ivan Salter, her sister's fiancé who she hadn't even met yet, and his recent promotion to head of security. She fantasized that Mr. Eyre would promote her over Olga. Fancy that, her giving orders to a princess! Mr. Eyre liked Olga very much, however. No, she'd have to be given some other kind of position. Like her sister, she'd learned how to type and take dictation in order to help their grandfather with the parish duties. Maybe Mr. Eyre would make her his personal secretary.

As she washed all her intimate nooks and crannies, though, she took a moment to cradle her stomach. She could already be expecting a baby, which would change everything. Thank goodness Les had received a promotion instead of the sack after the drama of Hull. Soon, they might need his extra income to offset her loss of work. She imagined herself strolling Primrose Hill around Christmas next year, pushing a pram with their baby in it, then chuckled to herself.

At least she knew enough about men to understand that once she'd been properly taken to bed, the activity was unlikely to cease. Even if she didn't have a baby inside her this time, one would come soon enough. Les had proven himself virile indeed, despite his claims. He was much better and it was her duty as a wife to continue to build him up, enhance his strength and endurance. She'd order liver for breakfast and make sure he limited his cocktails in the evening. During her off hours, she'd borrow wifely magazines from the Reading Room downstairs and learn how to take care of her husband, rather than dancing the night away in the Coffee Room like the unmarried Emmeline. No, she had a higher calling, whittling away at anything preventing Les from achieving perfect health and well-being so he could care for his family.

Sadie reached the basement staff lounge five minutes before her shift began, early for her. Arriving at work was infinitely easier when she merely had to travel down the lift. Olga met her by the bulletin board, which held an assortment of notices and the daily, already in-famous "Greetings from Peter Eyre" memorandum. Today's topic was instructions for what to do if you found a guest's missing be-longings.

"I'd like a word," Olga said, gesturing her toward the elderly arm chairs in the far corner.

Sadie followed her to the chairs, still flying from her night of marital bliss. She put her hands to her cheeks, feeling like she wore a giddy smile on her face, but apparently it was internal. "Yes?"

"Mr. Eyre was pleased with your actions yesterday," Olga said.

"I'm honest," Sadie told her.

Olga nodded. "I am glad to hear it. We took you on based on your sister's word, you understand, and then you didn't appear here to work."

"I did try as soon as I was able to come to town."

Olga patted the armrest. "I've heard the story. Your husband's ac-cident, then you came to town the day of the bombing. Despite all this, and two days of missed work so early in your career with us, you do good work, and as you say, are proving your honesty. There-fore, you've been promoted to the second guest floor. That is, the third floor."

"How nice," Sadie exclaimed. Now she knew she was smiling. She had a sense that Olga considered the promotion unearned, some-thing better saved for a single girl, but she knew she'd do a good job. And she'd even be seeing Mr. Eyre so she could thank him. "Are the facilities exactly the same there?"

"Yes, nothing changes until the fifth floor. So you can start today."

Olga's gaze had sharpened on a point on the wall. Sadie followed her supervisor's eyes to a crooked painting. She liked the small water-color, which depicted a dancer with a pearl necklace dangling down her back. Jumping up, she straightened it. When she turned back, Olga's shoulders had relaxed. She waved Sadie on, and Sadie left the room to join the other chambermaids at the service lift.

The day went quickly until Sadie arrived back at their room to at-tempt to dress for dinner. She had nothing suitable for dining with a film star, not even a strand of jewelry to make her clothing more ele-gant. For a young bride, however, did she really need anything more than her perfect, flashy wedding ring? Not to mention the confidence that came with a sexy new marriage?

While her dreams of promotion hadn't elevated her from maid duty yet, at least she had been promoted, and after such a short time. A good sign.

Les came out of the bathroom, steam billowing behind him. In a dressing gown, he smelled peppery and still patted his cheeks. She went up to him and stroked her fingers down his face.

"So soft," she murmured.

"Not as soft as all that lovely hidden skin of yours, darling," he said, bending his head for a kiss.

Long moments passed as they curved their bodies against each other. They kissed deeply and swayed to a rhythm they both instinctively understood. She broke away, breathless when black spots began to swim behind her closed eyelids.

As she gulped air, he said, "Don't you know to breathe through your nose when you kiss?"

She rubbed the offending organ. "I'm stuffy."

He frowned. "Do we need to cancel dinner?"

She squeezed his arm. "No. I'll run a hot bath. The steam from yours will help. I'll be fine."

He nodded. "Very well. I'll dress and be ready to go down when you are. Oh, and a box arrived for you. I put it in the wardrobe."

"That must be Alecia's dress. I cabled her this morning to see if she had something I could borrow for tonight." Mindful of the time, Sadie only rested in the hot water until she could breathe better, then dried off and went to look at her sister's dress. Her mouth fell open when she saw the lovely dress. She pulled it from the box. A piece of notepaper fluttered to the floor.

She scanned the note and read that it was a designer piece Alecia had ended up with courtesy of her former employers, the Marvins. The sleeveless high-low hem dress had a pink silk lining that would show from the front, and embroidered flowers across the waistline relieved the black shell. Sadie hoped it would suit her as it was more fitted than the average flapper style. She shimmied her way into it, then ran into the sitting room to show Les.

He was fiddling with a painting when she came into the room but turned quickly. She thought she heard the snick of a lock being engaged, as if the door had opened and closed, but no one else was there.

"Why are you frowning, darling?" Les asked, coming toward her, already dressed for dinner. "Head aching?"

"No, I just thought I heard something."

He glanced around. "No, I don't think so." He reached her and took her hands. "My, but you're a siren in those rags. Where did your sister acquire a dress like that?"

She smiled. "Courtesy of the stage actress Sybil Marvin."

"Ah, the infamous Mrs. Marvin. I understand they've set up shop near Gainsborough Studios as Mr. Marvin is filming a movie there now."

"From here to Islington is a bit of a comedown," Sybil said. "But Alecia said they've rented a furnished garden flat on Arlington Square. Mrs. Marvin wrote her. Sad, really, that she wants to keep up an acquaintance after her own husband tried to rape Alecia. I gather she isn't working herself, and is attempting to do her own housekeeping."

"Stay away from those people," Les said in a flat voice. "No matter how glamorous they are."

"Oh, I wouldn't. Not the Marvins." If nothing else, she was loyal to her sister. "Surely you don't think the Teddy Fortresses are the same sort of people. Mr. Eyre is very particular. He removed the Marvins the second he could, but the Fortresses are still here, and very much part of the social whirl at the hotel."

"I wish Mr. Eyre was as perfect as you claim," Les said, "but this hotel is so large, no one person can oversee everything. He needs to loosen the strings a bit and let others become experts in the hotel."

"It's difficult to start over with an entirely new staff," she agreed as he opened the front door of their suite and escorted her into the hall. "But at least he's quick to promote those he can trust, to begin to create a hierarchy."

"Like your future brother-in-law?"

"Yes, and now me." She grinned.

Les lifted his brows. "Congratulations, darling. What has happened?"

Finally, she'd had an excuse to share her news. "I've been promoted to the third floor, and after such a short time. I realize the quality of guest doesn't really change until the fifth floor, but still."

"It's a step in the right direction," he agreed, kissing her forehead as the lift opened. "I'm so proud of you."

She felt the warm glow all the way down, as she chattered happily, speculating about how long Lord Walling was willing to pay for their suite on the seventh floor. Les didn't comment. They were escorted to a table in the Restaurant without any waiting. Mr. Eyre and Emmeline were present already, a bottle of champagne waiting on ice for their first guests. The Fortresses arrived five minutes later. Miss Page wore a mink stole draped casually over one shoulder and a gold dress that plunged revealingly in front, plus another one of her sparkling headdresses, this one a gold band with sequin-dusted feathers and a glittering brooch attached.

Sadie admired the actress's considerable style. Would Les let her spend money on something so frivolous?

Miss Page showed her essentially good qualities by praising both her dress and Emmeline's. Emmeline wore a turban and looked wonderful in it, her strong features somehow softened, and the constant stream of cigarette smoke made her look mysterious. Eyre, on the other hand, seemed to have developed some type of secret connection with her husband and Sadie thought they shared several significant glances. For herself, she traded quips and impersonations with Teddy Fortress, enjoying herself immensely. It helped that Les gave her frequent approving glances throughout the meal, except when she attempted to imitate Irina Kozyrev's Russian accent.

"What?" she asked, catching his frown.

He waved his champagne glass. "Darling, your Russian needs improvement. I'll have to teach you some of the actual language, so that you can get a sense of the accent."

"Do you speak Russian?" Miss Page's eyes, already huge and mysterious looking with their thick lashes, probably fake, and Cleopatra-like lining of kohl, widened.

Les rattled off a phrase or two then grinned at her astonished face.

"How fascinating," Miss Page exclaimed in her flat American tones. "Too exciting. My darlings, I must have your help. I am playing a Russian in my next film."

"But your films are silent. No one can hear you speak," Les said, taking a sip from his glass.

"Of course I do," Miss Page said. "You can't hear me, of course, but I do speak. If you could teach me a few little phrases of Russian, perhaps when you are instructing your own sweet bride, I would consider it such a pleasure."

Sadie wiggled with excitement. "Why don't you come for tea in our suite on Sunday? Les can give us a lesson."

Miss Page looked thoughtful. "Too perfect, my darling. I shall arrive at four."

"Excellent," Teddy Fortress exclaimed, rubbing his large hands together. "More golf time for me."

Miss Page rolled her eyes expressively. "Usually I use my husband's golf time to shop." She stroked her fingers down her mink.

The famous comedian did a creditable imitation of a dying man. Sadie saw Les's frown and realized he didn't see the humor in it. However, the moment soon passed and she could hardly contain her excitement after they separated from the couple in the seventh floor hallway after dinner and went into their own suite. She'd held her own with the rich and famous, and her husband had done the same. The Lester Rakes were an up-and-coming couple. All she needed was a wardrobe of her own to match her husband's custom suits. The lingerie had been an investment in their private relationship but now she needed gowns.

Exhausted after her effort at socializing with film stars, she didn't mind when Les said he had to run back downstairs and thank Peter Eyre again for their evening. Her stuffy head returning, she went to take another bath.

The next morning, she woke with total resolve. She'd work at her position cheerfully, and plan to use every penny toward freshening up her wardrobe. Why shouldn't she fit in among the Teddy Fortresses of the world? She and Les were young and attractive and well-placed in the best city in the world. They could be anything they wanted to be.

First, however, she had to be a chambermaid. One who had eaten a lot of rich food the night before that hadn't digested properly. She felt a little dizzy as she cleaned the morning's allotment of rooms. The third floor seemed to be full of commercial travelers on their own, like Les had been, and emptied early because the men had to go to work.

Olga came down the hall just as Sadie pushed her trolley out of the last room on her list. "Done so soon?"

"An early bunch. I didn't need to clean around anyone," Sadie said.

Olga pulled a list from her apron pocket and perused it. "Why don't you have a long lunch? Then meet me in the break room and I'll find something for you to do."

"Are you sure?"

Olga frowned. "You're a bit pale, Sadie. I think you pushed too hard. I know you can clean, but I prefer thorough to fast, unless we are short-staffed."

"Yes, Olga," Sadie said, perfectly willing to put her feet up and leaf through one of Les's magazines for the next two hours. She went upstairs, to find her husband holding a fountain pen and an open book.

"What are you reading?"

"*The Mark of Zorro*," Les said, closing the book and capping his pen. "What brings you up? Is it lunchtime already?"

"Only for me. I worked quickly this morning." She heard a click in the wall between the suites. "Did you hear that?"

"What?"

She pointed to the wall. "I wonder what those Russians do all day. I hear the strangest noises."

Les shrugged. "I was too engrossed in my book to notice."

Sadie set down her apron and sat next to Les on the sofa, opening his book. She read the opening paragraph of the book. "This prose is so explosive that I can see why you can't hear anything. Beat? Shrieked? Puffed? Showered? All in the first lines?"

He chuckled. "It's rip-roaring stuff."

"'Tis a night for evil deeds!" she read, giggling.

"Thankfully our storms in London are not quite as descriptive," Les said, wrapping his arm around her shoulder. "Shall I shower you with my love? So that you may shriek?"

"Sir, you are quite puffed up," she said, tongue in cheek. "I should beat you back."

"But you won't." Les lowered his mouth to hers.

Chapter Fifteen

Nearly two hours later, Sadie rushed off the service lift to meet Olga in the basement staff lounge and receive the list of her afternoon duties. When she went past the four lonely bathrooms, she decided she'd better take the time to duck in and check her hair, since Les had done a very thorough job of loving her. Even her vision had been blurry afterward, not to mention her hearing. But the ride downstairs had cleared her senses somewhat.

She opened the first bathroom door with one hand, while shaping the hair at the back of her neck with the other, trying to give her locks some curl. Going straight to the mirror, she frowned at the flyaway strands in a nimbus around her head. She turned on the water, wishing she'd taken the time to check her hair upstairs.

When she saw the man in front of the open service closet across from the toilet, she stopped in shock. "My apologies." She backed away from the sink, bumping the door with her back.

Tall and broad, the man filled the space as he turned to face her. His reddish beard, though neatly trimmed, dominated his face as it grew high up on his cheeks. When he stared at her though, his eyes dominated, though they weren't large, but deep-set and piercing, a strange jumble of streaked blue and gold. Oddly enough, his hair was dull blond. Dye, maybe, as it didn't match the beard in the least.

"What?" he barked.

"My apologies," she repeated. "You didn't lock the door, but I'm quite sure you don't belong in the service cabinet."

His skin curved around the thick bones of his cheekbones as he sneered. "What business is it of yours, little girl?"

Russian. The man had a Russian accent. After the last few weeks, she'd have recognized that under any circumstances. She squared her shoulders. "I work here, and I know you do not."

He stepped forward. "I am new."

She shook her head, sliding her back along the door. "I don't believe you."

He reached out his hand, but she darted into the hallway then backed down the hall. She heard the door lock as soon as it was closed. Dashing down the hall, she was out of breath by the time she reached the staff lounge and Olga.

"Olga," she cried, as soon as she reached her supervisor. "There's a very scary Russian man locked in the first bathroom from the service lift!"

Olga looked up from her clipboard. "What is this?"

Sadie repeated her words, punctuated by pants. Olga then stood, and Sadie remembered that this woman was a princess. She had the fierce, piercing gaze of a Cossack.

"Show me," Olga growled.

Sadie grabbed a dry mop from a bucket as she passed it, wanting some kind of weapon in her hands. Olga pulled her keys from her apron pocket when they reached the bathroom, then put her ear to the door.

"Nothing," she reported, trying the door.

"Locked, right?"

"What if he is using the facilities?" Olga asked with distaste.

"He said he worked here, but that's not right. You and Ivan are the only Russians, correct?"

"Not true. There are two or three Russian immigrant waiters, and one of the page boys is Russian, though he was just a little thing when his family brought him here. Not to mention the Jewish Russians who have been here for a generation. We have at least one attending in the Reading Room, and Rachel, the fourth floor chambermaid, is also a Russian Jew."

"It didn't occur to me," Sadie said. "Glory, I hope this man isn't one of the waiters. He'd scare anyone off his dinner."

Olga pounded on the door, then put her ear to it. She waited thirty seconds then shrugged and found the master key for the bathrooms. The lock turned easily and she pushed open the door. Sadie held her mop in both hands, not sure of how she would use it as a weapon.

The bathroom seemed to be empty. Sadie frowned. "There aren't any windows."

"Maybe he left while we were talking in the staff lounge," Olga said.

Sadie stepped in. "Perhaps." She turned in a circle. The toilet tank wasn't running, and the sink and bathtub were dry. "But he didn't use anything."

"Now what?"

Sadie pointed at the storage closet. "He had that door open. What's in it?"

"Paper goods?" Olga shrugged and tucked her keys away.

Sadie turned the closet door knob. The door opened easily, exposing a dank cupboard with nothing in it. Olga peered over her shoulder.

"I can't see much." Sadie stepped out of the way and Olga lit a match, holding it out.

"Do you see that hole?" Olga pointed at the back of the closet.

Sadie went back in and put her finger in the hole Olga had seen. "This is just a sheet of wood." She realized it as she hooked a finger around the back of the hole, and easily tugged the wood to the right.

Olga muttered something in Russian when a tunnel was exposed.

"Glory," Sadie gasped.

"I had no idea this was here," Olga said. "Put the sheet of wood back into place."

"But the man will come back."

"Maybe not," Olga said. "I will tell Mr. Eyre about this. I'm sure he'll want to block off the tunnel."

"We could lock the closet door."

"If he's a large man as you say, he'll just break the door down," Olga said with a philosophical air. "No, we'll let Mr. Eyre take care of this. It is his job, not ours."

"What about that man? Why was some bearded Russian man wandering about the hotel basement?"

"I don't know. Remember, we don't know that he wasn't one of the waiters."

"I really don't think so." Sadie's words had a shaky undertone. She realized she was in shock.

"We'll lock this door and the bathroom door from the outside," Olga said. "I will report to Mr. Eyre immediately. You go and have a lie-down, Sadie. I don't like your color. We'll see you in the morning."

Sadie nodded. Her head spun as she did so and she walked out of the bathroom carefully, heading for the lift. She'd tell Les. He'd know what to do, if they should even stay at the Grand Russe when there were strange men in the basement. What if he was a Bolshie? There had been that bomb threat. Alecia had told her quite a bit about the story, and that the bomber was missing. What if that man was a Bolshie bomber attempting to blow up the hotel again? With her in it. And just when she'd begun to dine with film stars.

Peter Eyre leaned forward and tapped his cigarette against his battered brass ashtray. He had circles under his eyes that hadn't been there the night before.

"Late night?" Les asked.

Eyre rubbed under his right eye with his free hand. "No, I think all this business with the Russians is giving me hives."

"If you are allergic to Russians this is not the business for you," Les quipped.

"Allergic to things out of my control, more likely." Eyre picked up his tea cup, which had the same green-and-red pattern around the lip that was stenciled in the Grand Hall, albeit in miniature.

Les picked up his own cup, filled with a fragrant Russian Caravan tea. The scent swept him back to his late mistress Natalia, and one of the better cabins in which she'd found refuge. She'd torn up an old petticoat to block chinks in the log walls, using mud as an adhesive. It had been cozy for a time, until the army camp had moved again. Whenever Les could come by, she'd brew tea in the open fireplace for him, no samovar, just a pot and the wood fire.

He rubbed his face. "I think the stress is getting to both of us. But tell me, has something new happened, or is this the same old fear?"

"Not at all," Peter said. "That's why I called you down. Your wife saw a man in the first bathroom off the lift in the basement less than twenty minutes ago and when she and Olga went to investigate further, they found a tunnel behind a false wall in a cabinet."

"Konstantin?"

"I'm not sure. This man didn't have any gray in his beard, according to Sadie."

"Easily managed," Les murmured. "What are you doing about it?"

"First, let me say that it occurred to me that the money your wife found was meant as a payment to this Russian she saw."

"You might be right. At least it was intercepted."

"Indeed. I contacted Detective Inspector Dent. His men should be here any moment. Olga was just here in my office. I sent for you when she left." He pulled out a piece of thick drawing paper and handed it to Les.

Les stared at the drawing. "Olga?"

Eyre nodded. "I had a set of colored pencils. As you can see, reddish beard, pale hair."

Les considered. "The build is right, but our big win here is the green eyes. We need to see if Ivan Salter can agree on the eyes, since he's seen Konstantin for certain."

"He'll be here in a few hours. We can telephone the greengrocer in his building and have him wake Salter up now if you like."

Les set the sketch down once he'd memorized every detail. "No need. This man is a problem for us, whoever he is."

Hugh Moth poked his head in the door. "DI Dent is here, sir."

Les inhaled through his nose. "I'll take him downstairs. I want to see this, too."

"Very well." Eyre stubbed out the last part of his cigarette and rubbed his eye again. "Is there anything else? Any news from your surveillance? I saw you had a delivery late this morning."

Les nodded. "I had a recording analyzed. The Russians were speaking about hotel towels and cricket among other things." Les scratched his chin. Eyre's fidgets were getting to him. "It didn't sit right with me."

"What did your men decide?"

"That they were speaking in code, but they need more data."

Eyre chuckled. "The government."

"Based on what we know, hotel towels could be these tunnels," Les said. "They were discussing the quality of hand towels versus bath towels."

"Did you tell your men that?"

He smiled at Eyre. "No. The idea just came to me. Let me use your telephone, will you? I'll just ring someone up, then go down."

"What about cricket?"

"Hell and the devil," Les muttered. "I wish I knew. An assassination tally? They mentioned a Bolshevik assassin whose daughter is definitely in England these days."

Eyre scratched again. "I'll let you get to it, but I must say, when I reopened the hotel, these are not the kind of problems I expected to deal with. We might as well be in a war."

Les cocked his head. "That could only be spoken by a man who has never been on the front lines. I have, I'm afraid. A foot soldier has none of these comforts on the battlefield."

"There is more than one kind of war." Eyre leaned forward, looking very hard. "And more than one kind of battlefield. As always, Rake, I am at your disposal."

Les gave Eyre his most ironic stare, then stood and left the room. He wondered how Eyre would have done as a spy. While he had the brains, there was a bit too much ego dancing behind those hazel eyes. He would have been an asset though, with an appearance that could be converted to any number of nationalities with only a little subterfuge.

He found DI Dent and led the man and his plainclothes Special Branch men downstairs, ruminating on the fact that he'd had to hear from Peter Eyre about his wife's fright. Very appropriate, of course. She'd gone to her supervisor, who had then gone to her supervisor. However, he felt a strange sort of unease. Whatever Sadie was to him, she was also now his lover. Still, he had a cover, and the fact that she didn't go to her secret agent husband meant his cover was working. He'd managed to fool his own wife for quite some time now. Well, he didn't have to like it.

"No McCall?" Les asked as they went down the stairs.

"We were afraid your wife would be hanging about. Mrs. Rake knows him as a friend of yours."

Les nodded. "A fair point."

Olga met them in the staff room and took them to the bathroom. Now she was one who would be hard to mistake for anything other than what she was: an ice queen, a Russian aristocrat. No matter how lowered, she would never lose that regal bearing.

"How long has it been since the tunnel was discovered?" Dent asked the Russian princess.

"About half an hour," she said, with a frown at Les.

He frowned back at her. "I'm starting to think my wife is not safe in Mr. Eyre's employ. I want to see this tunnel for myself."

Olga glanced from Les to the three other men and shrugged. Les doubted she was fooled, but that didn't mean she'd share her suspicions with Sadie.

When they were inside, the junior detectives both pulled out pocket torches and illuminated the tunnel. Dent turned back to Olga. "Thank you for your help. You may return to your duties."

"Should I escort Mr. Rake upstairs?" she asked.

"That won't be necessary," Dent said calmly. "You may go."

Olga stared hard at Les, then left the bathroom, shutting the door behind herself. The detectives vanished into the tunnel.

"Terrifying woman," one of the detectives said, sticking his head out of the closet.

"A Russian princess, of all things," Les told him, assessing the longevity of the spider webs in the corners. The room looked like it had been cleaned a week or ten days ago.

The man shook his head. "That poor Romanov family murdered, bless them."

"The bloodshed is far from over," Les said. "Let's try to keep it off our own soil, eh?"

The second detective reentered the room. "I followed the tunnel. It goes into the wing you found before, where the explosives are."

Les frowned. "We know there is a way out from there because we followed it before, but the man shouldn't have been able to escape. It's been blocked off."

"He might have left through the hotel," Dent said. "We've had half an hour where no one was really watching."

"Maybe he exited through the employee entrance," Les suggested. "It can't be locked down unless they give every employee the key to the door."

"I'll tell Eyre to consider it. It would have to lock from the inside," Dent said. "What I don't get is, how did we miss this tunnel before?"

"The other side was hidden behind a panel, like this one," the detective said. "It's a fair miss in the darkness."

Dent frowned. "Incompetence is never fair. We have to be smarter than these people. I want you to comb every inch of this tunnel. What if the piece we miss is a spot where explosives are being held? Then what?"

The detectives nodded solemnly and went back in. Dent put his hands on his hips and turned to Les. "You have anything useful to tell me?"

"I suspect the trade delegation staying in luxury upstairs knows about the tunnels," Les said. "But it's conjecture. We've a poor operation."

"No staff," Dent agreed. "Government doesn't realize we're still fighting a bloody war. They knocked the teeth out of all the budgets of the intelligence operations."

Les nodded. "Meanwhile, we still have our work to do. There is a possibility Konstantin is freely roaming the halls. My wife found a bundle of cash upstairs while she was working that might have been intended to be a payment to him."

"Bloody frustrating. I'll be in touch."

"Yes. I should return to my microphone," Les said. "Though they weren't in their suite earlier. And my wife is up there now."

Dent laughed without humor. "Did you really need a wife for this operation?"

"She was meant to help me with my cover in the trade unions, and with the Kozyrevs. We'd hoped I might be able to develop her as a source since she works here, but it will take time to get her into a position where she can hear anything useful." Les paused. "She's already been promoted once. I could press for more, but the princess is suspicious as it is."

"Why don't you develop her instead of your wife?"

"We need to dig into the princess's loyalties," Les agreed, especially since his own erotic interludes with Sadie might limit her length of employment. "I'll bring Olga to the attention of my section head. A good thought, Dent. Thank you."

Sadie thanked the chambermaid who came to the door with fresh towels and declined her offer to tidy up. She had nothing better to do than tidy up herself. There was nothing much to tidy anyway. Since Les didn't smoke, there weren't any ashtrays to empty, no ground debris in the carpet, smells to air out of the suite. If it wasn't for Les's books, magazines, and papers lying about, a chambermaid would hardly know anyone was staying there.

She hummed to herself as she stacked his magazines and fashioned a bookmark for his Zorro book out of an unused piece of paper. Books shouldn't be left open. It damaged the spine. She smacked her lips, imitating the beat of the song running through her head, then regretted it. Her lips were chapped and sore from the hotel's dry heat. Half an hour later, she was out of chores again, and contemplating the basket of fruit on a side table. She picked up an apple and set it down, then saw a lemon nestled underneath.

While she wasn't hungry, she remembered reading a beauty article about the uses of lemon on skin. She could use the lemon to exfoliate her lips, and if she had darkened skin on her knees or elbows the juice would lighten them. If she had any sunlight she could use the juice to lighten her hair. That would be the best, but pouring lemon juice on her hair and walking outside in February was worthless. She decided to exfoliate.

In the bedroom, she found Les's rather wicked looking pocket knife in a drawer. He had two of them and had sheepishly told her it was a "man" thing when she'd noticed the pair. She cut the lemon in half, then put it on a towel and went back to the sitting room. A mirror hung above a comfortable reading chair and she could get closer to it than she could to the bathroom mirror, which was blocked by the sink. She crawled up on the chair and faced the mirror, then delicately began to rub the cut half on her lips.

"Ouch!" The juice stung her lip. She hadn't realized it was cut. Her hand jerked and the lemon half fell on the neat stack of books. A drop of juice fell on the face of Zorro. She snatched up the lemon and picked up the book so she could wipe it with her sleeve, then she checked the pages around the outside to make sure she hadn't dripped on them.

With a sigh, she decided to give up on exfoliating, and settled back with the book. She'd already read page one over Les's shoulder, so she flipped to the next page.

A scraping noise caught her attention. She glanced up. Something was being pushed under the suite door. She set the book down, using the lemon to hold the book open, and went to pick up the envelope. When she opened it, she found a thick piece of notepaper confirming her afternoon tea plans with Miss Page for Sunday afternoon. Miss Page extended an invitation to dine with both her and her husband that evening after Mr. Rake instructed the ladies in Russian.

Sadie grinned and clutched the paper to her chest. She danced around the room. Dining with the Fortresses, and not even Emmeline or Mr. Eyre would be along. The Rakes had arrived.

She read the note again, noticing that Miss Page's writing displayed her lack of education. Her lettering was not the most elegant, but she had other qualities. Finally, beginning to feel tired after a rather strange day, Sadie collapsed back into the chair and picked up Les's book, wishing she'd thought to order tea.

"Oh no!" The lemon had turned on the book, dribbling juice down the margin. She shook the lemon off the book and tried to wipe up the page with her handkerchief, but words were bleeding through the paper from the backside. Cheap paper. She lifted her handkerchief. The words were still there, even clearer. *And handwritten.* She picked up the book and held it close to the light. How odd. The book was new. She'd seen Les unwrap it. The hidden message was impossible to read, because it was in Russian. Why was her husband in possession of a book with a secret Russian code in it?

Sadie dropped the book to the chair and stood without even realizing what she was doing. She wrung her hands. Had she married a Russian spy? Her sister was engaged to a man whose sister had been part of a political group, and now she had accidentally married a spy? What was wrong with the two of them?

She stared around the room. When she noticed the painting of the Firebird on the wall, she remembered the strange clicking behind it and how Les often seemed to be near the painting. She crept over to it, not knowing why she was trying to keep the noise down, and stared at the painting. A beautiful Russian woman. Had she been fooled by Les's male beauty into marrying a full Russian, when he claimed to only be a quarter Russian? Memories of his behavior when they'd first met flitted through her mind. That strange Kozyrev couple. The parties. The rally. The changing accent.

Feeling around the painting, she half expected to find an envelope with foreign passports instead of money. Instead, she felt a piece of metal. She pressed her cheek against the wall, trying to see what it was. It appeared to be a hinge. She stepped around to the other side of the thick frame and pulled at the painting. Nothing happened. She stared at the side as best she could, then pressed her fingers alongside it. Eventually, her index finger found a button, and when she pressed it, she heard a click and the frame separated from the wall an inch. She pulled it further away. It was held up on the opposite hinge. Behind the painting was a ledge with what looked like a small gramophone, with wires heading into the wall.

While she had no idea what she was really looking at, it was obvious that Les was spying on the Russians on the other side of the wall. Frightened suddenly, she pushed the painting back into place.

The Firebird stared down at her, an ethereal smile on her face. She was a fantasy creature, and so was Sadie. A wife married to a man she didn't know. Was Lester Rake a real person?

She grabbed her coat and went back into the bedroom. In Les's collection of belongings in his dresser drawer she found the keys to his flat. Her fingers chose the knife before she even picked up the keys, and she put both into her coat pocket. She left the suite and took the stairs all the way down to the ground floor, then had Johnnie Miles get her a taxicab.

"You alright, Miss Sadie?" he asked.

She stared at his open, friendly face, almost wishing she'd have accepted a date with him instead of marrying Les. "I'll be fine," she said. "It's been a trying day." She described the man she'd seen in the basement bathroom. "Have you seen anyone like that?"

He shook his head. "No, but I'll keep an eye out."

"He's a bad man, Johnnie. Be careful."

Johnnie grinned and flexed his biceps. "Don't worry about me, Miss Sadie. I can take care of myself."

A taxicab pulled up and he opened the door for her. She smiled at him and climbed in, giving the directions to Primrose Hill.

When she let herself into the dark flat, she wondered if she would find Les there. She had no idea where he was. He hadn't been in the suite as he usually was. Now she knew why he was there all the time. He'd lied about his job. He'd probably been sacked for missing work. That was why she'd had to keep working, because he planned to rely on her income.

She quickly toured the flat. What if he'd put it up to let without even telling her? She didn't know anything about his lease. But that didn't seem to be the case. Nothing seemed to have changed or been disturbed, though there wasn't any mail anywhere. Les must have been coming by to pick it up on a regular basis.

She examined everything she could think of, feeling under mattresses, drawers, checking the few art pieces. Her feet tapped floorboards to see if any of them were loose. She investigated the toilet tank and the ice box. Two hours later it was dark outside and she was out of ideas. She cast herself down in a chair in the sitting room, then realized she hadn't checked there.

The envelope was taped underneath the sofa. She collapsed into the down cushion and stared at it. What did it hold? Fingers trembling, she undid the string clasp and let the contents fall into her lap. Not a Russian passport but a British one. Various papers. Memberships. Everything was made out to Leslie Valentin Drake. She stared at the passport. It was her husband's face, his birthdate. Everything matched but the name.

He wasn't Lester Rake, but Leslie Drake. And his fake Russian first name, Valentin, was his true middle name. She stared at the passport, feeling more confused than ever.

That was when the front door on the floor below opened. She clutched the documents to her chest, too numb to move. When footsteps clicked on the stairs, she had the presence of mind to pull out the knife. She'd been there for hours and hadn't even taken her coat off. Her fright had left her very chilled.

Les appeared in the doorway of the sitting room, his shadow cast hugely on the wall. But when he reached her, he was the same handsome man she knew, not slight exactly, but slim and deft. She'd never seen him smile like that though. It was an uncertain expression, which appeared strange on a face that always seemed so sure of itself.

He gestured to the papers. "Opening letters, Sadie? I have a proper letter opener. Would you like me to get it for you?"

"There wasn't any mail when I arrived." Her voice rasped. She waved the knife. "Who picks it up? Your handler?"

"Handler?" he asked, his voice even.

She noticed how carefully calm his voice was. "I know you're a spy, Leslie." Her fingers tightened on the handle of the knife.

Chapter Sixteen

Les watched Sadie's fingers tighten on the knife. He debated how strong she might be, how deft. She worked with her body, but had been out in the world, away from her family home, less than two months. He doubted his wife had much in the way of knife skills. Still, he didn't want to disarm her, not yet. She wasn't the enemy but the average English girl. His best weapon was charm.

"You know I'm a spy, Sadie," he repeated. "What do you think you know?"

"I saw the secret writing in your novel. I found the equipment behind the Firebird painting. And now I know Lester Rake isn't your real name."

He saw she was holding his passport. *Clever girl.* "Spies use invisible writing," he agreed. "And I am performing surveillance on those Russians."

"Who are you?"

"Not an enemy, darling." He forced a smile. "I'm one of the good eggs."

"How do I know that? You can speak Russian. You are supposed to start teaching Miss Page and me on Sunday."

"I didn't lie. My grandmother was Russian. I learned from her."

"What were you really doing when we went to Hull?"

"Building a relationship with the Kozyrevs. Her father is an assassin and we don't know where he is. I was supposed to research printers but events overtook us."

"Who is we?"

"The British government."

"You're a British spy?" Her voice held incredulity.

"Yes, darling." He took her moment of shock as opportunity. The second he dropped into the seat next to her, he swept the knife from her hand. She didn't resist. "It's not just the enemy who has to have spies. Oh, there aren't nearly so many as there were during the war, but you know as well as anyone that we still have enemies. So we still have people like me."

She blinked slowly and pressed her empty hand against the papers she still held to her chest. "Are we in danger?"

He was sorry for her sudden loss of illusions, but he had done this to women before. *Natalia.* "What do you think? You saw that man in the basement just today."

Her mouth dropped open. "How do you know?"

He shook his head, showing his amusement to her. "That's exactly the sort of thing I would know, don't you see? Peter Eyre told me. I went down there with Special Branch officers to investigate."

Her jaw quivered. "Why did you mix me up in this?"

He used his most gentle voice. "You already were, darling. Your sister is involved because of the position she held with the Marvins, and her fiancé."

She swallowed hard. "Oh. Is he a bad man? Should I tell Alecia not to marry him?"

He rubbed his chin. "I have no reason to think Salter is bad, but we do think he, and maybe your own sister, helped his sister escape the country. And Salter's sister, Vera Saltykova, is not necessarily such a good person. We really don't know her story."

"I don't know anything about that," Sadie said. "I've been such a fool, haven't I? Trusting you. Marrying you."

"No. Most people only see the surface. Usually, that's all there is." He tucked the knife away where she couldn't reach it, then put his arm around the back of the sofa. She stayed rigid, not allowing herself to touch him.

She squeezed the papers. "Now what?"

He kept his voice calm despite the churning of his insides. "It would be helpful to go on as we are. You might learn any amount of useful information as a chambermaid, and I need to keep an eye on the Russians."

"What do you think they are doing?"

"We're concerned about an attempt to bomb Marconi House. We're concerned about Bolshies using the Grand Russe to hide weapons. And of course, they did try to bomb the hotel recently. They might try it again. That money you found, it might have been a payment meant for a Russian criminal."

Her hands tightened until they vibrated the papers. "Were you thinking all along that you were going to use me?"

"You saved my life. You were staying in my flat. We couldn't go on like that, and I couldn't lose you."

"So you fell in love with me?" She let her hands drop to her lap. The papers and his passport fluttered down on top of them, topped by the envelope.

She'd obviously searched the place. Was this all she had found? He plucked the envelope from the top of the pile and slid his identity papers into it, then laced the string around the clasp. "How could I not fall in love with you, Sadie? You were my angel of mercy." He let his fingers dangle down on the sofa so that they touched the back of her neck. He used his other hand to slide his envelope under the sofa cushion. She'd become more important to him than he dared admit to anyone, even himself.

"I was, wasn't I? You could have had us both killed in that mess in Hull, but I rescued us."

"Mobs are dangerous," he agreed. "But the Bolsheviks are worse. We can't let them take control, and trust me, darling, they want to. This country needs to remain diligent. If you doubt me, talk to Ivan Salter, about how the Bolsheviks killed his parents. They will destroy us too, if we let them."

"I didn't know that," she said. "Alecia and I haven't spoken a great deal because she's so busy with Mrs. Plash."

"Georgy Ovolensky, who is in the suite next to us, head of the trade organization, is Ivan Salter's distant cousin."

Sadie's mouth formed an O. "Does he know that?"

"Yes, of course. And while the trade aspect is real, it's obvious that there is more going on. Ovolensky is behind the deaths of Ivan's parents. He's a bad man with blood on his hands. And we know people in his delegation have ties to the Russian bomber, Konstantin."

"What about that assassin you mentioned?"

"Mikhail Lashevich," Les said. "We do not know where he is, but he is known to the group. We're trying to sort out the code they are using in the room."

She trembled. "At least you won't have to hide your spying from me any longer. No more jumping away from the wall when I come in."

"That will help," Les agreed.

Sadie let her head fall back on his arm. He let her rest for a couple of seconds, then pulled her close to him. While his conscience still warred with his work in relation to Sadie, as an agent, he knew he needed to cement their relationship under the new paradigm. And it must be admitted that he wanted her. Her hair tickled the back of his hand, and her scent did the same to his nose. "My angel darling," he said softly. "You aren't too angry with me?"

She tilted her head and rubbed her cheek along his arm, then looked up at him, her eyes huge under her lashes. "I don't know what I think exactly, but I want you to be a good man."

He could never be that, not in this game, but he wanted her to have the illusion. "You know I'm a British spy. Why else would I be spying on the Russians? You've met Robbie. He's Special Branch. And Lord Walling, he's Secret Intelligence Service like me."

"Oh," she said. "What is Semyon Kozyrev, exactly?"

"He works on subverting the trade unions for the Bolshies," Les said. "But you know what? For once, we are here, alone, quiet. Let's enjoy it."

She was still innocent enough to ask. "What do you want to do?"

He grinned. "I bet we could both fit in the bathtub if we tried."

"But we'd be naked." Her eyebrows lifted. "Oh? We could? In there? Without drowning?"

"It's time I teach you a new position," he said. "Astride. I think you'll like it, and it will be easy for you in the water."

She blushed. He kissed along her hairline, then drifted gently down her nose, tiny kisses. When he nuzzled her nose, she turned up and found his mouth with hers. Something about the conversation had aroused her. Her kisses were open-mouthed, frantic, searching. He slipped his hand under her skirt and found her hot, moist, ready for him. She was back on his side. He'd won.

"Darling," he murmured. "I don't think I can wait for the tub."

"After," she said. "After."

He tumbled her down on the sofa and tugged off her knickers, not bothering to remove the rest of her clothing. She stared greedily at him while he ripped off his coat, loosened his tie, then dragged his trousers down his legs, not even bothering with his shoes. He entered her with no gentility, his tongue taking equal command of her mouth. But she arched against him, accepting it, grabbing at his bottom with surprisingly chilly fingers. For the first time, she moved against him like a proper lover. Obviously, she was a quick student in the arts of love.

"Sadie, oh God," he muttered, not expecting her hips to buck and cant, giving him everything, ratcheting him higher.

Her response was to kiss him hard and pull at his shirt. He could feel the bottom button begin to tear away from the fabric as she pulled from the back, trying to pull it up his skin. The demand of his body was too urgent to stop and help her take it off. Grimly, he kept to his task. Her hands loosened, then clutched at his head. She pulled at his hair and found his mouth again. He felt her body clench and lost control completely as she shattered. Down he went, following her, at her mercy. A man could never survive two masters, but he had two now.

Sadie stumbled as she stepped off the bus down the street from the hotel on Saturday morning, remembering the night before. She and Les had eventually left the sofa and went down to his bedroom. For the first time they spent the night together in the flat, in the master bedroom. The air in the room had cooled down dramatically through the night, which had woken them up. They'd warmed each other up before falling asleep again for a few hours. Then Sadie had woken in a panic. Her alarm clock was at the hotel, but her concern woke her half an hour early. The rustling of the sheets had woken Les again and he'd pulled her into her warm embrace. All the unaccustomed erotic activity had left her simultaneously over-relaxed and somewhat shaky.

She grabbed a lamppost to right herself, leaning her head back against the cool surface. Maybe it wasn't the lovemaking, but the night's revelations that had her so on edge. Either way, she couldn't think about it now, or she'd be late for her shift.

That man in the bathroom came to mind as she went down the stairs to the staff entrance of the hotel. The door didn't open when she turned the handle. Confused, she knocked. It was opened by a man she didn't recognize.

"What's this?"

"New security," the man said. He was dressed in the red coat and fancy cap of a Grand Russe employee. "The door will be locked from now on."

"Very well. I'm Sadie Rake."

He leaned back into the entry. "Just checking the clipboard. My apologies. I'll know all the faces soon enough."

"Your name?"

"Norman Johnson. I was on the night watch, but I've been changed to days. One of the original employees when we reopened."

"Lovely," Sadie said. "I'm newer than that." Two other chamber-maids lined up beside her, so she stepped around the watchman and went to put on her fresh uniform, which had been hanging on her peg.

Her Saturday shift lasted five hours or until her assigned rooms were completed. She thought about what Les had said, and paid special attention to who was in her rooms. But no one was Russian, or anyone of interest. She'd have to tell him to make Mr. Eyre promote her to at least the fifth floor if he wanted to make use of her. She day-dreamed about finding something important in a wastepaper basket, or overhearing something exciting. In her daydreams, it was juicy stuff, not anything dangerous like bombs and assassins.

But, by the end of her shift, as she went down to the staff lounge, she realized that all the fun of espionage aside, the real business was with the Russians who were already on the seventh floor. She came up with a list of things to offer to Les, such as writing a note to Irina Kozyrev, inviting her for tea when she was next in London. She should also make contact with that English bride of the Russian man that she'd met at the Chelsea party, Doris Ikanov.

Lastly, she could pay some attention to their neighbors, Georgy Ovolensky and his delegation. If she had to be married to a spy, she might as well make herself useful to him, and help keep the Russians from hurting anyone else. Why, she might have already foiled a plot by finding that money. She could do more.

She took the staff lift to the ground floor, then walked to the guest lift in order to return to their suite. Les would probably be there, spy-ing on the Russians if they were in their rooms. When she walked up to the lift entrance, she found one man already waiting. She recog-nized him as one of the Russians, twelve or fifteen years older than herself, a handsome man with dark hair and mustache. He bowed his head to her when he saw her approach.

"You are staying in the suite next to mine, no?" he said. While he had a strong accent, he was easy to understand.

"Yes, I'm Mrs. Rake," she said, glad that she'd taken off her apron and put her coat on over her uniform.

"I am Georgy Ovolensky," he said with a small bow.

So this was Mr. Ovolensky. She looked him over, a big man, like his cousin Ivan. Alecia had described her fiancé at some length. Ovolensky didn't have the face of a villain, despite what Les had told her. Sadie wondered if he'd ever killed anyone himself, or merely given orders, but since he was old enough to have been in the war, he probably had. Most men over thirty had been killers, even some younger.

Now that she knew what Les was, he was no doubt a killer as well.

"Do you have a chill, Mrs. Rake?" Ovolensky asked.

She nodded, not wanting to tell him the real cause for her shudder. In response, he tore his muffler from his neck in an extravagant gesture. She realized he wore golf attire and wondered at the weather, but of course, he was Russian and used to harsh conditions.

"Allow me." He draped the wool around her neck, careful not to touch her skin.

"Thank you." She forced a smile.

She tucked the ends into her coat as the lift descended to the ground floor.

"After you," Ovolensky said.

She stepped toward the back, then had to do an awkward dance as he insisted she stand in the front, then continued their conversation with her facing away from him.

"Do you spend much time in the Coffee Room?" he asked. "I understand there is often dancing there in the evenings."

"Seven nights a week. We don't recognize religion here at the Grand Russe."

"Ah. And you? Have you abolished religion as well, Mrs. Rake?"

"Of course not. My grandfather is a vicar."

"Yes, of course. Some little birdie told me you are Miss Loudon's sister. She is to marry my young cousin."

Sadie kept her face turned toward the lift gate with difficulty. But of course the man was a spy, or a subversive or something. He'd know everything there was to know. Perhaps even more than she did. "I had been given to understand that Mr. Salter was your cousin, but I admit I do not know him."

"How odd. He knows your husband. I've seen him on our floor."

"He is the head of security now. Perhaps you had not learned of his promotion?"

"I always knew Ivan had a brain. He went to University you understand, studied philosophy for a brief time."

She bit her lip until she knew she would break the skin if she continued. No doubt his studies had ended when his parents were murdered. "What about his sister?"

"He has one living sister. There were four of them, the Saltykovs, when we were young. One boy died young, drowning. Then Catherine, the oldest, became a subversive and attempted to murder Vladimir Lenin."

"And lost her life," Sadie said flatly.

"Indeed. Such an unpleasant topic on a rainy London day."

The lift ceased its ascension and the operator opened the gate, his expression carefully neutral. Sadie thanked him and stepped out. The Russian was close behind. She could smell his tree-scented cologne, or perhaps it emanated from the scarf still wrapped around her neck.

The lift was between her door and his. She stopped at the wall and unwrapped his muffler, folded it neatly and handed it back to him as a door opened down the hall. "Thank you very much."

"You may keep it, Mrs. Rake. A lady must stay warm, even when her husband doesn't dress her properly."

She kept her expression neutral despite the insult to Les. "I wasn't outside, Mr. Ovolensky, but downstairs. I assure you my wardrobe is perfectly adequate to our local weather."

He took the scarf with a nod of his head and an amused smile playing underneath his mustache. "Why don't you have a cup of tea with me? I have an excellent blend."

"That's very kind, Mr. Ovolensky, but I'm certain my husband is expecting me. Why don't we both join you?"

He chuckled. "Ah, you are adorable, my sweet. I have no interest in your husband."

"That makes one of us," Sadie said, sliding along the wall. She turned her head and saw her suite door had opened.

Before she could take another step, Ovolensky reached out and took her by the arm, firmly, though not rough exactly. "Come, you must join me for tea."

* * *

Les heard the exchange, and his thoughts warred between wanting a legitimate reason to enter Ovolensky's suite, and the thought of his wife in Ovolensky's clutches. How odd that he'd invite a woman in. During his surveillance he'd never heard a woman's voice in there.

He stepped out from behind the open door just as Ovolensky grabbed for Sadie's arm. The look on her face made Les's vision go red. He leapt forward and ripped her arm from the Russian's hold.

A fist came out of nowhere, headed toward Les's face. He ducked. The fist missed his jaw. Instead, it collided with his nose. His head snapped back. Blood spurted. His head came forward. He bit his tongue. The copper taste of blood overwhelmed his senses. Outside of the pain, he heard Sadie scream. His heels slammed against the wall. He stayed upright, balancing against the wall.

Sadie swore like a Billingsgate fishwife at the Russian. Ovolensky held up his hands and stepped away.

"Instinct," the man said. "I do apologize."

Les fished for a handkerchief. He held it to his nose.

Sadie stared at Les. Tears filled her eyes. She put her hands to her face. "I'll get a towel. Oh, Les."

"Allow me." Ovolensky moved around her and went toward their door.

Sadie's gaze met Les's with horror. She followed the man, hurling imprecations at him. "You are not welcome!" she screamed. "I'll have you removed from the hotel for this!"

Ovolensky stopped in his tracks and slowly turned around. "Pardon me, madam. I was attempting to help your husband."

"You are not welcome," Sadie said, standing her ground. "Come along, Les. I do not care to converse with this blackguard any further."

Les blinked. His vision swam a bit as he stood under his own power instead of having the wall hold him up. He put up his hand when he reached Ovolensky. His urge was to strangle the man, but instead he pulled the muffler dangling from the man's hand and smeared a bloody mess across it before dropping the striped wool to the carpet.

He stepped over it as he walked through his door. Sadie shut the door behind him.

"Sit down and lean forward so that you don't swallow all that blood," she instructed. "We need to get you some ice. That horrible man."

He sat on the sofa, rueful that he'd be damaging the beautiful white furnishings. She ran out of his line of sight, then returned with a towel, also snowy white, and laid it across his lap.

"I'll call for the lift and get help," she said.

"Leave the door open," he instructed, then spat into the towel. He had blood all over his hands. It reminded him of too many times that the same thing had happened. He'd broken his nose before, but it had never amounted to much.

"These so called gentlemen are animals," Peter Eyre growled, restraining the urge to throw his cigarette case at Detective Inspector Dent. The two men stood in the Artists Suite on the seventh floor. Chambermaids had just finished removing blood stains from the premises and now were working on the carpet in the hallway between this suite and the Piano Suite, where the Russians stayed.

"I understand your anger," Dent said, his gaze moving from artwork to artwork.

"Ovolensky might have raped my employee, who is incidentally, also a guest."

"I doubt it."

"He was using superior force on Mrs. Rake," Peter said. "Thankfully her husband heard what was happening in time."

"I am sympathetic, Mr. Eyre," Dent said, "but you and I both know that the Rakes are not ordinary people."

"I don't know that," Peter said. "Yes, I understand Rake is the government's man, but what about his wife? You can't tell me Sadie understands the situation."

Dent's gaze returned to Eyre. "A wife's place is with her husband, and she chose the man. If she's in danger, that is his fault and not ours."

"The entire operation, my family money, all our guests. The Russians are putting everything at risk. We have Konstantin or someone like him nosing around in the basement."

"That has nothing to do with the trade delegation," Dent said.

"We don't know that." Peter wanted to open the drinks cabinet and pour himself a drink, but he had a long night ahead of him as it was, and in these times, it behooved him to remain clearheaded. He folded his arms and opened the curtains so he could stare down at the street, all the taxicabs and pedestrians going by on a windy Saturday evening, heading to the theater, to restaurants, to nightclubs. None of them were aware of Russian explosives probably hiding in tunnels below.

"If you ask me," Dent said, "this is the safest hotel from Bolsheviks in London right now. In fact, I've heard Number Ten wants to use your first floor for meetings next week."

"That's the stupidest thing I've ever heard," Peter snapped. Why hadn't he heard about this? Someone on his staff must have. Hadn't he been paying enough attention? He had to admit he was behind in reading his reports. "We've found explosives here twice, and now that man is running around. The devil only knows what he hid that time."

Dent's attention flashed to the hallway when one of the chambermaids laughed, then returned to him. "You also have Secret Intelligence on site, as well as a police presence. Any building as prominent as yours is a possible target, but at least this is being protected. And Bolsheviks aren't going to blow each other up."

"They won't mind if they have the chance to kill British government ministers. They proved that last month."

Dent stepped over to the window and pulled aside the curtain. "One does have the sense that Ovolensky is not a popular man."

"He is a murderer and a rapist."

"No different than our average Bolshie," Dent opined.

"For whatever reason, Konstantin, at least, and whoever is running him, is willing to sacrifice the trade delegation. They have plenty of time to ship more men out. The actual meetings aren't until April."

Dent shrugged. "Nice suite. I wish I could be assigned to live in luxury."

Few people could afford such an elevated setting. Peter glanced around in pride. The trick would be keeping it in such immaculate condition over time. "You'd have to take up undercover work."

Dent pulled a cigar from his pocket and stuck one end in his mouth as he let the curtain drop. "I don't care that Ovolensky is an animal. Do what you have to in order to keep your chambermaids safe. I would suggest not allowing any of them to speak to the Russians is an excellent first step."

"I agree. I'll write a memo, and I'll find a man to clean their suite. Not that this is where the problem originated."

Dent chewed on his cigar. "You having trouble with any other guests on this floor where the Russians are concerned?"

It irritated Peter, looking at the uncut end of the cigar hanging from the man's mouth. Uncouth. "Not recently. We had a noise complaint before the Rakes moved in. They haven't had any wild parties since."

"Wild parties can be a cover for other business," Dent said thoughtfully. "But we did send our men through the suite recently, when the microphone was installed."

"Our real trouble is the basement, not up here," Peter pointed out.

"We'll catch Konstantin. Assuming the man down there was him, he's spending too much time hanging about one location. It's foolish for someone like him."

"I'd like to have faith in that," Peter said.

"We'll sweep the first floor before the Number Ten meetings," Dent said. "I'm honestly not worried about the hotel being bombed. Whoever this Konstantin is, he's not going to catch Ovolensky in his crossfire again. He may be on the run because of what he did before."

Peter's mind reeled with that logic. If Ovolensky wanted Konstantin dead for the man's attempt to bomb the hotel, then wouldn't Ovolensky want to kill him before he tried again?

Chapter Seventeen

On Sunday, Sadie woke to find Les's side of the bed empty. He had not been able to sleep well since the doctor packed his nostrils to stop the bleeding and he wasn't supposed to remove everything for twenty-four hours.

As she finished her morning ablutions twenty minutes later, her heart raced. She took a deep breath through her nose, trying to calm her nerves, but it didn't work. Restless, unsettled, she considered a quick inspection of her clothing. Then she would go to Montagu Square and see if Alecia wanted to attend services with her, if she could leave Mrs. Plash. After that, she had tea and Russian lessons with Miss Page, if Les was able to manage with his nose in the condition it was. She suspected they would have to cancel their second film star dinner. Such a pity, but he'd been injured defending her. She had to take comfort in that.

Folding her arms across her jumper against the morning chill, she went into the sitting room, expecting Les to be spread across the sofa with the coverlet from their bed tucked over him. But the blanket was tossed across one end and Les was nowhere to be found.

She went to the wall and pulled open the Firebird painting like he'd taught her and put on the headphones. No one was talking on the other side of the wall. The Russians were probably still asleep. She made a notation in Les's notebook, seeing that he had last checked himself a couple of hours before. Where had he gone after that?

She proceeded as planned. Returning to the bedroom, she went through her clothing. She had four day dresses and two evening frocks, all in good repair. Kneeling on the floor of her room, she polished her shoes carefully. Les left his outside for the hotel to clean them, but she liked to do her own. Then, she examined her accessories for needed repairs. For a girl to look her best on a small budget, everything needed to stay in perfect condition.

She hummed the theme song from one of Teddy Fortress's movies as she resewed the edge of one of her scarves, then put it away. As she put her now-dry shoes back in the wardrobe, starting to feel hungry, she saw an envelope pushed toward the back and opened it. Wedding documents.

Oddly enough, she'd never seen their wedding license. She pulled it out, still humming, admiring her signature, 'Sadie Elizabeth Rake.'

Her mouth snapped closed so quickly that she caught her lips between her teeth. 'Sadie Elizabeth Rake.' Wait. 'Rake' wasn't really Les's last name. The paper fluttered from her fingers to the floor. She fanned out her hands and stepped away from the wardrobe. Her pulse throbbed in her throat.

With a wail, she snatched up the license and stared at it again. Les had married her under a false name. They weren't married at all. He'd turned her into his mistress.

She could be expecting his child. Her. Sadie Elizabeth *Loudon*, a vicar's granddaughter. Could it be? Was that right? She didn't know marriage law.

She'd been caring for this man, feeling sorry for his injuries on his behalf, and it had all been a lie. He'd been so dishonest. His injuries were because he'd insisted on putting her right next to a group of evil Russians, and then tugged at her heartstrings so she'd try to help him in his investigation, without any training at all. He'd risked her life, her reputation, her future, and he hadn't even really married her!

She ran to the bed and pulled her ancient valise from underneath, grabbed a bathroom towel and wrapped her shoes in it, then tucked them into the bag. After that, she surrounded the shoes with all of her meager possessions. Oh, she'd have to keep her position, but she couldn't stay here in Les's suite.

Never had she wished so much for the mother she'd lost when she was not yet ten years old. *Alecia.* She would go to her only sister.

Frantic, Sadie raced into the sitting room, desperate to leave before Les returned from whatever errand had him out on a Sunday morning with a broken nose. She took his *Mark of Zorro* book and tossed it into her bag, with some disordered idea of being able to prove he was a spy by the secret writing in the margins.

Not that she wanted to hurt him. Or get him killed. Or anything really. "Glory," she muttered.

Making matters worse wouldn't help. Maybe she wasn't really his wife, but she certainly didn't want to be his widow. She took the book from her bag and tossed it on top of the blanket on the sofa, then grabbed her hat from its peg in the small entryway. She started to put on her muffler, then realized he'd given it to her. She tossed it on the floor, followed by the gloves he'd also gifted to her on her birthday. Jamming her hat on her head with one hand, she clutched her bag firmly with the other and marched out of the suite.

She saw the lift was down on the third floor. Not able to stand still, she opened the door to the staircase, letting it slam against the wall, and marched downstairs, wishing she hadn't left her old knitted mittens in a drawer at Les's flat. Hopefully Alecia would have a spare pair.

Johnnie wasn't on duty near the taxicab stand. She'd better not spend money on cab fare anyhow. While the air chilled her bare hands, the walk was only half a mile. She hoisted her valise, feeling extremely ill-used, and headed north.

Halfway, the rain started. By the time she trudged up the steps to the boarding house door, water dripped off her hat onto her coat. She wished she hadn't left her muffler. Her hand was frozen to her carpetbag handles. She used her elbow to push the doorbell, fuming while she waited for it to open.

An ancient-looking man opened the door after a couple of long minutes. He wore three sweaters, layered over a yellowed shirt and food-stained tie. "Yes?"

"I'm Alecia Loudon's sister. I'd like to see her," she announced.

"I'm afraid she's out, miss."

She wanted to wail. "How can that be?"

"She's gone for the doctor. Mrs. Plash is in a bad way."

She forced herself to register that someone else was in crisis. "I'm sorry to hear that. Can I wait for her?"

"She won't have time to see you today, if ye want my opinion. Best to come back tomorrow."

Sadie's upper lip trembled. "I don't have anywhere to go."

As tears welled up in her eyes, the man looked alarmed. "Now, look here, miss, it's not so bad. She'll be here soon enough, it's just that she has to take the medicine to the old lady, and it's hard to get it down her. I've heard the lady's daughter complain about it."

"I don't have anywhere to go," Sadie whispered. But she did, of course, her grandfather. Did she have money for the train? She thought frantically. No, she didn't. When they'd moved into the hotel, she lost her access to Les's stash of money on the top of his chest of drawers. She'd neglected to retrieve her own pay envelope. The distribution had been Friday afternoon when she'd been upstairs recovering from the man in the basement drama.

Someone came up the steps behind her. Sadie wiped at her eyes.

Olga, dressed in a shabby coat but rather smart hat, frowned at her. "What's wrong, Sadie?"

"It's all a lie," Sadie whispered.

Olga lifted her eyebrows as she saw Sadie's bag. "Have you left Mr. Rake?"

Sadie nodded and began to cry again.

Olga shook her head. "Can we please come in, Mr. Dadey?"

"Of course, miss," the old man said, and shuffled backward. "Will you be taking charge of the young lady?"

"Yes, she's my employee."

"Why don't I fetch you both a good cuppa? Beastly day." He wandered away.

Olga pushed her into the hallway. "Take off your things," she said briskly. "They can drip on the linoleum." She set her umbrella into the brass stand and unpinned her hat, then unbuttoned her long wool coat.

Sadie hung up her coat and hat. "My sister is out running an errand and Mr. Dadey said she'd be too busy to see me."

"Mrs. Plash is dying," Olga said in her no nonsense fashion. "I'm sure your sister is being run off her feet."

"Should I call you Your Serene Highness when we are outside the hotel?" Sadie asked. "I know you are a princess."

"It seems rather silly here in England," Olga said. "You need not do so unless we are in public. And not during work hours, of course."

"Thank you," Sadie said.

Olga led her into a sitting room, dominated by a large gramophone. "Now, what is this business about lies and leaving your husband?"

Sadie sat on the edge of the worn sofa next to a fern, hoping she wasn't soaking the fabric. It didn't look like the elderly chintz would need much encouragement to disintegrate. She placed her bag at her feet and opened it, then pulled out the envelope she found.

Olga took the envelope and opened it. "Your marriage license. The special license. What of it?"

Sadie froze. She didn't want to tell Olga the truth but she needed someone to confide in. "My marriage is invalid."

Olga stared at first the marriage license, then the special license. "Yes, I see what you mean. The Archbishop's seal is an obvious fake."

"W-what?" Sadie said, shocked. "It is?"

"Yes, that's not the seal. The real one has lettering around the outside and this one doesn't. Terribly inept job. If your special license wasn't issued by the Archbishop's office, you are a concubine, not a wife."

Sadie's mouth dropped open. "I am?"

Olga shook her head in disgust. "Was your husband sold this on the black market? Too eager to wait to call the banns?"

"I-I don't really know."

"You'll have to remarry. You're right to leave him until it's sorted. After all, what if he changes his mind now? You could end up with an illegitimate child."

Sadie closed her eyes. "I thought he loved me."

"Did he explain how he came to have a false special license?"

She could imagine, but she couldn't tell Olga. "No. I haven't seen him. I found the papers and then I packed and left."

"Did you leave him a note?"

Sadie's eyes filled with tears again as she shook her head. She fished for a handkerchief and held it to her nose, letting the tears drip down her cheeks.

"He can't fix anything if he doesn't know what is wrong," Olga stated.

"I'm certain he knew the license was a fake," Sadie whispered.

Olga frowned. She did that a lot. Sadie wondered if the princess would give herself premature wrinkles as a result. Olga's life couldn't have been easy. A shabby boarding house when she should be living in a grace-and-favor apartment at Kensington Palace or somewhere like that. She wondered what the story was.

"You must think the best of Mr. Rake," Olga said, as if instructing her. "I am sure you do not want to be unmarried now that you did marry him. You do not want to start over, right?"

Sadie balled the handkerchief in her hands, not answering.

"Think about it. He has a good position and a nice flat. Very handsome and charming, and he has Mr. Eyre's ear."

"Mr. Eyre's ear?"

"Yes, I've seen him come out of the office. And Mr. Eyre does not suffer fools."

"Are you sweet on Mr. Eyre?" Sadie asked.

Olga lifted one brow. "Don't be daft, Sadie. The man is a roué of the first order. My father was also such a man."

"But you respect him, surely."

"Yes, I do. Definitely, but I do not desire him. I've seen how you look at Mr. Rake. I told you I do not trust him, and my fears were warranted, but you are in love with him."

"Am I?"

Olga nodded soberly. "It is a misfortune to fall in love, is it not?"

Sadie stared at the silent gramophone, wishing music soothed her the way it did Alecia. She shook her head. "Sometimes, certainly. Only time will tell what the truth is for me."

Les felt the tender skin under his eyes as he waited for the lift. He'd seen the Secret Intelligence Service doctor and he'd cleaned away the work of the hotel doctor. His nose felt better without the packing and it had stopped bleeding. He'd even avoided the double black eyes, though his head would be aching without the doctor's magic pills. Nothing appealed to him but a nap, cradled in Sadie's arms. Could he teach her to make love with her on top? That sounded marvelous, since their sex life had been going so well.

Fedor Verenich stood in the hallway outside of the Piano Suite. Usually the Russians were not obvious enough to keep a guard outside of the suite. In fact, they often left the corridor completely empty. Something had increased their paranoia. Les considered the possibility that they'd discovered the microphone, but if that were the case, Verenich probably would have already shot him where he stood.

In fact, the Russian nodded at him politely. He had no idea that Les had interrogated him after he'd been caught near the Russian Tea Rooms. Les had been careful to use a tough Cockney accent that he'd perfected for just such occasions, and of course Verenich hadn't seen him, since the police had ordered him to turn around while they spoke.

He went into his suite to find it empty. His novel had been moved, as if Sadie had been reading it. Maybe she'd finished all the magazines. She liked to read them in the bath. He checked the bath: empty. Then, he went into the bedroom. The bed was made, but slightly mussed as if heavy objects had been strewn across it and removed.

He still wore his coat. After pulling it off, he went to place it on the entryway peg and found Sadie's coat missing. However, her scarf and gloves were still there. How odd.

A light tap came on the door. He checked himself in the mirror. While he could run his hands down his hair, that was the only improvement he could make.

"Darling!" said Miss Page when he answered. "Whatever happened?"

Les blinked. Even that hurt a bit. "I defended my wife's honor and took a fist to the face for my troubles."

"Who hit you?" she gasped.

"One of the Russians. Stay away from them, Miss Page. They don't appear to respect matrimony."

"I will." The beautiful film actress gave him a little pout and stroked the fox stole lying across one shoulder. "You're giving me tea today. Did you remember?"

"Yes, of course," he forced a smile. "I'm so sorry that Sadie isn't here. Some kind of emergency with her sister."

"I understand her sister is very beautiful," Miss Page said. "I don't remember her, myself."

"She lived on the fifth floor for a month or so," Les said. "Give me a moment to order us a tray."

"Oh, you naughty thing," she said playfully. "Won't your wife mind if we are alone?"

"I promised you both a Russian lesson. I won't deny you," he said. Sadie would kill him for canceling with the star when she returned, so he didn't. "Please come in."

He led Miss Page to the white sofa in the center of the room. She sat, gracefully. Then, he wrote a note ordering tea for three, in hope of Sadie's return, and reopened the door, then slid it into the box by the lift. The floor butler checked the box every few minutes.

"Now, what should we do?" Miss Page asked, allowing her stole to slide down her arm. Underneath she wore a white silk dress with a spear point brass necklace. Her shoes had very high heels. She was much more petite than she seemed. The shoes disguised her height and the fur accessories hid the fragility of her shoulders. The makeup disguised her youth. He'd thought her in her late twenties, but now, up close, he revised her down to twenty-two.

"Let us begin," he said briskly, seating himself in the closest armchair. "How much education do you have?"

"Why?" She stroked her stole.

"Do you understand how to diagram a sentence? I wonder if I should teach you simple phrases, like polite conversation, or if you want to understand how Russian is constructed?"

"Oh, phrases, definitely. I need the accent, you know, for my role. I want to know how my mouth should look." She pursed her lips.

"Generally, I would take a firm and negative approach. No flattery, no batting of the eyes."

Miss Page followed his instructions, sitting up straight and dropping her hands into her lap. Her heavily mascaraed eyes centered on his.

"Yes, delete coyness from your vocabulary. The Russians like to say no. They enjoy drama, so use those facial expressions you do so well. But take a stand, be definite. No fluttering."

"Act like a woman, not a young girl?" she suggested.

He nodded. Unexpectedly, she stood, and began to pace the room. After three turns, she stood before him, shoulders thrown back, head at an arrogant angle.

"Say 'love me' in Russian," she demanded.

"To say 'I love you' to a man, you would say, '*Ty mne ne bezrazlichen*,'" he said.

She dropped to her knees in front of him, a move that displayed her youth as nothing else could, and held her hands out to him. A tear ran down her cheek, but throughout, she kept the proud angle in her body. "*Ty mne ne bezrazlichen*," she said, then repeated it.

He smiled and clapped. "Very nice, Miss Page."

She bounced up, wobbling a bit on her heels, then sat next to him on the armrest. "Let me tell you the scenario of the film."

An hour later, Les was exhausted as he escorted the actress from the suite. Sadie had never arrived, and while Miss Page had not attempted to make love to him, he'd much rather have spent the hour napping instead of playacting her movie scenario. He'd better go downstairs and speak to the front desk staff about his wife. To miss this she had to be doing something important. He'd had to cancel their dinner plans with the film stars, which, under ordinary circumstances, would have been a huge disappointment to Sadie.

First though, he needed to change his shirt. It was sweat-stained and crumpled from his painful adventure with the doctor. He went into the bedroom closet. Half of the contents were missing.

"Hell and the devil." He realized the importance of Sadie's coat being gone while her gloves and scarf remained. She'd left the presents he'd given her behind and taken everything else.

His fake wife had deserted him. A woman who knew what he was. *A spy.*

Lionel Dew, the night manager, was already on duty at the front desk. A stout woman in a tweed suit and pearls turned away with a handful of envelopes as Les approached him. She inclined her head and marched away.

"Did my wife hand her key in?" Les asked the impassive manager.

"One minute, sir, I will check." Dew turned around and ran his finger down the row of keys, then turned back. "Yes, sir, it is here."

Les stared at the desk. The swirled pattern of the marble top entranced him. "Then she meant to leave. Is Ivan Salter on duty yet?"

"At seven, sir. I came in early today."

"Have you heard anything about Mrs. Plash's condition?" Les asked.

"We have not seen Miss Plash as often as usual, so I expect that is a bad sign for her mother," Dew said.

Meaning it was a good sign for the hotel, not to have Emmeline Plash and her drama distracting Peter Eyre. "Very well. Is Mr. Eyre about?"

"I will see." Dew disappeared into the back for a couple of minutes, then returned and nodded at Les.

Les found Peter Eyre poking through a filing cabinet behind his massive desk, his usual cigarette wafting a thin trail of smoke through the air from its perch on the edge of the battered ashtray on his desk. Gershwin's "Rhapsody in Blue" played on a gramophone in the other corner. It was the kind of music that sped a man's heart rate, and Les wished he could turn it off.

"What?" Peter asked, frowning as he caught sight of his visitor.

"Sadie's missing."

"Meaning what?"

"She's taken some of her things. We had tea planned with Miss Page, and I can't imagine Sadie giving up time with a film star."

"I wouldn't worry about it. Women are a mercurial bunch."

"That's all you have to say? You know what's going on."

"You think the Russians took her and her clothing? More likely, she took clothes over to her sister. Mrs. Plash is at her end, and I doubt Alecia has time to do her wash."

Les gritted his teeth as the tempo of the song increased. A tinny horn blast rattled his bones. No, Sadie wasn't being helpful in the way he had hoped, bringing him hotel news. The one thing she'd seen, the Russian in the basement bathroom, hadn't come to him until it had gone through hotel management. But, damn it, he wanted her back, his headstrong, caring, fake wife. What had happened after she tended him and his broken nose? Would she have skipped her film star tea to sit with a dying woman?

He realized he hadn't spoken in a bit when the piano part of the song started up again. Before the horns could resound, he walked behind the desk and pulled the needle off the record.

"Pardon me?" Peter said. "I was listening to that."

"I can't think with it on."

"It does settle into one's bones," Eyre said, closing his file drawer and setting some papers on his desk.

Les couldn't help glancing at them sideways. Some kind of construction company bills. "Planning to wall off the tunnels?"

Eyre snarled and shoved the papers into a desk drawer and slammed it shut. "Bloody spy. Why don't you let Sadie go? She deserves better."

"I'm better off with her than without," Les said without thinking.

Eyre picked up his cigarette. "But what about her? She can't be better off with you. Let her have a divorce if that's what she wants."

"I thought you were so certain she was merely bringing her sister a change of clothing."

He shrugged. "What do I know? I'd never even met a Loudon girl until December."

"I know you don't know Sadie terribly well. What about Alecia?"

Eyre stared at the cigarette burning down between his fingers. "I flirted with her a bit, but she hadn't flowered yet. Didn't know what to do with me, and of course, part of the reason Emmeline stays in my life is because she scares off others who might attempt to make love to me."

"You're hardly a victim." His nose had started to throb again. He wondered if it was time for another one of those magic pills.

"No, never that. Laughable, really. I'll be sorry to see the old girl go, though. Mrs. Plash was something else in the old days. So was Emmeline, really. The war broke her."

"And Mrs. Plash is just old."

"We'll all be there in time. Us, our beautiful girls. Someday we'll be looked at with pity and derision." He ground out his cigarette. "If you've nothing else, I do need to make some decisions."

"Of course," Les said. "I suppose I hoped for some kind of ordinary explanation, that Sadie had left me a note at the desk or something."

"No, but you should check your microphone to be absolutely sure she's not with the Russians."

"I did that. Nothing suspicious."

"If you think she's in danger, I'll do everything I can, but you need to check Montagu Square. I'm sure that's where she is." Eyre glanced up, and Les was sure he saw his own exhaustion mirrored in the other man's eyes.

He stood and walked away, his face throbbing.

Sadie crawled out of bed on Monday morning. Olga had allowed her to stay in her room so she could sleep in a bed instead of on a sofa. Since Olga had gone down the hall to wash up, occupying the only washroom, Sadie went downstairs and made tea with what was available in the Plash shelf in the boarding house kitchen. She carried the heavy tea pot upstairs, realizing she'd gained strength in her arms and muscles after a few weeks of being a chambermaid.

Emmeline opened the door when she knocked. The woman looked knackered and had a thin brown stain down the front of her embroidered Chinese wrapper. She stepped aside and Sadie set the teapot on a trivet on the low table in front of the loveseat in the sitting room.

Emmeline gathered teacups from the sideboard. "Don't you need to dress for your shift?"

"Why should I go to work?" Sadie shrugged and poured the tea.

"Don't be stupid," the other woman said crossly. "Work gives you options, keeps you from feeling worthless."

"A few days ago I was so excited about being promoted to the next floor, but it's still the same work," Sadie grumped. "I don't see any meaning in it. It's empty."

Emmeline sat next to her and took up another teacup. "Go back to the hotel, Sadie. Any husband is better than none. You don't want to end up in limbo."

"Limbo?" Sadie asked.

"Divorced? You're too passionate to live without love and sex. No man is perfect, but at least you have someone."

"He's deceived me. Olga doesn't even think I'm really married."

"What does a Russian princess know about English law?" Emmeline asked. "Tell your Mr. Rake you think you're going to have a baby. I'm sure he'll shore up any irregularities quickly."

Sadie's mouth drooped in shock at idea of such falsehood. "But if he did it on purpose?"

Emmaline reached under the sofa and pulled out a red tartan tin of shortbread. "Who forges a special license? Who even could? There's got to be a good explanation. You need to give him a chance. He could have been fooled. We're raised to think men have all the answers, but they don't. Not about anything, really."

Sadie wasn't about to explain Les's lifestyle. "That's a depressing thought."

Emmaline opened the tin and took a piece of shortbread, then passed the tin. "I'm quite a lot older than you, Sadie, and I've done my share of disappointing men, and had them return the favor. Don't assume malevolence when incompetence might be to blame."

"But if you always look for the best in people you can be badly hurt," Sadie said. Her tea was already gone though she didn't remember drinking it. She took a piece of shortbread then handed the tin back. Behind the door, she heard a series of wheezing coughs.

"That's my mother," Emmeline said, wincing. "Poor dear. Your sister is a wonder at keeping her calm. When I go in, she wants to tell me something and becomes so agitated."

"Do you have any idea what it is?"

"No, but her life is an open book. What could there be that I don't know?"

"Does she ramble? Maybe Alecia will have some clue."

"No, she's mostly silent now. The coughing. It's pneumonia, we think. The doctor comes in, but since we can't get her out of bed, it's just settled into her lungs."

"Maybe she wants the bliss of heaven, and just can't wait any longer."

Emmeline pursed her lips. "Who can blame her?"

Sadie set down her teacup as a rap came at the door. She went to open it and found Olga, already in her coat and hat. Her supervisor frowned at her dressing gown.

"You're going to be late," Olga snapped.

"I'll change quickly. There's plenty of tea left in the pot if you want to sit with Emmeline for a minute." Sadie stared hard at Olga, hoping she'd keep company with the grieving daughter for a few minutes.

"Very well." Olga swept past her in the doorway, somehow managing, in her regal way, to keep any part of her from touching Sadie.

Sadie smirked, despite the sadness of the day. It took all kinds. Both women had a lot to teach her, even though she'd been raised to believe, like all girls did, that marriage was the attainment that mattered, and therefore, she was superior to both of them.

Except she was probably a fallen woman, a concubine. Sadie squeezed her eyes shut hard before stepping out. She went to gather her clothes and wash up. Les had a lot to answer for. It wasn't just a broken heart, he'd broken her life, too.

Chapter Eighteen

"Brandy," Les muttered, setting down his headphones. Why were the Russians discussing brandy at ten A.M. on a Monday morning? He rubbed his hands over his face. Between his runaway wife and his sore nose, he hadn't slept well.

He put the painting back in place and paced the sitting room, running associations with the word *brandy*. Nothing came to him. Finally, he forced himself to let it go because he and Robert McCall were meeting in the basement to explore the hidey holes one last time before Peter Eyre had them sealed off.

Les hoped to see Sadie somewhere in the halls, but even though he ducked into the staff lounge to make sure she'd signed in to work, he didn't see her, or Olga. The night before, he'd reconnoitered at the boarding house on Montagu Square and he'd seen her through a first floor window, so he knew she had gone there as Peter Eyre had suggested. It hadn't helped him sleep but at least he knew she was safe.

His worst fear initially had been that she'd run afoul of the Russians. He thought about that as he went through the obscure door that led to the passage under the business office on the hotel's ground floor. Could *brandy* have something to do with kidnapping?

"Smuggling!" he exclaimed aloud.

"Excuse me?" Robert McCall stepped forward, a dim, solid figure in front of the door to the room where the explosives had been found.

"Upstairs the Russians are discussing brandy. Do you think they might be talking about smuggling something into the country?"

"Like explosives?" McCall said in a sarcastic tone.

"They can buy those from the miners. They have good connections due to their rabble rousing."

"What are you thinking?"

Les pulled out his lock picks and went to work on the locked door. They needed to check all the walls for false panels like the one in the bathroom closet. "What if they are planning to bring in Mikhail Lashevich?"

"Wouldn't he be likely to come in through Hull? Why would Russians here in London be concerned with that?"

"I haven't seen anything in my drops relating to Semyon. Rather odd that I haven't heard from him." Les straightened and tucked away his picks, then opened the door.

"Is Special Branch up north monitoring his activities?"

"I'm sure. He's a known agitator."

McCall took out a notebook and pencil. "I'll check on it. Brandy, huh. What was the context?"

Les told him what he'd heard as he ran his hands along the walls.

"It sounds rather salacious," McCall said, drumming his pencil on his notebook.

"Yes, but they were making fun."

"Would they smuggle in Russian women? Prostitutes?"

"I can't imagine why. They can get plenty of those here."

"Guns?"

McCall finished his note and put his pad and pencil away, then returned to the wall. "Perhaps."

"We still have a tail on Fedor Verenich," McCall said. "I'll make sure we don't have any holes in the surveillance."

"I think Ovolensky should be tracked as well."

"You would," McCall said. "Let's check the passage. There's nothing here in the room."

Two hours later, Les was dusty and covered in sticky spider webs. "I don't think the Grand Russe is being used right now."

"No," McCall agreed, picking a long trail of ants mummified in spider webs off of his coat sleeve. "Not by the Russians. We've scared them off."

"See what you can do to watch all of the members of the entourage," Les said. "I'll listen closely and see if I can gain any sense of the time factor in this brandy situation."

"You'd best be in place upstairs then. I hear Sadie's been brought into the fold. Is she listening for you?"

Les's body seemed to sink into itself. "No, she's left me."

McCall grinned as if Les had been joking, then the smile slowly melted away. "Whatever for? That girl is silly over you. I still remember her adoring gazes at the Russian Tea Rooms."

Les failed to summon a chuckle. "I don't know. I haven't seen her. Eyre tells me that Sadie's sister might need her due to the woman she's caring for being about to die, but Sadie didn't leave a note."

"Could it have fallen underneath a table or something?"

"I'll look. I was hoping to see her around the hotel. She is working today."

McCall ran his fingers down the lines developing along the side of his mouth. "Do you want me to speak to her?"

Les clapped him on the shoulder. "No, I can handle my own domestic dramas. The truth is, we aren't really married. I don't know what the future holds."

McCall bit down on his lower lip and stretched his mouth into the rictus of a grin. "Do you think she figured it out? The special license, I mean?"

Les's feet rooted to the ground. What if? "Come upstairs with me."

McCall followed him to the service lift. A couple of waiters passed them, with curious expressions at their filthy clothing, but no one troubled them. Another one of the Russians was in the hall again, but studiously ignored them.

After Les closed the door to his suite, McCall said, "They didn't used to post a guard, did they?"

"I think it's because of Sadie, and me."

"Because Ovolensky tried to drag her into his suite?"

"Yes. Either they are trying to protect Ovolensky from himself, or Ovolensky from me."

"Yet you're the one with the broken beak," McCall said with a smirk.

"I'd like to dump him in the Thames with a bag of bricks tied to his feet," Les muttered.

"Why are we up here?" McCall surveyed the sitting room.

Les waved two fingers in the direction of the bedroom. "In here." He went into the closet and searched the drawers of the built-in chest, then swore.

"What?"

Les stared at the detective. "She took our marriage records when she left."

"She's suspicious," McCall said.

Les rubbed his forehead. His head was really starting to pound now. "I married her under the Rake name. That doesn't matter. It's the license that keeps us from being legally married."

"How would a young girl recognize the forgery?"

"Vicar's granddaughter," Les muttered. He brushed past McCall and went into the bathroom for his pills.

McCall followed him and leaned against the bathroom door while Les swallowed the gray oval pill. "Those look homemade."

"Only the doctor knows what's in them, but I could kill a bear when it's in my system," Les said. "And I don't hurt."

"Probably kill you in under a year if you keep taking them."

"They didn't give anything like this to me after my head injury," Les said. "This is just for the nose."

"Lay off as fast as can be advisable. I find getting drunk is much safer than pills."

"You're right," Les said. He shook the pill bottle. He had five more of the pills. After he tossed the bottle back in the drawer, he stared at McCall in the mirror. "Sadie is a vicar's granddaughter. She's probably seen a special license before."

"Well, bugger that," McCall said. "You were doomed from the start. Still, it might be time to move someone else into the suite and be done with your fake marriage. A certain devilish young detective comes to mind."

Les stared at McCall blankly as he lifted his coat collar like a dandy and paraded around in a half circle. "You're a disgrace."

McCall dropped his collar. "What are you going to do?"

"I didn't marry her for this assignment. She was meant to help me with the Kozyrevs."

"She isn't going to be much help now. At least, not unless you marry her for real."

"Would that be the worst thing?" Les asked.

McCall's thick reddish eyebrows rose to his hairline. "You want to be saddled with one woman for the rest of your life? A life like yours?"

Les sat on the toilet lid. "She is one to go with the flow of a man's life, up to a point. She saved me, Robert. Literally saved my life."

"Right-o." McCall leaned against the sink. "Do you love her?"

"I loved Natalia." Les cleared his throat. "I was with her in Russia. She's dead now."

"So you're capable of the emotion. I think most men in your profession are dead in this region." McCall made a circle around his heart.

Les had thought himself inoculated against the emotion after Natalia's death. Was he wrong? "Sadie's a game girl. And when I'm with her, intimately, well, there's nothing like it."

"She's very young."

"I'm just twenty-five," Les said. "I only feel older."

"All I can say is you'd better clear it with Glass if you want to marry her for real. It might be the only thing that saves your relationship, but it does put her life in danger. Plus someone can hurt you, compromise your missions, through her."

"I've already pulled her into this life. But I want to keep her safe. She's equal to it." She'd proven that, and he'd let her down with lies and subterfuge.

"I like her," McCall declared. "Maybe it's the right thing to do. She's wasted as a chambermaid. I fear for any spy with children though."

Les nodded and folded his arms over his chest. "I hear you, but healthy young bodies and all that. It might already be too late."

"I'd like to say we play a gentleman's game, but the truth is we exploit weakness to get what we need. Watch your own weakness."

Les glanced up and met McCall's eyes. He nodded and the other man pushed away from the sink.

"I'll be on my way."

"Can you take my disks to the drop?" Les asked. "Then I can stay in."

"Certainly." McCall waited while Les packaged up what he had and changed the active disk, then departed.

Les spent the rest of his afternoon listening to the Russians, wishing he could have a telephone installed to relay information instead of counting on messages sent through the floor butler and watchmen. Discussion about "brandy" continued in the Piano Suite. His ears pricked when he started to hear information about three cases. Whatever it was, there were three of them, and the information pushed the Russians into motion. Doors opened and shut as men left the suite and returned in short order. They must have gone no further than downstairs.

Then, he heard that the cases needed to be picked up in the next forty-eight hours. That did it. He needed more men in the suite to live-monitor next door. Surveillance was brutal at the best of times and one man couldn't remain vigilant around the clock. Whatever was happening with these three cases, it would be happening soon. Surely Glass could spare the manpower for a couple of days. He sent another message through the waiter who turned up with a pot of tea, an arrangement he'd requested to occur on the hour all day so he could have messages picked up. At seven P.M. a knock came at his suite door.

He was standing to answer it, hands on the headphones, when one of the Russians mentioned the West India Docks. Devil take it. The cargo was flowing in through London. After thirty seconds, when nothing more telling was said, he carefully closed up and went to open the door.

He recognized another Secret Intelligence Service agent, Bill Vall-Grandly, at the door. "Hello, old boy. Here for that game of whist you promised me." The short, rotund, yet surprisingly athletic youngest son of a family who'd made its fortune in the previous era with patent medicine, held up a bottle of brandy.

"Well done, my man," Les said, for the benefit of the Russian keeping watch in the hallway. "Just what I need to cheer me up."

Bill set the bottle down on the small table next to the door and took off his coat. "Glass sent me. Sounds like someone should be manning the headphones at all times, eh?"

"West India Docks in the next forty-eight hours," Les said. "The information keeps coming in."

"Does Glass know?"

"Not about the location. It just came in a minute ago."

"I'd better get the headphones on. Why don't you stretch your legs and have a bite to eat? We can spell each other in shifts. I'm good for at least four hours."

"I'll telephone Glass from the manager's office before I eat," Les said. "I'll stay in the hotel." He quickly shared his arrangements with Bill then left so he could make his call.

The hotel did not bustle on a Monday evening like it did toward the end of the week, though many well-dressed couples, mostly past their first youth, were drifting across the Grand Hall between the Restaurant, the Reading Room with its bar, and the Coffee Room.

Entirely unexpectedly, he saw Princess Olga and his wife exiting the Salon together in casual frocks just as he passed by.

Sadie did not look relaxed and happy like most women did after receiving high-end beauty treatments. He saw her fingernails had been freshly buffed and her hands had the sheen of lotion of them. Her mouth was tight though, and her cheeks looked wind-chapped.

"Ladies," Les said, bowing his head.

"Mr. Rake," Olga said in an imperious tone.

He turned to his wife. "Would you allow me the pleasure of escorting you to dinner? I haven't seen you all day."

She opened her mouth, then closed it again. At least her gaze didn't leave his face. She didn't turn to the Russian princess for guidance. But then, her shoulders slumped as she nodded. "I suppose we should speak."

He nodded to the other woman. "Your Serene Highness." He took his wife's arm and turned her around, then steered her toward the Grand Russe's opulent Restaurant. Sadie turned her head back and mouthed something in the Russian's direction.

She was silent at his side, not even responding to the derision in the maître d's eyes when Les asked for a table for him and a woman not dressed for the location. They were seated discreetly out of the view of most diners, behind a moveable Russian pine and fabric screen that probably kept tables with dangerous liaisons hidden from the more proper guests. Sadie seemed willing to say nothing and simply wait for their food. She kept her gaze on the dancer's image painted on the screen, his face half hidden under a turban overlaid with feathers.

"I'll order for us," he suggested, and she did nothing but incline her head.

Twenty minutes later, they had finished off a plate of stuffed mushrooms, and their main course of beef with Yorkshire Pudding and roasted potatoes was in front of them.

"Princess Olga has been very kind to you," Les said as he picked up his knife.

"Alecia has been too busy caring for Mrs. Plash to see me for more than a few minutes," Sadie said.

"Do you want to explain why you left?" Les cut into his beautifully marbled meat, but couldn't summon up the hunger to take a bite.

"As if you don't know." She popped a tiny potato, dotted with rosemary, into her mouth.

"I saw our marriage papers are missing from the room," he stated. "But you are still wearing your rings."

She finished chewing and set her utensils down. "Are we really married, Les? Or has this been a sick game all along?"

"Sometimes we make hard decisions for the good of the country," he said.

"You don't look well," she commented. "What is this life costing you?"

"We must protect England from the Bolsheviks," he said. "Look how close the danger came to us. Ovolensky tried to abduct you."

"Why does it bother you? I'm not really your wife."

"You are mine." The words startled him, as did the guttural tone that had come from his throat.

She looked surprised as well, and set down her water goblet without drinking. "Your what?"

She might be young, but she was tough. "My wife. How do you plan to prove otherwise?"

"The seal is a forgery. Olga said so."

His training kept his expression neutral. That bloody princess. She'd caught them out. "You trust her over me?"

Her sardonic smile was older than her years. "I can't imagine why." When she picked up her glass again, she drank deeply.

He let her cut into her meat before he spoke again. "We'll sort it all out. I understand you don't want to stay in the hotel while the Russians are in residence. Unfortunately, they are here for another couple of months. I'll move back to the flat as soon as I can. Why don't you go there?"

"That puts me back into your control."

"I'll be here. You still have your position and can save your earnings. That gives you freedom. Why not stay in a nice flat? You can't be comfortable on someone's lumpy sofa in a boarding house."

"I was comfortable with you, sleeping with my head on your shoulder." Her sad gaze singed his.

His own eyes burned. "I never wanted to hurt you, Sadie. You saved my life. I care about you more than I ever thought I could."

Sadie pushed her plate away. She'd eaten two bites of meat at best, not enough to keep an active girl well fed. "I told Olga I'd meet her in the Coffee Room as soon as we were finished."

"I'll go with you." He wiped his mouth and set his napkin beside his plate.

"You haven't eaten."

"Neither have you. Pull your plate back. Ten bites." He pointed at her fork.

"You as well. You need to keep your strength up."

"Chewing makes my nose hurt," he admitted.

"Dip your pudding into the meat juices and eat that," she advised briskly. "It won't be so hard to manage."

He smiled and followed her suggestion. "You always take such good care of me."

"Men are pitiful," she muttered, but managed to finish off most of her food before he had swallowed the last of his pudding and steak juices.

He finished off his single glass of wine, mindful that he had a long night ahead behind the microphone. Until the Russians slept, he would not either. "What shall we do now?"

"I told you where I am going."

"Then I will escort you, Sadie." He'd decided never to admit their marriage was false. A deceiver to the end. After gesturing a waiter over, he signed their bill to the suite and helped Sadie with her chair. Several other diners noted his damaged face with curiosity and he realized the maître d' may have been disdainful of his condition, not Sadie's clothing, when they entered initially.

The Coffee Room was just across the Grand Hall and looked to be full to capacity. The band was playing a fast piece of dance music that made Les's head pound, but he forced a smile and brought Sadie to the dance floor before she could search for the princess. She didn't smile, but followed him easily as he led her in the dance, understanding his signals almost before he chose his next step.

"Thank God," he muttered, as the band finished their song and began a slow waltz tune. He heard a nearby couple mutter in disgust but he was saved by the stately dance. It didn't jar his head. Sadie had beautiful form in his arms. He could imagine her in a ball gown from the last century, her skirts belled out as he twirled her around.

He felt a tap on his shoulder. "May I?"

Les turned his head and saw Georgy Ovolensky, smirking under his mustache. He pulled Sadie closer. "Not on your life."

Sadie's eyes grew wide and he felt her hand tremble. He twirled her away. Ovolensky smiled genially at another couple and the man offered his partner. The Russian pulled her into a smooth grip and began to dance with finesse. The un-partnered man went straight to the bar and ordered a drink, apparently grateful for the respite.

"I'm ready to leave," Sadie said into his ear.

"We've only danced half of two songs."

She glanced uneasily at the Russian. "It was enough. I don't want to be here if he is."

Les agreed, thinking he could have a nap if the chief Russian had left his room. He danced her toward the edge of the floor. "I'll put you into a taxicab. Please return to our flat instead of going back to the boarding house."

"Our flat?" she asked.

"Yes, no matter what, darling. I know that you don't want to stay here and I don't blame you. I'm sorry our exciting visit to the seventh floor has turned out so badly."

"You haven't called me that all night," she said. "Darling, I mean."

"You are my darling." He had stopped dancing, which he hadn't realized until he was bumped by another couple. "Where is your coat?"

"Oh, there's Olga. I didn't see her before." Sadie waved to the princess, who stood by the tray of food on a sideboard.

Les wondered if she was dining on that food instead of spending her money on a meal. She shouldn't be too terribly poor, however. As head of the chambermaids, she should be making more than Sadie. Perhaps she had debt from before she took the position. He spotted Sadie's coat on a chair near the food and picked it up, then approached his wife.

She chatted to Olga while he helped her into her coat.

"Sadie's things are in my room," the princess said to him after Sadie explained what he wanted her to do.

"She has the rest of her possessions at our home," he said. "She'll be fine. I'm sorry our disagreement impacted you."

Her gaze upon him was cool. "Is that what you call a forged special license? A disagreement?"

Blasted woman. At least Sadie hadn't told her he was a spy. "I will sort it out at the Archbishop's office tomorrow. If we have to re-marry, so be it."

Sadie's eyes were as cool as Olga's. But of course, she knew bet-ter than to trust him. "I'll return home for tonight, but thank you, Olga. Have a lovely evening."

Les put his hand under her elbow and escorted her out, feeling Olga's gaze stabbing at him as he walked.

"There you are, Sadie." Peter Eyre stood up from a battered arm-chair, his natural grace evident.

Sadie glanced up at the clock in the staff lounge the next morning, her hands frozen on her coat buttons. No, she wasn't late for her shift. Why was Peter Eyre here? He almost never came down. That thought was interrupted by a banging sound down the hall. "What is going on?"

"A construction project. Nothing to worry about, but stay out of the basement as much as possible today. It's going to be terribly dusty and dirty."

"I see." She hung her coat on her hook.

"One of the chambermaids just took a position as lady's maid to a guest," he said. "So you'll be moving to the fourth floor today."

"Glory," Sadie gasped. "Staff turnover is considerable here."

"Life at the Grand Russe is still shaking out," he admitted. "We've been reopened such a short time." He batted a piece of dusty spider web from his otherwise immaculate charcoal-gray sleeve.

"I'm happy to be assigned to the fourth floor."

Eyre pulled out his cigarette case. "What about the seventh? I un-derstand you aren't staying with us any longer."

"I'm sure you know what happened with Mr. Ovolensky. I don't feel safe with Russians hovering in the hallway all hours."

"I'm sorry I can't boot them out of the hotel."

"I understand. They are important guests."

"I want to." He pushed an elegant curl off of his forehead. "I'll find a reason eventually."

"I hope no one else has to be injured. Poor Les."

"I know you know who he is," Peter said softly. "In a way, it's better that they remain here so that certain people can keep an eye on them."

She stared at him. "What am I going to do? Les seems to be mul-tiple people."

He smiled. "There's a spark there between you. Don't give up."

"A spark, maybe, but danger, too."

"Given who your husband is, don't you think he reacted the way he did with Ovolensky out of sheer jealousy? He's unlikely to lose control ordinarily given his training." He pulled a cigarette out and tapped it on the case.

"I suppose I was somewhat responsible for creating the situation by flirting with Ovolensky. I never suspected he'd try to physically overpower me. I was merely trying to strike up an acquaintance to help."

"Be careful with these Russians. They are animals." Eyre smiled briskly. "Now, we're very busy the next two days. There is a diplomatic lunch taking place the next day in the first floor meeting rooms. The work going on down here today is meant to increase security."

"Very well."

"Today, have Olga show you the new floor duties. She's upstairs already. Then tomorrow I'll need you to do them double-time, then help on the first floor."

"Yes, sir."

Eyre nodded. "Very good. I'm glad we had a word."

Les unlocked the door of his flat and walked into the entryway, tired from his long day. He'd shared the findings regarding the smuggling operation at a Special Intelligence operational meeting and men were moving into the docks to keep watch. Early that morning, the Russians had received a telegram with a ship's name, and had been foolish enough to read it aloud. After the meeting, he'd been forced to meet with Glass and demand that he be furnished with a real special license to marry Sadie.

Glass had laughed merrily at that and refused. So Les had gone to Doctors Commons to obtain one himself. Then he'd gone to Montagu Square and met Sadie's sister Alecia for the first time. She'd helped him pack Sadie's belongings, although she only had a couple of minutes free from her duties. He had the brief impression that she was quieter than Sadie in every way, but intelligent and full of hidden, unspoken emotion. Not an easy woman to know in a brief encounter. Back at his flat, he set Sadie's valise on the floor by the stairs, then went to look for his wife.

His clue as to her whereabouts came when he smelled the rose bath salts hovering in the air by the radiator. He peered into the bathroom.

Sadie had her short curls piled on top of her head, held in place with a navy scarf. It made her blue eyes even bluer, like the color of the Mediterranean Sea as it laps the shore in Nice. She didn't seem to register him for a moment, then she sat up, pulling her legs in and covering her breasts with her hands.

"Don't hide yourself from me, Sadie," he said, sitting down on the edge of the tub, his hands in his overcoat pockets. "I need you."

Chapter Nineteen

Sadie stared at him but didn't move her hands. Les wanted to throw off his clothes and join her in the bathtub, but she'd have to invite him first.

"I need you too," she said. "I'm sad without you, but we aren't married."

"I'll fix everything," he promised. He took a deep breath of the rose-scented air. Rose wasn't really a Sadie-smell, she needed something lighter and more agile. Did husbands buy their wives bath salts? "Just give me time to sort out the details. I'm sorry for all the mistakes I made."

Her eyes were troubled. "Are you? Or were they just part of the job?"

He did his best to project honesty to her. But he spent his life telling lies. How did he even know what the real truth looked like anymore? "You know the answer to that. My work involves deception. But you were never my target, even if you became mixed up in the lies."

She blinked hard. "It was never about me."

He'd said it wrong. "Please don't cry. I couldn't forget about you, that girl at the inn. When I originally asked you on a date, it was not about my job. In fact, I was meant not to have a date that night."

"No?" She rolled over and perched her elbows on the edge of the tub, then dropped her chin into her hands.

Thank God. She'd moved closer to him. "Though that changed fast enough, I'm afraid. You were aiding me without realizing it. You were my cover once we came across Semyon Kozyrev."

"Why?"

"Because you became tangled in my lies, Sadie. Lies I'd told before I ever met you, in an attempt to protect myself."

"What lies?"

He wanted to run his fingers across the creamy expanse of her shoulders, test the bumps of her spine. "That I was married. I told Semyon I was married because I didn't want to go in too deep. I've never been one of those spies who gets his work done in the bedroom. And he'd offered me a woman, you see."

"You didn't want one?"

"No, not from him, a source I was developing. That's one part of my life I wanted to be pure. I didn't want to be with a woman I didn't genuinely care for. Honestly, I never even meant for you and me to become lovers." He let one of his hands dip into the tub and skimmed a finger across the bubbles. "I meant to stay away from you, but you are irresistible to me."

Tears glistened in her eyes. "I don't want to be hurt anymore. I want life to be simpler."

"It won't be," he warned. "But between us we can be honest. I can promise that. You know the truth, after all. My father married my mother deceptively. He was a spy, too, and she never knew the truth. But you do."

"Do I?" she asked, rotating her neck from side to side. "It's always shifting. Even the reason for me working at the Grand Russe."

"I don't want you to work there anymore," he said, realizing it was true. "I want us to start over as soon as I can receive an assignment change."

"Why?"

"The goal was always for you to become chambermaid on the seventh, but that can't happen now."

"I was just promoted to the fourth floor," she said, a fiery hint of pride in her eyes.

"But you can't go to the seventh. You're known to the Russians now. Ovolensky has his eye on you. You're not really safe in the hotel. Konstantin has seen you in the basement. At least we think it's him."

"You had me confused with the Kozyrevs. So many Russians."

"We should go back to concentrating on them. This London mess was a temporary assignment. Why don't you give notice tomorrow and I'll work on my superiors to transfer me north to monitor the Bolshevik agitators."

She shook her head. "Now you want me to give notice? After all Olga has done for me, after Mr. Eyre continues to promote me?"

She had a face as strong as it was lovely. "Trust me. Your place is with me."

She allowed him to take one hand in his and lever her upwards, until she stood in the tub.

"Close the door," she said. "You're making the room chilly."

While he was turned away, following orders, she wrapped a towel around herself and pulled the plug from the drain. The water gurgled down as she stepped from the tub.

He wanted her to drop the towel. To hell with modesty. He wanted all of her. Instead, he found himself staring at her, doing nothing.

"What?"

His voice was hoarse when he spoke again. "I should tell you that you are not the first woman I've lived with."

"No?" She put one hand at the top of her towel, knotted just above her breasts. The other was wrapped tightly around her waist.

He blinked hard. "Her name was Natalia. If she'd lived I might never have spoken to you."

"You loved her?"

He felt like he was choking. Swallowing hard to move the lump down, he said, "Yes, but it was a hard life in Russia. She didn't survive a long, bad winter."

"Do you prefer a Russian woman?" she whispered.

He shook his head. "No, it was just her. Like it's you, now."

"But you loved Natalia." He couldn't see Sadie in the mirror. Steam had coated the surface.

"I mourn Natalia." He mimicked her, crossing his arms. "I don't want to mourn you, living or dead. Sadie, give me a future with you. Please, I know I'm no good. I'm a liar and I'm dangerous, but I love you."

He could hardly see, but he could feel. Her arms closed around his waist. Her hair smelled sweet against his cheek. He let his tears drop onto the crown of her head as he wrapped his arms around her shoulders, trying not to crush her soft form.

When he felt like he'd regained some of his strength, he picked her up, cradling her. She kissed his neck and jaw, murmuring words of love as he carried her into the master bedroom. He wanted to hear every word and paused in the doorway, staring into her eyes. "You love me? The broken, lying mess that I am?"

"I don't see you that way. You're battered, my hero, but you're hardly done in."

He smiled and carried her toward the bed. She pulled back the coverlet and the sheet just before he set her down, her towel losing its grip on her breasts.

He knelt at the side of the bed and covered the sweetly tipped mounds with his hands. She wriggled the damp towel out from beneath her and dropped it to the floor, then giggled.

"I should know better than to do that. More work for the chambermaid."

He kicked the towel to the wall. "Don't worry about it. No chambermaid is on duty tonight."

Her lips parted as she stared up at him, impossibly lovely, her short hair scattered on his pillow. "Now what, Mr. Rake?"

"Drake," he corrected. "It's Drake, darling. When I marry you again it will be as Leslie Valentin Drake."

"I like that better," she said, reaching for him.

"I should say no," he whispered as she drew him down. "I should be honorable and wait until we are married again."

"No, you shouldn't. You should do what I want." She pressed her palms into his cheekbones and stared into his eyes. "I want you to make love to me. Something about you staring at me naked makes me crazy."

He grinned. Her fingers tunneled into his hair and he was able to kiss her in earnest. "Darling, I do love you."

"Show me," she whispered into his ear, then licked the outer contours.

He couldn't remove his clothes fast enough.

Sadie woke in dim winter light. Her hips and inner thighs felt sore, reminding her of the three times Les had made love to her through the night. She smiled and reached for him, thinking she could just manage to love him again. But no one was in the bed next to her.

She sat up and turned on the bedside light. A dent in his pillow proved he'd been there, but his side of the bed was frosty cold. She shivered, and realized she was naked. When she jumped out of bed, the only thing to cover herself with was the towel from her previous night's bath, but it was still damp. She opened his closet door and pulled out a shirt and put it on. Feeling deliciously naughty, she crept into the passage and went upstairs, but Les was nowhere to be found. He'd left her again.

She heated water for tea. Though she didn't have an alarm clock on, she knew she had plenty of time to reach the Grand Russe without being late. They'd gone to bed very early. However, she wouldn't give notice as Les had requested. Despite the night's passionate love-making, he'd left today without as much as a note. How could he still play these mysterious games?

The Grand Russe was a flurry of activity when she arrived. Peter Eyre and Olga were both in the staff lounge, firing orders to everyone that passed by.

"Sadie!" Peter called. "I need you on the first floor. Help Monica set up the meeting rooms for the government luncheon."

"Luncheon?"

"Yes." Eyre's hair drifted over his forehead in disarray. "We didn't know they were dining at the hotel today. You and Monica need to convert Meeting Room C into a dining room for sixteen. Arrange the tables into a square, commandeer dishes from the Restaurant, set the tables, lay out glasses. It's going to be a three-course meal."

"Won't the dishes come up with the food?"

Eyre's gaze moved in first one direction, then the other. "Talk to them. Find out about the menu. Get decorations. You're in charge."

"Where is Monica?" Sadie asked.

Olga stomped by. "She's on the fourth floor, doing your job. Get upstairs, girl."

"No, she needs to work on the dining arrangements," Eyre said.

"By myself?" Sadie asked.

Olga threw up her hands. "I'd better go help Monica."

Sadie finished pinning on her chambermaid cap. "Is anyone in the Restaurant at this time of day?"

"Of course," the manager said, pushing his hair out of his eyes. "Go speak to them, but make decisions quickly. There is no time. They want luncheon rather early, at exactly noon."

The next two hours passed in a whirl of action, but Sadie was pleased to see she had the room reorganized and ready for luncheon well before ten in the morning. She'd done so well that she could start with her duties on the fourth floor, so she went to look for Olga, who she'd last seen hovering in the passage outside of the government meeting room, waiting to go in to clear the tables of ashtrays and tea cups.

No one was in the passage so she cracked the door of the meeting room. She saw fifteen or so men in expensive suits, layering the air with cigarette and cigar smoke, but no uniformed maids hovering about. Where had Olga gone? Back to the fourth floor? Down to the basement? She didn't want to leave this floor without permission with all of the important people around. There were a couple more meeting rooms on the floor so she decided to check them for her supervisor.

When she opened the first door on the opposite side of the passage the room was completely empty. Next, she tried the door to the room just past the occupied meeting room. At first, she thought that was empty, but then she heard a rustling sound.

She pushed the door open wide and went in. A man was kneeling on the floor, the upper fourth of his body inside a built-in cabinet on the outer wall nearest to the wall adjoining the next meeting room.

He didn't wear the red uniform trousers of the Grand Russe Hotel employees, but dark tailored ones. Her palms itched as she considered how to react. She couldn't help but remember the bomb story from the command performance the month before.

Screw up your courage, Sadie. "Hello?" she called out. No response. "Are you supposed to be in here?"

Slowly, the man came out from the cabinet. He turned, exposing long canine teeth. She recognized the dark hair and even darker eyes. His name was Verenich, and he was one of the Russians.

Heart pounding, she backed up into the open doorway. "You need to leave," she told him. "I'll call security."

He sneered at her, then turned back to whatever he was doing. She knew she couldn't overpower him. She needed Les. No one was around except the waiters serving at the meeting and she couldn't disrupt it.

Running down the hall, she took the steps to the ground floor two at a time, then walked as quickly as she dared to the reception desk.

Hugh Moth was on duty and thankfully wasn't helping guests. "Send someone to get my husband to the first floor," she cried. "There's a Russian doing something next to the government meeting room."

"What?" he asked.

She wanted to shake him. "Send someone to fetch Les! He'll know what to do."

Peter Eyre appeared behind the counter. "What is the problem, Sadie?"

"That Russian Verenich is in the room next to where the meeting is going on. What if he's setting up a bomb?"

Eyre stared at her for half a second, then picked up the telephone and demanded to be connected to Detective Inspector Dent at Special Branch. Hugh Moth snapped his fingers at a bellboy and sent him to the seventh floor. Sadie waved over the hall porter.

"Is anyone from hotel staff on the first floor?" Eyre asked her after he set down the telephone.

"I was only looking for Olga. I didn't find her. There are a couple of waiters in the meeting room."

Eyre shook his head from side to side. "I wish I had a gun."

"I thought you had to be nice to the Russians."

Eyre gritted his teeth. "I want to be done with those bastards." He lifted the hinged part of the desk so he could step out, and crossed to the other side. "Come with me, Sadie. Show me."

"Oh, sir, you shouldn't," Hugh Moth protested.

"My hotel might be in danger, along with all the souls in it," Eyre said. "I have to."

He strode briskly away. Sadie hesitated for a moment, her body trembling like a railway platform just as the train comes in. She followed Eyre, unable to stop herself, wishing Les would appear. He'd know what to do.

Eyre took the steps two at a time. She'd never realized he had an athletic side. He'd seemed the sort to always have a cigarette and a glass of champagne in his hand, but he wasn't breathing hard when he crested the top of the stairs. She followed him down the passage. He put a finger to his mouth when he saw the two waiters lounging there.

"Has anyone gone by since Sadie left?" he asked them.

The two men shook their heads. That meant the Russian was still in there.

"Past the room the ministers are in," she said. "He was in the cabinet just to the right of the window."

Eyre stopped just outside of the door. "I don't know what's going to happen. Stay back."

She clenched her fists to stop the shaking, then picked up a serving tray that was covered in used glasses and gently dumped them on the floor. She could use it as a weapon or a shield. Eyre would forgive her for staining the carpet under the circumstances. Staying two steps behind the hotel manager, she attempted to peer around his broad shoulders.

"You there," Eyre said, stepping briskly toward the room. "Get out of that cabinet."

She could finally see. Verenich was still half-buried in the open cabinet. Eyre grunted his displeasure and went directly up to the man.

Sadie gasped as Eyre reached into the cabinet and wrapped his arm around the Russian's neck, so that his elbow must have gone in front of the man's windpipe. She rushed to his side, holding the silver tray high, ready to bash the man's head in if necessary.

Eyre wrenched the man out of the cabinet. Verenich jerked back. He hit his head on the ceiling of the cabinet, then fell to the carpet. Eyre reached over him and ripped out a microphone on a wire. He threw it across the room, then pulled out a small gramophone. Sadie recognized the setup as something similar to that of Les's on the seventh floor.

"There's probably a hole in the wall," she said.

Verenich lifted his head and moved his arms. He was obviously about to stand. She slammed her tray into the back of his skull and he collapsed onto the carpet again.

Eyre chuckled as he leaned over the prone body and peered into the cabinet. "You are correct."

Running footsteps sounded in the passage. Sadie turned and saw Detective Inspector Dent, who she'd seen before meeting with Eyre in his office, and two men in dark suits and gray overcoats, who had the look of the police.

"What's happened?" Dent asked, gasping.

"He was recording the government session," Sadie said. "I knocked him out."

Eyre patted Sadie on the shoulder. "We have a new Boudica at the Grand Russe."

Sadie knew Les had instructed her to give notice, but at that moment, she wanted to pledge herself to the hotel's service forever. Peter Eyre's bravery made him a man she'd want to follow anywhere. And where was her husband?

"This must be the ship," Robert McCall said, pointing up at the enormous vessel that they had watched dock earlier in the morning. "It's the only one that's come in during the past twenty-four hours."

So far, no one had departed and they'd had a miserable morning watching from under the dripping eaves of a warehouse across from the dock. Finally, they saw a man coming their way, dressed in a heavy coat, a cap pulled down low. Something about his bulk seemed familiar, though. And his shoes were Russian.

Les swore and swiped at his neck. "Recognize that man?"

McCall followed the movement of Les's chin. "I don't know his name."

"Neither do I, but I've seen him on the seventh. I wonder who he is meeting."

"Would you recognize Mikhail Lashevich?"

"If he looks anything like his daughter," Les said. "She's a rare kind of beauty. Like a Venus fly trap."

"We'll see who comes down from the ship, then arrest and interrogate them all," McCall said. "You'll want to leave before we start that phase of the operation."

"I definitely don't want Ovolensky's man to see me here," Les agreed.

They waited two hours more before men came from the ship. There were four youths. Les didn't recognize any of them. They were all too young to be Lashevich, which only gave him more ammunition with which to persuade Glass to send him north again, to discover what was going on with the Russian assassin.

Les slinked back into the warehouse shadows as McCall's men swung into action, then left for Special Branch, ready to be involved in the interrogations. It would be a very long day, but at least the men hadn't entered London undetected. The operation in the Grand Russe Hotel had been a success in this instance.

Sadie's wrist ached from her determined swinging of her serving tray weapon that morning. She sat in an elderly armchair in the staff room, next to Olga.

"What are you going to do now?" her supervisor asked, closing the cover of a tattered magazine.

"Go back to the flat and pack." Sadie sniffed. "Les missed everything that happened today. What if it had been a bomb again? I could have died and he still wouldn't know about it."

"His company must have called him into an all-day meeting," Olga said. "He's in management now, right? All they do is attend meetings."

"He should have left a message. Or he could have called the hotel and relayed his whereabouts to me. I'm tired of this disappearing act," Sadie said. "I'm done with it."

"You're tired and overreacting," Olga said. "It's been a terribly frightening day. I still can't believe you followed Peter into that room."

"Someone had to help him. He should sack Hugh Moth for cowardice. Where were you?" Sadie asked. "I looked for you before I ever went downstairs."

Olga stared at the wall then shook her head. "I went to the fourth floor. One of the guests had spilled the contents of their suitcase across the floor just in front of the elevator. Some very personal items, including a glass jar of lotion. It was a mess."

"Ah," Sadie said. "Not nearly as exciting as a Russian bugging a British government meeting."

"The life of a chambermaid isn't glamorous," Olga said. Her laugh sounded forced.

"It is sometimes." Sadie flexed her wrist and groaned. "I'm going to soak my arm in a hot bubble bath before I pack, though."

"Are you going to move in with me?"

"Probably. Are you going straight to Montagu Square?"

"I was supposed to measure the Coffee Room," Olga said, pulling a measuring tape from her apron pocket. "I'm curating an exhibit for the space."

"I hadn't heard about that."

"Russian art," Olga said, tucking the measuring tape away again. "Although I don't know if Peter will want to do it now."

"He can't abandon the Russian theme," Sadie said. "It's imbedded into the hotel. I doubt he'll cancel it."

Olga yawned, hiding her mouth with her hand. "Don't come to the boarding house until evening, then. Take your time and enjoy your privacy. I'll still be here for a while."

Sadie nodded. "I'll take my time at Primrose Hill. Since Les is missing anyway, he won't know that I'm enjoying his bathtub again."

"Why are you so insistent on being hurt, Sadie?" Olga asked. "This man of yours is not perfect, but you have a nice roof over your head from all reports, and his company obviously values him. If he's willing to marry you again, legally this time, what's the point in making yourself miserable?"

"It's because I love him that I need to stand my ground," she said. "It's too easy to let him do whatever he likes. If I just go along with him because I love him, I'll lose myself. He wants me to give notice here."

Olga raised her fine, pale eyebrows. "That's an enormous change."

"I know," Sadie said. "I'd be so isolated. We might leave London."

"Oh," Olga said. "That really is a change. Is he being transferred?"

"Maybe."

"That could be why he's been gone all day. He's making preparations."

Sadie nodded. "You're right. I don't want to leave London and my position, and my sister, unless I'm sure everything is honest and aboveboard. I need to know I can trust my husband."

Olga sighed. "It's a rare woman who gets to make that decision twice. Usually we marry once and are stuck with the consequences."

"I wonder how many women would marry the same man again, given the opportunity to walk away," Sadie mused.

Olga's attention had shifted. Sadie saw Peter Eyre had entered the room. He nodded when he saw the two women. Sadie stood and offered him her chair.

"I'm about to leave," she said.

Eyre smiled and lowered himself to the chair. He patted his coat as if looking for his cigarette case, but didn't reach into his pocket.

"Are we still going to do the art exhibit?" Olga asked.

Eyre rubbed his chin. "That's your vanity project, Princess. I won't stop you. But I also can't bring myself to care."

"None of the artists represented will be Bolsheviks," Olga said. "We're representing the oppressed, not the oppressors."

"Very well, then. You'd better get to work." He nodded at her.

Olga stood up, all her vitality restored. She nodded at Sadie then left the room.

Eyre gestured to the chair the princess had vacated. "Will you sit?"

Sadie sat down in the opposite chair.

"Did you ever hear what happened to your husband today? I haven't seen him."

"No," Sadie admitted. "He's vanished."

"Strange," Eyre said. "I don't understand the work he does. He has to stay in the shadows. That's a hard thing to do. Never recognized, rarely rewarded."

"What if it had been a bomb, Mr. Eyre? We might all have been killed."

"You and I might have been killed, attacking Verenich like that," Eyre said. "We were lucky to catch him red-handed with his equipment. No one will doubt us. Verenich will be expelled from the country. We'll probably get formal letters of thanks from Whitehall."

"As you say." Sadie couldn't summon any excitement at the thought of the prime minister learning her name. She wanted to know where her husband was. Well, not her husband really. She'd expected some grand gesture after their lovemaking, a new special license, something. Not this lack of anything, this silence. "Are you going to boot the rest of Ovolensky's party from the hotel?"

"I've been asked not to." Eyre smiled ironically. "We've been doing such a good job of keeping them in check, you see. I understand your husband's surveillance has been very successful, though I don't know the details of the latest operation."

"Neither of us does," Sadie said. "I'm going to return to Les's flat. He's told me to stay away from the seventh floor."

"Yes, don't go near Ovolensky. It's not worth the risk given what happened. It's obvious I need to hire more daytime security after today. You shouldn't have been my backup. Those waiters were worthless, but what do I expect from waiters?"

"Hire ex-soldiers," Sadie said. "They'd be better in a fight."

Eyre chuckled. "It never occurred to me to hire staff who'd be good in a fight, but we bought ourselves a packet of trouble when we renamed the place the Grand Russe."

"At least you haven't had any starlets murdered since the grand reopening," Sadie said.

"Not yet," Eyre said with an edge of desperate cheer. "Give us time. We have enough film types coming through here."

Chapter Twenty

Sadie finished washing her dishes and dried them, then carefully tucked them away in the cupboard. Dinner had been cheese on toast, given that she hadn't had a reason to do any food shopping. Now, though, it was getting late and she needed to make a decision. She could listen to Olga and Emmeline, or even Mr. Eyre, who said to stick with Les. Her instincts told her to hold her ground and leave the man who'd made love to her then disappeared before she'd even woken up the next morning. He'd been unavailable for over twelve hours now.

But, instead of going to pack what little was left of hers in the flat, she went and took that bubble bath she'd promised herself, and soaked her sore wrist until the water went cold. Only after that would she find her luggage and survey the drawers in the guest room. And didn't that say it all, that she'd never moved her things into Les's bedroom? Maybe she should, and take possession instead of giving up.

She was just finished bathing when she heard a knock at the front door. Quickly, she threw her dress over her head and pulled it down her body. It wouldn't be Les. He wouldn't knock. Should she risk opening it? What if the Russians had found her? She told herself not to be silly. That would require someone having followed her home and waiting for a couple of hours before knocking. Besides, the building had a locked front door. It had to be one of the neighbors, hoping to borrow an egg or something.

Nonetheless, she reached for the sharp letter opener on the hallway table and concealed it in her sleeve before opening the door. She didn't recognize the man standing there.

"Mrs. Rake?" he inquired politely.

"Yes?" She clutched her hands together behind her back, all too aware that she had nothing on under her dress.

He handed her a box with a florist's name emblazoned on it, and expensive-looking envelopes in two different sizes.

"Thank you," she said, confused, then shut the door and locked it. She took the items upstairs to the kitchen. When she cut the string on the box, she found a dozen hothouse roses, a truly extravagant purchase. A small card lay atop the stems. She opened it and squealed in delight.

"Sadie, darling, will you marry me?" she read aloud, then clasped the card to her heart.

She used the letter opener to cut open the envelopes. The larger held a special license, which appeared to have the proper seal affixed to it. The other held a wedding invitation. To her own wedding! At the same place as the first one had been, it was scheduled for tomorrow.

"He's not wasting any time," she muttered to herself, then laughed aloud. He'd been missing all day because he'd been making arrangements. Oh, Les. He did love her.

She picked up her roses and danced with them around the room, humming to herself. What was she going to wear? She couldn't ask Emmeline for help under the circumstances. No, she'd need to find something in a shop during her lunch hour the next day. She was finally going to be Mrs. Drake. All thoughts of packing vanished.

Late that night, Les paced in the passage outside of the interrogation room at the police station. When he reached the far end he saw Glass come out of the stairwell.

"What's the news?" the section head asked.

"Blank stares where Mikhail Lashevich is concerned," Les said. "But I'm not convinced we can't get a lead on Konstantin."

"You've been out of pocket all day and missed some mischief at the Grand Russe." Glass flashed him a quick, roguish smile.

"Sadie?" Les asked, fear gripping his throat.

"A real heroine. Clocked Fedor Verenich in the head."

Les felt cold dread. "She was in danger? Hell. I told her to give notice."

Glass raised his eyebrows. "What about our plan to use her?"

"I want a transfer," Les said flatly. "Send us back up north."

Glass lifted his eyebrows. "What's this about?"

"I can't lose Sadie. I want a real marriage, not the illusion my parents had. We need a fresh start."

Glass twisted his lips. He knew Valentin Drake's service history. "Are you hoping she'll be a full partner in your work?"

"That's up to you. But every day that passes shows me something new about her. How did she end up fighting a Russian? Did Ovolensky attempt to abduct her again?"

"No, Verenich was bugging the government meeting at the hotel. She and Peter Eyre pulled the plug on his operation."

"By themselves?"

Glass shrugged. "I know. A foolhardy couple. Maybe they are best separated before they do something similar again."

Les ran his thumb and forefinger down his face. "I can just imagine what they might do if the hotel was in danger again."

"Dent said she was looking for you before she ran after Eyre."

"I was at the docks instead of at her side." Just like his father, far away during his wife's crisis. Les's cheek twitched. "Listen, Glass, I think London is too much for us right now. Too complicated. Between her work and mine, the constant way the Grand Russe gathers trouble to itself, we can go days hardly seeing each other. I don't want that anymore."

"Every time one of my operatives falls in love it's the same way," Glass said. "I'm never going to be stupid enough to do it. Too distracting."

"I wasn't expecting love," Les admitted. "Just a bit of flirtation, a good time with a pretty girl. How it came to this I can't say."

"You fell into her bed," Glass said. "Girl like that? You were all done in from that moment."

Les smiled. "I couldn't stay away despite my best efforts."

"She's one in a million," Glass said, scratching the scar in his eyebrow. "I'll think about our operational needs."

The door to the observation room opened and Robert McCall poked his head out. "We're getting into the Konstantin business now."

"You will deport me no matter what I say," Ovolensky's man Fedor was saying as Les and Glass walked behind the two-way mirror in the observation room. "There is no point in me saying anything."

"You're wrong," Detective Inspector Dent, down to his shirtsleeves, said. "I don't have to send you back to Moscow in one piece." Casually, he pulled a set of brass knuckles from a trouser pocket and fitted them into his fist.

Glass chuckled. "Man makes a good point."

"Now, what do you know about Konstantin?" Dent asked casually.

"Common name," Fedor sneered.

"The bomber that tried to blow you and your friends up last month," Dent said.

"Obviously he's no friend of my organization," Fedor said.

"He's a Bolshie from all reports. Likes to lurk in the Grand Russe basement. Your friends from the docks bringing him supplies? Interesting collection of ammunition we found in one of the cargo holds."

Fedor said nothing. Dent, expressionless, took careful aim at the Russian's face, pulling back his elbow. When he began the swing, Fedor flinched and jerked his head back. Dent caught him on the shoulder as he went over backward, his chair legs upending. The Russian shrieked when his full weight fell on his bound hands underneath his back and the chair. Dent stood and walked around the table, then stood over him.

"Konstantin," he said.

"Help me up," Fedor whispered in agony.

"Konstantin."

"Novikov," Fedor wheezed. "That is his surname. That is all I know."

Les frowned and turned to Glass. "I've heard that name recently."

Glass shook his head. "Does it seem significant to you?"

In front of them, Dent had placed his foot on Fedor's chest and pressed down. Fedor shrieked.

"Where is he?" Dent asked. "Konstantin Novikov. Where is his hidey hole these days?"

Fedor wheezed. "I don't know."

Dent pressed again and repeated his question.

"He has a room near the Natural History Museum."

"He's fled from there," Dent said.

"No," Fedor shrieked as Dent pushed in his heel again. "It's a new room."

"These men you picked up today. Are they part of Konstantin's organization?"

"No, they were going north to work in the mines."

Dent grunted. "Labor agitators, not Konstantin's kind of business. What about the ammunition?"

Fedor spoke in labored breaths. "Separate deal. Not Konstantin. Only bombs. All bombs with him. Very specialized."

Dent pulled his foot from Fedor's chest. The Russian rocked his body and rolled to his side, coughing. Dent pulled a knife from his pocket and flipped the blade open. Fedor's eyes tracked the movement.

"He's in his room every night at ten," Fedor wheezed. "Untie me."

"The address?" Dent asked crisply.

After the Russian gave it, Dent sliced through the ropes binding his hands to the chair with one flick of his knife. He held the knife over Fedor's face. Fear flared in the Russian's eyes. Les knew he was reflecting on the obvious sharpness of the blade.

Without speaking further, Dent stepped around the man and left the room. Wisely, Fedor stayed on the floor, sweat, tears, and snot beading on his face.

McCall and Dent stepped into the observation room and faced the two Secret Intelligence Service men.

"Ten P.M.," Dent said.

Les checked his watch. "It's after that now."

"Go anyway," Glass said. "Take McCall."

The police detective nodded and Les followed him out of the room. McCall requisitioned a car and they drove through the wet, dark streets toward the Natural History Museum.

"What are you thinking?" McCall asked.

"Well after ten now."

"Understood. What else?"

"I'm thinking about remarrying Sadie tomorrow night," Les said. "Then I'll be leg-shackled for real."

"I meant about Konstantin."

Thinking about Sadie reminded Les where he had heard the name Novikov before. Princess Olga's surname was Novikov. "Devil it," he muttered.

"What?"

"I've found our link between Konstantin and the Grand Russe."

McCall whistled. "What is it?"

"The Russian princess who supervises the chambermaids. Her name is Novikov. Olga Novikov."

"That can't be right," McCall said, pausing to let a crowd of revelers cross the street. "A Russian princess and a Bolshevik bomber?"

"It may be nothing, but it's quite a coincidence. Konstantin could be using a false name."

"What about the princess?"

"Odd that she uses the masculine form of her name, but she doesn't like being called by her title either. Has a mind of her own."

"A princess could have a mad relative. That's common, right?"

"I suppose."

"A savant of bombs."

"Precisely."

"Madness runs in royal families," McCall repeated. "All that inbreeding."

"Quite."

"Have to bring her in for questioning," McCall mused. "A princess. That's going to be rough. We'll have to consult with the higher-ups."

"With any luck we'll get Konstantin tonight, save ourselves the trouble."

"Or be blown up," McCall said cheerfully. "And right before your wedding, too. Bloody bad luck, I call it."

"Bastard," Les muttered. "I've put Sadie through enough for one week."

They parked a block away from the building of modern studio flats where Konstantin was supposedly staying, then surveyed the windows. Les counted up and across. "If that's the one, it doesn't look like anyone is home."

"It's nearly gone eleven," McCall said. "Sleeping? Out carousing?"

"This may be his meeting place. He may not actually live here. Fedor might have lied, too."

"Let's break in through the back," McCall said. "See what there is to see."

Les picked the back door lock. The building was silent except for one crying infant as they ascended the steps. They verified the number on the door of Konstantin's flat. McCall pulled out a revolver while Les went to work on the lock. When he was done, he opened the door silently.

Light from a street lamp illuminated the room through the thin curtain. The space was sparsely furnished. No bed.

"A meeting place only," McCall said.

Les pointed him toward the left, where there was a door, while he checked the right wall. The door opened to an empty closet. There was nothing else.

"Nothing really to search," McCall said.

"No, just surveillance. Hopefully we can pick him up tomorrow at ten."

"Not you, lad. You'll be thrusting your way down the River Drake."

Les grimaced. "I don't know that Glass will see it that way."

"You'll get the night off, boyo. Glass can come with me himself. He'll enjoy a spot of my company."

Les chuckled. "Let's depart before we're noticed. We don't want anyone getting wind of us."

McCall nodded and they left, relocking the door, and crept down the stairs. They left undetected.

At the end of the work day on Thursday, Olga pulled Sadie aside and handed her a package. "This is a hand-me-down from one of my wealthier relatives. You should wear it tonight."

Bemused, Sadie followed Olga into one of the three basement bathrooms that were still in use after the tunnel discovery, and opened the package. She opened the string and paper, her eyes opening when she uncovered the delicate lace.

"Chanel," Olga said with satisfaction.

"Don't you want to save it for your own wedding?" Sadie touched a finger to the bodice.

Olga smiled. "You aren't likely to damage the dress when you'll only be wearing it for a single evening."

Sadie threw her arms around Olga and kissed her soundly on the cheek. "I knew we were friends. I'll take good care of it."

An hour later, they arrived at the chapel after a quick stop at Primrose Hill to retrieve her roses. Les waited inside. He wore a slim navy suit and a natty tie. Sadie could tell he was nervous, because he held himself even more motionless than usual. She reached for his hand, finding it icy cold, and squeezed. He smiled at her.

The space looked much the same, except a row of candles were lit across the altar, giving the room a hushed feeling. The minister left the altar area, where guests waited, and came up to them.

246 • *Heather Hiestand*

"Where are your friends?" Sadie asked curiously, after Les had shaken the minister's hand.

Alecia, Emmeline Plash and Olga had all turned up for her wedding, but the party was somewhat bereft of men, the opposite of her first ceremony. Ivan Salter was required at the Grand Russe, as was Peter Eyre. She hadn't invited her grandfather because she didn't want him to know she hadn't been really married all this time. Oddly enough, Teddy Fortress and his wife had appeared, and Teddy offered to act as best man.

"Are you ready for a photograph?" asked the photographer Les had arranged. A large chap with brown hair and wire rimmed glasses, he smiled at her in a professional manner.

The door to the chapel swung open and Peter Eyre and Ivan Salter rushed in, bringing the chill February night with them just as the room had warmed up. Alecia cried out with joy and gave her fiancé a hug. Emmeline smiled at Peter.

"Our original wedding guests had to work," Les said, smiling at Sadie. "I was given special dispensation because of my prescheduled event."

"What was more important than our wedding?" Sadie asked, wondering if the Grand Russe was in danger again.

"They are trying to catch the man you saw in the basement of the hotel that day. The best chance is at ten tonight."

Sadie shivered. "I hope no one is injured this time." She touched Les's cheek. The swelling around his nose had just started to subside.

"There is always a risk in this kind of work. Are you sure you want to marry me?"

Sadie smiled at him as the photographer cleared his throat. "I have to marry you. I love you too much to stay away."

"Well, then, let's have that photograph. Everyone crowd around. It will take the attention off my battered face."

They all crowded into a group photograph, then broke into pairings that the photographer posed in front of a wide navy and gold banner that hung down one wall. Family only, then Les, Sadie, Teddy Fortress and Alecia, then finally, just Les and Sadie. She saw Les was beaming just as delightedly as she was.

When they were finished taking the photographs, the minister rubbed his hands together. "Let's do this properly, shall we?"

Les winked at the man. "Checked the special license this time?"

The minister tucked a finger into his clerical collar. "You won't fool me twice."

Sadie suspected the man was in the pay of Secret Intelligence, but she didn't care as long as the wedding was legal this time. Olga had assured her the paperwork looked right. She'd allow him to marry them a second time.

Les took her hand and they stepped in front of the altar. Alecia took Sadie's bouquet from her. The minister stood in front of them. "Life has given the two of you a second chance. For myself, I am happy to see two people I married once be willing to go through the ceremony again. It gives me hope for a blessed future for you both."

Sadie nodded. Les looked solemn now, as he stared into her eyes. They repeated the simple vows and were married again, under his real name.

Sadie laughed when it was over. "We can do this again next month!"

Everyone chuckled, and Teddy Fortress added, "I hope you don't mind, but I'm going to use this scenario in my next film! You must tell me what went wrong the first time."

Sadie smiled and mimicked buttoning her lips.

After the wedding, Peter Eyre invited the group to return to the Grand Russe.

Sadie gasped when he directed them into the Coffee Room. The usual crowd had been cleared out, and the sideboard held only champagne, lemonade, and a beautiful two-tier wedding cake decorated with sugared lemon slices.

"It's a special family recipe," Eyre said, smiling at her. "I'm glad you were part of the Grand Russe family, Sadie, even if it was only for a short time."

"Me too," she said, clasping his offered hand. "You're a good man, Peter Eyre."

He winked at her then lifted his hand to the band. A female vocalist Sadie didn't recognize walked between the musicians and smiled at the small crowd. The musicians began the opening bars of the popular song, "Tea for Two" and the woman began to sing.

Les bowed to Sadie and took her hand. They danced alone together for half of the song as their guests watched, then Eyre took Emmeline's hand and joined them. Soon, everyone danced but Olga, who watched Sadie and Les with a wistful smile drifting around her lips while she drank champagne.

Sadie listened to the lyrics, about the happiness of raising a family together, and wondered if that would truly be the life they lived. Would glamor, and danger, be followed by that baby boy and girl? She had no idea, but she happily committed herself to the adventure.

After an hour of dancing, followed by champagne and cake, Sadie lounged happily, perched on Les's knee, and watched the others dance. About eleven-thirty, she felt her new husband stiffen, and she glanced away from the sight of Ivan and Olga dancing the polka together to see men at the door. She recognized her original wedding guests, looking worn out and not party-ready. Lord Walling desperately needed a shave and Robbie O'Donnell's suit had wilted around his stocky frame.

Eyre walked up and bent over Les's ear. "You can meet in my office."

Sadie stood so that Les could greet the guests. Surprisingly, he walked them over to the sideboard. The waiter served them both champagne and cake. Then, Les gestured to Sadie, holding her hand as they left the party and went to Eyre's office. The new arrivals followed, holding their glasses and plates.

Peter Eyre unlocked his door then turned to the men. "Is this anything I should stay for?"

Lord Walling shook his head. "No good news, I'm afraid. Konstantin slipped the knot yet again."

Eyre put his hands on his hips. "I'm sorry to hear that."

"We'll get him next time." The man's face transformed with a surprisingly boyish, naughty smile. "I guarantee it."

Eyre nodded and departed. The tall man went behind the desk and sat down. Les gestured Sadie and Robbie to the other chairs and leaned against the wall.

The tall man rubbed his chin. "I'm Walling, Mrs. Drake, as you know. But I'm also known as Glass, in the Service."

"Yes, my lord," Sadie said, shocked.

"You know Detective McCall from Special Branch?"

"Not under that name, my lord."

"Call me Glass, like everyone else in the Service," he said evenly. She nodded.

"Can you speak in a convincing Russian accent?" Glass asked.

She turned to Les, who held out his hand to her. "Give it a try."

"But we never had time for the lessons," she protested, then in a smaller voice said, "I'd like the samovar, please," attempting to thicken her voice and roll her Rs like Olga would.

Glass shook his head sadly. "You'll have to play an Englishwoman after all."

"I can practice," Sadie said. "I didn't know what you needed, or really, that I needed to do anything."

"Given your issue with Georgy Ovolensky, you aren't going to be able to stay here," Glass said. "But Peter Eyre knows the way the wind blows these days, and I think we can get what we need from him."

"Where does that leave us?" Les asked.

Glass stroked his chin again. "You will be moving to the Newcastle area to monitor labor unrest."

"Glory," Sadie exclaimed.

"You remember the Russian assassin's daughter you met in Hull, Mrs. Drake?"

"Yes. Irina Kozyrev."

"We'll want a relationship there. Your job is to befriend the wives of labor leaders because some of the best intelligence comes from loose-lipped wives."

Les smiled. "That shouldn't be a problem. My wife is one who knows how to keep a secret."

"I'm going to be a spy?" Sadie asked.

Glass nodded. "Will you serve your country?"

She nodded. "Of course, sir. As long as I can be with Les."

"That goes without saying. There's no point in separating newlyweds unless it's due to wartime."

"Glory," Sadie repeated. "We really are married this time."

Les chuckled as Glass said, "I am sorry about that, Mrs. Drake. But you're one of us now. No need to tell anyone you are doing anything but enjoying being a wife, of course."

"No, sir. I was never the most dedicated chambermaid. My friends are aware of how much I wanted to be Mrs. Drake and take care of my husband and home. They won't be suspicious."

"Excellent," Glass said. He reached into his overcoat and pulled out a slim leather portfolio, then handed it to Les.

Her new husband opened it up and then raised his eyebrows. "Train tickets and arrangements for a hotel in Cornwall?"

"A honeymoon?" Sadie squealed.

"Training," Glass corrected. "You'll need to learn the basics of weapon management and hand-to-hand combat, Mrs. Drake, along with the basics of spycraft. A month of hard work should do it, then you'll be off to the north before spring."

She shook her head. "You're not just a husband, darling, you're a calling all of your own."

Les nodded. "I couldn't have found a better woman to share my life with."

She jumped out of her chair and wrapped her arms around him. "I never thought, when we first came to stay at the Grand Russe, that I'd be so eager to leave. But I am."

"Tomorrow, darling. Let's have a proper wedding night first at our flat."

Sadie blushed, and Les saluted the other two men. "If you don't mind."

McCall and Glass both jumped to their feet as Les escorted Sadie out the door. Glass held up his champagne glass to them both. "To an abundant and exciting future."

McCall grinned and lifted his own glass. "May you live and may you wear it out!"

Sadie gasped as Les laughed uproariously. "You Irish bastard." He shook both men's hands, and McCall bussed Sadie on the cheek, then Les all but hauled her from the room.

Sadie leaned against the other side of the wall and put her hands to her cheeks. "I'm still blushing."

Les stepped very close to her and kissed the top of her head. "It won't be an ordinary life."

She ran her hands from his shoulders to his waist. "I wouldn't have it any other way. I'll marry you again in Newcastle if I have to."

"Maybe it can be arranged," he said with a wink. "Anything can happen at a wedding."

Keep reading for a special sneak preview of the next Grand Russe Hotel novel, Lady Be Good, available in September 2017!

And don't miss the first in the series, *If I Had You*, on sale now, along with all of Heather Hiestand's Redcakes series:

The Marquess of Cake
One Taste of Scandal
His Wicked Smile
The Kidnapped Bride
Christmas Delights
Wedding Matilda
Trifling Favors

Chapter One

Though Lord Walling was his true title, some days it served as an alias. Douglas "Glass" Childers, Viscount Walling, reflected on the irony of his new posting as he surveyed the Artists Suite on the seventh floor of the glorious Grand Russe Hotel. His Hermès steamer trunk, shoe case, and vanity case were piled against the wall between the entryway and the sitting room, along with his Louis Vuitton hat box and a couple of *porte-documents voyage*. All of the accoutrements of the modern travelling nobleman, whether he was a spy or not. He had only needed to transport his luggage a short distance; from Knightsbridge, in fact, where he lived just below Hyde Park.

Not that he liked people to know that. As far as his network of agents was concerned, he worked and possibly even lived, out of a one-bedroom flat in Cosway Street, Marylebone.

"Nice digs, eh?" said Bill Vall-Grandly, one of his operatives. He'd been posted here for a few days, and his less impressive luggage waited just inside the suite door.

For now, Glass's usual activities were curtailed due to the threat to national security presented by certain hotel guests. Higher priorities prevailed and he had to take his place as a spy instead of a spymaster. Surveillance came first. "Indeed. Show me the operation."

Vall-Grandly, a rotund man with a kindly air who nonetheless possessed the steely nerves and stamina required of intelligence work, went to the inside wall of the sitting room and found the clasp holding a painting against the wall. As he opened it, he said, "Behind this is a shelf created by Secret Service technicians. It holds our listening equipment." He pulled on the headset for a moment to ensure that the recording device trained on the Russian trade delegation next door was working properly, then pointed out the features to Glass.

Normally, Glass supervised secret agents, rather than acting as one himself. But staff had been thinned to unacceptable levels since the war ended. The present government didn't want to believe there were any present threats to Great Britain worthy of the expense of spy-craft. Glass knew better. The service monitored German intriguers, Irish anarchists, and worst of all, Russian bomb-makers, among others.

For now, he'd had to pass management of his section to his own chief and dig into the daily work of a spy himself. He'd lost his last operative installed here full-time in the suite to matrimony and an assignment in the north, monitoring the infiltration of trade unions by the Bolsheviks.

"Thank you. Have you heard anything new regarding this so-called trade delegation's dabbling in human smuggling?"

"No, but they've only been here a month. Plenty more time for mischief before their official meetings commence." Vall-Grandly pressed the painting back against the wall.

At least staying at the listening post should be uncomplicated work. Only last month this hotel had nearly been damaged by Bol-sheviks, but they'd caught wind of the plot in time. The Metropolitan Police's Special Branch had sealed off the tunnels beneath the hotel proper, which had once harbored the tools of the bomb-maker's trade, including a nice little nest where at least one Russian had been hiding. The hidey hole in the basement had been dank and dark, as unpleasant as any Great War trench. Nothing like the rest of the hotel.

"I'll be going now, Glass. I have a dead drop that I have to moni-tor rather closely to pick-up time, or the messages tend to be de-stroyed. Waste bin near a nursery playground. You need a break, just let me know. I'll be happy to give up a few hours of sleep to keep the operation going."

"Thanks, Bill. It is men like you who are going to keep these bloody Russians from wreaking any more havoc on London."

Lines creased diagonally under Vall-Grandly's eyes as he smiled. "Thank you, sir." They shook hands before the operative picked up his modest bag and glanced over the sitting room one last time.

Glass's gaze took in the luxury of the Artists Suite as he stepped away from the Russian-style painting of a dancer dressed as the Firebird. The furniture glowed starkly, all white, in order to harmonize with the richly decorative Russian artwork on the walls. He had no knowledge of the artists' names or styles, but he could appreciate the sheer exuberance of the jewel-tones. Reds, purples, blues, greens, all blazed as brightly as any stained-glass window letting in the sun. The stenciling high on the walls of the hotel's public spaces was absent here, so the eye could feast strictly on what was inside the frames.

"Be a pity if this place was destroyed," Vall-Grandly ruminated. "I've been told that ballet is the primary theme of the hotel, but art in general is a strong second."

"I recognize the Firebird as being a character in a ballet, but I have no idea who the sleeping lovely in the next painting is meant to be," Glass said. In a blue and white ball gown, the sleeper rested on a dainty pillow, her blond curls done up in a sapphire ribbon. The settee holding her petite body was upholstered in blue, pink, and cream stripes. It would never work at the Grand Russe Hotel, which had been decorated in reds and greens. He took in the rest of the painting at a glance, having trained his eye to detail. Olive walls, floral screen, gold occasional table. A window, the bottom half of a painting. A bookcase.

A knock at the door made him turn away from his fledgling art appreciation. The floor butler, he expected, or the hotel's head of security, ready to verify his communication needs. He opened the door, ready for one of these men.

Instead, he found a tall, ash blond beauty in a severe black dress. A serviceable dress. Despite the bearing of an empress, she must be an employee.

"Yes?" he asked.

"My lord," the woman said in an imperious Russian accent, stepping in. "My apologies. I have come to collect a painting from the suite."

Vall-Grandly smiled broadly at the woman and laid a finger next to his nose before sliding out of the door, shutting it behind him.

The Russian accent lifted the tiny hairs on the back of Glass's neck. Yes, some of the hotel employees were Russian, but that didn't mean they were above suspicion. "Who are you?"

"I am Olga Novikov, the head of housekeeping," she said calmly.

"Novikov," he said slowly. "Shouldn't it be Novikova?"

"The English do not feminize their surnames so I do not either."

She was trying to prove a point, but he had no idea what it was. Unfortunately for her, Novikov was also the surname of the bomber his section was searching for. This woman could be a connection to the man he sought, but the cool beauty did not appear to be a woman who would give up her secrets easily. "I've heard of you. Serene Highness, correct?"

"I am a great-great-great-granddaughter of Nicholas I," she said, tilting her head.

"A distinguished lineage," he murmured, noting the perfection of her nose, the slim neck. He suspected a chain of ancestors who only married the most beautiful women in Russia. "I have just moved in, Your Serene Highness. The suite is satisfactory to me as it is."

She frowned. "I am merely Olga here. Titles are for guests, not staff."

He let his eyebrows settle over his eye sockets, knowing that when his eyes narrowed it gave him a most forbidding look. "If you say so. Are you the only Novikov on staff here, or is it a common name?"

"I have no relatives at the Grand Russe."

"Did many of your family escape the Revolution?" he inquired.

"My family can be of no interest to you, Lord Walling." She took a step closer to him, enough that he could smell bleach and orange oil. "If I could collect what I need I shall leave you to settle in."

"A distinguished name doesn't mean I can allow you to take a painting from the suite."

She placed one hand over another, on top of the keys that she wore at her waist. "Not only am I head of housekeeping, I am also a personal friend of the hotel owner."

"And your point?"

"I am curating a Russian art exhibit for the hotel. I require the Firebird painting."

Glass might have let her take a painting, but not that one. He was glad to know the woman, with her suspicious surname, had no idea that the Firebird had been permanently installed over the surveillance equipment. "I am convinced that the hotel manager did not give you permission to take that particular piece. It is the centerpiece of the room."

The princess drew herself up. "I'm well aware of the importance of

Mr. Bakst's work," the princess said. "But it is not the room's center-piece. That is the Konstantin Somov watercolor over the fireplace."

Glass stiffened at the name "Konstantin." Konstantin Novikov was the name of the bomber. He could not bring himself to merely send away the self-assured princess. "Let us take a look and see if I agree with you."

He stepped back so that she could enter the foyer, then went into the sitting room. Above the fireplace was the work she had mentioned.

"It is a study for Somov's masterwork 'Echo of Bygone Days,'" she said, gesturing. "You can see the bodice is unfinished, as is the garden off to the right, yet the pale dress, and the dark walls to her right, make this the perfect painting for this room."

Glass said nothing, merely stepped toward the Firebird, grateful his equipment didn't make any noise, at least until the recording device came to the end of the disk and turned itself off. "How can you say such a thing? This Echo girl is nothing but a bland apparition next to the doll face of the Firebird. Look at the dark eyes. And her dress! All those vibrant oranges and reds."

"You are teasing me, my lord," she said. "While I am a mere house-keeper now, I assure you that I know art. Removing the Firebird will harmonize this room."

"I don't want it harmonized." He forced the corners of his lips up, then turned them down again, knowing she was intelligent enough to pick up the falseness of his expression.

"My lord." She attempted to stare him down.

"Don't be headstrong," he chided. "I am a guest in one of the most expensive suites in this hotel. I expect my wishes to be respected."

Very deliberately, she bobbed into a curtsy.

"I must say, you are far more beautiful than any of the women depicted in these paintings, though I can see the resemblance between you and this painting next to the Firebird. A relative of yours?"

The princess went to the sleeping beauty painting. "It is another Somov," she said. "But I do not know its history. Somov was a part of the *Mir iskusstva* group and I didn't know any of those artists."

"Why not?" he asked. He observed that the fiery light behind her eyes had softened. She'd gone deep, into the past.

"The artists I knew were Symbolists, friends of my fiancé, not the homosexual crowd Somov ran in. They are mostly in Paris now, the survivors."

"Why aren't you there?" he asked.

"I—" She swallowed hard. "It is a long story, my lord. And I am taking too much of your time."

His smile flashed genuine this time. "I assumed you would refuse to leave until you had what you wanted."

"No, I need to return to work. I had a break, but that is long past now."

"Then you will have to leave empty-handed."

Her gaze sharpened again, the melancholy faded.

Now he remembered there was a time when it was suggested she be developed as a source for the Secret Intelligence Service. Now, her surname made her more of a point of suspicion rather than someone they'd pay money for information from. Besides, he had no one to run her as a source. He'd have to take her on himself. Before he could consider what that might mean, she spoke.

"I insist we discuss the matter of the painting with Peter Eyre," she said, all show of obsequiousness departing the lines of her statuesque, Athena-like body.

"I am sure the hotel manager will side with me," Glass said, "but I will not object to the conversation. Do you want to take the time now?"

She hesitated. "I should have someone come and unpack for you."

"That is the floor butler's duty, surely."

Her head swiveled toward the door, just as he heard a click behind the Firebird painting. The disk was full. But she didn't seem to notice the out-of-place sound. "I can't imagine why he hasn't stopped by."

"Busy with other guests. All those Russians next door must keep his schedule full."

She shook her head. "I do not understand why that party has not been removed. Boorish, my lord. They are not our kind."

He inclined his head. "Thank you for the advice, Olga. I shall endeavor to steer clear of them."

"Let us go downstairs if it pleases you, and see if Mr. Eyre is available."

"Excellent. I am very curious to know exactly how close your friendship is."

Her gaze darted frantically to his face, a quick movement of her eyes, a trapped bird trying to escape the otherwise serene expression. What was she afraid of?

All of a sudden, his curiosity was thoroughly piqued. The princess had secrets.

Heather Hiestand was born in Illinois but her family migrated west before she started school. Since then she has claimed Washington State as home, except for a few years in California. She wrote her first story at age seven and went on to major in creative writing at the University of Washington. Her first published fiction was a mystery short story, but since then it has been all about the many flavors of romance. Heather's first published romance short story was set in the Victorian period and she continues to return to historical fiction. The author of many novels, novellas, and short stories, she has achieved bestseller status on Amazon and Barnes and Noble. With her husband and son, she makes her home in a small town and supposedly works out of her tiny office, though she mostly writes in her easy chair in the living room. She's probably sitting there right now!

For more information, visit Heather's website at www.heather hiestand.com. Want to stay in touch with Heather and receive exclusive information about her new releases?
Sign up for her newsletter at http://heatherhiestand.com/newsletter/.

HEATHER
HIESTAND

IF I
HAD YOU

THE GRAND RUSSE HOTEL